MW01285260
The Far Ridges
Darknight Canyon
Hell's Glacier
Hælđrekys Peaks
Ribcage Fjords
Spine River
Keeper's Gate
Kalva
The Rapier
Cinereal Sea
The Ashen Narrows
Eravon
Nomaden
Ruby Peak
Irisi
Florence
Forest of Lost Souls
Laudon
Zayel
Esvaine
Vairian Sea
Carantic Ocean
Charlet
River Sarvane
Tourden
Verdivenne
Old Forest
Hills of Deminat
Amuilly's Vale
Bellandry
Hollow Pass
Tarsa
Suva
Crescent Cape
Havenwood
Almere
River Nos
Augurwood
Lunes
Hamren
Gulf of the Six Wars
Lake Quissari
River of Dragon's Tears
Marayat
Sultan's Shore
River Coreen
Starlit Dunes
Wolfwoods
Cardubar
Shadow Basin
Halriel's Hill
Oasis of Truth
Mountains of Promise
River Zeluar
The Diqar Desert
Zitra
Eqora
Assassin's Bay
White Desert
Pons Aelii
Aelii's Oasis
Serat
Twin Mesas
Valley of Life
Horizon Hills
Teyet
Devil's Dunes
River Jadir
Armarga
Marble Bay
Golden Bight
Drummer's Bay
Soral
Sabariel's Fangs
Kiru's Lagoon
Bokolan
River Kohi
Nomarea
Empress River
Koura
Koumagara Mountains

BY L. K. STEVEN

Silvercloak

FOR YOUNG ADULTS
(AS LAURA STEVEN)

Our Infinite Fates

Every Exquisite Thing

The Society for Soulless Girls

SILVERCLOAK

Silvercloak

L. K. Steven

NEW YORK

Published in the United States by Del Rey,
an imprint of Random House, a division of
Penguin Random House LLC, 1745 Broadway, New York, NY

Del Rey and the Circle colophon are registered
trademarks of Penguin Random House LLC.

Hardback ISBN 978-0-593-97399-8
Ebook ISBN 978-0-593-97400-1

Printed in China on acid-free paper

randomhousebooks.com
penguinrandomhouse.com

2 4 6 8 9 7 5 3 1

FIRST EDITION

Book design by Barbara M. Bachman

Title page illustration and endpaper map by Francesca Baerald
Other interior illustrations from Adobe Stock

The authorized representative in the EU for product safety and
compliance is Penguin Random House Ireland, Morrison Chambers,
32 Nassau Street, Dublin D02 YH68, Ireland. https://eu-contact.penguin.ie.

For Chloe Seager,

who took all my wildest dreams

and made them true

SILVERCLOAK

CLASSES *of* MAGIC

. . .

COMMON

Enchanter

Brewer

. . .

UNCOMMON

Wielder

Healer

. . .

RARE

Compeller

Foreseer

. . .

EXTINCT

Timeweaver

PROLOGUE

• • •

TWENTY YEARS AGO

THE KILLORANS' FRONT DOOR CHANGED COLOR DEPENDING UPON who knocked.

Sky blue for a charming acquaintance, heart red for a lover present, past, or future. Clover green for a spiteful enemy, or a rich, jammy plum for an old friend. Mustard yellow for family and, due to a slight inaccuracy with the spellwork, traveling salesmen.

The day the Bloodmoons paid a visit, the door turned as black as the bottom of a well.

Mellora had just returned home from a long shift at Saint Isidore's, the nearby hospital for magical maladies, to find her husband, Joran, and daughter, Saffron, giggling with glee. Joran was slowly and methodically turning everything in the house into sausages, including but not limited to the taps in the kitchen sink, all the cutlery in the top drawer, several house plants, the cat's furious tail, and his own high-bridged nose.

"Good afternoon to thee," he said earnestly, as Mellora shrugged off her violet Healer's cloak. His tone was a little nasal, on account of having a sausage for a nose. He tapped it once with his spindly cedar wand, and his handsome aquiline features returned.

Saffron stood by his side, arms wrapped around his leg, weeping with laughter. Her wild silver-blond curls tumbled over her face. "Daddy, stop! I can't breathe."

Warmth swelled in Mellora's chest.

Oh, how she loved them.

The Killoran family home was a round, ramshackle building overgrown with wildflowers, and Joran had charmed every inch of it with their daughter in mind: bookshelves that never ran out of new stories, miniature stars trapped in lanterns to form tiny constellations, a kettle that whistled the Serpent's Shanty once the tea was boiled. Carpets that took off at random and whizzed Saff around their small village, whooping and hollering with delight. Favorite of all was a spiral staircase that became a slide whenever Saffron approached the top—a not insignificant piece of conditional transmutation that would floor most ordinary mages.

Mellora was entirely more earnest than her husband—she'd always been unfalteringly sincere, even as a child—but it made her appreciate Joran's whimsy all the more. She could not imagine a better father for her only child.

Crossing to the cabinet of honeywine, Mellora poured herself a large goblet. As the sweet, sharp nectar hit her tongue, she felt her well of magic—depleted after a long day of healing—begin to refill.

Power was a finite thing, easily drained, and could only be replenished through rich pours of *pleasure*. Scented clove candles were eternally lit around their home. Gentle violin music echoed in the ceiling rafters, and the walls were adorned with glorious artwork. A feast for the senses, designed to restore.

Of course, the other thing that bolstered power was *pain*.

While pleasure swelled the *quantity* of magic at a mage's disposal, pain improved the *quality*. An ancient survival mechanism, one that made magical wars as brutal as they were unpredictable.

But the Killorans wanted nothing to do with pain. Not after everything Joran had been through.

"You're wasted tinkering away on this house," Mellora told him, as he enchanted a knife to chop vegetables into neat inch-wide chunks. "You should be in the King's Cabinet, protecting the realm. Or lecturing at a university. Even magical cure research. I know the Academy for Arcane Ailments and Afflictions is looking for—"

"Maybe joy is enough," he replied simply, brushing a corkscrew curl away from her face and planting a kiss on her lips. His own long blond hair was tied back with a worn leather string. Mellora had the sudden desire to run her hands through it, to seek pleasure the *other* way.

And then came the knock at the door.

Both of them turned at once.

At the sight of the ink-dark wood, Mellora blanched, setting down her goblet with a trembling hand.

"Saff, you have to hide."

Every word was a shard of bone in her throat.

"But Mama," Saffron protested, big brown eyes flitting from her parents to the door and back to her parents. She was six years old and doleful as a fawn. "Who is it? I've never seen the door black before."

"Please," said Joran, hoarse as he laid down the half-charmed knife. It skittered on the chopping block in confusion. "Please, Saffy."

They didn't know who was on the other side of the door, but they *knew.*

Another knock, more insistent this time, with the air of a final grace.

Joran took an envelope from his cloak pocket and stuffed it into the top drawer of the nearest cabinet, running a mournful finger over the cursive name on the front of the parchment. Mellora watched him, dread gnawing at her belly. Her husband was afraid enough for a farewell letter, and Joran was so rarely afraid.

"Saffron, we love you," Mellora whispered, kissing her daughter on the cheek. Saff tasted of creamy butter and strawberry jam. "We'll see you soon."

Joran ushered their daughter into the corner of the room. The pantry was enchanted to conceal any Killoran hidden inside, making them invisible and inaudible to anyone but another Killoran.

For once, Mellora was glad her genius husband *wasted* his time tinkering with their home. It might just be the thing that saved their daughter's life.

As the pantry clicked shut, the front door slammed open, hanging loose and frightened from its hinges. Slowly the color—the magic—

seeped out of the wood, until it was once more a plain brown teak. A few inches below the silver fallowwolf knocker, the imprint of an opening spell faded slowly.

Two hulking figures stepped over the threshold, cast in a wedge of fading daylight. Their cloaks were a deep scarlet, pinned at their throats with round ruby brooches, the moon phases embroidered down the lapels in black and gold thread. Everything else was black—the knee-high boots with gold buckles, the neatly laced tunics, the billowing breeches, the look of death in their eyes.

Mellora's stomach clenched like a fist.

Bloodmoons.

She took a few protective steps in front of her husband.

"Can we help you?" Joran said, the words cragged and uneven.

"We need a necromancer," said the shorter of the two men. He had a low, heavy brow and a scratchy voice. He twitched with a kind of fraught energy—whatever order they'd been given, haste was of the essence. And there was nothing so dangerous as desperation when it came to the Bloodmoons.

Joran squared his shoulders. "You won't find one here."

"Won't we?" The taller mage narrowed his gray eyes, a kind of rapacious hunger pulling his lips wide.

They both stared straight at Mellora.

Everything inside her seized with fear. She considered casting a desperate *praegelos* charm, to buy herself precious thinking space, and yet what good would thinking do when the devil was already upon them? The only thing that could save them now was the teleportation spell, and such a thing had been outlawed long ago.

Joran glanced back at her in confusion. "Mellora?" His knuckles were white as he gripped his wand. "My wife is a Healer. Easy enough to prove." He lifted his wand to his palm and made a slicing motion. "*Sen incisuren.*"

A cut opened—*too deep*, worried Mellora, *he's gone too deep*—and bloomed dark red. He didn't so much as wince.

Mellora raised her sleek willow wand and muttered, as she had a thousand times before, "*Ans mederan.*"

Heal.

Though her well of magic had been scantly replenished by a few sips of honeywine, the wound inelegantly knotted itself back together. It would scar, if they lived long enough.

The Bloodmoons stared disdainfully at Joran's hand.

"Either you know as well as we do that necromancy is a sub-class of healing," said the tall viper, "or you're entirely as moronic as you appear."

Joran's pale cheeks heated with anger, and Mellora silently willed him to not throw bait at the feet of wolves, yet she couldn't quite convince her mouth to form words, to urge him to keep his head.

True to form, he did not heed her wordless plea. He only lifted his wand.

But the Bloodmoon lifted his faster.

"Sen ammorten."

The killing spell landed true on Joran's chest, and he fell to the ground like a sack of bezoars.

Mellora let out a strangled cry, feeling the expectant weight of the intruders' gazes upon her. They knew what she would do next, and so did she.

Because she could not let Joran, her *Joran,* die at her feet.

After decades of running and rigging enchanted gamehouses, the Bloodmoons were experts at forcing players to show their hands.

The strand linking Mellora's mind to her body snapped.

She moved without thought, sinking onto her haunches and tearing open the fabric of Joran's tunic. There was a star-shaped scar over his heart where the spell had struck, and when she laid a palm over it, it was ice cold to the touch, like liquid silver. Magical death had a unique scent to it—not blood and rot, but smoke and ash and something honey-sweet.

She kept one palm resting on Joran's unbeating chest and raised her wand with the other.

"*Ans visseran,*" she incanted, self-hatred pluming inside her. "*Ans visseran. Ans visseran.*"

Revive. Revive. Revive.

A sense of utter depravity clutched at her with gnarled fingers.

Necromancy was not just unlawful—it was sacrilege. It went against nature, against all the various gods and Saints upon which Ascenfall was built. Something essential of the human spirit was lost in death, and it could not be brought back through the veil between *there* and *here,* no matter how skilled the mage.

But this was Joran. She had to try.

"Ans visseran. Ans visseran. Ans visseran."

Nothing happened immediately, but these things took time. Time to coax the heart back into thumping, time to cajole the blood into flowing. An inescapable law of physics: whether magical or not, an object in motion wanted to stay in motion, and an object at rest wanted to stay at rest.

Surely Joran's heart doesn't want to be at rest, Mellora thought pleadingly. *Surely it bucks against its very stillness. Surely it can sense me just on the other side.*

The Bloodmoons watched as she incanted the spell again and again, but there was no telltale lurch beneath her palm. Desperation surging, she bit down hard on her tongue until she tasted blood, letting the pain stab and swell in her mouth.

If pleasure worked like rest to *restore* magic, then pain worked like adrenaline to *enhance* it. A short, intense burst of energy, granting extraordinary power in the most dire of situations.

And Saints knew Mellora needed it.

"Ans visseran. Ans visseran."

Joran's heart remained a stone.

But it *had* to work. This was Joran. Saffron's dad.

Saffron.

Mellora prayed to Omedari, the patron saint of healing, that her daughter had not witnessed her father's murder. She was still concealed in the pantry, but if she pressed her eye right up to the keyhole . . .

Focus lapsing dangerously, Mellora's gaze flitted up to the pantry—

—just in time to see the golden doorknob begin to turn.

No, roared everything inside Mellora, but the handle kept twisting. If the Bloodmoons saw Saff, they'd kill her too.

Mellora spun on her heels, squaring her wand. She had never cast a killing spell, but to save Saff, she would do anything.

"Sen ammort—"

Her curse was severed by the two killing spells striking her heart.

The golden doorknob stopped turning.

The room rocked still.

For several moments, silence sprawled out like nightfall. Wordlessly, the intruders burned crescent moons into their victims' lifeless cheeks, the skin bubbling a grotesque burgundy beneath the tips of their wands.

If a death did not serve its original purpose, at least it could spread fear.

When the Bloodmoons departed, they left the door hanging off its hinges like a rotten tooth.

And when Saffron Killoran finally opened the pantry door—it could have been moments later, or hours, or days—the living room smelled of charred flesh. Of smoke and ash and something honey-sweet.

She opened her mouth to scream, but no sound came out.

Hunched over her mother's body were two mages in long silver cloaks, pinned at the neck with sapphire brooches. One mage drew a chalk circle around her father by hand, while the other examined the ruined door. Their wands were scrawling in notebooks suspended mid-air, and they talked in low voices.

At the sight of Saffron, one detective looked up. She was pale, narrow-nosed, thin as a spire, and for the briefest of moments, pure, unfiltered grief flashed across her face.

"Oh, sweetling," she murmured to Saffron, shielding the corpses from view. "Come here. You're safe now."

PART
ONE

—

CADET

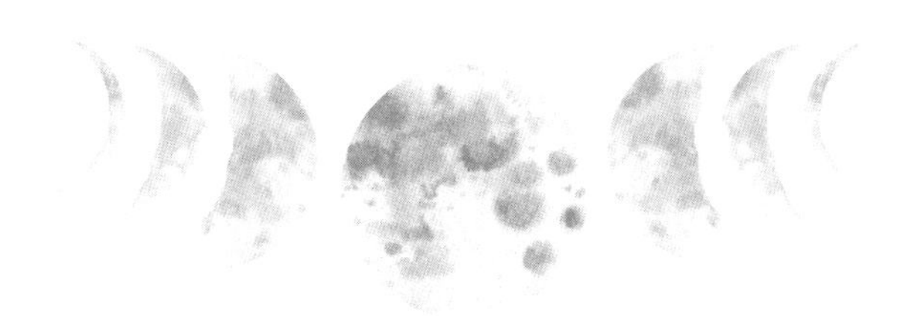

1

...

The Cohort

Saffron's cloak would turn silver by sundown—if she wasn't caught in a lie first.

A mere quarter hour stood between her and the final assessment.

Twenty years of grief and determination distilled into a single sequence.

She arranged her features into a neutral expression and set down a winning polderdash card. The priestess on the front winked coltishly.

Her opponent, Gaian, groaned like a dying hog.

"A whole year of having my hide whipped, and still I take the bait." He slid a pearly ascen over the bench, and Saffron pocketed it with a smirk. "You must have more coin than the city treasury at this point."

Not far from the truth. Saffron had spent most of her adult life gambling rather fruitfully against her peers and countrymen. Everyone else was so *bad* at card games.

Shuffling the deck idly in her hands, Saffron cast her gaze around the brewing lab. Orange-gold sunlight poured through the mullioned windows, turning dust motes to fireflies. The high walls were lined with shelves holding glass jars of common tincture ingredients: herbs and spices, ash and earth, fallowwolf claws and mourncrow beaks, flesh and blood and bone. Six long wooden benches ran parallel down the middle of the lab, each topped with pewter cauldrons and an array of gilded instruments. Along the benches, two velvines stalked and purred. Slender cats with purple eyes and black fur, their satin-cool breath sent ripples of pleasure across bare skin. They patrolled the Silvercloak Academy day and night, replenishing the magical wells of drained-dry mages.

The six cadets had gathered in the lab ahead of the final assessment, so that Auria and Sebran—the only Brewers amongst them—could stopper their tinctures. Though the cohort had spent twelve months competing against one another for the top rankings, they had become unexpectedly close-knit, and though none of them would admit as much, they all wanted to make the most of their last moments together. Before they were sent to far-flung corners of the continent for their first postings, before they no longer lived in one another's pockets.

Assuming, of course, that they all passed.

Tension hung heavy in the room. The cadets stood on the cusp of an ending and a beginning, and they all felt the knife-edge beneath their feet.

"Look alive, folks." Auria beamed, bright and earnest, her eternal vim never wavering. "We're all going to turn our cloaks silver tonight. I can feel it." A velvine brushed against her arm, purring pleasure over her throat as she notched three final vials into her tincture belt.

Nissa hung out of the arched window, smoking a hand-rolled achullah. It smelled of orange and clove and an earthy type of tobacco grown in the hottest part of the Diqar desert.

"Have you ever, even once, believed things wouldn't work out?" Nissa drawled, blowing out a smoke ring. Black hair fell to her waist in a sleek, shining sheet. "Despite all evidence to the contrary?"

Auria flashed another sincere smile. "No, not really."

Nissa's own lips curled. "You know, in Nyrøth they consider blind optimism a sign of low intelligence."

"Good thing we don't live in Nyrøth," Auria replied cheerily.

In truth, Saffron found Auria's sunny veneer comforting, but she didn't say as much. Despite overcoming her six-year stretch of silence when she was twelve, she still preferred to stay quiet.

From across the room, Nissa caught Saffron's eye with a private smile, and it felt like grabbing a fistful of gallowsweed—as though everything in her blistered at once. Saff and Nissa had been ensnared in a clandestine relationship for the last few months. It began with simple, stress-relieving fucking, and slowly bloomed into something richer, softer. A stroke on the cheek, a flower left on a pillow, *I saw this and thought of you.*

Then, a couple of weeks ago, Nissa had ended things. Said that they needed to focus on their futures, and the very real chance that they'd be posted hundreds of miles apart. Nissa believed that the best Silvercloaks cut off sentimentality at the root. But for Saffron, the entire reason she was at the Academy was an emotional one.

She looked away from Nissa, gathering up her playing cards and tucking them back into her white cloak.

Tiernan—a tall, uncertain Healer, mainly at the Academy to appease his father—stopped his frenetic pacing to shoot Nissa a withering look. (Well, as withering as it was possible to be, when he'd sooner perish than insult someone.)

"I, for one, appreciate Auria's positive spirit." Tiernan blushed, raking a hand through his pale brown curls. He and Auria were mutually infatuated, and yet both believed their feelings to be unrequited. "Her love of the game makes it easier to reconcile the fact we're both teammates and competitors."

He had a point. The final assessment was not just of the Silvercloak cadets as individuals, but of how they worked together as a field unit.

The Academy was reserved for the best of the best, and there were only six mages in Saffron's cohort. There was Saffron herself: stubborn, quietly cunning, relentlessly single-minded, even more relentlessly sweet-toothed, and frighteningly good at gambling. An Enchanter, in the eyes of the Academy—if not in truth.

Shy, awkward Tiernan, whose father was in the King's Cabinet. A talented Healer, albeit a perpetually nervous one.

Auria, a bright-eyed bookworm, a rule follower, with lofty ambitions of becoming a Grand Arbiter someday. Uncommonly gifted with three mage classes—Enchanter, Brewer, and Healer—her work was precise, if not especially imaginative, and she had an encyclopedic knowledge of *Modern Potions & Tinctures: Volume IV.*

Nissa, the elemental powerhouse of a Wielder. She was smoking hot and smoked a *lot*, but only so she could wield fire at any given moment, and certainly not because she was in any way addicted to achullah. Her dragonesque command of smoke and flame was revered by everyone in the Order—even Captain Aspar.

Sebran and Gaian, each of whom held a single classification—Brewer and Enchanter respectively—but made up for their moderate magic with unfaltering bravery in Sebran's case and a sharp, almost frightening intellect in Gaian's. The latter had the uncanny ability to spot lies; his interrogations always yielded confessions, even without truth elixir. And yet he still couldn't beat Saff at cards.

"You're the competition, pure and simple," said Sebran, stoppering a dark purple tincture that smelled of aniseed. He was broad and brawny, with dark brown skin and a close-shaven head. He never spoke of his family, his home. Nobody quite knew where he had come from, other than the military academy. "I'll get that Pons Aelii posting even if it kills me."

"Not a chance," Gaian said coolly, tying his long blond hair neatly out of his face. "It's mine."

Nissa ran her forked tongue over her bottom lip. "Or they could give it to the *actual* half-Eqoran."

The graduate assignments had been posted on the noticeboard the previous week—and there had been only five vacancies listed for six cadets.

Three were run-of-the-mill detective postings here in Atherin.

One was a stationing at a border outpost in Carduban, guarding the ascenite-rich Mountains of Promise from the lustful eyes of the neighboring Eqora. (None of them wanted this posting, since the Eqorans hadn't made any meaningful moves toward the mines in decades, thus the mission would largely involve mediating disputes between mountain goats.)

The last was an undercover field intelligence operation in Pons Aelii, the capital of Eqora itself. Nissa, Sebran, and Gaian had waged war over the posting for days. *Going undercover* held a certain level of prestige—if they performed well on such a high-stakes first assignment, they'd likely go on to great things in the Order of the Silver-cloaks. (Plus, it just sounded sexy.)

But Saff wasn't interested in Pons Aelii. If she wanted to destroy the Bloodmoons who'd stolen her childhood, she had to be in the city where their roots were laid—here in Atherin.

"Are you alright, Saff?" Auria asked. "You're quiet. More so than usual."

Saff peered through the wide double window. The pale-stoned Academy was perched on a hill just on the outskirts of Atherin, and the capital's skyline blurred with heat, smudging together the purple sapphire domes of Augurest temples, the towering crimson-and-gold obelisks honoring the patron saints, the carved marble pantheons with sapphire spires, the gleaming emerald tiles and pale sunbaked walls of the slouching townhouses. A sultry, jewel-toned riot of a city, built upon pleasure and violence in equal measure.

Lunes, the quaint northern village she'd grown up in, had never felt farther away. Her heart panged at the memory of overgrown wildflowers and cobbled courtyards, shabby cloaks and warm faces, the scents of rosemary and honeywine.

"Fine," she replied vaguely. "Just mentally preparing."

As though she hadn't spent two decades doing just that. As though she hadn't spent two decades planning and calculating, scheming and rerouting, overcoming every obstacle thrown at her by nature or circumstance, biding her time with the big *why* always in the forefront of her mind.

"That's what's driving me mad." Tiernan's teeth worked at his bottom lip. "We *can't* prepare when we have no idea what the assessment entails."

"Like real life." Sebran had a soldier's gruffness; there was little emotion behind his hazel eyes. "You're hardly going to get a detailed memorandum before every dangerous situation, are you?"

"As long as I get a job at the end of all this . . ." Tiernan fiddled nervously with the strings of his tunic. "My father will decapitate me if I come home without a posting. Even Carduban would be preferable."

"I'll let Aspar know you volunteer," smirked Nissa, stubbing out her achullah on the stone windowsill.

Deep down, Saff shared Tiernan's sentiments. Though she'd rather not be a glorified border control officer, she'd still take that over missing out on a posting altogether.

After everything she'd done to claw herself here, she couldn't fail now.

Twelve years of mage school. Four years at the Northern University of Novarin, earning her Knight's Scroll in Modern History. Five years of patrolling Atherin on the streetwatch, as all prospective Silvercloak candidates had to do, acting as first response to gory crime scenes, rounding up robbers and crooks and killers and hauling them off spitting and cursing to Duncarzus, accumulating injuries and trauma and hard-fought wisdom, knowing all the while that whatever innocence had survived her parents' slaughter was being slowly eroded, maturing into the understanding that evil was everywhere, so commonplace it was banal, and now that she knew this, she could never unlearn it.

And then there was the simple fact that all this experience was built on a foundation of lies and illusions.

She only had to maintain the fallacy for one more day.

One more hour.

THE SIX CADETS STOOD outside the Grand Atrium, staring at the words levitating over the threshold.

Candidates only—assessment in progress.

Beneath the sign stood a pale, raven-haired professor who had drilled them endlessly in the art of combat, leaving their flesh bruised and their muscles sore. When they'd protested that they wouldn't have to use physical strength with a wand at their fingertips, Professor Vertillon had retorted that unless their wands were surgically attached to their palms, they had to be prepared to lose them. A disarmament spell could be thrown at them at any moment, or in the heat of the skirmish, they might simply drop it out of sheer nerves and ineptitude.

Professor Vertillon gave Sebran a terse nod—the professor had trained him at the military college before accepting the teaching post at the Academy—then pressed his lips into a flat line to greet the others.

"The final assessment is upon us," he decreed, in his low baritone. "Though we can prepare for such events to the ends of the earth, we still must take into account the slippery element of chance. A wand snapped during a raid, a tincture belt shattered on the ground, compromising injuries, and conflicting information."

He held up six cream-colored envelopes. "As such, you will each draw a different hand for this exercise. Three of you will have no disadvantages. One of you will lose your wand. One of you will have a limb temporarily frozen. And one of you will work on different information than your peers. Cards will be drawn in alphabetical order of surname."

Vertillon fanned the envelopes in his weathered hands, then offered Sebran the first pick. Sebran pulled an envelope, opened it, and nodded woodenly. Tiernan drew next, then Saffron.

You have no disadvantages.

It wasn't quite true—she had her own temperamental magic to contend with—but it was a relief nonetheless.

As Auria then Nissa drew the last two envelopes, Saff looked up at Tiernan, whose foot jittered uncontrollably. The sea-green tinge to his cheeks had only intensified. He'd clearly received a disadvantage.

And he was already terrified of letting his notoriously cruel father down.

Saffron would never forget their first week on the streetwatch. A vicious gang of thieves called the Whitewings had cut the tongues out of the mouths of several children who'd accidentally witnessed a robbery, then burned said tongues with magical fire so they could not be reattached. Saff, Tiernan, and Auria had been first on the scene, and Tiernan had spent the first twenty minutes vomiting into a gutter.

When word got back to Tiernan's father about his son's weak stomach, Kesven Flane had chained Tiernan to a chair and forced him to watch vivid reenactments of torture, animated with the kind of illusionary magic Saff used to hide her secret, every night for a month.

Then Kesven had brought home an inebriated Ludder—a person born without magic—and sliced their tongue out for real, forcing Tiernan to practice healing it. Over and over and over again, until the Ludder blacked out from the pain and a small piece of Tiernan's humanity died.

And now, during the final assessment, the last show of strength before jobs were assigned, Kesven would see his son weakened. An embarrassment to the family name, even though it was through random chance, no fault of his own. Kesven would not see it that way.

"Switch with me," Saff whispered under her breath.

Tiernan twitched in her direction. "What?"

"Swap envelopes."

After a split second of indecision—clearly trying to discern whether Saff was trying to pull one over on him—he slipped his envelope into her hand. She reciprocated. Professor Vertillon was none the wiser.

Saffron read her new fate.

Your leg will be frozen for the duration of the assessment.

"I have no disadvantages," announced Auria.

"Me neither," said Tiernan, shooting Saffron a grateful look.

"Nor me," confirmed Gaian.

"No wand," muttered Sebran. He rubbed at his cheek, as though checking he'd shaven well. "But I suppose I can keep these?" He patted his tincture belt, and Vertillon nodded confirmation.

"It's a bit on-the-nose to give the foreigner false information," muttered Nissa.

"Not false," pointed out Saff. "The professor said *different.*"

"And besides, it was drawn at random, Nissa," said Auria hotly. She took any criticism of the Academy personally, though she had no familial ties to it, just a fundamental reverence for the rules and the establishment. A future Grand Arbiter to her bones.

"What's the information?" Gaian asked.

"Don't know. I assume I'll be given it during the exercise?" Nissa asked.

Vertillon nodded again. "Indeed. Sebran—I mean, Cadet Aduran—will have his wand removed as he passes the threshold of the Grand

Atrium. At which point Cadet Killoran's leg will also freeze." He took a step to the side. "You may enter."

"This is it," whispered Auria, patting her tincture belt for the thousandth time, eyes glowing with anticipation. She wholly and genuinely believed everything was going to work out. Saff envied her that easy faith. The world hadn't yet beaten it out of her.

Saffron checked her own belt. She was no Brewer, so it wasn't notched with vials but instead with an array of weapons and equipment they always took with them on the streetwatch: ropes, manacles, a tourniquet, a baton. Matter could not be created from nothing, no matter how strong the mage, and so some things had to be analog. She also carried a rune-engraved blisblade notched in a leather holster—daggers unique to the Silvercloaks, enchanted so that even a shallow self-inflicted wound provided an enormous full-body ripple of pain-pleasure. A fast way to replenish the magical well in a pinch.

Not that it had ever worked for Saffron. Nor did velvine breath.

She had to seek pleasure the old-fashioned way.

On the other side of the enormous double doors, a muffled din of chatter swelled. Who would be judging from the raised gallery on the southern side of the atrium? Captain Aspar, of course, and their other superior officers, but Auria suspected higher-ups from the King's Cabinet were here to cherry-pick the most sparkling candidates for House Arollan's own court.

Not that Saffron would accept any other offer.

She was fated to be a Silvercloak.

That fate was her god, her faith, her church. That fate was the only reason she was still standing. It had been written in the defining moment of her life—she believed that with her whole being.

Saffron shoved open the high double doors and gasped at what lay beyond.

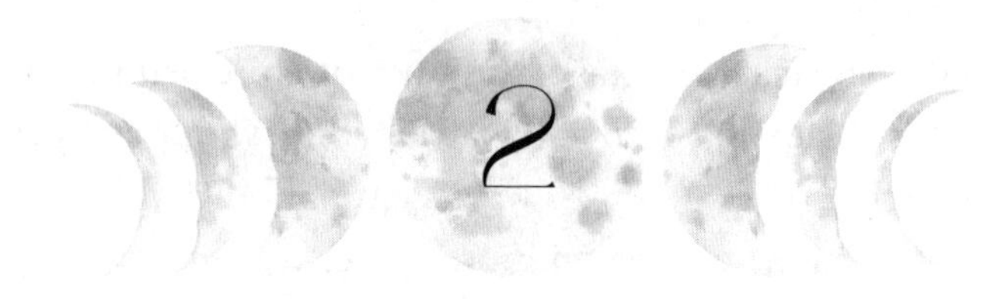

2

...

The Final Assessment

INSIDE THE CAVERNOUS GRAND ATRIUM STOOD A RECONSTRUCTION of an Augurest temple, hewn from pale stone and surrounded by red-leafed trees.

Augurest temples were shaped like an open eye: two curved outer walls sharpening into points where they met, with a domed purple roof. Inside was a winding spiral of a corridor, like an iris, leading into the central worship chamber—the pupil. They were designed to honor the prophetic power of the Five Augurs but were famously a hostage liability. Once intruders entered the spiral corridor, the worshippers in the central chamber became trapped.

Sure enough, this looked like a re-creation of a hostage situation. Two burly men flanked the arched entrance, wearing long scarlet robes with the moon phases embroidered in black and gold, the unmistakable ruby pins at their throats.

Bloodmoons.

Everything in Saffron bristled at the sight of them. Even though she knew these men were just Silvercloaks playing dress-up, even though she knew this wasn't real, her body rose to the threat like the hairs on a fallowwolf's scruff standing on end.

All at once she was six years old again, watching the murder of her parents through a narrow golden keyhole. The charred flesh, the reek of ash and honey. The slump of her father's body as it hit the ground. The surge of raw horror in her chest.

Instead of shaking it off, she leaned into the pain of the memory. She could either suppress it, or she could *use* it, and she'd already come this far with the latter.

The cadets crossed the Grand Atrium's threshold as a unit, and Sebran's pine wand soared into Vertillon's outstretched hand. Nissa cupped her palm to her ear, receiving her alternative information.

Saffron's leg, of course, did not freeze as it should. But she was used to pretending.

She altered her gait, dragging her left foot behind her like a corpse.

"Welcome, candidates," boomed Captain Aspar, their commanding officer, though she was nowhere to be seen. The room's acoustics had been enchanted to amplify the voices inside it, and her words tremored, slightly distorted. "In the worship chamber, there are twelve hostages. The temple has been taken by an unknown number of Bloodmoons. You are to rescue the hostages with as few casualties as possible. As always, no killing spells—use *effigias* to turn your foes into statues, to represent death, but only when strictly necessary. The best cohort in the Academy's history retrieved all twelve hostages while taking every Bloodmoon alive. That is the standard you should be aiming for. Good luck."

The six cadets all turned to stare at one another.

"Taking every Bloodmoon alive?" muttered Nissa, dropping her hand from her ear. "Why would *that* be a priority?"

"Intelligence," replied Gaian. "You know, the reason we're here."

"And so that innocent hostages aren't murdered in retribution." Auria's voice was hollow, echoey—their voices too were amplified by the room's enchanted acoustics. She tucked a lock of frizzy ginger hair behind her pale ear. "At first glance, I think this is a reconstruction of the Temple of Augur Amuilly, in the apothecary district. It was built roughly seven hundred years ago, meaning its walls are approximately forty-eight inches thick, and it won't have an escape tunnel, like some of the newer temples. Could you burrow one, Nissa?"

"I'm not a fucking *mole,*" Nissa seethed.

A frown notched between Auria's brows. "No, but Wielders can manipulate earth. I don't know why you have to be so—"

"Not sure that's the best solution." Peacemaking Tiernan scratched his head, looking up at the glittering purple dome. "My father always impressed on me the importance of community relations. What if we accidentally damage the temple? What if we burrow too hard or deep and destroy its foundations? If the whole thing crumbles to the ground, not only have we killed the hostages, but we've also decimated the Silvercloaks' reputation amongst the Augurest community."

Nissa rolled her eyes. "Fuck the community."

Gaian smirked. "You know, it's never clear what you're arguing for or against."

"Maybe I just like arguing." Nissa's fingers twitched to her lips, as though smoking a phantom achullah.

Saffron swallowed hard and looked away, trying desperately hard not to remember how their naked bodies felt intertwined, Saff's soft edges pressing against Nissa's hard planes, candle wax dripping over her bare hip—that tantalizing line between pain and pleasure, where the finest magic bloomed.

"What information were you given?" Auria asked Nissa.

Nissa paused for a second. "I'm not sure I should share."

Auria clenched her fist around her slim wand. She and Nissa clashed so often that Gaian had started a tally.

"Let's think about how we'd take this building from a military perspective," said Sebran. He'd served in the Vallish infantry before enrolling in the Silvercloak Academy. "There are two Bloodmoons manning the entrance, and likely at least two in the central chamber guarding the hostages. Another four or five spaced out in the spiral corridor to block our way." He tapped his bottom lip with his forefinger. "Nissa's wind could provide a lethal weapon when combined with *effigias*. Take out all the Bloodmoons in the tunnel in one fell swoop."

"We're not supposed to kill the Bloodmoons," Auria said, with the air of a parent trying not to lose patience with an unruly child. "We need to think about this as sorcerers, not soldiers. What spells could we use to extract the hostages without ever encountering the Bloodmoons?"

"What are you going to do, roll your little vials through the spiral corridor for them to sip at?" Nissa laughed, but not kindly.

She had a point. There were no windows into the central chamber—it was sealed off from the outside world. How could they cast spells with any kind of precision when they couldn't see the targets? Magic was far more directional than that.

"We could take invisibility elixirs," Auria suggested. "They'd help us sneak in and disarm the Bloodmoons."

"Use your head," Sebran replied, irritated. "The guards would see the front doors open. And even if we weren't instantly killed, the odds of us accidentally firing curses at one another . . ."

As the cohort bickered, Saffron's mind spun like a roulette wheel.

She always did this, thought while others spoke, weighed every word or action carefully before committing to it. Because Saints knew what happened when you *didn't* think it all the way through. When you turned a doorknob a quarter of an inch, and your parents were slaughtered between one heartbeat and the next.

In any case, they were all thinking about it the wrong way. Shallowly, one-dimensionally. Putting too much weight on the solution without giving the problem its due diligence.

Forgetting one very simple question: *Why?*

Interrupting Sebran's rant about the acceptable number of civilian casualties being higher than zero, Saff said, "Look, why would the Bloodmoons hold up an Augurest temple in the first place? Don't we need to understand their motives first?"

"We're not fucking diplomats," said Nissa, golden eyes boring intensely into Saff, a stare that carried an almost physical heat. There was a rumor that Nissa's grandmother was a dragon, but Saff couldn't quite wrap her head around the logistics.

"Auria, could there be anything of great value in Augur Amuilly's temple?" Saff asked. "Something *worth* this level of Bloodmoon manpower?"

Auria pursed her lips. "Some of the older worship chambers contain relic wands from the era of the Five Augurs. Not the wands belonging to the Augurs themselves, but from other Foreseers in that time period. Followers believe these relics still contain old power, and that in the right hands, they could be used to cast new prophecies."

Saff nodded intensely. "So maybe we focus on extracting the relic, not the hostages. Draw the Bloodmoons away from the innocent people they have no real interest in."

"I like that idea." Auria's blue eyes crinkled. "But the relics would likely be in underground vaults. If they were in plain sight maybe we'd be able to levitate them out, but . . ."

"This is ludicrous." Sebran shook his head in disgust. "You're intentionally misinterpreting the assignment. Following orders is critical in a hierarchal institution. The captain told us to extract the hostages—not a relic that might be completely irrelevant, that might not even *exist.*" He projected his voice a little more clearly than usual, as though he wanted the higher-ups to hear.

"Would you like me to fetch a straw, Sebran?" Saff asked earnestly.

Sebran frowned. "Why?"

"For all your sucking up."

"*Sen effigias,*" came a sudden command from beside Saff. Then again, "*Sen effigias.*"

In a burst of impatience, Nissa had struck the two guards flanking the entrance.

They stood still as statues, their bodies turned to ash-gray stone.

For the purposes of this exercise, they were dead.

"Shall we?" Nissa asked sweetly, starting toward the entrance, and Saff was knocked momentarily breathless by a surge of anger.

"What the hell?" hissed Auria.

Nissa turned on her heel, exposing the vertical column of runes tattooed up the side of her neck. "There's only one way into the temple, and they were guarding it. We'd have had to do it at some point."

"No, the captain said it was possible to complete the task with all Bloodmoons and hostages taken alive." Auria's cheeks were pink with rage. "I can think of countless enchantments we could've used to get past them. *Exarman,* to disarm. *Vertigloran* to make them dizzy and disoriented. You didn't need to ruin the assessment before we even—"

"I'm going to make a wind tunnel," Nissa interrupted. "Who's coming?"

Sebran gave her a mocking salute and followed, wandless. Gaian hesitated for a moment, pale skin looking particularly white, then tailed Sebran toward the entrance.

Auria sighed, shoulders sinking. "So now our choices are either to split up the group and get a low score for teamwork, or go along with this reckless insanity."

Saff clenched her jaw. "Nissa was the one who sacrificed any notion of working together. Let's do our own thing. Prove that we care about doing this properly."

Auria nodded in agreement, while Tiernan looked anxiously from Nissa to the temple and then up to the viewing gallery where his father sat.

"Sorry," he eventually said, rubbing the back of his head. "I don't see a better way."

And then he stalked off after Nissa, Sebran, and Gaian.

"You're better than this, Tiernan," Auria muttered. Some of the shine had slipped from her demeanor.

Nissa yanked open the doors to the temple, and an echoey voice yelled from inside: "*Sen effigias.*"

She ducked the curse, and it struck Tiernan square in the forehead.

Every inch of him turned to gray stone, and a skirmish broke out between Nissa, Gaian, Sebran, and whoever was on the other side of those doors.

"Well, I'm glad that went horribly for him," Saff snorted. But in truth, she was pissed off he'd squandered the switched envelope. "While they're distracted, let's do a lap of the perimeter. There must be something we haven't thought of. A back entrance, an open window, a tree we can scale to get a better vantage point."

Auria nodded, casting one more disdainful glance in the direction of the others. Sebran lay prone on the floor behind the statue of Tiernan, the vials from his tincture belt scattered and smashed on the flagstones around him. Nissa and Gaian were nowhere to be seen.

As they walked, Saff reminded herself to drag her leg behind her like a useless slab of meat. It was uncomfortable—her left hip was overcompensating, and a dull ache already throbbed in the socket—but as Professor Vertillon always reminded them, this was how it might be in the real world. She might have to fight for her life with a horrible injury.

She knew better than anyone that these things were rarely fair.

The Academy had gone to great lengths to make the scene feel real. Around the perimeter of the temple, vendor carts sold pleasure-evoking refreshments: apricot pastry crescents and almond nougats, frothy caramel coffee and spiked hot chocolate. A pair of horses grazed at a hay bale, and a group of elderly mages sat at a fold-out picnic table playing polderdash, a card game in which the suits of Saints and priests were prone to changing colors and loyalties midway through proceedings. A young, handsome lute player with fiery red hair twanged the Bone Queen's Lament, eyes closed in feigned sorrow, fingers blurring over the strings. The mournful music was sweet and sad, pure and clean as bellsong, and as the lament built, Saffron's well of pleasure felt a smidge fuller than before.

Yet for all the scene's painstaking details, neither Saffron nor Auria spotted any alternative ways into the temple.

"Shame *portari* is no longer an option," Saff muttered, but under her breath, so that rule-loving Auria wouldn't hear.

Portari, the teleportation spell, had been outlawed several decades ago—stripped out of every wand in the land—and Saff was usually glad of the prohibitions. It meant fewer criminals evaded capture. But right now she had to wonder why the Silvercloaks hadn't been given special dispensations.

Slowly, however, another plan was forming in Saff's head.

"The roof," she said, looking up at the magnificent structure. The bulbous purple glass shimmered like a dragon's hoard. "It's mostly opaque, but we might be able to carve a couple of holes in it. We'll be able to see the central worship chamber. Maybe even cast some enchantments through it."

"*Yes,*" agreed Auria, so vehemently that the horse nearest to her startled. "I brewed three levitation tinctures—knew they'd come in handy."

A low yell echoed inside the temple, followed by the distinctive *ping* of a spell ricocheting off a stone wall. Auria pulled out two pearly white potions neatly labeled *ascevolo*. She handed one to Saff, unstoppered her own, and gulped it down in one.

A few moments later, Auria's feet floated several inches off the ground.

Saff knew the elixir would not work on her, but she had to maintain the lie. She swallowed the gritty potion confidently, as though fully expecting it to have the desired effect.

But of course, nothing happened.

Auria, now six feet above the ground and gripping onto a tree branch, frowned down at her. "Did you take it?"

"Yes." Saff feigned confusion. "But I don't think it's working."

"That makes no sense. I brewed them from the same batch."

"Strange."

"Maybe I didn't mix it well enough? There could be too much elm ash in yours."

Saff studied the nearest tree. A long, spindly branch jutted low on its trunk.

"*Sen efractan,*" she muttered, and it snapped clean off. Magic might not work on *her,* but she was still able to enchant other people, other objects.

Next, she gathered a bushel of straw from the horses' stash—with grunts of effort, to maintain the impression her left leg was not cooperating—and bundled it together, holding it to the end of the branch.

"A broomstick!" Auria called gleefully. She had a genuine, almost childlike adoration for magic.

Saff unlooped a thin rope from her belt and secured it around the bundle of hay. Finally, she opened the third levitation elixir and spread it over the length of the branch. Gravity immediately loosened its grip, and Saff mounted as it floated upward, making sure one leg drooped more clumsily than the other. For the smallest of moments, her stomach swooping as the broomstick rose from the cobbled ground, Saffron shared Auria's delight in the simple art of a well-executed spell.

As they drew level with the purple dome, Auria and Saff grabbed onto the corniced rim of the curved stone wall and hoisted themselves onto it with a grunt. The broomstick continued skyward before clattering against the high ceiling of the Grand Atrium.

Saffron perched on the ledge, breathing hard. The dome was mostly opaque, but there was a vague swarming and shouting of shadowed shapes in the worship chamber below—which meant at least one cadet had made it that far.

"*Sen aforam*," muttered Saff, pressing the tip of her wand right up to the thick, tempered glass.

A burst of horn-shaped magic shot from her wand, piercing a small round hole in the dome. Auria mirrored Saff's spell, and they both looked through.

The scene fifty feet below was carnage. Nissa was a statue in the doorway, while Gaian had been struck a little farther inside. Both stone faces wore stunned expressions, like they couldn't believe they'd been hit. Sebran, the trained soldier, was the last cadet standing. Using Gaian as cover, he fired haphazard *effigias* spells into the chamber, striking Bloodmoons and hostages alike.

A quick tally showed that five hostages had been "killed," as well as four Bloodmoons—though there could be more in the spiral corridor. The three surviving Bloodmoons, using hostages as shields, strode across the room to where Sebran crouched. Sebran drew his blisblade and sliced urgently into his palm, shivering with the surge of pain-pleasure, but it was too little, too late. He was badly outnumbered.

"What a bloodbath," Auria groaned in dismay.

Forgetting her voice was magically amplified.

It boomed through the wand-hole and echoed around the chamber below. All three Bloodmoons glanced up at the purple dome. One fired an *effigias*, striking the pane Auria perched on. The glass smashed inward, and she turned into a solid statue.

And then she fell through the dome.

Fast, hard, and made wholly of stone.

As she hit the mosaic tiles below, she shattered into a hundred pieces.

3

. . .

The Relic Wand

SAINTS, CURSED SAFFRON, STOMACH TWISTING VIOLENTLY AS she ducked out of sight.

What did that kind of obliteration mean? Could such damage be repaired? Once Auria was reanimated, would she still be in a hundred pieces? Limbs and organs spread over the mosaic-tiled floor like a spilled coin purse? She wouldn't be the first candidate to die in a Silvercloak assessment, but it was rare.

Yet one of the first things Saffron had learned in life was that when the worst *could* happen, it usually did. It was this cynicism that made her a great detective—she was very difficult to catch off-guard—but also prone to gloom and misanthropy.

Somewhere far below, the Bone Queen's Lament picked up pace, lute strings twanging fervently beneath the musician's deft fingers. A second *effigias* curse flew in Saff's direction, shattering another section of the glass roof. It wouldn't actually turn her to stone, of course, but she couldn't let the Academy know that, or her forged Enchanter accreditation would be exposed.

She could cast one of her illusions, if circumstances became truly dire. Her father had taught her the rare art of illusionwork when she was a child, so she could cast a shimmering glamour to make the others *believe* she was hewn from stone. But such spells were difficult to wield and costly to hold for more than a few seconds, draining the magical well faster than almost any other kind of enchantment—which is why so few modern mages used them.

Below, Sebran fired disarmament spells at the Bloodmoons. One landed true, sending a wand careening across the rounded room. The other Bloodmoons turned their attention away from the figure on the roof and closed in on Sebran, their faces thunderous, their scarlet cloaks drifting behind them like shadows.

Two *effigias* curses struck Sebran at once, and he turned to stone.

Saff was on her own.

How should she play this?

How could she salvage this ruined assessment to come out on top?

She could disarm the Bloodmoons one by one from the roof, but that wouldn't buy her enough time to free the hostages. She would have to cast to kill—or, in this case, turn to stone. Yet she badly wanted to prove there was a way to execute this assessment without crude slaughter. Even if she could take *one* Bloodmoon alive, they'd be a valuable source of information.

She ran through her arsenal of enchantments, landing on one Auria suggested before everything went wrong. *Vertigloran,* to make a target dizzy and disoriented.

Could she use that? And then cast an illusionary version of herself to trick the Bloodmoons, distract and confuse them while she approached from behind? It would drain all her magic almost immediately and expose her knack for illusions to the Academy, but both would be worth it to emerge from this trial as the sole survivor.

Then the Atherin posting would have to be hers.

In an ideal world, she'd have plenty of time to stop and consider every potential ramification of her plan. But this was not an ideal world, and hers was not an ideal life, and with all other cadets neutralized, the Bloodmoons turned their attention on her.

The remaining purple panes of glass shattered one by one, and then she was falling.

Her wand-free hand flailed above her, finding purchase on an unexpected solid length. Her enchanted broomstick gradually lowered itself from the ceiling, the levitation potion wearing off.

Hanging on for dear life as she descended, Saff yelled, "*Ans vertigloran!*" into the chamber below. It struck true on the first try, making her glad for the hundreds of hours of target practice they'd gone through earlier in the semester.

One Bloodmoon staggered and fell to clumsy knees, but the other two wore murderous expressions. The shorter of them fired another *effigias* spell up at her. It narrowly missed, but the next one likely wouldn't.

"*Ans clyptus,*" Saff bellowed.

A shimmering spellshield formed just in time to repel another *effigias.*

The spellshield shuddered and nearly dropped, and Saffron trembled with the effort of keeping it up.

While matter could not be created from nothing, certain Enchanters could use raw magic to maneuver intangible forms, such as illusions and spellshields—a rare sub-class of enchanting known as mattermancy. Thanks to her father's tutelage, Saffron was the only cadet at the Academy with any sort of grasp on mattermancy, much to Auria's chagrin.

The mattermantic shield would not protect Saffron from a fist or a sword, but it would repel most charms and curses. It was, however, incredibly costly, and Saff felt her power drain with alarming speed, as though a sinkhole had opened beneath it.

With the spellshield raised, she couldn't cast another spell at the same time—magic being a well with a single bucket—but it bought her precious seconds in which to think. Should she cast to kill? Conjure an illusion, even though it was likely too late, now that she was mere moments from the ground? Keep firing *vertigloran* and hurry out the remaining hostages in the confusion?

But now the other two Bloodmoons trained their wands on her, and she couldn't shield herself from all angles.

"*Sen effigias,*" bounced and echoed around the chamber, sparks flying, her shield flickering dangerously.

And then she was struck.

The spell grazed her shoulder just as her boots hit the tiles. She sucked in a breath, half preparing to be turned to stone—would she still be conscious, just unable to move?—but of course, it never happened.

Her heart thudded against her ribs like a battering ram.

Everyone would have seen that spell hit her.

Everyone would *know*.

The lapse in concentration caused the shield to evaporate.

The three Bloodmoons closed around her in a circle formation, one still wobbling from the disorientation spell. The end was nigh. She couldn't disguise *three* spells striking her square in the chest.

"*Ans vertigloran,*" she shouted, and this one found its target, but while the struck Bloodmoon keeled backward, the other two approached with menacing glares.

Both cast *effigias* at once.

Saff pointed her wand at her boots and called, "*Et esilan.*"

One of her favorite tricks.

The boots leapt from the ground as though on springs, and Saffron sailed forward on the momentum, clearing the Bloodmoons' heads—and overshooting quite dramatically.

Slamming into the opposite wall, she crumpled to the ground.

Rolling over to face their backs, she raised her wand, but they were already above her, the word *sen* hovering on their twisted lips.

Desperation cresting, Saff remembered a rare spell her mother had admitted to using on occasion. It would freeze a scene exactly as it was, if only for a few moments. Mellora sometimes used it to buy herself time when a patient was bleeding out, or if they had precious few seconds in which to diagnose and heal—she said it bought her invaluable thinking space.

Worth a shot.

She raised her wand, unsure what to aim at. "*Ans praegelos.*"

Nothing happened, but the Bloodmoons spun their heads wildly, a strange expression on their faces. Something like fear, or revulsion, or disbelief.

Saff sharpened the intent in her chest to a single defiant point. "*Ans praegelos.*"

Still nothing.

Was she pronouncing it wrong? Had she misremembered the word?

Or was the prefix the wrong one?

Magic was commanded verbally, and when casting a spell, one had to announce one's intentions. *Ans* represented honorable intentions, while *sen* represented ill. An important distinction, a built-in fail-safe, making it difficult to injure or destroy by accident. There were a couple of other prefixes—*don* for the elements, which didn't particularly care for human notions of right and wrong, and *et* for the practical every-day magics—but neither of them fit this scenario.

Why wouldn't *ans* be the correct prefix? Saff believed her intentions were honorable: save the hostages. Get Auria medical attention. But magic was as elusive as it was pedantic, and it had its own ideas as to what constituted good and evil. Some commands were inexorably linked to a prefix, such as *sen incisuren,* because the magic would always consider cutting and severing to be a destructive act.

Did it have similar preconceptions about *praegelos*?

The Bloodmoons recovered their composure, raising their wands simultaneously.

"*Sen praegelos,*" Saff bellowed with as much ferocity as she could muster.

There was a burst of blue-silver light, and the world fell silent and still.

All except Saffron.

The hostages ceased squirming and fake-sobbing, and the Bloodmoons froze in place, one of them in the middle of a backward stagger, the tilted angle of his body defying gravity, the ruby brooch at his throat shining like a pearl of fresh blood.

Even the distant muttering from the viewing gallery fell to nothing.

Every inch of Saff's body shuddered and coiled with the effort of holding it, an immense pressure pushing at her from all angles.

Time was not a beast that took well to being bridled.

Not wasting a precious second, she grabbed the three outstretched Bloodmoon wands and tossed them into the corner of the room. She used the two manacles looped to her belt to fix the three Bloodmoons together, knowing the restraints might not hold once she unfroze the world, but it would be enough to buy the surviving hostages time to escape through the spiral corridor, enough to seal herself as the clear winner of the final assessment.

Dizzy with the effort of holding *praegelos,* every fiber of her being willed her to let it drop, the bottom of her well exposed and scraping, but something else bothered her. She had to know if her initial instinct was right—that the Bloodmoons had a motive for holding up an innocent temple.

Searching the chamber for a potential vault entrance, she spotted a large, well-worn rug arranged rather precisely over the apex of the round room. Another small yank in her stomach—something she'd come to realize was a gut instinct. She followed it to the faded blue rug, pulling it back from the mosaicked tiles of forest green and star white and amethyst purple.

Beneath the rug was a hatch. It blended almost seamlessly in with the rest of the tiles, but it was an unmistakable hatch nonetheless. She dug her fingernails around the edges, trying to haul it upward, but it was too heavy, its seams too smooth. And while holding time still, she couldn't use magic to open it. Remembering a trapdoor with a spring-loaded mechanism in her own family home—devised by her father, in case magic should ever fail them—she pressed her palms against two opposite corners and pressed down *hard.*

The hatch swung open, and Saffron blinked rapidly, forcing her vision to clear.

She'd half expected a spiral staircase leading to a vaulted cellar, but there was just a small round compartment no wider than a horse's cart, no deeper than a grave. At its center was a purple velvet cushion with a wand-shaped indent in the middle—but no wand.

Validation surged in Saff's chest. She'd been right. They were here *for* something.

Where was it now?

She only had a few more seconds left in her, and she used them to study the room.

There. Tucked into the waistband of the mid-stagger Bloodmoon.

Another wand. Short, chunky, made of a warm-hued wood Saff didn't recognize.

Saff reached for it. Just as the *praegelos* charm fell, Saffron's quaking fingers closed around the tip—

—the world bleaches white.

A figure emerges through the blank mist.

No—two figures, mid-kiss.

One is Saffron.

The other is tall, pale, dark-haired, with a chiseled face and a scar bisecting his lower lip. His fingers are laced through the back of Saffron's blond curls, every hard line of his body pressed against hers.

They both wear Bloodmoon cloaks: flowing folds of scarlet, moon phases embroidered in black and gold.

The kiss deepens, intensifies.

Saff digs one hand into the hollow of his hip, and the man lets out a soft, rough moan.

Her other hand presses her wand against the man's stomach.

"Sen ammorten," *she says.*

The killing spell leaps, a fork of lightning, a death kiss, and the man staggers back, eyes wide with horror.

He slumps to the ground, dead.

Something hard struck Saff in the face, and the mist dissipated. The worship chamber materialized. She was flat on her back, relic wand in hand, stars in her eyes, temple aching from where she'd hit the ground. The Bloodmoons above her struggled with their bonds. Auria lay in scattered stone shards all around her.

"*Go,*" murmured Saffron at the hostages, her voice distant and watery.

The hostages clambered to their feet, escaping past their captors into the spiral corridor.

Was it over?

What just *happened*?

Saff wiped her sweating brow on the sleeve of her cloak, focusing on the final assessment and not the white-hot relic wand in her hand.

She had saved more hostages than the others had killed, and taken three Bloodmoons alive. In a real scenario, they'd be invaluable sources of information to the Silvercloaks.

One of the Atherin postings was hers. It had to be.

Her cloak would soon be turned silver.

Saff looked blearily up at the viewing gallery, expecting a round of rapturous applause once her assessors had realized what she'd done.

But instead she was met with a cold, stony silence.

4

...

Healing Stone

IT TOOK SEVERAL HOURS OF PAINSTAKING WORK TO PUT AURIA back together.

Tiernan and Saffron sat by her bedside in the hospital wing as a swarm of Healers and Enchanters tried—and failed—to reassemble her shattered parts. There was cursing and blaspheming, low mutters and furrowed brows, and a mounting sense of worry that the brightest mage to walk these halls in a decade would not leave this room in one piece.

Beyond the arched windows, the sun dipped over the horizon of Atherin, washing the purple domes and gold obelisks in a pink-peach light. Dust rose between the buildings, and there was the distant clang of bells, the roar of drunken crowds, the rapid clop of hooves.

A chariot race.

The streets would be shifting and reversing in order to trick riders into wild detours, and a crew of Wielders would be creating vicious hailstorms and torrential gales in a bid to unseat them from their steeds. The competitors rode wandless, to avoid the temptation to maim their rivals, though they were permitted to enchant their own horses prior to the race. Last year's Vallish Grandstand had been won by a beast the approximate size of an Augur temple, with eyes that could see through walls. Several important government buildings had been trampled by its carriage-size hooves, but it was so entertaining that nobody seemed to mind.

Saff used to bet on such races every week, until the Academy consumed her life. At first, she had used gambling as a kind of exposure therapy for her fear of the unknown, hitting the gamehouses night after night, rolling the dice and learning to live with the outcome, however unfavorable. She used it to blow off steam, to allow herself a brief respite from careful planning and controlled execution.

She wasn't expecting to be quite so *good* at it. Not necessarily at the simple bets, like the roulette wheel or the chariot races, but in the more intricate, skill-based games. Her tightly guarded emotions aided her nicely in the polderdash hall; her constant vigilance allowed her to read her competitors' every muscle twitch—she was used to studying subjects closely, so that she might recreate them in an illusion—and her natural inclination toward nihilism led to big risks with big rewards. Her bank vault was suitably lined with the fruits of her frivolous labor.

She wrapped her hand around the ascen she'd won from Gaian only a few short hours ago. Everything was about to change. Everything had *already* changed.

"I'm annoyed the others aren't here," Tiernan admitted, as a broad-hipped Healer gently removed his hand from Auria's stone wrist. "Thanks, Saff. For this, and for switching envelopes with me."

Nissa, whose fury over the final assessment had caused literal smoke to billow from her nostrils, had taken herself away to the pleasurebaths to replenish her well. Sebran and Gaian were drowning their sorrows in the Glory's Edge—a dimly lit, musk-scented tavern down the street from the Academy—while trying not to think about the fact that the job postings would be pinned to Captain Aspar's bulletin board in mere hours.

"Of course," Saff said vaguely, but in truth her ears were still ringing from the post-assessment silence.

The silence, and what had come before it.

What *was* that, when she touched the relic wand?

It had once belonged to an Augur—the temple was named for

Augur Amuilly, if Auria's knowledge was correct (which it usually was). Augur Amuilly had been the first of the Five Augurs, casting the original world-shaping prophecy a thousand years ago. Saffron was fairly certain his own wand was in a tightly guarded display in the Museum of Verdivenne, back in Amuilly's homeland of Bellandry.

What had Auria said? *Not the wands belonging to the Augurs themselves, but from other Foreseers in that time period. Followers believe these relics still contain old power, and that in the right hands, they could be used to cast new prophecies.*

The wand Saffron touched could've been one such relic, hailing from the era in which the art of foreseeing was at its height. But why hadn't the Academy just used a replica? Surely they hadn't brought in a genuine relic wand for what was essentially a training exercise?

Assuming the relic was real . . .

Did that mean it had cast a prophecy?

Was Saffron fated to kiss—and then kill—a Bloodmoon?

And had the rest of the room also borne witness? Or was the vision for Saffron's eyes only?

She wished she could ask Tiernan whether he'd seen anything, but he'd spent most of the assessment as a grim statue outside the Augur temple.

Her first instinct was to tell him everything, yet she felt somewhat ashamed of the whole thing. When she thought of herself in a Bloodmoon cloak, horror tugged viscerally at her guts. Horror, but also . . . intrigue. She was strangely compelled by it, picking at the image like a fresh scab, examining every tiny detail. The sleekness of the cloak, the rough edges of those moans. It was like walking in on yourself fucking someone you shouldn't.

"I'm worried about Auria, you know," Tiernan murmured, shaking Saff from her thoughts. "And not just because she's currently a pile of rubble. She's going for a fourth mage classification, on top of everything else. Because it's not enough to be an Enchanter, a Brewer, *and* a Healer. She wants Wielder too—probably because she can't handle Nissa having something she doesn't. She's working herself to the bone all hours of the day, endless library studies, endless drills from Aspar in the dark of night. She's a shadow of her former self."

A fourth classification? *Saints,* that was almost unheard of. Three was exceptional enough—only a few mages in a generation achieved such a thing. Even Aspar, the highest ranking Silvercloak in the Academy, only had two. Magical abilities mostly followed ancestral lines, and if you didn't have a natural talent for a class, it was incredibly toilsome to force the matter.

"Is that why you're following her around like a lost puppy?" Saff smirked. "To provide restorative pleasure upon request?"

She'd meant it as a joke, but Tiernan's face fell. "I honestly don't know. Maybe she is just using me."

Saffron remembered one night a few weeks ago, when Tiernan had returned to the common room after a meeting with his father, sporting an ugly welt across his cheekbone. *Healing practice,* Kesven liked to call it. Storm clouds had darkened behind Auria's furious gaze, but instead of trying to bring assault charges—as she had so frequently threatened to do—she went straight to Tiernan, healed the wound herself, and then clasped his jaw in her trembling palms.

My father is right, Tiernan had said miserably. *I do need to toughen up.*

Your softness is the best thing about you, Auria had whispered, as though nobody else were in the room. *It's what makes you a great detective, and a great person. The world would not be so broken if everyone were like you.*

And she was right. Saff often envied Tiernan for the way he'd never hardened against suffering. Surely it was a good thing to still be so horrified by violence that you lost your dinner. Surely it was a good thing to always believe the best in people.

Saff smiled warmly at him. "Auria is not using you. I promise. And when she inevitably becomes Grand Arbiter one day, your father had better flee the country." A taut beat. "Have you spoken to him yet? After the assessment?"

Tiernan paled and shook his head.

"You should be in a place like this, you know." Saffron gestured around the hospital wing. "Healing, not catching criminals."

Tiernan nodded. "I know. Maybe once my father's dead. Hopefully he's assassinated soon."

Saffron barked with laughter. "I'm sure that could be arranged. Nissa would do it just for the sport."

For a few moments, they watched the Healers work in amicable silence. The hospital wing flickered with golden lanterns, and enchanted orchestral music played in the air. Intricate murals covered each wall—glorious depictions of temples and fruit bowls and Saints and orgies. Four-poster beds were strewn with layers of soft blankets and fur pelts, and there were bowls of sweet treats *everywhere.* Candied citrus peels and honey-roasted chestnuts, huge purple grapes and dark chocolate truffles. Velvines purred on windowsills, licking at their own underbellies.

In Vallin, pleasure was not just pleasure—pleasure was a force of nature, as vital as water, as integral as air. Pleasure healed, nourished, enlivened. Pleasure was downright constitutional.

Pleasure was magic, and magic was pleasure.

But pain was also magic, and magic was also pain, and therein lay the problem.

The Order of the Silvercloaks had been founded two centuries ago in an attempt to bridle the chaos and debauchery wracking the country. Ever since the founding of Vallin, there had always been a streetwatch, always a trial-by-jury system and always a crude dungeon into which criminals were tossed, but House Veliron were the first rulers to truly explore what magic could do in the prevention and solving of major crime.

Because in a world built on pain and pleasure, there were always going to be those who pushed the very outer limits of it—who exploited the fact that magic could not exist without those twin pillars. Street gangs who peddled narcotics to mages desperate for pleasure, Compellers who manipulated other mages into intimacy and submission, torturers who tried to siphon the potency of their victims' pain for themselves.

Enter the Silvercloaks.

How could enchantments be used to gather forensic evidence, so that the trial process was more robust, less reliant on hearsay? How could truth elixirs be built into the country's constitution, so that it was impossible to lie in a court of law? How could the Order develop powerful tracing spells to follow a killing curse back to its origin?

The latter was still a work in progress, and the Grand Arbiter had repeatedly voted down any motions to bring truth elixir into the courtroom (purportedly under the guise of protecting state secrets). But the Order did what they could regardless.

The air in the hospital wing shifted as Detective Tenébo Jebat—a fierce-faced, middle-aged mage with an utter mastery of enchantments—swept into the room, silver cloak billowing behind him like smoke. Hailing from Sinyo, a lush country of mountains and rainforests, he had deep brown skin and an arc of gold-and-ruby jewelry hanging from his septum.

"Step aside," said Jebat, his accent kissed with the gentle lisp of Cape Fala, Sinyo's capital.

The wall of Healers parted as he pushed toward the stone rubble of Auria. In the last few hours, they'd only reassembled part of an arm and the rippled folds of her cloak.

Jebat rubbed his temples. "The ineptitude is astounding, frankly."

He raised his palm-wood wand, closing his eyes and swaying to the orchestral music. A velvine leapt from the sill to his shoulder, purple eyes flaring, caressing his throat with cool, potent breath. Pleasure washed over him, and his skin glowed brighter from within.

"Ané-akouventa."

Though Jebat spoke perfect Vallish, magic was always strongest cast in one's mother tongue.

The jagged debris leapt at the command, scurrying into a sensible order like soldiers into formation, and in moments Auria's full form reassembled—all except her left ear.

Curse words rippled around the Healers.

"Find the ear," said Jebat, tucking his wand inside his cloak with a satisfied grimace.

As he stalked back out of the hospital wing, several Enchanters followed, heads bowed.

"So what happened in the assessment?" Tiernan asked Saffron, leaning back in the cushioned armchair with a sigh. He couldn't tear his eyes from Auria's statuesque form. "After I 'died.'"

Saffron scanned the room, but after Jebat's whirlwind, there were only a couple of Healers left behind, tending to another patient in a faraway bed.

So she told Tiernan everything.

Everything, except for her magical immunity. That card had to be kept close to her chest.

But he listened, enthralled, as she described the battle, the *praegelos* spell, the relic wand she'd found not in its original compartment but tucked into a Bloodmoon's waistband.

At this, Tiernan groaned. "You were right. To think of the *why.* I should've listened to you and Auria."

Tiernan was the most self-chastising person Saffron had ever met. She understood why—with a father like Kesven, he was so excruciatingly aware of his every flaw—but it became quite boring after a while.

"Obviously. But there's something else," she muttered lowly, before she could talk herself out of it. "When I touched that wand, I saw something. A prophecy, I think? And I don't know if it was real or not."

A small part of her twitched nervously. Should she be sharing all of this with Tiernan? He was a good person, and a good friend. She trusted him implicitly. And yet there was always the threat that he might share sensitive information about his cohort to win favor with his father. There was no precedent for this—as far as Saff was aware, he hadn't shared so much as Auria's tea preferences. But the staunch cynic tucked in the back of Saffron's mind always wondered what it would take for Tiernan to betray her trust.

Surely he wouldn't. Not after she'd switched envelopes with him in the assessment.

Tiernan blinked, pushing his owlish glasses up the bridge of his nose. "What kind of prophecy?"

"It was about me, and it was bad." She pressed her lips together. "Do you think it could've been a genuine vision? I'm no Foreseer."

Tiernan's brow furrowed. "Auria's the one with the comprehensive knowledge of such things. If anyone's going to know about a relic in Augur Amuilly's temple, it's her. But I do know that genuine prophecies are rare, these days. Other than the King's Prophet, there aren't many legitimate Foreseers left in Vallin. Although you know as well as I do that frauds abound."

The streets of Atherin were rife with wheeled carts decked in flowers, where shawled old mages charged four ascens for a fate. But most of them were known nonsense, and it was mostly tourists and Ludders who fell into their trap.

"Say it *was* a real vision." Saff's thoughts pirouetted as she tried to make sense of them. "Once a prophecy is cast . . . is it guaranteed to come to pass? Or is it more of a warning? Is it saying, *If you continue down this path, this will happen?* Or will it happen no matter what you do to try and stop it? No matter how hard you try to shift onto a different path?"

Tiernan gave a bitter laugh. "If we knew that, it would have prevented a lot of wars."

Stomach sinking, Saffron knew he was right. The question over whether prophecies were airtight had plagued the Augurests for a thousand years. Tiernan's homeland of Bellandry had endured plentiful civil wars over the very subject, while the two aged prophets who sat the thrones of Esvaine and Tarsa perpetually clashed over their differing opinions on what the future may hold.

Tiernan passed Saff the bowl of dark chocolate truffles, and she palmed three into her mouth at once. As they melted over her tongue, a shiver of pleasure rolled through her, the feeling of fallow ground being watered after a long drought. Still, she'd need a lot more to replenish the well in full. *Praegelos* had been so taxing to sustain that exhaustion burrowed all the way to her marrow.

Perhaps Saffron would seek Nissa out later. Her forked tongue could revive magic like nothing else. Besides, she craved Nissa's solidity, the way she never yielded beneath the weight of Saff's pain.

Because while Saffron loved Tiernan and Auria, she did so in a guarded sort of way. She never let them all the way in, never let them see how broken she was—not out of self-preservation, although there was an element of that, but to protect *them*. She worried that her dark outlook, her lack of faith in humanity, would somehow damage them. She'd never forgive herself for tarnishing Auria's shine, for eroding her faith in karma. During Auria's impassioned tirades about all the good she wanted to do for the city when she became Grand Arbiter, she genuinely seemed like she'd never entertained the notion of failure.

And Tiernan . . . Tiernan could barely handle his own negative thoughts, let alone anyone else's. He was a sweet man, but there was a kind of innate fragility to him that alienated Saff—although she supposed he hadn't survived his father's brutality for this long by accident.

Such was the appeal of Nissa. She was robust enough to bear witness to Saff's innermost despair without withering beneath the black gloom of it. Saff never worried for a second that Nissa could be tainted.

Just as Saffron and Tiernan were finishing off the truffles, an auburn-haired Healer entered the hospital wing, shaking her head defeatedly.

"Summoning spells are coming back empty, even for Jebat. The ear is nowhere to be found. Probably nothing but dust. We'll have to reanimate without it."

"Alright," said Paliran, the chief Healer, tucking their chin-length, caramel-colored hair behind an ear and rolling up their violet cloak sleeves. They had dozens of gold and silver bangles stacked up to the elbow, each engraved with the names of obscure healing charms, but Paliran didn't need to refer to the bracelets for this. They'd been reanimating fake hostages and Bloodmoons all afternoon. "Are you ready?"

Tiernan turned to the six-sided golden teapot on the bedside table, pouring out a cup of hot ginger tea for Auria's awakening. She was never without a flask of the stuff.

Relief coursed through Saff like a pulse. They were going to bring Auria back, and she was going to be alright, less for a missing ear, and Saff might be able to glean some answers about the prophecy before the job listings were posted.

Auria had always been generous with knowledge, never hoarding it for herself so that she'd appear brighter than everyone else. She left annotated notes on Saff's desk during exam season, helping her out on the subjects she struggled with, sharing strategies and shortcuts for remembering common law. She quizzed Sebran, the other Brewer, on elixir ingredients until they were both ready to drop with exhaustion.

She picked up rare books from secondhand shops in town, wrapping them in brown paper and gifting them to Nissa, her sworn enemy, because even sworn enemies deserved good reading material.

She was prim and sanctimonious, yes. Relentlessly assiduous, irritatingly upbeat, and often judgmental. A veritable stick up her backside at least seventy-four percent of the time. But she was also warm and smart and wonderful, with a fierce underpinning of righteous anger and a fundamental faith in the world.

And just like Saff, she always held a grudge.

Paliran raised their wand with a long, slow intake of breath, bangles clinking on olive-skinned arms. But before Saffron could bear witness to her friend's reanimation, there was a sharp touch on her shoulder.

One insistent tap, like a mourncrow's beak.

Saff swiveled to see Malcus, the captain's straitlaced assistant, standing behind her. A Ludder, but an excruciatingly thorough—and naturally deferential—one.

At the sight of him, dread sank into Saff's gut, the childish feeling of being caught just when you thought you'd gotten away with a misdeed.

That stony silence in the Grand Atrium still echoed in her ears.

"Captain Aspar wants to speak to you," Malcus muttered, voice low and grim. "Alone."

5

. . .

The Five Augurs

As SAFF WAITED OUTSIDE HER CAPTAIN'S CHAMBERS, HER hand went to her necklace.

Hung on a delicate gold chain was a wooden oval pendant, made from a small corner of her parents' once enchanted front door—still a faded teak, its magic stripped out by the force of the Bloodmoons' opening spell. Set into the wooden oval were two gleaming jewels, one emerald green and one purple sapphire.

The remains of her parents.

In Vallin, bodies were not dug into the cold, dark earth with their cloaks and wands, as they were in Bellandry and the Eastern Republics. Nor were they turned to stone and ground into sand, as was the Eqoran custom, so that their souls might return to the desert. The Vallish tradition—one that transcended religion—was to purify and heat ashes with raw magic until they compressed into glistening jewels, which were then set into all manner of jewelry. It was said that whatever color of gemstone emerged reflected the true soul of the deceased.

The honor of who got to *wear* their dead was a hotly contested thing, the most crucial part of any will and testament. Her Knight's Scroll in Modern History had taught Saff just how many civil wars had broken out over who bore the diamonds of slain queens. Jilted lovers and bitter exes, siblings and sons and daughters, all of them clamoring for the crown that carried the jewels of the past.

But nobody had fought Saffron's right to carry her parents with her.

The wooden pendant warmed beneath her grip, and it anchored her, brought breath back to her lungs.

Exhaustion pressed her eyes closed, despite the foreboding over what awaited her behind those chamber doors. As she teetered on the brink of sleep, she thought of her father, and of the day he taught her, at five years old, how to cast illusions.

"Listen to me, sweetling." Joran had knelt on the rug before her, palms rested on her narrow shoulders, the heat of the ever-burning fire pressed against her apple-round cheeks. "I know it stung you that old Renzel was reluctant to sell you a wand. But the fact you're immune to magic is a good thing, alright? No terrible curses will ever befall you. You'll never be rendered mute or immobile by magic, never be compelled to do anything against your will. But you're old enough now to understand that there are dark mages out there who may try to exploit your gift."

Fear had bucked in her chest; she was not yet hardened against it. "Dark mages?"

Joran's thumb had stroked the crook of her neck. "There might be times in which you need to create the illusion that a spell or curse has landed true. That you have been turned to stone, or shrunk to palm-size, or . . . I don't know, turned blue. And I'm going to teach you how. But it's challenging work, alright? Illusionwork is some of the costliest magic you can produce, which is why it fell out of favor a long time ago. And it's also why nobody will suspect you of using it."

"But *why* can't magic be cast on me?" Saffron had asked, for possibly the thousandth time since the wandmaker's snubbing.

A cloud had passed over Joran's face. "I'll tell you one day, my love. But not today."

They'd practiced mattermancy for several hours, and by the time Saff was able to conjure even a fine mist of an illusion, every bone in her body had ached with exhaustion. Joran had kept her replenished with sticky date tarts and milky hot chocolate, jubilant choral music and delicate hand massages, but Saffron's bucket had scraped the bottom of her magical well long before an experienced mage's would. When she could cast no more, Joran had scooped her up in his broad, steady arms and carried her all the way to bed. She'd rested her fire-warmed face against his chest, thinking that this was all very silly, indeed.

Why would she ever need to defend herself? She would always feel safe with her father by her side.

"Cadet Killoran."

Saffron jolted upright. Had she been asleep? "Yes?"

Malcus had emerged from the captain's chamber with a stony expression. "She's ready for you."

Letting her hand fall back to her side—the imprints of her parents etched onto her palm—Saff followed.

Captain Elodora Aspar was a renowned Wielder, and her chamber was a riot of the elements. Because *something* could not be created from *nothing*, Aspar had to keep plentiful supply at hand should she need it. Flames danced on the tips of silver candelabras, licking but never burning the floral arrangements climbing up the bookshelves. Wind chimes tinkled by the open arched window. A raised cauldron overflowed with earth and rocks, and a small water fountain shaped like a Serantic sea serpent burbled in the corner. It was carved from ascenite—a shimmering, pearl-like material, also used in the royal mint to make coins.

Ascenite had a lightly amplifying effect on magic, and wealthier mages adorned themselves in jewelry made from it. It was one of the only known substances that could not be magically enlarged, which made it the perfect currency. And while there was no true poverty in Vallin—food was always in abundance, and housing could be internally expanded to provide endless shelter—ascenite still held its allure, thanks to the way it augmented natural magical ability.

And unlike pleasure or pain, ascenite never lost its potency. Once you had it, you were bolstered until it was taken from you. Little wonder the Bloodmoons pursued and hoarded it so doggedly.

Aspar was a statuesque mage in her late fifties, with shaven hair and spiraling Augur pupils tattooed onto her eyelids: a mark of her devoutness, a show of faith in the first prophets to guide her when she herself could not see. Her silver cloak was pinned at the throat not with the usual sapphire but with a crystal-cut diamond—a mark of her tenure and seniority. Combined with the pale cream of her wrinkled skin and the ridged bones of her exposed skull, the palette was spectral, almost ghostly.

"Cadet Killoran." Her voice was smooth as seaglass. "Please, take a seat."

Saff's pulse drummed in her temples as she lowered herself into a stiffly upholstered chair.

Aspar aimed her wand—a narrow, neat mahogany—at the small coffee press on her desk. "*Et limus.*"

The golden top plunged through the dark, rich liquid. Aspar uttered another spell and the cafetière poured the nutty, caramel-scented coffee into a wide-rimmed goblet, which floated over to Saffron's open palm on a gentle breeze, dribbling a little onto the mosaic-tiled floor. All of this could easily have been accomplished by hand, of course, but most mages were afflicted with an occupational laziness when it came to doing things the Ludder way.

"Tell me, Killoran." Aspar leaned back in her chair—a huge throne-like thing with navy cushioning. She stroked the purple-eyed velvine purring in her lap, the dozens of silver rings on her fingers clinking together. "Do you honor the Five Augurs?"

Saff frowned, confused by the conversational direction. A beat too late, she noticed a weather-worn copy of the Divine Augurtures cracked open on Aspar's desk. A doctrine over which countless battles had been fought.

"No," said Saffron cautiously. "I was raised a Patron."

Unlike most northerners, her parents had taught her that a court of Saints had come together to make the world of Ascenfall—and all its forms of magic. As an Enchanter, Saffron's own Patron was Naenari, though she couldn't remember the last time she'd engaged in any sort of worship.

"We were never all that devout," she added, in the name of honesty.

"That is not what I asked. The beliefs of the Patrons are not fundamentally incompatible with Augurest worship. One can believe that a court of Saints made the world, while also believing that the Augurs foretold the future. Foretold the *truth*."

The beliefs were not inherently incompatible, no, but most mages fell into one of the two camps. There were atheists, of course, and several fringe religions—such as Draecism, whose followers were subservient to dragons, and the Disciples of Halantry, who worshipped the eccentric necromancer Halant—but the Patrons and the Augurests made up most of the population.

There were plentiful reasons the sects rarely overlapped. One was that the Patrons still honored Aevari, the patron saint of timeweaving, as a founding member of the court, which made them abhorrent in the eyes of most Augurests. Another was that the Patrons' Six Laws of Virtue expressly forbade genocide, which was not entirely unreasonable, while the Augurests had murdered Timeweavers in the thousands. The other reasons were more granular and largely not worth getting into, other than to say tension between Patrons and Augurests had historically oscillated between moderate and world-ending.

And Aspar knew this perfectly well. So why was she needling at a cadet with opposing beliefs?

"Are you asking whether I believe in the foundational prophecies?" Saffron asked measuredly. "I believe they were cast, yes."

A hard stare. "Just not in their teachings. Not in their *truth*."

Saffron had to tread very carefully.

The five foundational prophecies had been cast a thousand years ago, when the Foreseer class of magic was far more common—and more celebrated.

In the first prophecy, the Augur Amuilly foretold that a new magical class, the Timeweavers, would rise with a terrifying power in their blood. The people and the Crown would delight in the promise of what this gift represented. A chance to undo fatal mistakes that led to war and tragedy, a chance to remake the world in line with their own whims and desires.

This had come to pass.

The second prophecy, cast by the Augur Nos, said that with all this cavalier writing and rewriting of time, the fabric of the world would wear thin and eventually fray. That mages with opposing views would force a moment back and forth through the great loom of the world, changing the outcome over and over again, until that moment—and all the mages inside it—ceased to exist at all.

This had come to pass.

The third prophecy, cast by the Augur Vaurient, said that most mages would be seduced by this new power, desperate to claim a piece of it for themselves, and that only the bravest would remain faithful to the Augurests' true purpose—eradicating Timeweavers altogether, in order to save the world from accidental destruction. There would be a slaughter, but a necessary one.

This too had come to pass.

The fourth prophecy, cast by the Augur Emalin, said that the devout Augurests would emerge triumphant, but a few ancestral lines of Timeweavers would slip through the cracks, and the Augurests would have to remain vigilant for centuries, awaiting the second uprising, ensuring they slaughtered every last one.

This had not yet come to pass.

The last big purge of Timeweavers had happened long before Saff was born. No stones were left unturned in the quest to eradicate the ancestral lines once and for all. Not even the highborn were spared—the entirety of House Rezaran, one of the four royal houses in Vallin, was slain outside the Palace steps.

No Timeweavers had surfaced anywhere in the world for centuries. There had been no second uprising.

"Maybe the prophecies are factually true," Saffron said carefully. "Three have already come to pass, I suppose. I just don't believe in executing innocent mages, no matter what they're capable of. We should have found a way to legislate and regulate timeweaving instead."

"Timeweavers will unmake the world," Aspar barked, thumping a fist on the Divine Augurtures like a judge hammering a gavel.

Saff met her captain's blazing eyes. "For all we know, they'll remake it soon after."

The fifth and final prophecy, by the Augur Sarcane, had been long lost. Nobody knew how the foretelling actually ended, although plenty of evangelists had "found" forgeries in forgotten temples. In the past thousand years, countless relic wands had been worshipped, fondled, coaxed, and caressed, trying to uncover that vanished prophecy. To no avail.

Aspar looked up at the ceiling, as though the final prophecy was playing across her own mind's eye. When she spoke, it was cool, quiet. "Imagine, if you will, a world where everyone and everything you've ever loved can be undone. Including yourself. Imagine a mage so powerful that they could go back and make it so that you never existed at all. Does that not terrify you?"

"I guess it just feels like a fairy tale," Saff admitted.

"I see. And do you think there's a place for devout Augurests, like myself, in the Order of the Silvercloaks?"

Saffron stilled, weighing her thoughts. Truthfully, she didn't think anyone with a eugenic agenda should be in a position of power, but she had read enough of Aspar's passionate manifestos to know that her captain believed the Order of the Silvercloaks was the best place *for* Augurests.

After all, imagine a world in which criminals could become uncaught? Imagine a world in which kingpins and killers could wind back the clock again and again until their nefarious plans unfolded according to their wishes?

To that Saffron might counter: *Imagine a world in which Silvercloaks could wind back the clock until they* did *catch their marks.*

Imagine a world in which I had never turned that Saints-damned doorknob.

"I believe in religious freedom," Saff replied steadily.

The captain leaned forward, almost hungrily. It unnerved Saffron, and she was not an easy person to unnerve.

"Did you see anything when you touched that relic wand?" Aspar searched Saff's face, as though studying an ancient map. There was an intensity to the stare that Saffron couldn't parse.

"No," lied Saffron easily. "It's just a replica, isn't it?"

There was a loaded beat. Then, "Yes. Just a replica." Aspar closed the Divine Augurtures, as though to signal the resolution of their theological debate. "Now, onto the next order of business. Where did you learn the *praegelos* enchantment?" Aspar's gaze was blade-edged. "It's a maligned spell."

"I read it in a book of fables." The second lie slid off Saff's tongue instinctively. "Why is it maligned?"

"Too reminiscent of timeweaving."

"I didn't weave anything. Just froze it for a while."

Any decently powerful mage could pause time, in theory, but only a Timeweaver could wind it back—or forward.

Aspar's eyes narrowed. "I gather that you yourself were not frozen, given that you glitched from one side of the temple to the other inside a single second."

So they couldn't see what she'd been doing while time was paused. "No, I wasn't frozen."

"Yet *praegelos* is supposed to freeze *everything*. Caster included."

Was that right? It had been twenty years since Saffron's mother had spoken about using it. But sure enough, the way she'd phrased it . . . it bought her *thinking* space. Not actual space.

Was Mellora frozen too, with only her thoughts left spinning?

"Maybe I cast it wrong," Saff said evenly, though her palms were sweating.

Aspar leaned forward in her chair, steepling her fingers on the desk. "Cadet Marriosan's levitation potion didn't work on you either."

"She must have brewed it inaccurately."

"Auria Marriosan has never brewed anything inaccurately in her life."

"You've obviously never tried her tea," Saff quipped, but there was an unspooling feeling in her stomach.

A strange pause. "Did you know that we have a Compeller in our midst?"

Aspar's words were a taut murmur, a precise side step.

At this, Saffron blinked in surprise. "A cadet?"

A stony nod. "One of your peers has been given a false accreditation to protect their true identity. It'll be extremely useful for undercover work."

Saffron's mind reeled. Who could it be? Sunny, bookish Auria? Surely not. Bumbling, awkward Tiernan? Nissa, the smoldering enigma with the wicked tongue? Brave, albeit brutish, Sebran, with the mysterious background? Gaian, with his quiet confidence, his keen intellect?

Nissa's wielding was so strong that she couldn't possibly be a Compeller too. And Tiernan had been struck down so early that he seemed an unlikely candidate. Auria . . . they'd stuck together the whole time. She'd had no need to attempt to compel Saff. And she already had three classes of magic. A fourth would be almost unprecedented.

That left Sebran and Gaian—the two cadets most hell-bent on the Pons Aelii undercover posting. Surely Gaian wouldn't have lost to Saffron at cards so often if he'd been capable of compelling her into losing. Then again, would he risk exposing such a rare gift for the sake of a game of polderdash?

And Sebran . . . well. Nobody knew very much about Sebran at all.

"The Compeller was ordered to compel each and every one of you in a different way," explained Aspar. "And yet despite their efforts, you did not bend to their will. In fact, I'm not sure their will even registered upon you at all."

Saints.

"And you know, it's funny," the captain continued. "Because I could've sworn I saw an *effigias* enchantment strike you in that chamber."

"It grazed past me," Saffron said weakly, draining the last of her coffee.

"You forgot to continue your little mime, you know." Aspar rose to her feet, smoothing down her long silver robes. The velvine pattered to the ground, then stalked up the windowsill and leapt out the narrow crack. "The frozen leg became remarkably unfrozen around the time the Bloodmoons started closing in on you. You used *et esilan* to make your boots spring, and landed rather too spryly for someone with a single working foot."

Saffron didn't know what to say to that. She knew she was caught.

"You know what's remarkable, Killoran?" The captain crossed around the desk, footsteps clipped and smooth on the tiles, and rested a palm on Saff's forearm. "I laced that coffee with enough truth elixir to make even the hardiest of Bloodmoons sing."

With a soft swiping motion, she pulled the fabric of Saffron's white cloak all the way up to the shoulder, revealing the unmistakable starburst imprint of a spell that had met its mark.

"And yet every single word out of your mouth has been a lie."

6

. . .

The Assignment

DREAD CIRCLED IN SAFFRON'S STOMACH LIKE WATER AROUND a drain.

"What lies?"

Aspar withdrew her hand from the cadet's cloak, white folds of silk sliding back down Saffron's arm. Now that attention had been drawn to the mark of a spell landed true, Saffron couldn't unfeel the ghost of magic's touch.

The captain crossed to the mullioned window and stared out at the hazy moonlight settling over Atherin. The back of her head was ridged with bones. "You *were* struck by that curse. You *were* impossible to compel. Auria Marriosan *did* brew the levitation potion perfectly." A meaningful pause. "And unless you find some honesty within yourself, you can pack your bags and leave the Academy this very second."

Saff was backed into a corner, but although the thought of airing the truth filled her with fear, it also carried a light, lifted sensation: relief. The feeling of laying down a heavy load she'd carried for so long.

"Magic has no effect on me," she started, keeping her voice clear of emotion, which Aspar famously abhorred. "Doesn't matter who casts it. Myself, a friend, an enemy. My body just . . . absorbs it. Repels it. Does something—or nothing—in a way I can't quite figure out."

A fairly unique quirk—Saffron had never met another mage like her. And she had spent a long time looking, researching, asking quiet questions over pints of bitterale, nothing ever yielding the response she craved: that she was not alone.

"I've made it as far as I have in the Academy because I have a fairly advanced grip on mattermancy," Saffron went on. "Illusionwork. I can make it look like an enchantment has affected me, if only for a short while. It costs my well immensely."

Aspar sat back at her desk, tapping her wand to a locked drawer with an *et aperturan.* She pulled out a fat black folder, from which she withdrew a familiar cream and gold document.

Saff's heart careened off a cliff.

The captain cleared her throat. "Your mage school certificate says you have an Enchanter accreditation. But that's not the truth, is it?" A hawkish glare. "If you cannot enchant yourself, you fall drastically short of specialization standard. So you had the record forged."

Saffron bowed her head. Aspar didn't just know about the lies Saff had told this evening—she knew about the *big* lie. The colossal lie. The lie that could have her thrown out of the Academy, or even charged with fraud.

Because while Saffron had graduated from mage school with a Mage Practer certificate—that was to say, she had enough grasp on the fundamentals of magic and the practical daily spells to officially be called a mage—she had fallen short of the excellency required for specialization standard. She had her strange immunity to magic and six years of silence to thank for that.

At first, she hadn't been too worried about not achieving a specialization. Back then, the Silvercloak Academy only required a Mage Practer certificate for a candidate to be eligible. But sometime during Saffron's university years—while earning a Knight's Scroll in Modern History, a non-magical subject—the commissioner, Dillans, had decided that he only wanted the best of the best in the revered silver cloaks. From then on, Mage Practers couldn't make it past the streetwatch without a specialization.

Which left Saffron in a bind. It was too late to go back to mage school (only attended between the ages of six and eighteen) and use her illusions to scrape a specialization. She was stuck as a Mage Practer.

And so her accredited Enchanter record was an illusion.

Illusions, of course, were designed to be held for a short period of time. They were hard to conjure and costly to maintain, and ordinarily Saffron's certificate would only be enchanted for the length of time she was able to hold the spell. But it wasn't good enough for the forged accreditation to simply pass first inspection—what if someone at the Academy took it out at a later date, only to see the words *Mage Practer* written clear as day?

In a moment of desperation, Saffron had done what very few mages were willing to do: made the spell permanent. Such things were possible—it was how magical objects were made to stay magical—but bore a great price. To make a spell last forever, the caster had to give up a part of their magical well forever too. No matter how much they refilled on pain and pleasure, the magic used to cast the permanent spell would never be replenished. For an illusion as minor as some text on a piece of parchment, it was a small, almost negligible part of the well Saffron had given up. But she had given it up nonetheless.

She would always be slightly diminished—because she'd uttered the words *medei perpetua* after casting the illusion. *Medei perpetua* had carried an awful, heavy anchoring sensation, then the feeling of something inside her breaking away.

And now the sacrifice had been for nothing. Would her father be ashamed of what she had used his mattermantic teachings for?

"How long have you known?" she muttered to her captain.

"Since your very first interview—we have every school certificate stripped of magic, of course. You're not the first candidate to lie your way through these doors."

A feeling of utter humiliation came over Saff, as though she'd been fixed naked into a pillory outside the Palace. She'd put so much effort into her training, her reputation, and the stack of lies that held it all up, but it was doomed from the start. Five years on the streetwatch, a year at the Academy, all of them for nothing.

"So why did you let me enlist in the first place?" She fought to keep the misplaced anger from her tone.

Something dark passed over Aspar's pointed features. "Once upon a time, I owed your father a great debt of gratitude."

Saffron's chest twinged. "You knew my father?"

"A story for another day." Aspar leaned back in her chair, spine straight as a rapier. "Do you know why you're a great detective, KilToran? Because you think and you act in equal measure. The likes of Auria and Tiernan do too much of the former. Nissa and Sebran throw too much weight behind the latter. You take the extra beat to look at every angle, *then* you run toward the danger. The perfect intersection of cunning, calculation, and courage. You hold your goal in your head, and you chart a path toward it, and even when an obstacle arises, you recalibrate intelligently and ruthlessly. You wend your way through the wilderness, no matter how long or arduous the journey. You never lose sight of why you're here."

Saff bowed her head, thinking of her parents' wake.

The entire village had piled into the Sleeping Wolf, a pokey tavern with a thatched roof and dark saintmoss climbing the arched doorways. As she'd perched on a long wooden bench near the crackling hearth, Saffron's hand had never strayed from the fresh wooden pendant around her neck.

"How're you holding up, sweetling?" her gruff grandfather had asked. Saffron barely knew her mother's father, who'd traveled north from the southern coastal city of Aredan when he'd heard the news. He was spry, one-eyed, bearded, pale-skinned, and quite astonishingly drunk.

Saffron had shuffled in her borrowed mourning cloak and taken a sip of hot chocolate. She hadn't spoken a single word in the week since her parents' deaths, and couldn't quite remember how.

"It's alright to cry, you know." Her grandfather had taken an almighty swig of bitterale, his cloak sleeves sopping with spilled drink. "You didn't shed a single tear at the jeweling ceremony. Don't feel like you have to be stoic for us old folks."

Saffron hadn't known what *stoic* meant, but nodded anyway.

"Let me tell you something about loss, sweetling." Saff had hated her mother's term of endearment on those ale-puckered lips. "You can either yield to grief, or you can *use* it."

Saffron had looked up at him, questioningly.

"Those are the only two choices, in the end. Grief can bury you, or it can fuel you." He'd leaned in closer. "That's what I'm going to do. Make those scarlet bastards pay."

Her grandfather had died not four months later, after drunkenly ambushing two Bloodmoons on the street. But his idea had seeded itself in Saffron, and she was willing to bide her time to execute it. She would not swagger into the situation with inebriated bluster. She would think, plan, think some more, plan some more. And only then would she act.

Aspar saw that in her. Had always seen it.

The captain slid the fraudulent certificate back into Saff's file, looking intently at her cadet. "Something happened when you touched that relic wand."

Another sharp diversion. Saff's knee-jerk instinct was to lie again, but what was the use in it now? All the polderdash cards were already on the table. She was about to be thrown out anyway.

"There was white mist across my vision." Saff remembered the sheer brightness of it, like she'd been in a dark cave for years and finally emerged. "Then I saw myself . . . killing a Bloodmoon. I wore a scarlet cloak."

For personal reasons, she kept the kiss to herself.

Aspar's expression hardened, a kind of keen Augurest hunger in her gaze. Her palm drifted to the clothbound cover of the Divine Augurtures, as though about to swear an oath. "And have you ever had such visions before?"

"No. I was horrible at foreseeing in mage school. This vision felt like . . . it came from the wand, not me." Saff rolled her own ugly wand in her palm, and even though it had been twenty years since Renzel had reluctantly sold her the near-useless thing, his clear disdain for her broken magic still stung. "Is the relic real?"

Aspar's lips pursed. "That's above your pay grade."

Saffron came at it from a different angle. "Fine. Say it was a prophecy—are prophecies guaranteed to come true?"

The captain fixed her with a long, contemplative stare. Then, quietly, calmly, she said, "Whatever you saw in that temple will come to pass."

Saffron disguised how unsettling she found the prospect.

She was going to kiss—and then kill—a Bloodmoon.

And if she was going to do that, it should be in service of a greater goal.

She leaned forward, forcing conviction into her tone. "Captain, couldn't it be a *good* thing that magic doesn't work on me? I can't be struck with a killing spell. I can freeze the world for a few seconds and dodge through it unscathed—because I'm immune to the *praegelos* enchantment, like I am to everything else. Surely that makes me an asset, not a liability."

"*Praegelos* is an abomination," Aspar snapped. "Cast it again and you'll be kicked off the force faster than you can say *Timeweaver.*"

Saff gritted her teeth. Her mother hadn't been a hallowed Timeweaver, and neither was Saff. She was just, for some Saintsforsaken reason, immune to magic.

Then her attention snagged on what Aspar had really said.

"I'm not being kicked off the force anyway?"

There was a long bolt of silence as Aspar considered her next words. Saff's gaze went to the leather-bound spines on the nearest bookshelves. Slightly apart from the others, as though recently reviewed, was *The Elusive Fifth Element: A Study in Lightning* by Philomena Driver. There was a scorch mark on the bottom corner, the leather melted and warped around the blackened curve.

Finally, Aspar laid down her wand and said, "You might have noticed that there were only five job postings pinned last week."

"Noticed? We were all half-demented over it." Saff smiled, but it died on her mouth as she intuited her captain's meaning. "There's a sixth?"

"A deep undercover assignment. And I mean *deep,* not just gathering intelligence from Pons Aelii, like Cadet Villar will be."

So Gaian had got the posting. Sebran and Nissa would be livid.

Could that mean Gaian was the Compeller, after all?

Aspar grimaced as she went on. "Cutting-all-ties-to-the-Silvercloaks deep. Agonizingly, life-alteringly deep."

Everything inside Saff went still.

"As I'm sure you know, we've been building a case against Lyrian Celadon for many years. Decades."

The Bloodmoon kingpin.

Saff's heart tightened in her chest.

"Every Silvercloak in Atherin knows that the Bloodmoons are the fount of most violent crime in this city, but their tendrils spread so far into our various institutions that bringing a case against them has been almost impossible. We were close last year, with evidence gathered by Marcel Vales—who sadly died in action—but Grand Arbiter Dematus refused to bring charges on behalf of the Crown."

Frowning, Saff replied, "The Grand Arbiter is corrupt? Or just afraid for her life?"

"Again, that's above your pay grade."

"It's what you're implying."

A meaningful stare. "You can interpret my words as you wish."

If it was true, it was the scandal to end all scandals.

Grand Arbiter was arguably the most important position of power in Vallin—in comparison, the monarchs were mere figureheads. Voted in by several high-profile councils and governing bodies, the Grand Arbiter was responsible for the writing and abolishing of laws, the shaping of public policy, prosecuting major criminal cases on behalf of the state, and providing legal counsel to the royal family and the Vallish military.

And now Aspar was insinuating that the Grand Arbiter was in the Bloodmoons' palm.

Was that why Dematus so staunchly resisted the introduction of truth elixir into the courts?

Saff's mind was a beehive. She'd known for a long time that trying to secure Bloodmoon evidence was like trying to pin a dragonfly by its wing. Her parents' murderers had never been found, despite the crude crescents charred into their cheeks. The Silvercloaks knew Bloodmoons were to blame, but not which ones or why. Forensic sorcerers were developing techniques to trace killing spells back to their casters, but progress was nowhere near fast or conclusive enough.

Slowly, everything slotted into place.

The prophecy—if that was indeed what it was—had shown Saff in a cloak of scarlet. A cloak of scarlet she would always associate with the smell of charred flesh, with the feeling of grief so raw and sharp she thought she'd die from the pain of it.

There was no other situation in which Saff would wear such a cloak.

"You want me to infiltrate the Bloodmoons."

"Truthfully, I was on the fence." Aspar massaged her own temple. "Your incomplete grasp on magic could well make you a liability. But, as you rightly pointed out, it could also make you an immense asset."

"How so?"

Another grimace. "Do you know what the Bloodmoon initiation entails?"

"Plentiful torture, I'd imagine."

Aspar nodded bleakly. "Torture, truth elixir—which we have established you're immune to—and finally a loyalty brand. A round stamp burned right over your heart. It sears the flesh dark red, resembling a Bloodmoon. It's how they got their name."

Fear cut through Saff like a scythe through wheatgrass.

"The advanced dark magic causes the beholder to perish the moment they betray the Bloodmoons. Once upon a time they'd brand any civilian who fell into their debt, hoping to amass an army, but mages recruited by force usually took their own lives—and the dead are not profitable to an organization like theirs. So now they only brand those who enter their service willingly, in exchange for the wiping of debt. Every Bloodmoon who walks the streets in a scarlet cloak has a brand on their chest.

"With you . . . the burn would take, but the enchantment would not. These measures—the truth elixir and the loyalty brand—are the reason we've never been able to successfully send Silvercloaks undercover into the Bloodmoons. It's why our evidence has always been peripheral, secondhand, easy to dismiss. We need evidence that nobody, not even a compromised Grand Arbiter, can sweep under the carpet."

Enter Saff. The mage with broken magic and an old grudge.

"What kind of evidence?"

"Nothing that can be contained to one or two bad apples. It needs to be the whole tree, and it needs to be tied to the kingpin at the root if we're going to rip the whole thing from the ground. And we also want to know *why*. Why they're so hell-bent on money and power, on vaults upon vaults of ascenite. What their end goal is."

A wry smile tugged at Saffron's lips. "I heard you had eyes on the commissioner role, when Dillans retires. Being the captain who brought down the Bloodmoons would seal the deal."

Aspar said nothing to refute the idea.

Dillans was a shriveled old mage who'd been in the Silvercloak commissioner post for longer than Saffron's parents were alive. His biggest legacy was spearheading the campaign to outlaw *portari*, the teleportation spell, since it had scuppered a number of critical arrests during his tenure. Saffron had spent a not insignificant amount of time wondering what would've happened if it had remained lawful. Would her parents have been able to *portari* out of their house the moment the front door turned black?

Saffron took a deep, steadying breath. "In the Bloodmoons . . . would I still be Saffron Killoran?"

"Yes. We'd keep your own identity intact, to minimize the risk of being caught in a lie."

"So they'd know I trained to be a Silvercloak?"

Aspar gave Saffron a look that bordered on sympathy. "A spectacle will be made of you. You'll be kicked out of the Academy and publicly denounced for your lies and forgery. Charged with fraud, and sentenced to some Duncarzus time, to avoid suspicion. Upon your release, you will enter a Bloodmoon gamehouse and gamble away everything. And then you will borrow more, and lose more, until nothing can save you except offering your soul and your service to the Bloodmoons."

Saints. "Will anyone else know the truth?"

Aspar shook her head. "Nobody outside this room. You will be a Silvercloak, yes, but in my eyes and my eyes alone."

A sour taste tanged at the back of Saffron's throat. She hated the idea that the friends she was supposed to graduate with would think her a crook, a fraud, an embarrassment. Nissa, Auria, Tiernan . . . she'd lose all respect, all dignity. She'd spend weeks or months in the filthy gutters of Duncarzus.

And on the other side, she'd face the most dangerous mission imaginable.

Yet bringing down the Bloodmoons was the reason she'd lied her way into the Silvercloaks in the first place. They had destroyed everything that had ever made her feel warm and safe and loved. They had robbed her of a childhood. They had sentenced her to life in a nightmare she'd spent twenty years trying to wake up from.

And Saffron knew her decision was already made, because the relic wand had shown her as much.

Her future was written—had perhaps been written the very day she turned that doorknob—and it could not be unwritten now.

Captain Aspar offered a ring-decked hand, and Saffron shook it.

PART TWO

—

CONVICT

7

...

One Year Later

SAFFRON BLINKED INTO THE SUN. AFTER SIX MONTHS IN the dingiest of Duncarzus's dungeons, the brightness felt like hot pokers in her skull.

The navy tunic and dark slacks she'd worn at her sentencing hearing now hung loose in tragic swaths. She'd borrowed a length of rope from the warden to loop through her trousers, but there wasn't much she could do to disguise the collarbones jutting through the laced-up neck of the tunic. The feel of them protruding through her skin made her cringe. Fuller figures were very much preferred on the continent—a mark of power, of a well generously filled—and she was chagrined to lose the charming tummy rolls she'd been rounding all her life.

Her leather boots, polished and proud while she was at the Academy, were dusty and wrinkled from their time in storage. She looked—and smelled—like a street rat. It would work in her favor when she entered the gamehouse later that afternoon, yet shame clung to her like tar and feathers. She had spent her whole life fighting the urge to become this person, the urge to give up on herself and the world, and yet now, here she was. Tragedy manifest.

The street outside Duncarzus was deserted, and there were no carriages to be seen. Not that she was likely to hail one. Any horse with the slightest bit of pride would whinny and flee at the sight of her.

She could always take a *portari* gate into Atherin—while the transportation spell had been stripped out of Vallin's wands, a series of interconnected and highly regulated gateways had been established using the same magic—but she craved the rhythmic patter of her footsteps, the sun on her bare skin after so many months confined to a cell.

There were two routes into the center of Atherin. Strolling down the wide boulevard of Arollan Mile would see her pass Clay's Cloakery, run by the two uncles who'd taken her in after her parents died. Mal and Merin Clay were by turns flamboyant and eccentric, married in a flower-filled riverside ceremony the year Saff was born. Wealthy customers traveled from all over the continent to buy a cloak from Clay's—and to hear the scandalous court gossip from its proprietors. Few paid much mind to the silent, wild-haired girl moving through the storerooms like a ghost, a clothbound novel tucked under her arm, its spine cracked and pages loose from over-reading.

Her uncles had attended Saffron's sentencing earlier in the year, after she'd plead guilty to all charges. Mal had wept in the gallery, while stoic Merin had worn an unbearable expression of resignation. As though he'd always known that Saff, with her crushing trauma and frightening single-mindedness, was fated for something like this.

There was a saying in the north: *misfortune begets misfortune.*

She was living proof.

When she'd been led away from the gallery in shackles, Merin had whispered three strangled words: *coradin se vidasi.* An expression from Ancient Sarthi, roughly translated as: "my heart will not beat until I see you again." From Mal she'd have dismissed it as campy melodrama, but from restrained, repressed Merin, it cut through her like a blade.

In Saff's last letter to her uncles from Duncarzus, she had lied about her release date. She couldn't bear for them to see her like this.

She chose the other route into the city.

It was early Sabáriel, the seam between summer and autumn, and the clement sunlight had a kind of buttery quality. Atherin's streets were narrow and winding, decorated with mosaicked tiles of dark blue and forest green, grand murals painted into shallow alcoves. The pale creamstone of the buildings had settled over the centuries, the townhouses slouching into one another like common drunks. Every so often a wall would fold in on itself, offering a shaded nook in which two mages could spontaneously fuck each other senseless. The omnipresent sounds of horse hooves and orchestral music were frequently punctuated with moans of desire.

The entire city was built upon this pursuit of pleasure. Flower shops and massage parlors and pavement cafés spilled into the streets, a riot of color and scent and incense, the fresh gardenias and praline cocoa almost enough to cleanse the Duncarzus stink from Saff's memory. Stray velvines stalked the cobbles, sipping at bowls of sweetened cream left out by grateful residents, leaping upon the shoulders of drained-dry mages and purring upon their naked throats.

Magic wouldn't replenish itself, after all.

Food and sex were the most potent sources of pleasure, so essential to the survival of the species that human bodies *craved* them, magical or not. Pleasurehouses were notched into every street, strung with twinkling red lights and black awnings and tangled ivy vines. No ascens were ever exchanged; they were a place in which sex flowed freely, joyfully, fueled by achullah and flamebrandy, bodies entwining against rough walls and satin bedsheets. Most of the King's Cabinet could be found in a pleasurehouse the evening before the Great Wards were recast around the city walls each month, filling their wells until they overflowed with raw power.

As a country, Vallin vastly preferred revelry and bliss over the grittier power of pain. Nyrøth, on the other hand, was a culture entirely devoted to the latter—beds of nails and carved-up forearms, spiked cuffs around bleeding thighs, streets lined with whipping posts and pillories, dark-windowed shops flogging thumbscrews and torture racks, government officials scarified from the neck down. It was a point of pride, amongst the Nyrøthi, to see how much they could take, how potent they could make their power.

There was a *reason* nobody would declare war on the tundral north—they were brutal, unconquerable, their military and their royals forged of steel and suffering. And this culture of sadism and masochism was bleeding farther south, into the Eastern Republics of Laudon,

Esvaine, and Tarsa, kissing at the edges of the devout queendom of Bellandry.

Atherin was idyllic by comparison, a work of hedonistic art, but Saff had spent long enough patrolling the city to know the Bloodmoon vise had grown tighter. Rows of shutters were closed despite the pleasant breeze, and a Wielder washed the cobbles clean of blood smears, cursing beneath wine-furred breath. A wizened mage with a braided beard installed deadbolts made of deminite—which nullified magic's power—to his front door. Such bolts might have saved Saffron's parents' lives, all those years ago.

As she walked, she felt horribly like she was being followed. The danger of her imminent mission was already toying with her senses. Paranoia blurred the shadows, making her smell smoke where there was no fire, until at last she reached her destination.

The Cherrymarket was a vast cobbled cacophony of stalls that never wound down, even in the dark of night. Named for the bountiful copse of ever-blossoming sweetcherry trees at its heart—forming a natural pavilion over the plaza—the plaza was boxed in on three sides by narrow townhouses, tall-pillared Saint halls, and a purple-domed Augurest temple. On the fourth it was sided by the gushing River Corven—the very lifeblood of the high-walled city.

Atherin was landlocked in the center of Vallin, and spliced along its belly by the Corven. The capital was flanked by mountains to the east, where the river's source was notched, and valleys to the west, which swept all the way down to Port Ouran. Trader boats sailed up and down the arterial river and sustained the capital with imported gold and silver, silks and cottons, cocoa and coffee and spices and salt.

Today the Corven was topped with dozens of riverboats in purple and navy and emerald. Beside it the Cherrymarket hummed with activity, its vendors flogging everything a mage could possibly require. There was a stall dedicated entirely to different types of feathers—raven and phoenix, owl and parrot and sirin—which were important for all manner of flight tinctures. One sold vials of waneweed elixir, useful if one wanted to temporarily shrink down to palm-size, while another sold luxurious bolts of cloak silk with different defensive and amplifying properties.

Papa Marriosan's Gelateria, run by Auria's kind-faced, potbellied Brewer of a grandfather, sold a vast array of enchanted flavors. Coffee and walnut, to literally put a spring in one's step. Bitter lemon-grapefruit, to put hairs on one's chest. Honey-pistachio, to make one more attractive to wildlife (invaluable for apothecaries seeking rare ingredients). Saffron's stomach grumbled at the heaped mounds of chocolate gâteau gelato, which promised substantial aphrodisiac effects, but she thought it might not be altogether prudent to mount her captain like a steed, so she decided against it.

She found Aspar by a hot chocolate stall, holding two red paper cups.

At the sight of Saffron, the captain held one out. "Your favorite."

Saffron took a long, rich sip of peppermint cocoa, struggling to contain the groan as her long-empty well of magic gradually filled. After six months behind deminite bars—nature's opposite to ascenite, suppressing magic rather than fueling it—the utter lack of magic in her body had felt like a gnawing pit. Like absence; like grief.

Aspar studied Saffron as though searching for evidence of corruption or disease. "How was Duncarzus?"

In truth, the stint had been mind-numbingly dull. After a fraught first week—she'd been accosted in the mess hall by a thief she'd arrested during her time on the streetwatch—she was moved into protective custody and given a cell all to herself. It was dark, cold, and lonely, but at least it was quiet. It gave her time to think, to prepare, to mull over the prophecy and the mission ahead. And part of her—the part permanently suspended as a traumatized six-year-old—had been secretly glad not to have to talk to anyone. She vastly preferred the solace of her own thoughts.

"Fine," she said, and it wasn't wholly a lie. She'd always possessed the kind of internal grit necessary to persevere through bleak times.

Never one to dwell on a subject, Aspar dug around in a dark leather pouch tucked under her cloak, pulling out a green velvet coin purse. "At the gamehouse, lose this money first. Preferably on the roulette wheel. Something that depends on pure chance, so you can't be accused of being skilled or unskilled, rigging the game either way."

A shadow by the nearest stall shuddered and shifted, and a paranoid heat spread up the back of Saffron's neck. Again came that cloying scent of smoke, lightly spiced, like the achullah Nissa was so fond of. The thought of her old lover sent an unexpected lance through Saff's chest.

"There's a loan shark booth in the southwesterly corner," Aspar continued. "Pular Sistan. A nasty Enchanter who operates out of the gamehouse with the Bloodmoons' blessing. Because the more desperate they can make their patrons . . ."

"The more ascens they make. The more power they build."

Because ascenite was not just money. It was the great magical amplifier. And the more the Bloodmoons had, the more dangerous they became. The harder they would be to bring down.

Aspar grimaced. "Borrow a further thousand ascens from Pular, to make sure your situation is truly dire."

Saff took the green coin purse, and a curious frisson darted through her. Not dread or fear, but anticipation. *Excitement,* even. She'd worked her whole life for this assignment, and nobody felt more at home in a gamehouse than her—although she'd always boycotted Bloodmoon establishments in the past.

"Once you've lost everything," Aspar continued, "including the additional ascens you borrow from the shark, plead futilely with the teller for a while, then sell yourself to the Bloodmoons."

"Do you know how or where it'll happen? How I'll be . . . initiated?"

Tortured. Branded.

"The Bloodmoon compound is a few streets away, connected by warded tunnels we've never been able to breach. I'd imagine you'll be taken there for interrogation and initiation, and based there throughout the duration of your assignment."

"How will we communicate?"

"Sparingly. Use *et vocos,* but don't jump straight in with intel. You don't know what company I might be keeping, and this mission is highly classified. I'm the only one who knows the truth. So start with a code word. *Dragontail.* If I'm free to talk, I'll say *rising.* If not, *falling.*"

"Why *Dragontail*?" The word sparked a glint of recognition somewhere deep in Saffron's subconscious.

Aspar looked at her then. Truly looked at her.

"If you come out of this alive, maybe I'll tell you."

"If?" Saffron laughed, but the sound was hollow.

"It's a dangerous mission, Killoran. I've never suggested otherwise."

Saffron drained the last of her cup and tossed it in a street can. Nausea clamped around her stomach from the sudden influx of sugar, but she felt more human—more *magical*—than she had in months.

"Bide your time." Aspar scanned the market warily. "Root yourself in the order of things. Make yourself useful until you have a deeper feel for how the organization works. Only once you have this base understanding should you begin to plot means of gathering evidence. If it's essential we meet in person, I'll be alone at Esmoldan's Baths every Oparling evening. Not an ideal location, since there are darkened alcoves in which pursuants could lurk, so make sure you aren't followed. And I'll be here at the Cherrymarket every Laving at noon. I'll swap forms with my familiar."

Her familiar, Bones, was a pissant of a white cat with a black smudge on its nose.

"Why don't you go undercover yourself?" Saff asked. "As Bones?"

"They don't let cats gamble."

Saffron snorted. There was something *humor* adjacent in the retort, which Aspar was not exactly known for. "You know what I mean."

"The compound is heavily warded. The dark magic guarding the territory will only yield to a Crown-decreed search warrant, which is why we need substantial evidence against them. To give the Grand Arbiter no choice but to issue the warrant. Otherwise, access is granted only to those with a brand."

Saff looked up into the sun, letting the warmth wash over her face. "So I guess this is it. The point of no return."

Aspar bowed her head. "Whatever happens, Killoran, remember . . . *cera belrère*."

It is written.

The Augurest expression—Bellandrian in origin—brought immense peace to followers of the religion. An inherent trust in time and fate, a sort of absolution of worry and fear. Whatever happened was always going to happen, for it was written by the prophets long ago.

While Saffron had been raised a Patron, and while she abhorred the Augurests' mass slaughter of Timeweavers in the name of this mantra, she couldn't deny feeling a certain comfort in the idea. Her fate was already written. She just had to follow it to the end of its path.

With a final nod farewell, Saff set off in the direction of Celadon Gamehouse, feeling once again that every shadow had eyes.

Until, outside a secondhand bookshop one street from her destination, a shadow did indeed blink. There was a strange hissing sound, like sputtering embers, and it dropped like a curtain.

Before Saff stood a figure she thought would never want to see her again.

A figure of fire and smoke and dragon-gold eyes, in a cloak of flowing silver.

Nissa.

8

...

Three Corpses

AT THE APPEARANCE OF THE SMOLDERING SILVERCLOAK, A pavement display of leather-bound romance novels yelped and leapt to one side. A violet tome fanned itself, as though the surrounding air had grown far too hot.

Nissa resembled the vault of a wealthy aristocrat. The gold of her eyes, the silver of her cloak, the sapphire of her brooch, the ruby of her lips, the Irisian emeralds on her fingers, all underpinned by the deep, earthen brown of her skin. The gold stud piercing, notched in the bow of her upper lip—an Eqoran custom. Eqoran culture was rich and pervasive despite its secularity, and the lip piercing was to symbolize that kissing an Eqoran was to kiss the entire land.

"Anything you want to tell me?" Nissa drawled, taking a drag on her achullah.

Saff stepped beneath the sunny orange awning of the bookshop, as though this would prevent them from being heard. "Aren't you supposed to be burning the borders in Carduban?"

Nissa had been purportedly furious with her first posting out of the Academy—guarding the ascenite mines the Eqorans had lusted after for centuries—and had passed the time by scorching complex strings of ancient runes into the ground. The *Griffin Gazette* had run a story on it, since a pair of mountain-dwelling farmers had believed the marks to be made by dragons—which hadn't been seen on the continent since the Dreadreign. Saff had read the story from her Duncarzus cell, after the guard had taken a liking to her quiet, unobtrusive presence and tossed her the paper each morning once he was finished with it.

"They transferred me." Nissa shrugged. "Sebran's there instead. A few skirmishes broke out on the border, and Aspar *said* she wanted someone with a military background there to get it under control. But I figure it's also because I'm Eqoran, and she doesn't wholly trust my loyalties."

Nissa's family were originally desertcombers from the remotest part of the Diqar, but when they'd lost Nissa's young twin sisters to a brutal sandstorm, they'd relocated to the marble-fortified city of Zitra, on the northern border. Once they'd arrived in the city, however, Nissa's curious heritage attracted too much attention from a band of dragonseekers, and after multiple abduction attempts, her parents fled over the border into Vallin, where the Silvercloaks immediately offered special protection.

Now she searched Saffron's face with a strange mix of emotion.

Saff knew she hadn't imagined the flickering of the shadows, the spiced scent of achullah, the hair-raising sensation of being watched. It was often said of Wielders that *those who brandish the flame may bend its shadow.* Saff should have known, should have trusted her instincts.

"Fuck, Killor." Nissa's nickname for Saff made her toes curl. "I knew something was off."

"I don't know what you mean," Saffron replied cautiously. Thankfully she had a *lot* of experience lying through her teeth.

"Save it." Nissa rolled her eyes. "I overheard your conversation with Aspar. You're going undercover? Into the *Bloodmoons*?"

"No." A vehement head shake. "You misunderstood."

Furious thunder broke across Nissa's face. "Don't patronize me."

"Why would Aspar let me go undercover?" Saff argued. "The trial was true. I am a fraud. I forged my Enchanter certificate."

Nissa mimicked, in an alarmingly accurate impression of the captain's northern accent, "*Bide your time. Root yourself in the order of things. Then plot means of gathering evidence.*"

Saff sighed, breath gusting out like her lungs were bellows. "Fine. I'm going undercover. Happy?"

Nissa simply stared at her, as though it were a stranger standing before her in a shabby black cloak.

Saffron averted her gaze, looking instead at a rack of garish pulp magazines. On one cover, King Quintan lay beheaded at the foot of an ogre-faced Bloodmoon. Piles of ascens lay discarded around them, as though the monarch had been shaken loose prior to his execution. The pulps always reflected public opinion, and public opinion of House Arollan had soured of late, thanks to the Crown's lack of action against the Bloodmoons.

"But you did lie your way into the Academy." Nissa refused to drop her glare. "You're not an accredited Enchanter, are you?"

Saffron shook her head. "Just a lowly Mage Practer. I can cast enchantments—damn well, in fact—but magic doesn't have an effect on me. I couldn't enchant myself, so I fell short of specialization standard in mage school. I forged my certificate, then got through the Academy with illusionwork."

Nissa's expression darkened. "So when I used dragonbreath charms on you in bed . . . you faked it?"

Saff laughed roughly. "That's where your mind goes first? Anyway, this quirk of mine means I'll be immune to the sick and twisted loyalty measures inflicted by the Bloodmoons. Great silver lining, I know."

Something fierce and protective passed over Nissa's face, those golden eyes shining like lit torches in a dungeon. For a moment, Saff felt as though she had won the breakup—she might have been left, but here Nissa was, a year later, still *caring*.

"What are they going to do to you?"

Nissa clenched her fist so tightly that her claws appeared. Long, sharp, obsidian talons that only paid credence to the rumor of Nissa's dragonesque heritage. Saffron had asked Nissa about her fabled ancestry a handful of times—her favorite book, *The Lost Dragonborn,* centered on a boy with dragonblood who was critical to a devastating war between mages and dragonkind—but her questions had always ended the same way: with Nissa giving her the cold shoulder for several days, and nothing even resembling an answer. Not wanting her lover to feel like a zoo exhibit, Saffron had eventually stopped asking. But she never stopped wondering.

Blinking away the memory of those claws digging into the arched round of her hip, Saff grimaced. "I'm sure whatever your imagination can come up with is only the half of it."

"Hells, Killor." Nissa tucked a lock of sleek black hair behind her gold-studded ear, displaying the column of runes Saff had so often ran her tongue down. "Do you *want* to do this? Or was your hand forced?"

"I want to do this. I've always wanted to do this."

Nissa's jaw hardened as she drew again on her achullah. "Because they killed your parents."

A memory rolled into Saff's mind, clear and glistening as a marble. She and Nissa talking in low voices, late at night by the fire in the common room, her head in Nissa's lap. Nissa sipping flamebrandy while Saff recounted, in painful detail, what happened the evening her parents died. Nissa hadn't said much, only stroked Saff's silver-blond hair absently as she stared into the flames, but that night had been some of the best sex they'd had. No longer just hands and lips and flicking tongues, but hearts and minds too. No longer just a careless fling, but something *deeper,* more urgent, a new texture to their relationship.

Nissa ended things less than a week later. Saffron understood why she'd done it—self-preservation, or perhaps cowardice—but it still stung more than she cared to admit.

"They killed my parents," Saff confirmed. "But Nissa, you can't tell a soul, do you understand? If this secret leaks, then—"

"You'll be dead. Got it." A hard pause. "Are you scared?"

"No," answered Saffron, and it was at least partly true. She'd always possessed a kind of nihilistic fearlessness, a bravery born not from heroism or gallantry but from the fact the worst had already happened. Yet she couldn't deny the churn in her stomach when she thought of what might be about to happen to her—body and mind. "Are you angry? That I lied?"

"No. I'm jealous as all hells." Nissa gave a grudgingly admiring smile as her claws receded. "Goodbye, Killor."

"Wait. The captain told me there's a Compeller in our cohort. I didn't think it could be you, since your wielding is so strong. Do you have any idea . . . ?"

Nissa's eyes narrowed, but she didn't seem wholly surprised. Perhaps she'd felt the guiding hand at her shoulder during the final assessment, the almost imperceptible voice in the back of her head saying *No, do this instead.* "I don't know. Gaian is in Pons Aelii and Sebran's in Carduban, but I'll keep an eye on the other two—we're meeting for drinks at the Jaded Saint later." Loneliness panged in Saff's chest. "Frankly I've always found Auria a little suspicious."

"Well, yes, but only because she's always on time."

Nissa nodded sagely. "Exactly. Suspicious."

Something else occurred to Saff. "Oh, and back in the final assessment . . . what was the alternative information you received? I've always wondered."

Nissa shrugged. "That the Bloodmoons were going to start killing hostages one by one, every minute on the minute."

Saff snorted. "That explains why you got impatient with our bickering and took matters into your own hands. But why didn't you just tell us?"

"And miss out on an opportunity to piss off Auria?"

Saff gave her a flat look. "Nissa."

"I don't know, Killor." Nissa stared at a fixed point in the middle distance. "I'm a private person. I learned early in life that once a secret is out there, it can never be taken back. Once the rumor starts about your heritage, it's hard to extinguish the fire. In the final assessment, adrenaline got the better of me, and I reverted to what I knew. Secrecy." A smile quirked at her lips. "And maybe I just wanted to win."

"Relatable."

"For what it's worth, Aspar annihilated me afterward. I almost failed the assessment for *incontrovertibly poor communication.* That's why she gave me Carduban. But worry not, my darling Bloodmoon. I'll claw my way back to the top." Then, with a flourish of her black ash wand, Nissa finished, "*Don umbracelon.*"

Shadows spilled from her achullah pipe in dark, inky whorls and swallowed her whole.

The sound of footsteps echoed down the street before disappearing entirely.

Saff exhaled slowly, as did the nearest row of books. She didn't know whether to be unsettled or relieved that Nissa knew of her assignment. It was one more potential leak in the pail, yes, but Saff found herself oddly comforted by the knowledge that it was no longer only she and Aspar who knew the truth. This way, if something happened to her captain, there was still someone inside the Silvercloaks who could vouch for her.

Pulling her drab black cloak more tightly around herself, Saffron rounded the final corner.

Celadon Gamehouse was bright and sexy and magical, every inch of it designed to lure citizens inside—and to disguise the rot at its heart. There was a beguiling feel to the place, a tug beneath the ribs, a primal desire to go inside.

Golden lights announced the name, and the merry jingle of coins sounded from the slots. Manning the front doors were not sinister Bloodmoons in scarlet cloaks but rather two neatly dressed bouncers with black three-piece suits and golden bowties. There was the distant sound of live up-tempo music—saxophones and trumpets, pianos and a distinctive Vallish flambone. The scents of spiked cherry sours and honey-roasted rivernuts mingled on the breeze. Beneath it all was something richer, more metallic, like achullah blended with coppery blood.

Notched into the outer walls were rows and rows of glass jars, inside which were hundreds of naked dancers shrunk down with waneweed elixir. Miniature mages put on the performance of a lifetime, twirling and leaping around their tiny vessels, gesturing pleadingly to the small slots in the side of each jar, through which patrons could slip ascens as tips.

Saff found herself watching the tiny dancers for far longer than she should.

As she stepped toward the entrance, there was a ground-shaking thud on the street behind her—the kind of sound you heard with your bones, not your ears.

A ripple of screams carried through the gathering crowd as Saffron swiveled.

Three naked mages had fallen from the sky. They were tied together at the waist, deminite shackles around their wrists and ankles, skulls cracked onto the cobbles like eggs. Their backs were inked with white wings tattooed over jutting shoulder blades, marking themselves rather heavy-handedly as Whitewings—a rival gang of thieves rapidly gaining power in Atherin, much to the Bloodmoons' ire.

The Whitewings bled from their eyes, their chests, the cavernous gapes in their heads. Their bodies were mottled with cuts and bruises and other signs of torture, including shattered kneecaps and missing thumbs. The oldest mage's mouth was agape, revealing empty, blood-soaked gums. Their final moments had been filled with agony—agony so intense that their magic must have churned with raw and monstrous power—but shackled by deminite, there was nowhere for the power to *go*.

Pain, the ancient survival mechanism, hadn't been enough to save them.

Saffron's mind reeled. There were rumors that some dark mages had found a way to siphon pain's potency away from the recipient. They could inflict torture, and instead of bolstering the victim's magic, they could steal the power without having to endure any hurt themselves. The Silvercloaks hadn't found any evidence to back up this theory, but if any sect was likely to have mastered such a thing, it was the Bloodmoons. Her detective's instincts urged her to examine the mutilated bodies, but she couldn't. Tonight, she was a simple patron.

And so she stood there, watching the carnage, feeling strangely, horribly detached. Not just because the most formative experience of her life was a violent one, but because her five years on the streetwatch spat out such nightmares every week. She had stared down the red holes of headless necks; stepped over the bodies of naked, humiliated Ludders; comforted innocents burned from head to toe with cruel blackfire; borne witness as children grieved parents and husbands grieved wives, so overcome with the sheer magnitude of the suffering that her body rejected it entirely.

It soon became apparent that she wasn't the only bystander to feel numbed to it. Already the echoing screams had died down. Three mages lay mutilated in the street, yet the patrons moved around them like a river around a rock. They filtered into the gamehouse, their eyes glazed and happy, their heels jumping with anticipation.

Two Silvercloaks approached the mangled bodies, and Saff jolted at the sight of them.

Auria and Tiernan, dressed in hallowed silver.

Neither of them noticed Saffron, who stood several yards away from the corpses, but she pulled the black hood up to disguise her distinctive hair anyway.

Auria crouched to the ground, futilely feeling for pulses, while pale-faced Tiernan hastily set up a perimeter around them. His days of vomiting into gutters were behind him, but he still looked like he'd rather be anywhere else. Saffron watched as he moved in concerted arc-like patterns, always making sure Auria was covered, peering over his shoulder at regular intervals to make sure she was alright. At one stage his palm found the hollow in the small of her back, and she looked up at him, grim-faced but smiling.

So they'd finally heeded their love for each other.

About damn time.

Saff ached at the sight of Auria's nose scrunched in concentration, at the reminder of Tiernan's nervous, puppet-like movements. She longed for the warm fire of their common room, for long nights spent poring over spellbooks and dog-eared case studies, for sunset dueling in the cobbled yard until they collapsed into their four-poster beds, breathless and exhausted and deeply fulfilled.

Her time at the Academy had been one of the brightest spots of her life. She cupped the memory of it somewhere deep inside, like palms protecting a candle from a breeze. The Silvercloaks were her home, and she would find her way back.

Nodding at the black-suited doormen, she took a long, steadying breath and stepped inside the gamehouse.

9

...

The Gamehouse

AFTER EXCHANGING HER POUCH OF ASCENS FOR A MODEST stack of gambling chips, Saff wandered through the gamehouse in a trance, gazing up at the vast domed ceiling. Painted upon it was one of the most beautiful murals she'd ever seen—dragons and griffins, warriors and Saints and priests, naked nymphs in glorious waterfalls, bare breasts and soft bellies, the whole thing a smear of color and skin and *want.*

Pleasure churned into her well at the mere sight, and it felt wrong, somehow, to experience such a thing in the devil's own lair, but perhaps the wrongness was part of the appeal.

Pushing farther into the gamehouse, she passed a barrel-shaped woman arguing with the polderdash cards in her hand—one particularly mean-spirited queen had decided to poison the other royals, which had brought the game to a standstill—as well as several rows of elemental slot towers, which were famous for periodically electrocuting players in quite an erotic way. A gaunt mage wept at the feet of a wheel of fortune, which apparently told real fortunes, since it had been enchanted by a Foreseer. Said fortunes were rarely flattering. In fact, the more cursed your fate, the more likely you were to win big.

Saffron decided to stay well clear of that game.

Instead of heading directly to the roulette tables, her feet carried her in the direction of the divine scent. The bar was vast and round in the center of the gamehouse, shaped and painted like a gigantic roulette wheel. Saffron notched herself into a black seat and caught the eye of a handsome young bartender with dark brown skin, a Sinyi septum piercing, and owlish gold glasses.

"I'll have one of whatever smells so good," Saffron said, feeling lightheaded.

The bartender smiled, his face dazed, placidly content. "A blackcherry sour."

He mixed the drink in a disaffected trance, his hands moving fluidly behind the bar, and Saffron lost track of all the different tonics and tinctures being poured. The drink was handed to her in a tall, thin glass with a single blackcherry skewered on a mixing stick.

She drank thirstily. It was at once sweet and bitter, frost-cold and butter-smooth, alighting each of her senses in turn. A shiver on the skin, a pleasant tinkle in her ears, the luscious flavor filling her mouth and nose. The edges of her vision flared and danced with stars, and a sense of enormous well-being spread through her like a parting of shadows. It wasn't a potion—it wouldn't affect her, if so—and yet it had a far more profound impact on her sensibilities than simple booze.

She downed the drink in one, ordered another, and then looked at the bartender expectantly.

"May I mix you a third?" he asked.

"I was just wondering how much I owed?"

"Oh, no." He gave her a strange smile of his own. "Blackcherry sours are on the house."

Saffron found this a little odd—wasn't the whole point of Celadon to rake in as many ascens as possible?—but felt no need to argue. She strolled over to the nearby roulette table, feeling infinitely more relaxed than she had a few moments ago.

In fact, it wasn't just relaxation. It was . . . arousal? No, more than that. Like teetering on the edge of an orgasm, those blissful few seconds before the starburst—except the sensation spread over her whole body.

Saints, she felt good.

Maybe she wouldn't go straight into her mission. Maybe she would treat herself to a few games of polderdash first. It had been over half a year since she'd flexed those muscles, and suddenly nothing in the world was more appealing than *winning*.

She found a spot on a mostly full table and the croupier dealt her in.

As she played—and won, over and over again—a memory came back to her, rich and textured.

A few months into the Silvercloak program, the cadets had coalesced in the common room to play polderdash around a low coffee table. The darknight moon shone through the arched windows, the creamstone hearth crackling with merry flames. Case files and textbooks scattered every couch, every desk, every spare patch of floor. They'd survived their first law exam that day, and were celebrating with a bottle of flamebrandy and an ancient, ale-stained pack of cards.

Well, *Saffron* was celebrating.

The rest were growing rather pissed off.

"How did you win *again*?" Auria had grumbled, pushing a significant stack of ascens toward Saff. "I follow the best strategies every single time."

"Because you aren't playing strategies." Saff had shuffled the deck with expert sleight of hand. "You're playing people."

"And do you enjoy *playing* your friends?" Gaian's pale brow had formed a perfect arch, his gray eyes glinting in the firelight. "Manipulating their emotions, homing in on their weaknesses?"

"I do." Saff had smiled earnestly. "One more hand?"

Auria and Tiernan had groaned at once. They'd been depleted to a mere handful of coins each.

Sebran had long since retired to bed. He'd claimed it was because he still kept a soldier's schedule, and arose at dawn to train every day, but in reality he had lost all of his ascens in the first few rounds and could not stomach the embarrassment of being outlasted by Tiernan, of all people. Though Tiernan was actually rather good at polderdash, on account of having no idea what was going on, and therefore being quite hard to read.

Looking around the room, a rich, golden pleasure had poured into Saffron's magical well, not through any physical sensation but from a kind of emotional fulfillment. It had been happening more and more lately, the longer she spent with her cohort, and it worried her, how much she was letting herself care about them.

Another soft spot into which fate could drive a blade.

Nissa had sighed and risen to her feet, stretching like a cat. The flames crackling behind her only accentuated her dragonesque features. "I'm going for a smoke."

Another dare of a smile had tugged at Saffron's lips. "If you win this hand, I'll keep you in achullah for a month."

Nissa had rolled her eyes. "I have plenty of achullah."

Saff's own grin had broadened. "Alright. I'll kiss your toes in front of everyone."

After a few moments of consideration, Nissa sat back down, sheets of silken hair falling around her face. "Fine. But only because I thrive on the humiliation of others." She held out a palm. "And I'm shuffling."

Shuffling didn't help. Nissa still lost.

Because that was the first thing Saffron had learned about gambling.

It wasn't reckless when you were *good.*

And so in Celadon Gamehouse, Saffron kept playing until she'd won a frankly irresponsible amount of ascens. By the time she eventually made her way to the nearest roulette table, her well was brimming with the pleasure of victory.

It was a little-understood facet of the magical well. If joy or grief were powerful enough to elicit a bodily response, then they seemed to replenish the well in a similar way to physical pleasure or pain. Whenever Saffron thought hard enough about her parents, a hard brick of sadness slammed against her ribs, and her magic was, for a brief spell, galvanized.

At the roulette table, there were two other players—older mages bickering about whether House Arollan would fall before they met their graves—and a short, neatly presented croupier of around fifty. He wore a purple cloak over a gold-trimmed waistcoat, sweeping chips soundlessly from the velvet table and gesturing for the players to place their next bets.

Saff set her chips over the table, covering black and red squares equally. As the croupier spun the wheel and rolled the silvered ball around its rim, a thrill built in Saff's chest until she thought she might detonate.

The silvered ball slowed down, and Saff stared at it, entranced. In certain lights, it resembled an eyeball rolling frantically inside a mirrored casing.

No, that's *exactly* what it was.

As it came to a stuttering halt, Saff picked out the red veins; the dove-gray iris; the wide, fraught pupil.

An unsettling illusion, surely.

"Red thirty-six," announced the croupier, placing a marker on the table and sweeping away all the losing bets.

Even though losing was the reason she was here, Saff felt an innate snap of disappointment. When she'd first started gambling—back before she discovered her excellency at polderdash—she'd stuck to the games of pure chance, games wholly and utterly out of her control, like roulette. And whenever she lost early and hard, she felt the need to keep going, to keep betting, in a desperate attempt to recoup the sunk cost.

This was how the Bloodmoons made their fortune, after all.

Gambler's fallacy—the idea that surely she couldn't *keep* losing, when it had already happened so often.

That familiar desperation awoke in her now, like a beast from its slumber.

Losing was the whole point, and yet it still felt *terrible.*

She placed her next bets even quicker, that drumming sensation building ever higher in her chest.

Everything went according to plan for the next half hour, and despite winning the occasional round—which brought with it a familiar surge of pure, raw pleasure—Saff whittled her chips down to the last handful. The two other mages lost all their chips and disappeared in the direction of the bar. Saff was laying her final bets when the croupier muttered something so fiercely staccato that she had to ask him to repeat himself.

"Walk away," he hissed. "While you still can."

Saff's hand froze over her chips. "Pardon?"

"I haven't seen you at my table before." He tucked his shoulder-length brown-gray hair behind his ear. His silver name tag read *Neatras*. "Leave now, while you still have your wits. I won't accept another bet."

Frustration—and truthfully, dread—prickled at Saff. "You're overstepping."

"Please." The word was laden with grief, its single syllable sagging in the middle. "I had a daughter your age, and I cannot watch another . . ." Neatras stared down at his liver-spotted hands as though they belonged to someone else. He wore a deminite cuff around one wrist. He peered up at her pleadingly through slate eyes winged with wrinkles. "You feel it already, don't you? The restlessness in the tips of your fingers, in the space behind your ribs. Like you won't be calm until you lay down more ascens. Until you win again."

Saffron searched herself and found him to be right. The initial euphoria from the blackcherry sour had almost worn off, replaced by a jittering disquiet. There were subtle aches in her body that hadn't been there before, and the craving for another drink, another gamble, was so intense she could think of little else.

But she had to lose all her ascens. It was crucial to the plan.

"Nothing will ever be enough for you again." Though his voice was low, quiet, he'd abandoned all effort to speak through his teeth. "You won't stop until the debt is too high, and the debt is *binding*. Do you understand the meaning of the word? You'll soon find yourself dancing naked in one of those glass jars, hoping that maybe in a few months or years or decades, the meager tips will finally be enough to clear your balance slip."

This is what finally got through to her.

The naked dancers . . . they were trapped there until tips paid their debts?

What if that happened to *her*? What if she wasn't offered the option of receiving the brand? What if they saw a young woman whose nude dancing would reap plentiful ascens and shrunk her down with waneweed before she could protest otherwise?

Would Aspar do anything to help her then?

"This is my daughter." Neatras picked up the roulette ball, and the eye—for it was definitely, unmistakably an eye—swirled to look at Saff. "She resisted the glass jars, and now . . . all that she is exists in this ball, and she must watch day after day as her father is complicit in this hell. And so I beg you one last time. Go home."

The final words were rough, desperate.

Saffron stood from the roulette table and walked away.

She needed to regroup, to restack her emotional defenses. One of the first things she'd learned on the streetwatch was that it's almost always better to take an extra beat to steady yourself before diving headfirst into danger. Professor Vertillon, a decorated colonel in the Wielder corps, said that an extra moment of inaction is usually safer than hastily executed action.

Catching her breath would not cost Saffron anything, in the long run.

She pushed her way toward a sign that read ACHULLAH TERRACE. The outside decking area was abuzz with gamblers sitting on beanbags around low tables, and the smoke choked in Saff's lungs. Dodging a waiter carrying a blown-glass pipe of ruby and bronze, Saff hurtled down several wooden service steps and onto the uneven cobbles of a dusk-darkened alley. It snaked around the nearest buildings, and Saff followed it until the chafing laughter from the terrace was a distant echo, and the loudest sound was the roar of blood in her ears.

Pressing back against a cold, rough wall, Saff clutched her knees and lowered her head, forcing her breaths to steady. Her vision canted sideways, terror throwing her off-kilter, but she focused on the rhythmic filling and emptying of her lungs until the stars across her gaze faded.

Slowly, doggedly, she forced her spiraling thoughts into tidy columns.

Everything was going to be alright. She *knew* that.

When she had touched the relic wand during the final assessment, it had shown her a vision so clear it could only be prophecy. And Aspar had confirmed that all prophecy was *real.* Yes, the captain was a zealot about such things, but Saffron had seen it with her own eyes, had *felt* it resonate in the deepest corners of her chest. She didn't understand how or why the prophecy had been cast, only that it had.

Cera belrère. It is written.

She was not going to end up in a jar. She was going to become a Bloodmoon.

The croupier was wrong. She had nothing to fear.

She wiped the arm of her cloak across her clammy forehead. Her thick silver-blond curls stuck wetly to the back of her neck, and the aches in her body grew deeper, more bruise-like. Saints, she wanted another blackcherry sour. She wanted it like she wanted air.

Standing up and turning back toward the gamehouse, however, she heard an echoing cry of anguish from a nearby alley.

No, not anguish.

Agony.

A roar, bloodcurdling and coarse.

Well-drilled instincts sparked beneath her skin. Saffron was a trained Silvercloak, and trained Silvercloaks always went toward the danger.

Heart thudding, she drew her wand and pointed it at the soles of her boots.

"Et aquies."

The muffling charm took immediate effect. She crept silently down the alley, rounding several corners before a muddle of human shapes came into view.

Night had fallen, the sky fading from lilac to indigo, and her eyes struggled to adjust. Tucking behind the nearest wall, she lifted the hood of her plain black cloak over her head, casting her face in shadow. Then she withdrew a palm-size mirror from her pocket, angling it so she could see around the corner without exposing herself. An analog trick—one she'd discovered because she couldn't perform augmentation magic on her vision, like her counterparts could—but effective nonetheless.

The silvered glass showed three male figures hunched at the far end of the alley, illuminated only slightly by an almost burnt-out sconce. Two of the mages wore scarlet cloaks, the moon phases embroidered in black and gold. One of them held down the third figure—a reed-thin mage in a green Brewer's cloak—while the other muttered spells under his breath.

"*Sen perruntas,*" incanted a tall, broad-shouldered Bloodmoon, his voice low, malignant.

The Brewer screamed as his hand was severed from his wrist. It fell lifelessly onto the ground in the alley, blood spattering across the pale creamstone.

"*Ans annetan,*" the same Bloodmoon called.

The hand leapt off the cobbles and clamped itself back onto the Brewer's wrist, magically reattaching, the bone and flesh and skin fusing not quite seamlessly, but convincingly enough.

The Bloodmoon must be a talented Healer—albeit a terribly cruel one.

Tilting the mirror slightly, Saff studied the scene for any evidence of a siphoning device, but saw nothing. The Bloodmoon didn't look to be stealing the victim's pain-power for himself.

"I can do this all night," he growled at his victim, who whimpered in the other Bloodmoon's grasp. "We can cut it off and mend it as many times as it takes to get you to talk. And when you black out from the pain of it . . . well. We'll be right here waiting for you to wake up. At which point you may find yourself missing certain other appendages."

"P-please, I d-don't know anything," the Brewer stammered, curling his body futilely around his crotch. He had deep brown skin with a purplish undertone, almost certainly hailing from Nomarea. "*Nibabayo,* don't you t-think if I did, I would end this? I—*arrrrrghhhhhhhhh.*"

The Bloodmoon muttered another severing curse, and the hand fell raggedly to the ground.

"Where. Is. Nalezen. Zares?"

The name sparked no recognition in Saff's mind, if indeed it was a name.

"You have the wrong person, I swear it, *nibabayo,* I have no—"

"*Sen ammorten,*" the spell caster snapped.

The screams and kicks stopped abruptly, though they echoed around the narrow walls for several haunting moments, an almost prayer-like quality to them, as though a whole congregation were murmuring a funeral prayer.

The Bloodmoon holding the Brewer in place dropped his limp body, and the spell caster kicked the errant hand so far down the alley that it rolled to a stop at Saff's feet.

The cruel mage lifted his head until half of it was limned by the dim sconce.

At the sight of his face—the dark hair against pale skin, the chiseled jaw, the strong nose, the scar bisecting his lower lip—a deep chill scraped through Saff, peeling the marrow from her bones.

The Bloodmoon from the prophecy.

The one she was fated to kiss—and to kill.

And he was staring straight at her outstretched mirror.

10

. . .

The Fated Bloodmoon

The Bloodmoon strode toward Saff, the hem of his scarlet cloak skimming along the blood-spattered cobbles, and a dark thrill hooked through her belly.

It was *him.*

A fate emerging from the shadows.

Now the games began in earnest.

The Bloodmoon barely looked at her as he reached the mouth of the alley, finding her crouched behind the nearest wall.

She should have run, perhaps. Should've drawn on a mattermantic illusion to shield herself. Yet a thrum was rising in her chest, like a roulette ball spinning around its wheel, and she found herself unable—or unwilling—to cower and hide.

As it happened, he did not even raise his wand.

"Kill the witness." He spoke over his shoulder to his accomplice, calmly, casually, as though placing a tea order. "Take both bodies to the incinerator."

As though Saffron wasn't worth the effort of killing himself.

Loathing carved through her like a hot knife.

Oh, how she would enjoy destroying this mage.

The accomplice turned his wand on her, but Saffron had trained all her life for this. To adapt, to reroute, to change course between one second and the next.

"*Sen ammorten,*" incanted the accomplice.

Saffron threw up the mattermantic spellshield just in time.

The next two killing spells ricocheted off it, but the shield shimmered and fell.

Saints. Saff's magical well had been drained by the blackcherry sours. A counterfeit pleasure, a trick of the light, a hat with a false bottom. She felt almost entirely depleted already.

"Sen ammort—"

She couldn't waste her dwindling magic on the fancy boot-leaping trick, so she ducked to the ground and rolled out of the way, mind whirring as she assessed her options, as quickly and cleanly as a croupier shuffling a deck.

"I have something you want," she said, as the hood of her black cloak fell away from her face.

"What's that?" he asked, bored, as though used to strangers begging for their lives.

But then, upon a second glance at her, something shifted in his posture. A subtle straightening, the briefest recoil. As though he recognized her, somehow.

Saffron dismissed the thought—he couldn't possibly.

"Information." A sense of calm settled over Saff, her training kicking in. "I used to be a Silvercloak. I can tell you everything they have on you."

The flicker of almost-recognition vanished, and his stone-hewn face betrayed nothing but disdain. "If the Silvercloaks had anything on us, we'd be having this conversation before our good friend the Grand Arbiter."

He was close enough that she could smell the flamebrandy on his breath, the leather of his belt, the mint leaves and lemon zest of his soap, the unmistakable scent of warm skin. Close enough to see that though his blue eyes were a pure cerulean, there was no real light behind them.

Something essential in him had died.

"But I could—"

"And now you just gave us even more reason to dispose of you." He shook his head, sighing, *scathing*, like she was a bitter disappointment, like he was terribly used to everyone being less clever than he was. "Why is a former Silvercloak sniffing around Bloodmoon territory, willingly offering themselves to us?"

"I lost everything on the roulette." Saffron's pulse skipped as the Bloodmoon raised his wand, her body reacting to the danger even when her mind held firm. "Went outside for some fresh air, heard the yells, and came running. Old habits."

"Sen ammorten."

The curse flew low and fast.

Saff rolled once more along the blood-slicked cobbles, dodging the spell.

Of course, it wouldn't *actually* kill her, but she could not allow it to strike. If the Bloodmoons knew she was immune to magic, they wouldn't even bother to brand her. They'd slaughter her the old-fashioned way: a knife to the heart, a blade to the throat, a noose around the neck.

A scarlet crescent burned into her lifeless cheek.

The murderous Bloodmoon swung around to face her. "*Sen—*"

"*Sen vertigloran,*" she hissed, aiming at his ankles.

He didn't dodge quickly enough, and the dizzying curse buried into his shin.

He stumbled backward but did not fall, palm pressed against the wall to right his balance.

"Nalezen Zares," Saff rushed out. "I can help you find Nalezen Zares."

There it was again: a shift, a recoil. The Bloodmoon's grip tightened on his thick oak wand. "How do you know of Zares?"

"I fucked her mother."

A reckless riposte, perhaps.

His brow furrowed. "You can't have. I *killed* her mother."

A quirk of her lip. "But you seem such a peaceful fellow?"

Humor, she found, was a useful way to disarm those who believed themselves more intelligent than everyone around them. A way of saying *Here, look, I'm as quick on my feet as you are, as mentally agile, as sharply observant. I'm a person worth your time.* Or, if they didn't believe the idea that humor correlated with intelligence, at the very least they might translate *shock* as *interest.*

Sure enough, something like intrigue quirked on his face. The banter was buying her more time—or more rope with which to hang herself.

"I don't know Zares," she admitted, a little breathless. "But I have an old friend in the Silvercloaks—the most gifted researcher I've ever known. If anyone can find them, she can."

As the Bloodmoon considered this, something hope-shaped bloomed in Saffron. Miners in the Mountains of Promise used a homing charm to locate patches rich with ascenite. This was how it must feel to find a promising spot of earth: a glow, a hum, an innate urge to keep pushing forth.

"What's her name? Your friend."

Guilt lanced through Saff at the thought of dragging Auria into this. "That I won't tell you."

A muscle feathered in his jaw, accentuating the cleft in his chin. "Is stubbornness worth your life?"

"It's worth hers."

This earned her a caustic eye roll. "The integrity of a Silvercloak, even in your final moments. Admirable. *Sen ammorten.*"

"*Ans clyptus,*" called Saffron at the same time, and one more shimmering spellshield materialized in front of her, absorbing the killing spell.

But as soon as the shield was struck, it collapsed inward.

Her well was drained; she was almost out of pleasure, only a few desperate dregs remaining.

Pain would have to suffice.

Letting her cloak sleeve drop to her elbow, she dragged her bare forearm along the rough stone wall. She hissed between her teeth as her skin grazed and shredded, blood blossoming in furious patches.

The last scraps of power in her brightened, deepened, the quality increasing if not the quantity. It was stronger, more potent, but she would have to spend it wisely.

Dodging another killing curse, she muttered an old faithful spell under her breath. "*Ans lusio dulipsan.*"

"*Sen ammorten,*" he incanted, louder and shorter than before, as though she was beginning to piss him off.

Only now there were two of her.

The illusion surged from nothing. From decades of practice, it looked even more real than her own body, which she had shrouded in a kind of pale mist to make it *seem* like the illusion of the pair.

Both versions of Saff dodged the killing curse, and then they split in different directions.

Sure enough, the Bloodmoon's gaze followed the illusion, wand still raised.

For a moment, Saffron was entranced by her own work. The illusion bore such an eerie likeness that it sent unease curling through her, like watching a mirror reflection act of its own accord.

Illusion-Saffron tucked her silver curl behind her ear and raised her wand to the Bloodmoon, parting her lips as though to utter a fresh spell.

"*Sen ammorten,*" the Bloodmoon snarled.

The curse landed true on the illusion's chest—and flew straight through, smashing against the wall behind her with a *chink*. Shards of stone scattered on the cobbles below.

The illusion smiled sweetly at the Bloodmoon.

The Bloodmoon swung around in confusion, gaze flicking between Saffron and her curious apparition.

Sweat beaded on Saffron's forehead at the effort of holding it. She couldn't cast anything else to disarm her enemy—the magical well, with its infuriating single bucket—but the moment of disorientation allowed her space in which to bargain.

"I can be useful to you in more ways than one," she said through gritted teeth. "I can find Zares, and I can also manipulate the Silvercloaks as you need. And as you can see, I cast some fairly convincing illusions."

Her last vestige of power withered and died, and her illusion vanished.

The fated Bloodmoon shot her a brief glare, then a disaffected shrug, but she could tell she'd rattled him. "You've shown your cards too soon. Someone in the Silvercloaks can help us find Zares. Now we torture each member of your old cohort in turn until one of them squeals."

"That Saints-damned integrity would never give for the likes of you. The approach needs to come from me."

The Bloodmoon's eyes narrowed, and he took a few steps toward her. "Do you take me for an imbecile?"

"I don't think you want me to answer that."

His eyes were blank, unblinking, and somehow that was more terrifying than hatred. It was like he felt *nothing*. "This all reeks of Silvercloak work. Your sudden presence, your neat solutions . . ."

Frustration bursting its banks, Saffron snapped, "I'm not a Silvercloak anymore. You can give me all the truth elixir in the world and that answer will be the same."

"I don't have any more truth elixir on me. Wasted it on the Brewer, not knowing he'd swallowed an antidote. Segal?"

Segal, the accomplice, looked rather intrigued by the whole thing, and simply stared at Saff as though he'd forgotten something that he was trying desperately hard to remember.

As Saff met his gaze properly for the first time, recognition slammed into her chest like one of Nissa's wielded gales.

He was one of the Bloodmoons who'd killed her parents.

The short, stout figure. The low, heavy brow. The scratchy voice, like a rat's claws against a slate. Twenty-one years had not been kind to him—everything sagged and snarled in a way it hadn't back in Lunes—but Saff would recognize him anywhere. Hatred pulsed through her, white hot and roiling, expanding outward so fast it might decimate the alley walls in an instant.

But she couldn't let it show. Aspar had advised her to keep that particular aspect of her history hidden, lest her captors become too suspicious of her willingness to join them. She couldn't let this *Segal* know that she wanted to flay him alive, wanted to pour acid into his wounds, wanted him to suffer as she had suffered.

Segal shook his head, still watching Saff intently. "No truth elixir on me."

He shouldn't be able to place her—she'd stayed hidden in that pantry all the while he was in their house—but Saffron had spent enough time staring wistfully into mirrors to know that she was the perfect blend of her parents. Mellora's tumbling curls and heart-shaped face, Joran's high, aquiline nose and mirthful eyes. Hopefully he'd taken enough lives in the last two decades that they all blurred into one faceless victim.

Saffron faced her fated lover with as much courage as she could muster. She was only an inch or two shorter than him, at nearly six feet tall.

"So brand me, then."

The very air in the alley seemed to solidify, as though struck by *effigias.*

"Brand you," he repeated slowly, scarred lip curling. "You'd bind yourself to the Bloodmoons—the decades-old enemy of the Silvercloaks—just to save your skin."

"I said my cohort's integrity wouldn't give. Not mine."

He made a *pfft* noise. "You're more cowardly than I thought."

"Perhaps I don't want to die for the simple crime of being in the wrong place at the wrong time."

The Bloodmoon stood perfectly still for a moment, as though calculating a complicated chess line.

"You could have killed me," he said evenly. "When I had my back turned, chasing down that illusion. Segal was distracted. You could have killed us both and fled, but you didn't. Why?"

Because the mission requires me to take you alive.

"Because I'm not naïve enough to think I can kill two Bloodmoons and then go about my life as normal. And because I didn't have enough magic left to cast *ammorten* once, let alone twice. The illusion took everything I had left."

"Good to know you're powerless right now."

Saffron squared her shoulders to him, taking a step forward, their eyes level. This close, she spotted the telltale signs of exertion: a quickness to the breath, a subtle sheen to the temple.

"Magic is not the only kind of power," she said evenly.

"It's the only kind that matters."

"And yet all the magic in the world hasn't led you to Nalezen Zares."

A pause, in which an ephemeral shadow flickered over his face. "Nobody has chosen the brand in years."

"Yet here I am, choosing it over certain death." She laid her palm over her thumping heart. "Is that so hard to believe?"

A long, sprawling silence, in which she could practically hear the cogs turning in his head. Behind him, Segal shifted uncomfortably, plucking at the fabric over his heart. Did it still hurt, after all this time? Or was it a kind of phantom pain?

"If I find out this is all a trick," her fated lover snarled, "I will not kill you. I will hunt down everyone you have ever loved and bleed them dry in front of you. I will spread their deaths out, so that your suffering is not one fast strike, but a series of fatal wounds you'll never recover from. And when you beg me to kill you, I won't. I will force you to live with the pain until your heart eventually dies in your chest. And I will *enjoy* it."

"Cute speech." Saff smiled, because she had won, and she did so love to win. "No notes. I accept your terms."

She expected anger to break across his face in response to her flippancy, but he did not rise to the bait. His eyes were so lifeless that he barely registered the goading at all.

"Very well," he said finally, holding out a palm. "Your wand."

With a surge of triumph, she relinquished her wand, leaving her exposed and vulnerable, crossing over some treacherous precipice, the chasm widening and fissuring behind her.

Nothing had gone as planned, but as the Augurests would say, *It was written.*

It was always going to happen like this. A chance encounter in a darkened alley.

And now she was going to be mutilated.

They'd endured torture training at the academy. A cold-faced Wielder with jet-black hair had waterboarded them for hours, ensuring they could not be coerced into treason unless forced by a particularly talented Compeller. The truth could be easily loosed by elixir, which is why so much intel was classified, but Silvercloaks could always be trained how to resist *orders.* Tiernan had failed the torture exercise over and over again until Auria sat in there with him, so he could focus not on the intense pain and fear but instead on her gentle face.

Saffron had passed on the first try, yet the silken streams of water seemed a kinder fate than the unrelenting, permanent scorch of a brand.

She knew she could survive the pain. She had plenty of experience locking herself away from suffering. Hells, she could barely feel the hot sting of her arm where she'd shredded it.

It was what the brand represented that troubled her. Since she was immune to magical healing, she would be marked forever.

She could only hope that in time, it would come to represent bravery, not evil.

"Er, Levan?" asked Segal in that craggy voice. "You still want me to take the Brewer to the incinerator?"

A missed-step yank in Saffron's stomach.

The doorstopper case file on Lyrian Celadon floated to the front of her mind, bright and clear as a beacon.

Levan.

The Bloodmoon in front of her was Levan Celadon.

The kingpin's son.

11

...

The Kingpin's Threads

Saffron's heart cantered unevenly in her chest as Levan Celadon led her through a series of warded tunnels. Dark stone walls dripped with a nameless black liquid. Inkmice scuttled, and lanterns flickered, and somewhere in the bowels of the building there was a marrow-curdling scream. Saff felt the reverberations of it in her ribs, in her spine, in the back of her own throat.

She was fated to kiss—and to kill—the kingpin's son.

And at that moment, she didn't know which part was more horrifying.

How could she ever lay her lips on this monster? He had mutilated and slaughtered an innocent mage in front of her. He represented everything she loathed in the world. A fatal knock on a beloved doorway, crescent moons burned into her parents' cheeks. Six years of silence, a lifetime of grief.

But there was also the fact that killing the kingpin's son represented a failed mission. She was here to take them all alive, and if she slayed him where he stood, a wealth of information would die with him. Not to mention that killing him would put an enormous target on her back—the Bloodmoons would hunt her down for the rest of eternity until they could avenge the death of Levan Celadon.

Yet there was still that unsettling *thrill* somewhere in her belly. She'd spent twenty-one years thinking about bringing down the Bloodmoons, and now she was finally acting. Despite the roil of fear in her gut, the prospect was rather exhilarating.

Levan strode ahead of her in silence, both wands clutched in his palm, while gargoyle-faced Segal took up the rear, his gait loping and uneven, as though he wore a wooden leg. There was an oppressive tamping sensation from the wards, a kind of muffled gravitational pressure. Saffron dimly wondered how she'd been able to enter the tunnels at all without the brand. Perhaps Levan had lowered them enough to let her pass.

The stone walls were etched with unusual carvings. At first, Saffron thought the markings were simple runes, or perhaps untranslated glyphs from the pangea below theirs, until she realized they told a story, like the cave paintings found by miners in the Mountains of Promise. To her chagrin, they were moving too quickly for her to make sense of them.

Too soon, they took a sharp left at a crossroads in the tunnels, and a narrow stone staircase lay at the end of the passage. At the top was a squat wooden door, and as they crossed over its threshold, Saff felt a curious force press in on her from all angles, then heard a distinct popping sound as the ward gave way.

The atrium beyond the doorway was grand enough for an emperor of old. An intricately coffered ceiling depicted a legendary dragonback battle, gilded chandeliers dripped in teardrop crystals, and hunks of black marble formed the walls and floor. A pearly staircase swept into the center of the room, hewn from raw ascenite. Huge hulking blocks of it more than likely sat in the royal vaults. A staggering display of wealth and power. *We're so rich we walk all over our money.*

Saffron scanned the room for threats and exit points, as was deeply ingrained in her by the Academy. Countless Bloodmoons bustled through the atrium, scarlet cloaks swishing ominously, but few paid her any mind. Perhaps they were quite used to the kingpin's son hauling street urchins into their lair.

None of the servants or Bloodmoons wore shaven heads or eyelid tattoos, which seemed an unlikely thing to happen by chance—

Augurests made up a third of the general population, after all. Did the Bloodmoons have a policy against hiring them? Why? Augurest beliefs weren't inherently oppositional to the Bloodmoons' pursuit of ascens. Perhaps the Bloodmoons didn't want to recruit anyone with a staunch belief system—someone whose loyalties would always belong first and foremost to five fabled prophets who lived a thousand years ago.

Were Patrons similarly shunned? Was atheism a prerequisite? Did the Bloodmoons consider themselves a religion unto themselves? They were fascinating questions—and not ones Saffron had ever considered in much depth.

As Saffron followed Levan up the sweeping staircase, which shimmered with power beneath her shabby boots, something enormous and black dived at her head. She ducked so fast she almost sent Segal careening backward. Looking up in astonishment, she saw a pair of huge ridge-backed dragons chasing each other around the atrium.

"Not real," muttered Levan, without so much as casting a look back. "One of my father's favorite illusions. He likes to make them fight each other. We're introducing sweepstakes into the gamehouse."

Something in Saffron curdled at the idea that Lyrian Celadon shared her gift for illusions. Her *father's* gift. Mattermancy had always felt so sacred to her. Any kind of link between her and the Bloodmoon kingpin felt damning, somehow.

After climbing several more staircases, winding through more opulent corridors into the quietest heights of the headquarters, Levan stopped outside a vast set of black double doors with ruby-jeweled handles. He raised a fist and knocked, knuckles clenched white.

"Whomst?" came an amplified voice from beyond the threshold.

"Levan. *Fair featherroot.*"

Saffron's attention snagged on the watchword. She made a mental note of it for Aspar, though it likely changed regularly.

The doors swung open, and Segal shoved her forward.

The kingpin's office was so lavish that it crossed firmly into gauche. The walls were paneled black, and almost everything else was either gold, crystal, or ascenite—the cauldron simmering in the far corner, the ornate candelabras, the gold-leafed book spines in the coved shelving, the tiles of the fireplace and the dragon statues on its mantelpiece. It was stiflingly warm, with heavy velvet drapes pulled over the windows. Two emerald-green dragon illusions—smaller than those in the atrium—wrestled midair above a stiff leather couch.

Behind a squat mahogany desk, Lyrian Celadon sat in a wing-backed armchair, flicking his wand back and forth to maneuver the dragons.

He was thin as a spire, his spine hunched and crooked, his crop of once dark hair now a shock of pure white. There were simple enchantments to fix such things, but he must have liked the white, the way it contrasted so starkly with the bloodred cloak, the way it made his dark, hooded eyes even sharper.

Loathing licked through Saffron like a naked flame.

This was the man who had ordered her parents' deaths.

Strangely, there were no clear sources of pleasure in the room. No grand artwork; no bowls of sweet, ripe fruit; no music or scent; no velvines stalking the rafters. Not even a concubine languishing on the fire-warmed rug.

Where did Lyrian Celadon draw his pleasure from?

The kingpin barely looked up as they entered, so entranced was he by the dragons of his own creation. Instead he simply asked, cool and disinterested, "Who is this?"

"A former Silvercloak," grunted Levan. He stiffened like a soldier standing to attention. "Says she can bring us Zares."

Lyrian's left eyebrow quirked upward as one fake dragon tore a chunk out of the other's scaly shoulder. The wounded dragon gave a convincing roar of pain. "*Former* Silvercloak?"

Levan shrugged. "We need elixir to be sure."

The dragons blinked out of existence as the kingpin's attention latched onto Saffron, and while she prided herself on her ability to square her shoulders in the face of evil, there was something so oily and rancid in his gaze that she had to look away.

Instead, she visually scoured the desk, which was topped with a bowl of shiny peppermint humbugs; a detailed drawing of a racing steed covered in razor-sharp blades; a handwritten letter signed by the Steel King of Nyrøth, which surely had to be a forgery; and a jeweled ashtray filled with the kind of entombed eyes Saffron had seen on the roulette wheel. All of them looked very much conscious, aware, the whites of them spidered with blood vessels, the pupils dilated and afraid.

"Vogolan," Lyrian said coolly.

At first Saffron thought this was some sort of curse, until one of the velvet drapes rearranged itself into the shape of a mage in a scarlet cloak. Saffron blinked in surprise as a pale, hook-nosed face materialized in the fabric—then stepped clean out of it.

"Yes?" replied the mage Saffron presumed to be Vogolan.

"Truth elixir, if you please."

Vogolan drew his moon-embroidered cloak to one side, revealing a leather Brewer's belt at his slender waist. He plucked out a vial of pale yellow potion, then crossed to where Saffron stood and held the vial up to her lips. She obligingly opened her mouth and swallowed. It tasted sickly sweet—far more so than Auria's.

"Your name." Lyrian leaned back in his armchair, steepling his gnarled fingers the same way Aspar always did.

Saffron steadied her breathing, leveled her gaze, and spoke. "Saffron Killoran."

There was something petrifying about the blankness of the kingpin's stare—so similar to his son's. As though his humanity had long since died.

"Are you still a Silvercloak?" Lyrian asked.

"No. I never truly was. I didn't pass the final assessment." Saffron added this last part to make the Bloodmoons think the elixir was uncovering lies.

Levan's cerulean eyes narrowed. "That's not what you told me in the alley."

She shrugged. "I wanted to seem useful to you."

"I already know about your fraudulence and imprisonment," said the kingpin, with a blasé wave of his hand. "It was all over the *Gazette*. What I want to know is why such an incompetent wretch could be useful to us."

Saff wasn't expecting him to already know who she was, and it rocked her balance. "I overhead Levan torturing a Brewer for information on a Nalezen Zares. I don't know who that is, but I believe an old friend from the Academy might be able to help."

Levan's lip curled viciously, victoriously. "Which friend?"

Saints.

She'd have to answer; she was supposed to be under the influence of truth elixir.

For a split second, she considered using Aspar's name. She had the clearance to research Zares, after all. But if anything went wrong and the Bloodmoons killed the captain, nobody but Nissa would know the truth of Saffron's mission. And if Nissa couldn't convince the Order that Saff was undercover this whole time, she'd be trapped in the Bloodmoons.

"I suppose you're thinking of Auria Marriosan," drawled Lyrian, before she could even speak.

Her heart missed several beats.

The kingpin gave a wide, cruel smile, as though this was an immensely fun game. "Oh, yes. I know every name in this city, and *especially* every Silvercloak. A clever mage, is Auria Marriosan. Perfect marks on her Knight's Scroll in Common Law, although the final Silvercloak assessment landed her in the hospital wing with a missing ear. Righteous, proud. No religion to speak of, which will be useful if she wants to be an impartial Grand Arbiter. Although she'd do well to cut the Flane boy loose. The flame-hearted Eqoran would be a more suitable companion . . . although you have your own soft spot for Nissa Naszi, do you not?"

Saffron struggled to bridle her fear.

How in the hells did the kingpin know so much?

She had thought herself prepared for this meeting, but he was twice as prepared, and he hadn't even known she was coming.

"Yes, Marriosan." Lyrian looked deep in thought. "Now, *she* would be a valuable card to keep in our pocket."

Levan cleared his throat. "Killoran made the point that the Silvercloaks wouldn't willingly cooperate with a Bloodmoon. Better for her to make the approach."

"Well, we're rather skilled at encouraging cooperation." Lyrian stroked his chin. "Marriosan. Her grandfather is a gelatier. Do you think he could still make banana cream pie without his hands?"

The words clamped around Saff's chest.

The thought of sweet Papa Marriosan tortured because of her . . .

He was old. The pain would likely kill him.

Auria would never recover, and she would certainly never forgive Saffron.

"In any case, we don't need Killoran." Lyrian climbed to his feet, crossing around to where she stood in front of his desk. He lifted his wand and pressed it in the soft hollow beneath her chin, jerking her face up to the chandelier light. "Didn't your time in the gamehouse teach you anything about showing your cards too soon?"

Saff struggled to swallow against the jutting wand.

Had he been watching her the whole time?

As if to answer her question, he let out a cold, rattling laugh. "Each of the roulette balls act as second eyes for me. I see *everything,* Filthcloak. I know *everything.*" A cruel grin. "*Sen doloran.*"

The torture curse.

It had no effect, of course, but Saffron was used to pretending.

She let out a strangled, half-suppressed scream, her limbs trembling, her eyes beading with tears.

"Hurts, doesn't it?" Lyrian murmured, and there was a look of sadistic pleasure on his face, as though seeing victims squirm was immensely erotic. "I'll stop when you beg me to do so."

"No," Saff all but spat. "Never."

For some reason, her refusal triggered a curious reaction in the kingpin. In an instant he dropped the wand to his waist and gave a sordid head shake, as though disappointed in himself for resorting to such crude measures.

Saff let out a breath of false relief, though she kept the trembling for effect.

"Pain has never been all that satisfying to me." His voice was quiet, sinister. "Fear is a more sophisticated beast, is it not? Pain stops when the spell stops, but fear . . . it burrows, it grows roots, it takes on a life of its own long after I have sown its seed. To wield fear is to wield the greatest power of all." A dismissive hand wave. "I have magic, of course, but my most valuable gift is my memory. Because you know, Filthcloak, I never forget a face. I never forget a name. Every person in this city is mapped out in my head. Every strand of love and kinship between them shimmers before me, begging to be plucked. The most efficient means of compelling, other than compelling itself, is to tug those threads until they *hurt*."

Saff said nothing, and he paced in front of the fire, his steps neither frantic nor impulsive, but rather slow, deliberate, quietly intimidating.

"Your uncles, Mal and Merin. Cloakiers, and fine ones at that. We've used them ourselves to purchase common cloaks, for when we wish to move through the city unmarked."

He gave a broad, cold smile.

"How kind of them to take you in, after we killed your parents in Lunes all those years ago."

12

. . .

The Croupier's Sacrifice

SAFFRON HADN'T EVEN HAD THE *CHANCE* TO KEEP HER PAST a secret.

She had prepared for this for two decades. She had studied and practiced and patrolled and studied some more, grown skin thicker than dragonhide and instincts sharper than wolf claws, learned everything she could about the Bloodmoons' operation, cooked up half-baked plans for exiling her uncles from the city if things went south, and none of it mattered.

She was still *losing.*

That was the true horror of Lyrian Celadon.

It didn't matter what you did—he was always several steps ahead.

Not for the first time in her life, words failed her entirely.

"So my question is twofold." The kingpin stopped and turned on his polished heel. "Firstly, why would the daughter of two of our most unfortunate victims willingly walk into our gamehouse in the first place? And secondly, does it matter? Because once you're branded, there will be no way for you to betray us without immediate and agonizing death." Lyrian shrugged impassively. "And so it doesn't matter if your motivations are not what you claim. We'll be able to control you regardless, fit you with a tight collar and a tighter leash, walk you down the streets of Atherin like a dog, should we so please. And if you resist our orders, I know exactly who to hurt. Auria Marriosan, Tiernan Flane, Nissa Naszi. Your dear uncles. The moment you stepped foot in that gamehouse, you brought all of them with you."

Terror tied a noose around Saffron's throat.

She'd been too brazen about this assignment, comforted by the knowledge that she was immune to the brand, to magical torture, and to truth elixir. But the same could not be said for her loved ones. She'd known from the beginning that she'd be dragging them into this perilous snarl of conflict—she knew enough about how the Bloodmoons operated to predict as much—but she hadn't expected it to happen so soon. She hadn't counted on the kingpin's terrifying memory, the way his cruel hands hovered over the city, tugging at the strings below.

Determined not to show Lyrian that he'd rattled her, she forced her chin high.

"If it doesn't *matter*, cut the prattling preamble. Brand me."

She felt Levan's stare pressing into her, but she did not meet it.

Lyrian studied Saffron with onyx coldness. "Very well. I've always wanted a pet Silvercloak. Perhaps we can use you to turn every last member of your cohort one by one." He tapped his wand on his palm. "Vogolan, fetch the prisoner from the cell next door."

Vogolan left the room, and as Saffron's gaze followed him out, she finally returned Levan's glare. His blue eyes were still blank and unfeeling, but there was the slightest flicker of his pupils, the sense that he was making calculations, analyzing her every word, her every move. As though he was intrigued by her, despite all his best efforts to appear otherwise.

She had to be careful not to let that intrigue ossify into suspicion.

When Vogolan returned, Saffron gasped at the sight of the prisoner—face beaten bloody, clutching something small in his palm.

Neatras.

The croupier who'd urged her to flee. He coughed roughly, spitting out a bloodied tooth, his hair slick with sweat.

I see everything, *Filthcloak.*

Lyrian's cold eyes gleamed. "The loyalty brand requires a living sacrifice in order to work. It seems fitting that Neatras be yours."

Levan handed back her wand. Neatras's head lolled dangerously, clinging onto consciousness for dear life.

Saffron stood frozen with horror, as though she'd been struck by *effigias.*

"I can't," she said, to nobody in particular, and sure enough, nobody answered.

Instead, Lyrian gave a contented sigh, and Saffron realized *this* was where the kingpin got his pleasure from: inflicting horror. It was written in the flare of his pupils, the soft timbre of his moan. She could practically feel it pouring into him, dark and potent. No need for velvines or concubines.

Dread slithered through her like a hailsnake, and she gripped her wand, contemplating what she would need to do.

She had never killed before. At least not intentionally.

There had been an incident in her fourth year on the streetwatch, when she'd cast a disarming spell with too much raw force—heightened power welling inside her from the pain of a leg wound. The impact had sent the Whitewing thief sailing off a roof, his spine crumpling on the pavement below, his neck snapping like a bird's.

It had taken Saffron months of Academy-mandated counseling to process the shame, the guilt. It was a *good* thing that she still reacted this way to manslaughter, the therapist had insisted. It was a *good* thing that she still had her humanity, no matter how much she believed she was immune to grief.

But killing Neatras would be so much worse. Because it was a choice.

"Just do it," came a grunt from Neatras. "I'm dead anyway. Save yourself."

Helplessness pressed in on Saff from all angles.

If the relic wand's prophecy was anything to go by . . . she survived this encounter.

Which must mean she took this life.

She killed Neatras. Killed? Kills? Will kill? The tenses smeared together in her head. Did the nature of the prophecy mean this had technically already happened? She felt herself unspooling at the prospect.

She had always known, intellectually, that going undercover would lead her down some ugly paths. She had known that to properly bed herself into the order of things, she would have to kill at their command. But there was understanding with your head and there was understanding with your belly, with your heart.

"Last chance, Killoran." Levan's voice was indifferent, almost listless, yet she caught the impatient twitch in his stance. As though he wanted this to happen more than he was willing to admit. As though he too longed for a Silvercloak pet. "I'll go after Auria Marriosan with or without you."

Saff didn't move. *Couldn't* move.

At her inaction, Levan sighed, shaking his head with disappointment. "Fine. But you'd have saved us a lot of time and energy if you'd just let Segal kill you in the alley."

"They're all like this, son," Lyrian sighed. "The Filthcloak beetles always refuse to die. But they are often so terribly useful that sometimes it's worth taking them alive."

Anger seared up Saffron's throat like blazing bile, but she swallowed her hatred. She would not be like her grandfather, killed by a scarlet cloak for an ill-judged burst of outrage. She would keep cool, play the game, make measured moves toward her goal.

An abyss opened in her chest as she turned her attention to the man slumped at her feet.

If she didn't kill him herself, the croupier would still die. Only she'd be incinerated with him, and this rare opportunity to gather Bloodmoon evidence would be lost. The Silvercloaks would be further than ever from bringing a case against them.

Kill or be killed.

Maybe this was how most murderers became murderers—not because of some deep-rooted evil, some innate bloodlust, but because they had no other choice.

A heretical idea, for a Silvercloak.

There was always a choice.

She just had to make the wrong one.

"I'm sorry," she whispered to Neatras, her tone almost pleading. "I'm so sorry."

Neatras's hand tightened around what remained of his daughter, raising his chin and closing his eyes.

Saffron unhooked her brain from her emotions and raised her wand, a hard stone lodged in her throat.

"*Sen ammorten,*" she whispered, distant even to her own ear, the incantation uttered for the first time—but certainly not the last.

Yet nothing happened.

No unmistakable forked killing spell shot from her wand—only a pathetic waft of colorless vapor. Deep inside her lay a bottomless hollow, the feeling of a vast and glistening lake dried to a desolate husk, her well wholly sapped after the alleyway skirmish with Levan.

Saints. Would the Bloodmoons think she'd failed on purpose? That the sheer force of will required for such a curse was absent, and thus the magic would not obey her command? Would they think her too weak to join them?

Panic started to jackhammer against her temples, but she drew on her almost arcane ability to focus under perilous circumstances.

There were other ways to take a life. Terrible, terrible ways. But ways nonetheless.

One of the first things Professor Vertillon had drilled into the cadets at the Silvercloak Academy: sometimes you had to do things the old-fashioned way.

Hand trembling wildly, she pulled a simple steel dagger from her innermost cloak pocket. Its walnut-and-leather handle was carved with a decorative pair of fallowwolf fangs, a gift from her father's father.

Gritting her teeth, she crossed to Neatras, cupped the back of his head as a lover might, and swiped the blade cleanly across his throat.

His flesh opened like a bloody mouth.

As he fell, he let go of his daughter. The encased eye rolled to Saffron's boots, gray iris wide with horror and grief, all of it smeared in her father's blood.

Saff clutched her hand to the wooden pendant around her neck, the familiar grooves of her parents' jewels biting into her palm. The grim reality of the assignment struck her then, sharp and raw as a killing spell. Even if she came back from this, she would never *truly* come back. Not as she was, as she had been.

A whimper wracked her chest, and she could not silence it.

"How touching." Lyrian's voice was cold as the Tundra of Bones, and in that moment, she wanted to slaughter him where he stood. Evidence was more valuable than a corpse, of course. But *Saints,* what she wouldn't do to see him dead. "Vogolan, restrain her."

She had almost forgotten what came next.

The edges of her vision starred and blackened.

"You don't need to restrain me," she said weakly, as Segal and Vogolan yanked her by the upper arms, hard enough to bruise. "I agreed to this."

"It's one thing to consent," said Levan, "and quite another to feel the pain. We need to keep you still. If you buck, the brand won't take, and we'll have to repeat it until it does." His gaze was not kind, nor was it hostile. It was just empty. "It's for your own benefit."

Saffron was struck once again by the desire to plead, but she knew it was no use. This was something that had to happen.

Besides, some part of her knew she deserved this pain. She deserved to writhe and scream for the life she had just taken.

Neatras's unseeing corpse watched as Segal dragged her to the wall.

Levan uttered an inaudible incantation, and Saffron's arms snapped wide, deminite manacles folding out from inside the stone wall and closing around her wrists. They pulled taut, yanking Saffron's hands so far apart that every muscle screamed in protest. Her feet only just grazed the ground.

Segal stood mere inches away from her, stale breath wafting over her face.

"*Et laceran.*" He streaked the tip of his wand down the front of Saffron's tunic and it tore cleanly in two, leaving her bare breasts and pale torso exposed.

Shame burned through her cheeks. She felt as powerless and humiliated as a hog on a spit. Sweat beaded on her clavicle, from the fear and the stifling heat of the room. Levan pointedly averted his gaze, and in that moment, Saff was grateful for the tiny show of humanity.

Lyrian rolled up his tunic sleeves. From a brass rack, he unhooked a poker with a solid circle on its end, then held the round stamp over the fire.

Saffron's breaths came fast and shallow. The sight of the brutish instrument glowing orange sent a fresh lance of dread through her.

Wand in his other hand, Lyrian muttered a conditional curse at the licking flames.

"Ver fidan, nis morten. Ver fidan, nis morten. Ver fidan, nis morten."

Saffron's brain worked frantically. She'd never heard magic cast like that before: a hiss, a litany, a serpentine snap.

The flames grew darker, bloodier, until they were the exact hue of Lyrian's scarlet cloak. The poker glowed furious white, and Lyrian withdrew it.

He stepped over Neatras's body, paying it no mind, and Saffron wondered then whether the murder had truly been necessary. The body had played no part in the spell; the poker had not been dipped in his blood or pressed against his unbeating heart. Did Lyrian simply enjoy watching her suffer and squirm, enjoy watching her wage war against her own humanity?

It doesn't matter if your motivations are not what you claim. We'll be able to control you regardless, fit you with a tight collar and a tighter leash, walk you down the streets of Atherin like a dog, should we so please.

Panic clawed up her throat as he approached.

She couldn't breathe, she couldn't breathe, she couldn't *breathe.*

Then the searing circle at its tip was upon her flesh, right over her heart. There was a split second in which she felt nothing, and then the agony cleaved her in two.

A frayed scream tore from her.

Her body violently rejected the scorching metal, legs bucking like a frightened foal in a bid to escape it, but the bindings at her wrists held firm, and she remained pulled taut beneath the torture, nowhere to go but inside the pain itself.

Still he held it there.

What began as a contained burning, a vicious shredding sensation like every one of her skin fibers was being pulled apart by lightning, became an all-consuming crimson. Her vision was cloaked scarlet, and her chest felt flayed open, flames licking at the exposed flesh inside.

Still he held it there.

Her other senses severed themselves one by one until nothing existed but the pain.

She folded in on herself like a dying star.

Still he held it there, the poker clamped against her skin, the surface fizzing and bubbling, but by now she barely saw anything but Lyrian's vague outline.

The world pressed in on her from all angles until everything sank into darkness.

13

...

Fallowwolf

SAFFRON AWOKE IN AN UNFAMILIAR BED, HER CHEST A CRUcible.

For a moment, she didn't understand where she was.

The scene was smudged in hazy blurs of cream and gold and red. She wasn't in the stony Duncarzus cell, nor in her cozy room at the Academy, nor in her late-childhood bedroom above Clay's Cloakery. She made out the frame of a four-poster bed, but though she was flat on her back, her limbs were not bound to its oak spindles. Her heavy palms found the thick, textured brocade of a bedspread.

A distant wail bled through the walls, interspersed with high pops of laughter and the low ooze of a saxophone.

A fallowwolf howled.

And then she remembered.

She had slain Neatras as Segal had slain her parents.

She deserved the seething char over her heart. She deserved to be peeled apart.

Consciousness came in fits and starts, like sunlight through a slatted window. When she slept, she dreamed of the common room at the Academy, of Nissa and Auria and Tiernan laying on their stomachs by the fire as they read fat manila case files, the whole scene basked red from a waxen bloodmoon shining through the window.

She dreamed of her uncle Mal's green eye in a marble ashtray, of a handless Merin's frantic whisper: *coradin se vidasi.* My heart will not beat until I see you again.

She dreamed of pain itself: a towering scarlet, a never-ending shaft of darkness.

Minutes or hours later, she awoke to a terse knock on the door.

A dark figure entered with the swish of a scarlet cloak.

At Levan's heel was a sleek, white-eyed fallowwolf, its fur a shimmering pale silver, its nose and ears starkly black. Saff flinched—her mother had been good with animals, but even she was wary of the fabled fallowwolves—yet it neither growled nor raised its hackles at her, only studied her with a careful curiosity, head tilted to one side.

Levan carried a silver tray topped with more food than Saff had eaten in six months. A cafetière of coffee with a little jug of sugared milk, a mound of flaky pastries stuffed with apricot puree and pistachio cream, a plate of pepper-crusted sheep's cheese and ripe halved figs, a platter of cured meats and glistening strawberries, half a loaf of sour-risen bread with a tiny bowl of salt-flaked butter. Enough to replenish Saffron's well in full, yet as Levan set it on a high table by her bedside, her stomach roiled, threatening to empty northward.

He also handed her a small pot of seafoam-colored ointment, sealed with brown paper and wax. "Salve. For the pain." He didn't meet her eyes.

Saff forced herself up onto her elbow, the room pitching around her.

The brand was bright and raw and burning, a hideous tugging sensation whenever she moved an inch. Her tunic had been stitched neatly back together, though her shabby black cloak had been discarded.

To make way for the new.

As she broke the seal on the salve, the scent yanked her back to her childhood home in Lunes—a cool, sweet mingling of buttermint, saintflower, and garnet sap. Her mother had made salves just like this.

Saff dug two fingertips into the soft putty, lowered the neckline of her tunic, and gingerly spread the salve over the crusted wound, trying very hard not to vomit—the texture was rough and pitted, like a chunk of coral from the reefs below Sarosan. She couldn't bring herself to look, but the brand felt like it was the size of a jam jar lid.

She didn't expect the salve to actually *work.*

Most were made with magic, and magic would have no effect on her. Yet this salve melted away the pain almost instantly. A cool spreading sensation, crisp and clean as the River Corven in winter. Perhaps it was made with simple, natural ingredients, with no spellwork to be seen. Saff spread more over the grazed, bloodied forearm she'd scraped against the alley wall, and the residual sting faded to nothing.

Levan stood with his back to the stone wall, his body a half-drawn blade. He gestured stiffly to the platter of food.

"You should eat."

Saffron ignored him, instead eyeing the smoothly carved wand holder on the bedside table. Her knobbly beech wand was notched into the groove—and why wouldn't it be? She wasn't a prisoner. She was a Bloodmoon. She was one of their own.

Levan took a pointed seat on a dark red armchair by the door. "Here, Rasso."

The fallowwolf lay obliging on the floor beside him. It moved with spectral silence, as though cloaked in shadow.

Fallowwolves were once known as the Timeweavers' most loyal companions, for the beasts could devour seconds and minutes as easily as they did their prey, but without their human conduits, their time-consuming powers had all but deserted them. Now they wandered Ascenfall aimlessly, attacking random mages for lack of anything better to do. Saff wondered vaguely how Levan had domesticated one.

"Now," said Levan, patience wearing thin. "Eat."

Saffron clenched her jaw. There was a fruity, almost alcoholic taste at the back of her mouth. A sure sign she was about to throw up. "Why do you care whether I eat?"

"You're little use to us without your magic, and judging by the fact you had to slit the croupier's throat the Ludder way, I suspect you drained your well with that little alley illusion of yours."

"That little alley illusion had you fooled."

He made an irritated sound but said nothing to refute Saff's victory. In fact, he looked very much like he'd rather not exchange words at all. As though, now they were no longer firing curses at each other, he had no idea how to interact with her beyond brusque instructions to fill her belly. As though practicalities were the only safe ground between them.

He looked downright *awkward.*

Saffron stared at him for several long beats. The lantern on the wall behind him limned his high cheekbones with a pale, threaded light. Wavy dark hair framed his face, falling to the sharp line of his jaw. It was curiously exhilarating to be in the same room as him, knowing he was the climax this mission would always build toward. His body emanated its own energy field, tugging at her like gravity, that strange urge to prod at a wound.

How would they get there, to that moment she had foreseen?

There was no denying he was attractive. He had the chiseled face and physique of the carved statues that stood outside Saints halls. If she met him as a handsome stranger in a tavern, she'd undoubtedly sink several flamebrandies and suggest they get a room. But he wasn't a handsome stranger in a tavern. He was a murderer, a torturer. Dark and cruel to his bones.

She'd just have to focus on the part that came after the kiss: sinking a killing spell deep into his stomach.

Propping herself farther up on the bed, Saffron tentatively plucked an apricot pastry from the tray. She brought it to her mouth, and a violent shudder of cold tore through her. An image had taken root in her mind: a rolling eye on a bloodstained tile, the grout seeped with scarlet.

"What did you do with the croupier's daughter?" She couldn't even bring herself to say his name.

Levan shrugged. "Took her back to the gamehouse."

"How long will she stay there?" The sailor's knot tightened around her belly. She was shaking from head to foot, and she hated that she was. "And where's the rest of her?"

His face remained impassive, gaze still averted. "Just focus on finding Nalezen Zares."

Saffron tore the pastry in half. The fallowwolf eyed it longingly, even though the beasts famously only consumed other animals' hearts. She lifted the pastry to her mouth, but nausea lurched up her gullet, and she laid it back down with a grimace.

Levan sighed. "Is there a problem?"

Saffron's jaw clenched. She didn't want to share her turmoil with this monster, and yet some part of her wanted him to know that she was still *good*. Or, at the very least, better than he was. She wanted her moral objections to be known at every juncture.

"Not all of us can take a life and still stomach our dinner."

The reply came whip-fast. "Better get used to it. We own you now."

The kingpin's words haunted her. *It doesn't matter if your motivations are not what you claim. We'll be able to control you regardless, fit you with a tight collar and a tighter leash, walk you down the streets of Atherin like a dog . . .*

Saffron shakily poured the coffee into a black clay mug, wrinkling her nose at the bitter scent. "I don't suppose you have any hot chocolate?"

Levan's brow furrowed. "Are you twelve years old?"

"Yes," said Saffron, deadpan. "I wonder what puberty will feel like. Apparently I'll grow hair on my—"

"Fine." Levan, less than amused, pointed his wand at the mug of coffee. "*Ans calacocar.*"

Saffron stared in amazement as the dark coffee faded to a milky brown, thickening and frothing of its own accord. "You can transmute?"

Turning one object into another entirely different object was one of the most challenging types of magic in existence, because the objects must have the exact same energy and mass. If the old object contained more energy than the new, there would be a rather dramatic explosion, and if the new required more energy than the old, the mage's own lifeblood would be drained to make up for the shortfall. Lesser mages died trying, but Levan only shrugged, no trace of pride on his face at the casually devastating magic he'd exhibited.

Saffron took a sip of the transmuted cocoa, discovering with mild annoyance that it was delicious. Mercifully, her stomach did not reject it. She swallowed down several mouthfuls, and some of the feeling returned to her extremities. With the replenishing of her well came a rush of pleasure, a kind of heat flooding to her core, and she sighed into it. The pain of the branding had given the power more potency, and now it coursed gorgeously through her, simmering, fizzing, begging to be spent.

And yet she had to keep it close for now. Saints knew when she might need to call upon it.

"Why did you kill that Brewer in the alley?" she asked, as though they were equals, colleagues, and she were merely curious. "Seemed like he genuinely didn't know anything. And I think you knew that too. You said he'd taken an antidote to the truth elixir, but why wouldn't you just take him prisoner until the antidote had worn off? The only reason to kill him would be if he was genuinely no use to you."

"Very perceptive," Levan grunted, stroking Rasso's head absently. "Yes, I soon realized that Segal brought me the wrong mage." He had a flat manner of speaking, free from inflection or sentiment.

"So why didn't you let him go?"

"He was evidence."

"Not very strong evidence. It would've been his word against yours."

"And the Silvercloaks would believe he magically amputated and reattached his own hand?" He shrugged, as though the situation irked him but didn't particularly pain him. Merely a set of unfortunate circumstances. "All magic leaves a trace, and the Silvercloaks are getting better at following said trace. You of all people should know that."

Saff reached for a strawberry, and the hot stroke of pain across her chest was so harsh and sudden that it bleached her vision white, so visceral that the salve couldn't touch it. The magic in her well brightened, sharpened.

Sucking in her breath, she dug her nails into the bedspread, trying not to cry out.

"Are you alright?" Levan asked, almost like a reflex he couldn't control. There was little warmth behind the question, but it was still surprising to be asked it at all.

"Fine."

She loathed the idea of the kingpin's son witnessing her like this, branded and hurt. Her pride bucked against the very idea. She'd come into this assignment feeling that she had the undeniable upper hand, and that if she could just grit her teeth through the branding, she'd be in full control of the situation, their defenses breached, their downfall inevitable; but everything that had happened since she entered the kingpin's chambers had put her squarely on the back foot. To show the kingpin's son her pain was to offer him a certain power over her. And she could not afford to lose any more power.

Yet her detective's instincts still snagged on something.

He had asked if she was alright—as if he knew what it felt like?

What had Levan said as Segal restrained her?

It's one thing to consent, and quite another to feel the pain.

"Do *you* have a brand?"

It was a little bolshy, perhaps. Too direct, too personal. Yet she got the sense this was a man who appreciated frankness. Conversation free from the usual trappings and obfuscations of most human interactions. The type who wanted you to say what you meant, without bells or whistles. He'd answered her questions about Neatras's daughter, after all, and about the Brewer in the alley. Because she'd asked him explicitly? Or because he saw no reason to withhold the information?

But this time, dark shutters dropped behind his eyes. A muscle twitched in his jaw, and she knew she had gone too far, too soon.

"I'm the kingpin's son." He stood abruptly, as did Rasso. "What do you think?"

Saffron's first instinct was *I suppose not,* but Lyrian seemed the sort to mutilate his son, just in case.

"I don't know," she said honestly. "That's why I asked."

The brief silence that spread between them was like a crypt, echoing and cavernous and cold. Rasso, the fallowwolf, glared at her, as though to say *How dare you ask insulting questions of my master?*

Levan crossed to the door. "Let's go."

Saffron blinked at him. "Where?"

"To find Auria Marriosan."

"Right now?"

"I'm not an especially patient man."

"But I can picture you doing needlework. Or knitting a long and complicated scarf."

She didn't know why her father's impish humor was rearing its head now. Perhaps she was using quick wit as a way to establish herself as an intellectual equal, as she had in the alley. Or perhaps she was trying desperately hard to prove to this man that she was not afraid of him. Pride was a stubborn beast.

Levan sighed, resting a palm on the doorknob. "The truth elixir should still be in your system. Do you know where Marriosan is?"

Saints. Another corner of truth she'd been backed into. "What time is it?"

Levan looked down at a gold wristwatch with a black leather band. "Quarter to darknight."

Auria would be drinking blossombeer with Nissa and Tiernan right now. Nissa had told her as much.

Saff swallowed. "The Jaded Saint. A tavern on Arollan Mile."

"Alright. I'll wait outside while you freshen up." He gestured to a small washbasin in the corner of the room—and to a scarlet cloak laid out on a trunk at the end of her bed. "We'll go together."

"Why?"

"Just in case things get out of hand."

"Pun intended?"

The joke landed flat. Levan and Rasso left the room without looking back.

Their absence rang in her ears like a bell fallen quiet.

Swinging her legs over the side of the bed, Saffron studied her wand in its holder for a moment. Should she mutter *et vocos,* try and make contact with Aspar? Let the captain know her position was secured? No. Some instinct told her to hold off until she knew how closely the Bloodmoons were observing, listening.

I see everything, *Filthcloak.*

Besides, she didn't have any real intelligence yet. She could warn Aspar that Lyrian knew everything about their cohort, but what good would that do? Aspar wasn't the type of captain to place detectives in safe houses so readily. She needed cloaks on the streets.

Saff shoved her feet into her boots and headed over to the small washbasin. She scrubbed her face and neck with the same lemon-mint soap she'd smelled on Levan, then lifted her tunic at the waist and dabbed her armpits with a cloth, but she couldn't bring herself to wash the rest of her body yet. That would mean confronting the brand, and she was nowhere near ready to do that.

Once she was dry, she grabbed the crimson cloak from the top of the trunk. It was light and silky, gliding through her fingers like ink. She shrugged it over her shoulders—wincing as the fresh brand tugged at her chest—and secured it at the neck with the ruby brooch.

Then, turning slowly on her heel, she eyed herself in the tall, wall-mounted mirror.

At the sight of herself in the infamous Bloodmoon scarlet, she felt a kind of profound disturbance in the very fabric of herself.

Her silver-blond curls corkscrewed in all directions—her mother's curls. The last time Saff had seen them on another mage, they had haloed Mellora's dead face like a mourning wreath. Now the very same curls fell onto the shoulders of a Bloodmoon cloak.

It felt like dancing on a grave with the person who had dug it.

As Saffron strode to the door, she felt the thread tying her to her old life shiver and snap.

PART
THREE

—

BLOODMOON

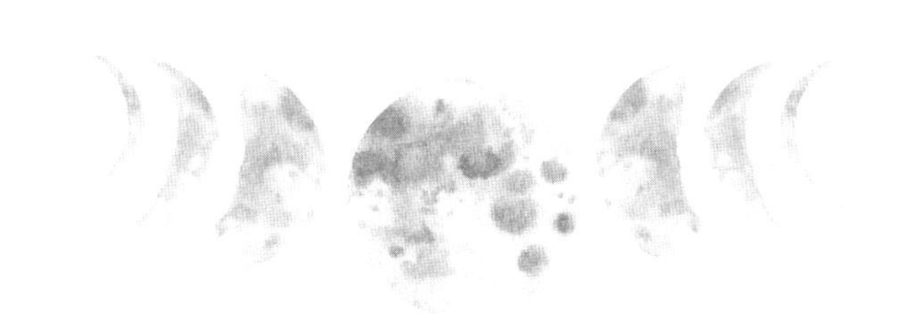

14

. . .

The Jaded Saint

THE JADED SAINT WAS A MOODY TAVERN FRONTED BY DARK BLUE awnings, flanked on either side by raucous red pleasurehouses. Indented into the tavern's creamstone walls were several shallow domed alcoves, each housing a marble statue of the patron saints of wielding. A jet of everflowing water shot from Quissari's fingertip, while eternal fire danced behind the eyes of Incinari. Thunder cracked above Etanari's head, while red roses sprang from seed to bloom and back again around Aterrari's feet. All of the Saints wore tormented expressions, staring at their respective elements with a look of existential horror. (There was no real reason for this artistic choice, theologically speaking, rather than a desire to lend a certain edginess to the tavern's aesthetic. According to Patron legend, the Saints had actually been quite titillated by their own acts of creation.)

Saffron and Levan stood across the street, outside an enchanted quill shop Auria adored. Arollan Mile flowed with a steady stream of civilians, all of whom avoided looking at the two tall mages in sinister scarlet cloaks. The fallowwolf's gaze fixed hungrily on the drinkers outside the Jaded Saint, as though wondering whom to tear to shreds first.

"Are you going to tell me who Zares is?" Saffron asked, disquiet swirling in her gut. "Or at least why they're important? Auria will need something to go on."

"Not if she's as skilled a researcher as you claim."

His tone signaled this was a closed matter.

And so Saffron sought victory elsewhere, a tiny grapple for control, no matter how small. A reminder that she was not the kingpin's dog, nor the fallowwolf trotting at Levan's heel. She was a powerful mage with her own agency, and she would not fall into step like a leashed animal.

"I don't think I should wear the scarlet cloak," she said matter-of-factly. "Auria won't cooperate if she knows I'm working with you."

Levan grunted his assent. "Fine."

"And you should wait outside. There's a chance you'll be recognized—Auria has a powerful memory, and if your face has ever appeared in connection with Bloodmoon activity, she will know. She has your father's file memorized cover to cover."

At this suggestion, Levan looked at her incredulously. "Let you go in alone? And leave you to say whatever you want to your old Silvercloak brethren?"

"Not whatever I want." Saff tapped at the brand. Despite the salve, it was raw and tender to the touch, the wound still bright and new. "Or I'll perish instantly. I have no choice but to act in the Bloodmoons' favor."

"You could just not do anything. You could go in and discuss, I don't know, the new translation of the Saints' manifesto, and I'd be none the wiser."

"And lie to you?" Saff gave him a pointed glare. "Wouldn't that constitute a betrayal?"

His jaw hardened. "You're not going in alone."

Saffron folded her arms. "If you're happy with Auria immediately clamming up and refusing to give you the information you want—or even trying to arrest you there and then—you're most welcome to join me."

"You've seen how far I'll go to convince—"

"We went through torture training in the Academy, and only three of us passed first time: me, Auria, and Sebran. You will never break her with pain or fear. You kept me alive for a reason. Because you need me to coax."

The street felt muted around them. Levan appeared to be grappling internally between logic—what was best for the mission—and a desire not to cede any ground. He wanted her afraid for her life, not ordering him around.

Finally, he relented, clenching his teeth. "Alright. But don't go thinking you'll often call the shots like this."

"Right. Tight collar, tighter leash." She put on a brooding voice. "*I will hunt down everyone you have ever loved and bleed them dry in front of you.* Et cetera."

Levan's face darkened. "As you wish. *Sen collaren.*"

With a swish of his wand, his leather belt unlooped from around his waist and leapt toward her throat. She blocked it with a swift, practiced forearm, and it clattered to the cobbles.

"Careful," said Saffron, grinning broadly. "You don't want to turn me on, do you?"

He squared his tight blade of a body toward hers, though his stare was fixed somewhere over her head. "I know what you're doing. You're trying to prove you're not afraid of me. You're cracking big jokes so you won't feel small. You're trying to wrest control of the situation, but the first thing you need to learn is that I control *everything*."

Well. He'd certainly gotten the measure of her fairly fast.

Saffron boxed her shoulders, grateful for the fact she stood at six feet tall. "I'm sure your father would love to hear that. Where I come from, that's called insubordination."

Something flashed behind those dead eyes, and for the first time, she got the impression her barb had landed. "Who do you think feeds my father all his information? Who do you think tells him exactly which strings to pluck?"

"Whatever gives you a reason to get out of bed in the morning," Saffron said blandly. "I'm going in. Maybe you could peruse some quills to pass the time." She shrugged off her scarlet cloak and handed it to him, as though he were a cloakroom attendant. "You seem the type to write long, flowery letters to loved ones."

As soon as her back was turned, he uttered the low sling of a curse.

Warm leather clamped around her throat. Levan yanked her backward so hard she lost her balance and slammed to the cobblestones, pain shooting up her wrists and forearms as her hands broke her fall. He knelt beside her, jamming his wand beneath her chin as his father had done mere hours earlier.

"You're not as clever as you think you are," he whispered, breath tickling her ear. "Because you know what you've just done? You just told me who *didn't* pass torture training on their first try. You've exposed your cohort's weak spots. And now my father will know exactly where to press if you don't stay in line. We can torture Naszi, Flane, and Villar for information, knowing that their torture will hurt *you*. Two ravens, one rock."

The belt dropped to the cobbles like a dead adder.

Levan offered her a hand up, an impenetrable look on his face. As their gazes finally locked, heat prickled across her cheeks, up the back of her neck. Loathing, or exhilaration, or a deep, dark mortification at the way he'd so effortlessly collared her on the street like a rabid dog. He had won control, had won *power,* as he had so many thousands of other times in his sinister life. And now those piercing blue eyes looked down on her from above, glittering with victory.

The only thought that steadied her, that mitigated the shame, was the image of that forked killing spell driving into his stomach.

She would overpower him eventually. She just had to bide her time.

Ignoring his outstretched palm, Saff climbed to her feet and stalked across the pale flagstones of the wide, tree-lined boulevard that was Arollan Mile. The long, leafy stretch leading up to the Palace was named for the house that currently sat the throne, though it hadn't been anything but Arollan for four generations.

At the center of the boulevard sat a vast water fountain in the shape of a sundial, mosaicked with tiles of sapphire and emerald. It was after darknight, but the sundial still somehow had a shadow. A young mage in a plain black Practer's cloak idly manipulated the impossible shadow, winding it back and forth as though toying with time itself. A pair of older Augurests with shaven heads and eyelid tattoos scowled at him as they passed, and one of them looked downright frightened. Since the Dreadreign and the subsequent slaughter of Timeweavers, tension between the Augurests and the Patrons was constantly simmering below the surface of the world. Saffron couldn't see that changing in her lifetime.

Naturally, there wasn't an Augurest to be seen inside the Jaded Saint.

In the dimly lit tavern, a bard sang an angsty tune of love and war. Dark ivy hung from the ceiling in tangled knots, and pale spores floated hazily across the air. The center of the wooden floor was carved with the Saints' symbol—an overflowing chalice inside a laurel wreath—and more rough-hewn marble statues were dotted around the tavern. Vesari, the patron saint of brewing, held a tray of complimentary flamebrandy shots by the entrance, which was probably bordering on blasphemy in the eyes of more devout Patrons. Thankfully, Saff had never been all that pious. She grabbed a shot and tossed it down her throat, relishing the after kick of spice and warmth.

Next, she performed her ritualistic scan of the room. There were two exits—the front entrance she came through and a small door behind the bar that led to the alley—and a couple of potential threats, in the form of overly drunk patrons and the furtive glances of a known pickpocket. But none of these threats were as great as the one seared into her flesh.

Her former cohort sat in the far corner, lounging in a booth, Auria and Tiernan laughing carelessly. In their gleaming silver cloaks, they all looked relaxed and proud, content in the knowledge that they were doing right by Atherin, by the world.

And now Saff was dragging them down into the city's dark underbelly with her.

She strode over with a false smile plastered over her face.

"Mind if I join you?" she asked, barely able to hear her own voice over the bard's song.

Nissa blinked up at her in surprise, her hands clutching an empty flamebrandy tumbler.

Auria and Tiernan exchanged a worried glance that made Saff want to wring their necks. Neither of them had attended Saff's plea hearing or sentencing. As soon as the truth emerged about her forged accreditation, they'd cut her off.

"Pull up a pew," said Nissa, though the words were strained.

"How are you all?" Saff asked too brightly, looking over at Auria and Tiernan as she slid into the booth.

Auria said nothing, her pixie-ish jaw clenched.

"Sorry, Saff, I can't be here," Tiernan mumbled. "My father would . . . You understand, don't you? Take care of yourself."

He climbed out of the booth, leaving behind most of his blossom-beer, and left the tavern in a hurry.

Auria visibly squirmed. "I'm going to the bar. Another flamebrandy, Nissa?"

"Two," said Nissa tautly. "One for Saff."

Auria left a beat of chagrined silence, ensuring her disapproval was felt, then said, "Fine."

Saffron tried not to betray how much the snubbing stung. After everything she'd just endured, *this* should not be the thing to break her.

Once Auria was out of earshot, Nissa's clawed hand squeezed Saff's beneath the table. "Are you alright?"

Saff nodded unconvincingly.

"What happened? Are you—"

"A Bloodmoon?" A stark image of Neatras's dead body hit Saff like a physical blow. "I am. It's done."

"So what are you doing here, if you're already compromised?" There was an edge of accusation to Nissa's tone.

Anger stabbed at Saff's temples, though she understood Nissa's wariness. It had just been a long night.

"What I have to do to stay alive," she said curtly, sliding out of the booth. "Excuse me."

"No, Killor, wait—"

Saffron ignored Nissa's protests and approached Auria, who stood straight-backed at the bar, focusing very hard on the dusty line of liquors.

"Auria," Saff said, her toes curling inside her boots. The mental image of Papa Marriosan without his hands was seared into her skull.

Auria didn't look at her. "Hi."

"How have you been?"

"Good." Her tone was pointedly flat. Saff struggled to reconcile it with the sunny, bright-eyed friend she knew so well. "Enjoying the posting."

Saff swallowed hard, resting her elbows on the oak-carved bar. It was sticky with honeywine residue. "How are you healing? After the final assessment."

She shrugged. "Well, I'm missing an ear. But the scars look more dramatic than they are."

"Can they do anything about them?" As she said it, Saff regretted it. The marks were oddly beautiful, an ethereal cobweb over pale, freckled skin. She didn't want to imply they were something that needed fixing.

"I don't want them to," Auria said, her teeth gritted. "It's a reminder to do the right thing, even if it leaves a mark." There was a loaded pause as she gestured to the barkeep. "Three flamebrandies."

He nodded, pouring viscous amber liquid into cut-crystal tumblers.

Saff cleared her throat. "I have a favor I need to ask."

"Do you think you're in a position to ask for favors?"

"No," Saff admitted. "And I'm sorry if you felt betrayed by the forgery. I just wanted to be a Silvercloak so badly, Auria. My parents—" Her hand went to the wooden pendant. "Anyway. I wouldn't ask unless I needed it."

At the mention of Saff's parents, Auria softened a little. "Go on."

Deep breath.

"I need you to look up a person for me."

Actually, Saff needed Auria to *find* a person. But she would take this one thing at a time.

Auria stiffened like she'd been struck by an *effigias* curse.

"I can't do that." Auria absently fondled the silky fabric of her silver cloak.

"Please," Saff pushed. "I need this information."

Auria shook her head impenetrably. "I'm sorry. I can't help."

Saff understood Auria's resistance—she wanted to be Grand Arbiter one day, to bring charges on behalf of the Crown, to shape mandates on what was good and right. She had a Knight's Scroll in Common Law and worked in the courts as a prosecutor before applying to the Academy. Why would she throw all that away now? Why would she go against her own rigid moral code for something so trivial, for a publicly shamed friend she seemed embarrassed to know at all?

Auria was the kind of person who, when a loved one did or said something she didn't like—something that challenged her shiny worldview—would rather end the relationship than try to understand or reconcile. After arguments, she would give the cold shoulder for weeks or months or forever, cutting the antagonism clean out. Self-preservation was the charitable explanation, but Saff often suspected it was to do with the desire for a perfect world, a perfect life. Auria could not handle imperfect people.

So how could she convince Auria without explicitly saying their lives were on the line? If Saff admitted she was here under duress, Auria would slip straight into Silvercloak mode, asking for details and possibly even pursuing a premature arrest of Levan Celadon—an arrest that would never stick to a charge, with the corrupt Grand Arbiter Dematus at the helm. On the other hand, if she warned that Auria herself was in danger, Auria would take it as intimidation, and Saff would probably wind up in Duncarzus before the night was through. That charge would certainly hold up.

Time to spin yet another lie.

"My uncle is in trouble. I just need to know how much."

Now Auria did return Saff's gaze. "Is the person you're looking for threatening him in some way?"

"I can't share the details."

"Well, your uncle needs to come to us, rather than sending you to elicit information illegally. I'd be happy to help him, Saff. You know we're good at what we do."

Please just take the Saints-damned bait, Saff screamed internally. "He won't do that. He's terrified."

The barkeep slid the three drinks over the bar, and Auria passed him three ascens. "Then there's nothing I can do. I'm sorry."

The words had a spine, and Saffron grudgingly respected them.

Still, she couldn't go back out there and tell Levan she'd failed. Her connection to Auria was the only thing keeping her alive.

"Is there nothing I can do to convince you?" Saff pleaded.

Something dark came down behind Auria's blue eyes. "Are you trying to bribe me?"

She almost spat the word *bribe,* as though it were the deepest insult she'd ever received. Auria was not particularly known for her venality.

"No!" Saff insisted. "Saints, no. I just . . . I'm desperate."

Auria swallowed her flamebrandy in one gulp, winced at the burn, then said with an air of finality, "I'm going to find Tiernan."

With a billow of her silver cloak, she left the Jaded Saint.

15

The Forked Tongue

Saff traipsed back to the booth, boots dragging, another grim plan forming in her mind. She slid Nissa the flamebrandy tumbler and folded herself onto the bench.

"Killor, please." There was no actual pleading in Nissa's tone, but there was a trace of kindness. This was significant, as Nissa was the sort of person who usually found kindness patronizing. "Tell me what's happening."

Saff shook her head vehemently, but it was all for show. "I can't involve you in this."

Of course, she would have to.

She loved—or *had* loved—Nissa. But there was nothing she would not do to bring down the Bloodmoons. If that made her an irredeemable wretch, so be it.

Nissa looked offended. "But you were willing to involve Auria?"

Saff hurled the second flamebrandy down her throat, the cinnamon-clove searing her gullet. "To my immense shame, she's already involved. I invoked her name under duress."

"Hells." Nissa raked a finger through her sleek black hair. "In what sense?"

"My new *colleague* needs information. I thought Auria could get it, but she won't cooperate."

"What kind of information?"

"A person's whereabouts." Saff ran the tip of her forefinger around the rim of the empty glass. "I watched a Bloodmoon torture and execute an innocent in the name of finding this person. So now *I* need to find them, or they'll . . ."

Nissa's gaze was hot as a dawning sun. "Torture and execute you."

"I might be useful to them in other ways, but if I can't help them manipulate the Silvercloaks, they might decide I'm more trouble than I'm worth."

Nissa drained her own drink without wincing. "So not only are you working the Bloodmoons for the Silvercloaks, you're now working the Silvercloaks for the Bloodmoons?"

Saff laughed bitterly. "A fantastic situation, I'm sure you'll agree."

And yet one she had worked toward for decades.

Several months into her year at the Academy, her uncles had sat her down over dinner and said they were worried about her. She didn't paint anymore, and she certainly didn't spend hours rereading those chunky *Lost Dragonborn* novels she used to love. Whenever she visited Mal and Merin at the Cloakery, she arrived late and left early, always muttering about coursework and case files, and even when she was present, they knew her mind wasn't in the room with them. She no longer went to watch the chariot races with her velvet pouch of coins and that hungry gleam in her eye. They'd never quite approved of the way she gambled on the winner week after week, but at least it had shown passion for something other than the Bloodmoons, the Bloodmoons, the *Bloodmoons*.

But if relentless singularity is what she needed to avenge her parents, to ensure no other child went through what she went through, it was a series of sacrifices she was all too willing to make.

Nissa sighed, the outward breath a billow of scorching steam. "I don't like this, Killor."

The bard struck up a new tune. Spores drifted in front of Saff's face, and she realized how exhausted she was. "Really? I get off on the danger."

"Well, yes, it's undeniably hot."

Saff laughed again, grateful, as she always was, for Nissa's solidity. For how unflinching she was in the face of trouble, for how Saff's hurt and grief passed right through her without ever leaving a mark. It was as though Nissa was born with a series of emotional culverts, draining any kind of sorrow or trauma before it could fester. She rarely spoke of her own anguished past, not because she was suppressing her unprocessed grief but because the loss of her sisters and everything that followed had long since bled away. Saffron, on the other hand, let pain pool and rot inside her, a body of stagnant water growing more mephitic with every passing year.

Not Nissa.

Nissa was indomitable. Dauntless, and bold, and unshakeable.

Saints, Saffron *missed* Nissa, and what they'd had. She missed having a person, one she could melt into at the end of a long day, one with whom she had private jokes and secret dreams, a sense of hope on the horizon.

The best Silvercloaks cut off sentimentality at the root.

Yet from the way Nissa was looking at her—through thick, fluffy lashes, her eyes rimmed in white and gold kohl, her lip piercing catching the light—Saffron suspected she missed her too. If Nissa was indeed capable of such emotions.

Then again, perhaps she just wanted to fuck.

All at once, Saffron remembered how it felt to have Nissa's forked tongue drawing neat circles between her thighs. Desire pooled low in her stomach. Her body made the decision before her mind caught up, and she tilted toward her dragonesque former lover, heat shimmering between them in waves.

Nissa drew her face closer, and as their lips met in a fiery-sweet clash of flamebrandy and lust, her claws pierced holes in Saff's trousers. There was nothing sweet or tender about it; pointed teeth dragged at Saff's lower lip, all the blood rushing to the surface of Saffron's skin at the touch.

Saff understood it then, the reason soldiers made love in the trenches of the last major war. Facing death and triumphing over it brought with it a rush of relief, of desire, of existential hurt.

It took everything she had not to melt into Nissa.

"We can't," she muttered against Nissa's parted lips. "I'm compromised. Cavorting with me puts you in grave danger."

And it was true. If Levan saw Nissa and Saffron kissing . . . Nissa would become his clear target. She'd already let slip that Nissa had failed the torture trials the first time—they'd played a cruel trick involving an illusion of her dead twin sisters—and so she was already in the kingpin's son's sights. She would become just another innocent to threaten—although Saffron suspected Nissa would abhor the word *innocent* altogether.

"Cavorting?" Nissa snorted. "Is that what you call letting me drip hot wax all over your body until you beg for mercy?"

Saffron's cheeks pinkened, although nobody would bat an eyelid if they overheard. Almost everyone in Ascenfall was attracted to all genders, and almost everyone was kinky as all hells.

Blame the magic; it was something of an aphrodisiac.

"I'm already in this, Killor. Might as well have some fun with it."

Hells, Saffron thought. She could die tomorrow. They both could.

That nihilistic fearlessness swelled and crested, and she ceded to it.

Their mouths met again, hot and wanting, pointed teeth and the hard gold of the piercing, a forked tongue flicking over hers, a palmful of claws digging into the narrow of her waist.

The nearest walls of the Jaded Saint folded into a pocket, a private nook, until there was a mere sliver of space through which the rest of the tavern could be seen. Their alcove was twined with ivy and hazy with spores, candlelight flickering, the bard's music both distant and immediate, the twang of strings rippling across the surface of Saff's skin.

Nissa's kissing intensified into hungry bites, digging into Saff's lower lip before tracing a path across her jawbone, her neck, her collarbone. Saff laced her hands through the silken sheets of Nissa's hair, a rough moan escaping before she could snatch it back, that bright, burning power from the brand surging and curling inside her.

Reaching for her magic, Saff whispered, "*Ans omnivolan.*"

The pleasure spell pressed *hard* at all the tender places in Nissa's body: the throat and the nipples and the inner thighs; the soft pulsing peak and somewhere deep, deep inside; all of it met with a sudden intense pressure.

Nissa gasped, breath hooking sharply inward, eyes widening.

"Saints, are you hurt?" Saffron muttered, pulling away. She realized too late that the searing agony of the brand had churned her well into something ferocious, something *monstrous.* Her magical well was overflowing, and the spell had been cast far too strongly.

But judging from the dilated pupils and the parted lips, Nissa had enjoyed the added potency.

"*Ans omnivolan,*" Saff murmured again, twice more, raw magic pressing over and over against Nissa's most tender places.

After everything that had been done to Saffron in the last few hours, it felt good to take control. She and Nissa were perpetually caught in this ravenous push-pull, a grapple of reins, a tug-of-war, neither of them naturally submissive, both of them hungry for power. Nissa usually won this tussle, but Saff still tried to assert herself anyway.

Saff pressed her mouth to Nissa's neck, feeling the frantic pulse against her lips, then pressed the tip of her wand between Nissa's legs. "*Ans vorticaloran.*"

Swirling heat.

Another gasp loosed from Nissa's throat, golden eyes fluttering closed for a moment, losing herself in the spell. The swirling heat still pulsing over her—Saffron wouldn't let the enchantment drop until it peaked and cascaded—Nissa pressed her own wand between Saffron's legs.

"*Sen laceran,*" Nissa purred, drawing a slit down the central seam of Saffron's trousers—and slicing clean through her underwear.

With her other hand, Nissa traced a claw downward, a stark line drawn over Saffron's *want,* both soft and hard, both painful and *good,* and a tremor rippled through Saff, more power rushing into her well with alarming force. Slender fingers circled and pressed, and their mouths met once more, Nissa breathing raggedly from the swirling magical heat between her legs. Saffron's pleasure towered and deepened, something vital inside herself coming back to life, a pool refilled, a humanity restored.

All at once, Saff was glad Nissa knew the truth about her immunity to magic, glad she could relinquish herself to the simple thrill of a hand between her legs, of knuckles pressed against her inner thigh, of a sharp claw probing the place where everything throbbed.

"*Et ascevolo,*" Nissa incanted, flicking the table upward with her wand until it pressed flat against the ceiling, tumblers shattering around them like rain. Then she sank to her knees on the shard-covered floor, kneeling in front of the bench and looping Saffron's legs over her shoulders. Through the slit in Saff's underwear, Nissa gave a single forked lick, every inch of Saffron shuddering and gasping.

Nissa clasped Saff's hips, tugging her closer as she drew flickering circles with her tongue, soft and wet and reverent, and Saffron leaned her head back against the wall, surrendering herself to the pleasure, trying not to think about searing pokers and wrists shackled apart, trying not to think at all. Trying only to *feel.*

The pleasure peaked with a shattering moan, and the table came clattering back to the ground, narrowly missing Nissa's head.

Nissa maneuvered herself back onto the bench, her lips red and swollen, the kohl around her eyes smudged. "Hells," she muttered. "Who knew being compromised could feel so good?"

Skin still on fire, Saffron repaired the tear in her trousers. "*Ans annetan.*"

Then she sighed deeply, pressing the heels of her hands into her eyes. Though the feeling of a replenished well was a welcome relief, she felt a kind of creeping sadness as reality edged back in. She would not be returning to Nissa's bed tonight, falling asleep with exhausted limbs entwined, embers and coal crackling in a grate. She would be going to face the Bloodmoons, face fear and torture and death.

As the walls of the Jaded Saint folded outward and the clamor of the tavern rushed back to greet them, Nissa read the dread on Saffron's face.

"Who do you need to find?" Nissa said carefully, arranging her disheveled robes. "Now that we've established I'm already in this, and it's rather hot."

Saff wanted to protest, wanted to insist Nissa shouldn't get involved any further than she had to. But of all the choices sprawling out in front of her, all the potential prongs in the fork, none of them seemed good.

If she wanted to stay alive, she had to find Zares.

And if Auria wouldn't help her do that . . .

Guilt soured in her stomach. She was making dark choice after dark choice, all in the name of self-preservation. No different than the royal houses, no different than the Bloodmoons.

"Nalezen Zares," she muttered. "That's all I have."

Nissa nodded once, stoic, then rose to her feet. "Meet me back here at the same time next week. I'll see what I can do."

16

. . .

Dubias Row

By the time Saffron left the Jaded Saint, Atherin had grown slack and wild.

The pleasurehouses sang with ecstasy, and laughter swelled from every tavern. Velvines lay languidly along purple awnings, and the air was scented with achullah and dark chocolate. Mages grouped together in clusters, some talking in hushed, urgent tones, others audibly arguing over religions and monarchs and which brand of whiteroot gave the best high when rubbed into the gums. Bright spellbursts erupted like fireworks up and down every street. Shutters twitched, and deadbolts clinked, and the air crackled with a curious anticipatory energy—one Saffron had come to know all too well during her time on the streetwatch.

The taut hum of trouble threaded through the streets like a pulse. Every Laving was like this—a day dedicated to using up all the spare magic left in the well after a long workweek. It was an ancient belief, and not an especially accurate one, that magic left too long could fester, turn rancid, and so tradition held that the sixth day of the week was a day to purge the old, to cast loose and largely unnecessary spells until the well was clean and empty. The last day of the week, Plenting, was an altogether quieter affair, built upon good food and great wine, long lovemaking by roaring hearths, refilling the well with fresh, pure magic once more.

Saffron used to love the weekly ritual of Laving and Plenting, but Duncarzus had smeared all the days together with little to mark them apart, and now the whole ritual seemed farcical, foreign.

Levan stood soldier-straight across the street, leaning against the quill shop window, broad arms folded between scarlet sleeves. Rasso had grown restless, galloping up and down the moonlit cobbles for no discernible reason.

At the sight of Saffron emerging from beneath the midnight blue awning, Levan pressed off the glass and raised an eyebrow in question.

Saffron gave a single nod.

They began walking back in the direction of the warded tunnel entrance, Rasso trotting at Levan's heels with a lolling, panting tongue. Saff's neck still smarted from the memory of Levan's leather belt coiled around it. She squared her shoulders, trying not to let the residual humiliation show as their bodies fell into step beside each other.

"Which Silvercloaks were present?" Levan asked, wooden and formal.

Saffron stared straight ahead, not wanting to share a damn thing with this murderous *vock,* but she was still supposed to have truth elixir in her system. She'd have to oblige.

"Marriosan, Naszi, and Flane. Flane left almost as soon as I arrived." It was strange to call them by their surnames, but it helped to create a sort of dissonance between her friends and the mission.

"And Marriosan's going to find Zares?"

"It's all in hand." She didn't want to admit that it was not Auria but Nissa who'd promised her the information. Papa Marriosan was already on the gallows, but Nissa's family should be left out of it for as long as possible. "We're meeting here again this time next week."

They walked past a young, handsome mage in a violet Healer's cloak, sprawled along the marble edge of a fountain and snoring quite emphatically. Water shot from Saint Quissari's rough-hewn wand and onto the Healer's face, but it did not rouse him from his inebriated slumber. A cloakless Ludder lurked a few feet away, sizing up the

Healer—as though about to pick his pockets—and Saffron had to tamp down her detective's instincts. Though she could stay vigilant, she couldn't intervene. Not anymore.

Levan didn't seem to notice the impending thievery. "What was it my father said about Marriosan's love life? *She'd do well to cut the Flane boy loose. The flame-hearted Eqoran would be a more suitable companion, although you have your own soft spot for Nissa Naszi.*" A neat grimace. "I won't bother asking if there's any truth to it. My father's intel is never wrong."

Saff pressed her lips into a flat line and said nothing, employing her well-practiced polderdash face, her long-perfected silence, but she still felt the pinkness in her cheeks from the pleasure Nissa had so recently wrought.

"You should bury any residual feelings you have for Naszi." Levan's footsteps were clipped and smooth on the cobbles. His pace was brisk, and Saffron was a little breathless as she tried to keep up. "You're on opposite sides now. And if we order you to neutralize her, you'll have to do so, or the brand will fell you where you stand. Cut off the emotion while you still can."

An almost eerie mirror of what Nissa had told her a year ago.

"Thank you for your sage counsel, great oracle of romantic affairs."

Better to lampoon painful observations than to let yourself recognize their truth.

"Tell me about the others in the cohort," Levan said. "Aduran and Villar."

"Gaian Villar is undercover in Pons Aelii," she said reluctantly, tiredness weighing her down like a lead blanket. The brand was already burning through the salve, and she clenched her teeth against the hot pain. "Strong Enchanter, terrible polderdash player. Great hair, even better interrogator. Sebran Aduran is a decent Brewer, trained in the Vallish infantry, generally brusque and reserved. I know nothing of his past before the military academy. He's down in Carduban, guarding the ascenite mines." Saffron paused uncertainly before continuing. "One of them is likely a Compeller. I believe it's Gaian—it would explain his interrogation skills, and the fact he won the most prestigious posting—but I can't be sure."

It had been playing on her mind, the fact that there was a Compeller in the cohort. If she crossed paths with them while undercover in the Bloodmoons, it could present some serious complications. Knowing for certain who the Compeller was would make it easier to steer well clear.

At the mention of a possible Compeller, however, Levan's expression darkened, his loathing for the Silvercloaks evident on his face. "Leave it with me."

Immediate regret calcified Saffron's lungs. Perhaps that was a misstep. The Bloodmoons would never abide a dangerous Compeller in the Silvercloaks.

Had she just put an irretrievable target on Gaian's back?

Sloppy. Unforgivably sloppy.

Her thought processes were usually far more stringent, rigorous. Pain and exhaustion were addling her analytical mind—it had been a perilously long day. She could barely see straight.

You're not as clever as you think you are, Levan had said less than an hour ago, shortly after collaring her on the street and slamming her to the cobbles like a misbehaving prisoner. Shortly after she'd revealed who failed torture training, and shortly after he'd pounced on the information.

The first thing you need to learn is that I control everything.

She had more than met her match, and she needed to be a lot more Saints-damned careful.

"Naszi's heritage," Levan asked, oblivious to her inner turmoil. "There are rumors that she's part dragon. Any truth to it?"

"I don't know," Saffron replied truthfully. "Never got a straight answer out of her."

They left the raucous Arollan Mile onto Dubias Row, a quieter street lined with shady shops favored by sneaks and mercenaries. The lamplights flickered a warm orange bronze, casting the entire row in a furnace-like glow. Black scorch marks licked up several ancient buildings—remnants from when dragons had burned up the city as a form of protest to the Dreadreign. The scorch marks could very easily have been removed by a simple spell, but the proprietors believed them to add character.

On one of the street's only unburned walls was an elaborate mural of Parlin the Great, raising his wand to the sky, dragons bowing deferentially in a semicircle around him. The historical figure hailed from two thousand years ago and was said to be the most powerful mage who'd ever walked Ascenfall. His list of credits included vanquishing a vast and omniscient evil, carving the world's first wand from the Elm of Eternity, and possessing a cock of unprecedented stature. In the dragon mural, the crotch of his trousers bulged beyond all feasibility.

Vallin was a land of people who lauded the hero figure. The neighboring Bellandry favored the underdog, the warrior with all odds stacked against them, the unlikely victor as a representation of triumph over adversity. The Vallish, on the other hand, loved the lore of undefeated champions and unassailable conquerors, of power and glory, of charisma and flair, of talent beyond all measure.

As such, Parlin the Great was as integral to Vallish culture as pleasure and flamebrandy, far more a symbol of the country's spirit than the flag could ever be. Three of the seven days of the week were named for his achievements, in fact. Elming, for the day on which the first wand was carved. Sording, for the defeat of the Sordai, his historic foe. And Oparling, for the mage himself.

"Naszi's silence on the matter only pays credence to the rumors," Levan said, slowly, as though deep in thought.

"What do you mean?" Saffron frowned, glancing at him for the first time in several hundred yards. The fiery lamplights illuminated the indented scar cutting through his lower lip, making it look deeper than usual.

Outside an almost deserted tavern called Cernašti's, a place renowned as a meeting place for the Disciples of Halantry, two black-cloaked women spoke in rapid-fire Tarsan, their words accompanied by the elaborate hand-speak native to the Eastern Republics. A pearl-colored pocketwatch lay on the table between them, emitting a high-pitched frequency that made Saffron wince.

"Well," said Levan, and there was a trace of genuine intrigue in his usually cold voice, "my reading on the subject tells me that the truly dragonblooded are bound not to speak of it, or said blood will freeze in their veins."

Interesting. Saffron badly wanted to ask more questions, but the longer they discussed Nissa, the more dangerous the situation felt. So instead she said, very wisely and maturely, "I'm surprised a Bloodmoon grunt reads at all."

Levan gave her an almost pitying look, and Saffron chastised herself for once again playing into his hands.

I know what you're doing. You're trying to prove you're not afraid of me. You're cracking big jokes so you won't feel small.

How had he so quickly and wholly got the measure of her?

She had the impish desire to do something, anything, to surprise him. To catch him off guard. To prove that she was not predictable, and that she *wasn't* afraid of him. But that was a flawed impulse, and she knew better than to indulge it. She was here for intelligence, not juvenile grudges.

"Anything else you want to know?" she said calmly, redonning her cool demeanor like a cloak she'd accidentally discarded. "Marriosan's foot size? Flane's favorite color? How many flamebrandies Naszi can sink without passing out?"

He shot her a sideways look. "Does—"

Three moon-white cloaks sailed down through the air.

They landed directly on top of Levan, who stumbled into Saffron, knocking the wind out of her belly. Her skull hit the cobbles with a blunt crack.

Everything became a blur of orange streetlights and pale fabric and pained grunts.

Spells flurried and sparked, overlapping and misfiring.

Saffron fumbled for her wand, though she wasn't sure what she'd do with it. Confusion mired with fear, and she struggled to orient herself.

"*Sen ammorten,*" Levan incanted, sounding almost bored.

One of the assailants slumped dead next to Saffron.

Vision unstarring, she hauled her legs out from beneath Levan's bulk and scrambled back on the cobbles like a beetle.

A white-cloaked assailant with raven-black hair stood above Saffron, jabbing her pine wand as her lips formed the word *sen.*

Before Saff could throw up a mattermantic shield, Rasso leapt onto the assailant's chest and ripped the vocal cords clean out of her neck, both tumbling backward into the gutter.

Saffron stared at the throatless corpse in horror, trying to make sense of the scene.

White cloaks usually meant Silvercloak cadets, but these faces were unfamiliar.

A new cohort, perhaps? Unless—

Levan straddled the third assailant, who'd lost his wand in the skirmish. He was a pale-skinned, redheaded mage with a purple scar carved from forehead to jaw, bisecting an empty eye socket.

"You slaughtered my uncles, you *vock*!" the scarred mage spat.

"They tried to rob us," Levan said quietly, coldly. "It's not personal."

"It's always personal." There was a hateful gleam in the assailant's remaining eye, something that shone with grim satisfaction, even in the face of imminent death. "You of all people should know that."

Levan's hand gripped his wand so hard that his veins bulged dark and angry. "*Sen ammorten.*"

The killing spell forked into the assailant's chest, and the scarred mage sagged limply to the ground.

Levan climbed off him, smoothing down his scarlet cloak, then resumed his long, quick strides down Dubias Row as though nothing had happened. Rasso cantered beside him, silver-white fur stained dark red around the jowls. His tail wagged merrily, as though grateful for a good feed and a chance to stretch his legs.

Saffron gave the white-clad corpses a final glance and then rushed to catch up with Levan, her heart hammering.

"What just happened?" she asked, studying the firm set of Levan's jaw, the defiant square of his shoulders. The way his fist still clenched his wand.

He grunted his distaste. "Whitewings made an attempt on the gamehouse earlier tonight."

Of course. The bodies she'd seen hurled from the roof.

And they hadn't just been killed. They'd been maimed beyond recognition.

"They've upgraded their cloaks since I was on the streetwatch," Saffron muttered, swallowing the acrid saliva pooling in her mouth. "Must be moving up in the world."

Rounding a final corner onto Beakpeck Place, they reached Zamollan's, an abandoned apothecary that had once specialized in dragon scales. Inside the old shop lay an entrance to the Bloodmoons' warded tunnels, entirely unguarded and yet nonetheless impossible to penetrate.

The Silvercloaks had known of the entrance's existence for years. Did they have eyes on it right now? Were they watching as Saffron and Levan ducked beneath the saggy green awning, bloody-mouthed fallowwolf at their heels? Did they spot Saffron's stark silver-blond curls and recoil at the sight of her in scarlet?

She lifted her hood over her hair, just in case.

Inside the apothecary, the air was stale and musty. Old, damp wood and brittle sawdust, dried feathers and something distinctly leathery. Levan pushed a large barrel to one side and lifted the trapdoor disguised beneath it. The steps below were pitch dark, but they shimmered with a strange translucent film—the wards themselves.

The wards the Silvercloaks had never been able to breach, until now.

Saffron paused before descending, studying the kingpin's son for any sign that he was rattled by the Whitewings' assault. For any sign of dismay that he'd just murdered twice in cold blood.

She found none.

But there was *something.*

Something tense and brittle in the hard line of his jaw. Something too straight in the steel of his spine.

"What did he mean, you of all people should know it's always personal?" Saff asked, voice echoey and loud in the derelict shop.

But Levan only shot Saffron a closed stare—one she'd been on the receiving end of once before, back in Captain Aspar's office.

One that told her the answer was above her pay grade.

17

...

Aterni Se Quiestae

After a wretched night of half sleep, Saffron awoke the next morning not knowing entirely what to expect from her brusque captor and his feral pet.

Would there be a formal debrief of the previous evening before a council of Bloodmoons, in which she had to relive everything that had transpired in the Jaded Saint—and subsequently on Dubias Row? Were they as thorough as the Silvercloaks in such matters? If she were still a hallowed detective, she would be doing a frankly unconscionable amount of paperwork at this very moment, only narrowly resisting the urge to feed herself through a meat grinder.

But there was no debrief. As it happened, she was largely ignored.

Not long after dawn there was a short rap on her door, but by the time she'd donned a robe and padded over to open it, there was only a tray of breakfast food left on the ground. A note, scribbled on a scrap of parchment, had been curled up and slotted between a bowl of dragonberries and a clay pot of sugarcream.

Stay in your chambers. I'll come for you later. —Levan

His handwriting was surprisingly neat, with swirling cursive letters and pin-straight margins. Saffron stabbed the note with her wand and muttered, "*Sen eriban,*" watching with satisfaction as the note shredded into ribbons. A waste of magic, certainly, but gratifying nonetheless.

She had nil qualms about recuperating in the privacy of her own bedroom all day, so she set the tray down on her bed and feasted—runny-yolked eggs and mapled bacon and sun-sweet tomatoes, toast with lashings of butter, and several helpings of the berries and cream. Levan had also given her another pot of salve, which she applied generously to her searing brand.

The relief, however, was soon followed by a whip-crack of self-loathing. She didn't deserve to have a full belly and a soothed wound. Not when Neatras had died at her hand. Not when his daughter had been consigned to a miserable eternity in that wretched gamehouse.

The mission demanded his death, she told herself. *You thought through every possible outcome. It was the only way.*

She thought of what Sebran had said with a soldier's gruffness during the final assessment—that the acceptable number of civilian casualties was higher than zero—but felt little comfort.

She spent the rest of the day debating whether or not to establish contact with Aspar. Her captain would want to know how the previous night had unfolded, yet Saff couldn't reveal that she'd compromised Nissa. Yes, she could share information on the Whitewings' failed heist and their later attempt on Levan's life—the Silvercloaks had likely found those corpses by now, one with its throat ripped out by a fallowwolf—but was that worth the risk of reaching out? The Silvercloaks were already well aware of the enmity between the Whitewings and the Bloodmoons. Without tangible evidence that Levan himself had murdered them, an arrest warrant would never stick.

No, it wasn't worth making contact. Not yet.

Saffron napped on and off for hours, dreaming that she was a silk-spider trapped in the center of a barbed-wire web, jolting in her blankets at every footstep echoing down the hallway.

Twilight came and went, but Levan never appeared.

Saffron grew restless.

Close to darknight, she lay staring at the gold ceiling rose above her four-poster bed, thinking of Lyrian Celadon and his fiendish memory.

The way he seemed to know every single citizen of Atherin, and the shimmering strands of love and kinship that connected them all. His innate understanding of how to pluck those strands to hurt the most.

How long until the Bloodmoons touched every life in the city? How long before they poisoned every existence? The degrees of separation would not stay separate for much longer.

Saff also thought, incessantly and agonizingly, of Neatras's daughter.

How long would she live in a tomb of glass, unable to move or speak? Most mages lived to be over a hundred. She still had so long left to suffer.

Unless . . .

So much of this assignment was out of Saffron's control, and yet here lay a pocket of possibility. Of goodness, of redemption. A risk, but she was built for risk. To assess danger, to forge a route through it to the other side.

First, what were the threats?

She would likely get caught. Lyrian had eyes everywhere.

What would he do if he found her stomping on the roulette ball with the heel of her boot?

It wouldn't be worth killing her over—they needed her to find Zares—but there were always the twin pillars of pain and fear to contend with.

Pain didn't scare her. She'd take the brand all over again if it actually did some good.

Fear, on the other hand . . .

They wouldn't threaten the Silvercloak cohort—whom they'd want in one piece, flipped and turned into assets one by one—but her uncles would be in danger. The Bloodmoons would want to send a message to Saffron, to let her know she couldn't undermine them so brazenly.

So they would likely hurt her uncles, but surely they wouldn't kill them over this. They needed Mal and Merin alive to keep her in line. They wouldn't waste their ultimate bargaining chip on the destruction of a roulette ball.

In any case, she was sure either of her proudly *good* uncles would take a blow to end the suffering of an innocent girl. And they would want someone else to do the same for Saffron, if she ever found herself entombed in a glass case.

Satisfied that she'd thought through the likeliest outcome—and that the likeliest outcome was not too devastating—she dressed in her tunic, slacks, and scarlet cloak; reapplied salve to her burning wound; and left the bedroom to a deserted corridor.

She kept her hand tucked around her wand, preparing to throw up a spellshield at a moment's notice. To freeze time if she had to. She ran through the arsenal of offensive and defensive spells she'd had to master to pass through the Academy, ready to cast them in the split seconds between life and death.

But to her surprise, Saffron moved through the mansion like a warm knife through soft butter. There were only a few servants around, dipping their heads in acknowledgment and continuing with their duties. The scarlet cloak afforded her an immediate respect, a kind of inherent power, and she supposed none of the underlings knew the truth of how she came to be here. None of them had heard her scream or plead as the hot poker melted her skin and flesh.

They simply saw the cloak and bowed.

Snaking back through the warded tunnels—she'd memorized the route on the way to and from the Jaded Saint—Saffron kept peering over her shoulder, expecting to see Levan or Segal or Vogolan on her tail, but nobody followed.

So much blind faith in the loyalty brand.

The arrogance.

Several minutes later, Saffron entered the gamehouse the same way she'd left it: through the smoky haze of the Achullah Terrace. As she moved through the domed atrium, the other patrons cleared a path, parting like water around a rock. They nodded their heads, giving tight, fearful smiles. One even curtseyed, as though she were royalty. It was a curious, almost intoxicating feeling, to be so powerful.

Because fear *was* a kind of power, far easier to wield than magic. A well with no bottom.

No wonder the kingpin found it so irresistible.

Even in the dead of the night, the gamehouse was still in full swing, but there was a looseness to it Saffron didn't like. Slack faces, empty eyes, veins pulsing darkly in throats. That same hunger and thirst had returned to her too: a draw toward the blackcherry sours, toward the pure, raw pleasure, the heightened euphoria.

At the roulette table where she'd gambled the previous evening, Neatras had been replaced by a young mage with olive skin, an upturned nose, and an Irisian griffin necklace dangling around her neck. Her name badge read *Venda.*

Venda set the wheel spinning and tossed in the ball, watching as it clacked and clattered in a silvery blur. As it slowed, a slate-gray iris took shape, narrowing hatefully as it spotted Saffron. The eye was glazed over, dizzy. Saffron felt the nausea secondhand, writhing and curdling in her belly.

As Venda swept the chips from the felted table, Saffron approached. The croupier purposefully didn't look at the scarlet cloak or the mage who wore it, but the visible pulse in her neck betrayed her fear.

Saffron aimed her wand at the roulette ball. "*Ans convoqan.*"

A simple summoning spell. The roulette ball sailed through the air and landed in Saff's palm. For a single shocked moment, Venda locked gazes with Saffron.

"Speak of this to no one," Saffron muttered, tucking it into her cloak pocket.

The croupier gave a single petrified nod, her fingers clutching the silver-and-sapphire griffin resting on her collarbone.

Saffron strode off without a backward glance, heart thumping against the cage of her ribs. Was Lyrian watching through the roulette ball? Or was it late enough that he'd be asleep?

She'd almost made it to the Achullah Terrace when a hulking figure stepped out from behind the slots.

Levan stared straight at her with an impenetrable look on his face, those blue eyes cold and cadaverous. At the sight of him, Saffron thought of searing flesh and bloody wrist stumps, pleading croupiers and wolves tearing vocal cords from pale throats. Her mother and father, dead at her young feet, corpses spread on the faded rug her father had once charmed into flying.

"Subtle." Levan glanced pointedly down at her pocket, then meaningfully back at the roulette tables.

Loathing bolted through Saffron like white lightning.

"There's no need for her to suffer anymore." She spoke in a low, hateful snap. "Her father is dead, and there's nobody else you need to keep in line. Leaving her here is just cruel."

"I've never claimed not to be cruel."

Levan took another step toward her, so close she felt the heat of his body. Even though the riotous gamehouse rattled and roared, it all faded into the background, her senses vignetting around him. Half of his face was illuminated by the blinking lights of the slots, flashes of gold and blue and green and white dancing over his sharp cheekbones and scarred lip, the chiseled lines of his face, the penny dent of his chin, the gloss of his cocoa-dark hair.

Loathe as she was to admit it, she was terrified of this mage, of how fast and free he flung the killing curse, of how he severed appendages in the pursuit of information. And yet the prophecy foretold that she would get the upper hand, eventually. She would lay her lips on his, and he would let out a soft, rough moan, and she would fire a killing spell into his stomach. And it would feel *good.*

"How did you know I was here?" she asked, stamping the fear resolutely out of her voice.

"I have my ways."

He glared at Saffron so harshly that she wanted to look away—he seemed either to not look at her at all, or to stare all the way down to her bones—yet her pride kept her gaze pinned to his. Smeared up the side of his throat was something dark and red.

Saff gestured to the unmistakable blood spray. "Busy day?"

"Empty your pockets," he muttered, ignoring the question.

"No." Saffron's hand closed around the roulette ball, but she didn't pull it out.

He scoffed. "This is not worth your life."

"That's for me to decide."

He pinched the bridge of his nose, impatient, and Saff felt a tiny glimmer of satisfaction. She rather enjoyed making his life difficult. He was used to getting what he wanted. He was *not* used to her stubbornness.

"Why would you do this?" he asked in a low timbre. "Why would you risk yourself for a girl you don't even know?"

She shrugged. "Are you going to collar me again? Or shall we skip straight to the part where you threaten or maim my loved ones?"

"You calculated the risk to your loved ones and acted anyway?" Levan frowned, as though he'd just heard one of her uncle Mal's impossible riddles.

"If I were trapped in that ball, they'd take any pain to free me. Neatras's daughter deserves the same mercy." Saff gestured to her chest. "And clearly the brand doesn't believe this to be a *betrayal* of the Bloodmoons, because I'm still standing."

It was bold, to invoke the brand, but the Bloodmoons' faith in its potency seemed unwavering, and she saw no reason not to leverage it.

Once again Saffron wondered whether a matching brand lay beneath Levan's tunic. If it did . . . she couldn't imagine going through that at the hands of your own *father.* It wouldn't be an excuse for the cruel killer Levan had become, but it would be a catalyst nonetheless.

Nobody was born evil, contrary to what Captain Aspar believed.

"How is your wound?" he asked gruffly.

"Fine," Saffron lied, hot blood simmering beneath the surface of the awful scab. She pulled the silvered eyeball from her pocket. The whites were mottled with spidery pink blood vessels, as though Neatras's daughter had been weeping. "Any threats you want to level at me before I do this anyway?"

More bolshiness. He could easily overpower her, if he so wanted to, but she was banking on the fact he wouldn't want to cause a scene in the middle of the gamehouse.

There was also a kind of wariness, a latent distrust, in his expression—as though he was remembering her startlingly convincing illusions, and wondering what sort of trick she might play next.

Or maybe he just pitied her. But she wouldn't let herself entertain that idea.

Levan looked down at the roulette ball, betraying no emotion. "Go ahead."

Victory dipped in Saffron's chest, and she set the roulette ball down on the floor. She lifted her foot and brought down her heel as hard as she could.

The glass casing didn't give. Didn't even *splinter.*

Instead, the ball skittered away in the direction of Levan's own leather boots.

He knelt to pick it up, and Saffron desperately incanted, "*Ans convoqan.*"

But Levan's fist had already closed around it, and her summoning spell was not strong enough to wrench it from his grasp.

There was a long, sprawling silence as he studied the roulette ball, like a jeweler examining an ascenpearl for imperfections. Saffron's breath hung suspended somewhere in her throat.

Eventually, Levan gave a stiff grunt. "You're right. The daughter's suffering serves no purpose. I am what most would consider a monster, but I have a code."

Saffron frowned. "You're going to free her?"

"She cannot be freed. Her body has long been incinerated. But I can end her suffering."

Saff searched the words for a catch—she had spent a lot of time observing interrogations, and had come to recognize the tiny tics that betrayed a lie, or an ulterior motive, or a trap about to spring—but found none.

Still he stared down at the roulette ball, deep in thought. But he did not move to act.

"Do you remember her name?" Saffron asked tentatively.

A terse nod. "I remember every name. Tenea."

Finally, his expression cemented itself, and he raised his wand.

The black elm hovered over Tenea's dilated pupil, flared so wide her slate-gray iris was eclipsed. A horrible lurch went through Saffron's belly, but the least she could do was bear witness to the girl's final moments.

He tapped his wand to the entombed eye. "*Ans casulan libreran, ans niman vanesan.*"

Saffron didn't recognize Levan's spellwork, but the cadence of it made her start. The precision, the mastery . . . it reminded her so viscerally of her father's magic, the way he linked together complex charms to form a compound enchantment. He'd always had a gift for alloyed spells.

An intense ache of grief spread between her ribs, wrapping around her lungs, her heart.

She watched in half awe, half horror as the glass casing opened at an invisible seam. The eyeball didn't squelch into Levan's open palm, but rather melted away into thin air with a tangible, passing *sigh.*

As the last vestiges of Tenea vanished into nothing, Saffron's brain scrambled to make sense of it. One of the cardinal rules of magic was that *something* could not be made *nothing.* Matter could not be made to disappear entirely, because it would upset the energy balance of the world.

"Where has she gone?" Saff breathed.

A simple shrug. "Elsewhere."

What did that mean? How was there still so much Saffron was yet to understand about magic?

Levan closed his empty palm and whispered something so quietly Saffron almost didn't catch it.

"Aterni se quiestae."

Saff jolted at the expression. It was something she'd only ever heard her uncle Merin say, something she couldn't remember how to translate precisely. It meant something like "eternal peace."

She blinked in surprise. "You know Ancient Sarthi?"

Two thousand years ago, when explorers of old knew only of the continent—and not of the vast pangea that lay beneath it—there had been only two known lands: Nyrøth and Sarth. Over time, the sprawling tundra nation of Nyrøth remained united as a whole, but bloody battles and terrible wars carved Sarth up into three separate territories: Vallin, Bellandry, and Eqora. The ensuing centuries saw the lands splinter further still—Bellandry lost the three Eastern Republics of Laudon, Esvaine, and Tarsa to a violent rebellion for independence, while the islands of Mersina and Irisi each became city-states. These countries' modern languages all had roots in the Ancient Sarthi tongue, but the original language had mostly been forgotten over the course of millennia—with the occasional exception of a linguistics fanatic like her uncle.

"I know languages most people have never even heard of." Levan shrugged, but something in Saffron told her he was inwardly proud of it—in a way he hadn't been when she pointed out the astonishing power of his transmutation. The pride of his languages gave him a subtle glow, a half smile, so at odds with his hard, stoic outline.

She found it oddly compelling, and wanted to ask him more about it, until she remembered who he was, everything he represented, and scoffed instead. "I wouldn't think you'd have time to casually study ancient tongues, what with all the torture and killing."

The half smile vanished as quickly as Tenea had, leaving behind an even darker, blanker expression than before. Levan turned on his heel, as though suddenly disgusted by the whole situation.

"We're finished here, Silver." And then, almost as an afterthought, "Speak of it to no one."

18

...

Rezaran Blood

SAFFRON SPENT THE NEXT COUPLE OF DAYS IN THE FOLDS OF her four-poster bed, slipping in and out of sleep. It was not a restful sleep, but rather a hostile, imprisoning one. She felt as though her mind were at the bottom of a lake, the surface glistening just beyond her bodiless reach. Like she had died and reincarnated as algae—an entity that did live and breathe, technically speaking, and yet lacked agency in any real sense.

When she did wake for a few moments, lifting her groggy head from the pillow, the room around her swayed and eddied. The brand left her weakened, feverish. Not herself.

Levan and Rasso appeared several times a day, at precisely punctual times, to proffer food. She didn't know why Levan felt the need to deliver the meals personally, rather than having a servant do it, but it was likely a means of intimidation, of surveillance. No matter. She barely had the strength to register his arrival, let alone interact with him in any meaningful way.

On the third morning, however, after bringing breakfast at precisely eight a.m., Levan announced that he had run her bath, on account of the fact she smelled like a reekhog's posterior. With an immense surge of effort, she traipsed obligingly behind him down the corridor and into a private bathing chamber.

The air in the chamber was opaque with steam, and the bath was sunken into the turquoise mosaicked floor, its contents scented with a rich rosehip oil. All the fittings were solid gold: the taps, the grates, the little wall hooks upon which a fresh cotton towel hung waiting for her. Next to the towel was a clean set of plain clothes—a black tunic, matching slacks, and new undergarments.

"I'll wait outside," Levan said.

Saffron rolled her eyes. "It's not like I'm going to make a run for it."

"I'll wait anyway." Rasso lay at his feet by means of confirmation.

As Saffron was about to cross the threshold into the bathing chamber, she hesitated. Her hand went to the tender burn on her chest.

"What's it going to look like?"

She still hadn't laid eyes upon it. Whenever she reapplied the salve, she stared resolutely at the ceiling.

He didn't have to ask what she meant. Didn't even seem surprised at the question.

"Like a dark, angry crust." He swallowed, not meeting her eye. "It'll fade."

The bath chamber was dimly lit with evercandles, and the clouds of steam mercifully obscured the brand, somewhat. She shrugged out of her clothes and hung them on the hook, and as she lowered her aching body into the bath, there was a fresh lick of fire, another poker sizzling against her skin, a pain so fierce and bright that a scream tore loose from her throat.

In an instant she was back at the mercy of Lyrian Celadon, wrists bound and flesh burning—

The door opened with a crash, and Levan's outline appeared through the steam.

"Are you alright?" he asked, voice gruff.

Saff went to hastily cover up her intimate parts. Shame filled her belly, like she'd been caught masturbating. "Fine."

"The brand?"

She nodded, fiercely blinking away the tears beading along her waterline. "The heat against it."

Saints, it throbbed. She had to focus on keeping her breathing steady, on not whimpering like a kicked wolf cub. Levan had already seen her at her weakest, her most broken. She had to maintain some semblance of pride.

Yet she was naked and in pain in front of him, and he made no effort to leave. Instead, he pulled the wand from his cloak pocket and dipped its tip into the bathwater.

"Don corzaquiss."

The water sizzled and cooled. It wasn't *cold,* but it also was not quite so scorching, so reminiscent of the brand. A long breath rattled out of Saffron, and the intense sear of her crusted brand ebbed slightly.

"Better?" Levan asked, the word rough.

"Yes," she muttered. "Thanks."

He nodded once and left. She stared after him, trying to reconcile this random act of compassion with the man she'd seen torturing an innocent Brewer and murdering . . . well, not *innocent* Whitewings. But he'd mutilated some and slaughtered others without a hint of remorse.

The kingpin's son seemed to have a weak spot for her brand. He'd been rattled when she first suggested it in the alley, and he'd looked away while it was happening, offering her a tiny shred of dignity and privacy. In the aftermath, he'd brought her salve and asked if she was alright, and now . . . this. All signs pointed to the fact that he too had been branded—perhaps young, perhaps against his will. Why else would he show such relative sympathy for her pain, when everything else he said and did was so unrelentingly cold?

I am what most would consider a monster, but I have a code.

Aspar had ordered her to uncover the Bloodmoons' elusive motive, the big *why* behind their pursuit of power and fortune. Saff would have to establish herself as a valuable confidante to both Levan and Lyrian if she wanted the answer. And of the two, Levan was much more accessible to her.

The rough edges of a plan sharpened, solidified.

When she was done bathing, Levan and Rasso escorted her wordlessly back to her room. Rasso glowered at her from the threshold, those unnerving white eyes as bottomless as they were blank.

"How do you have a fallowwolf?" she asked Levan, sitting cross-legged on the bed. "I thought they only bonded with Timeweavers, and since the Timeweavers were eradicated, the fallowwolves went feral."

He paused with his hand on the doorknob. "You know a lot about fallowwolf lore."

"My old commanding officer was an Augurest."

Levan tensed like an arrow nocked in a bow, pulled back and quivering with the effort of staying still. "I have a fallowwolf because I have Rezaran blood."

All the blood rushed to Saffron's head.

"Impossible," she breathed. "The whole house was slaughtered a hundred years ago."

Levan shook his head grimly. "Not the whole house. There was a bastard son nobody knew about."

Saffron reeled at the revelation.

His ancestors had once sat the throne of Vallin.

House Rezaran's fifty-year Dreadreign had almost unmade the world. The royal house had written and unwritten time so frequently and indiscriminately that the very fabric of the world wore thin. Careless rewinds and redoes created paradoxical knots, and it took an immense amount of ascenite to smooth them out again. Entire days and weeks went missing from time, fraying and disintegrating, while others repeated in frantic loops. Mages vanished between the cracks of *then* and *now,* never to be seen again.

As the Augurests had predicted.

The dragons—the longest-standing allies of Timeweavers—scorned this cavalier manipulation of time, and so they deserted House Rezaran, fleeing north to the ice-capped mountains of northeastern Nyrøth. House Veliron, who were proud Augurests, used this weakening of House Rezaran to take the throne, executing over a hundred Timeweavers outside the Palace.

House Rezaran was eradicated in its entirety—or so the world believed.

Not that they had been mourned.

And now there stood a mage before her with their blood running through his veins.

The fourth prophecy from Augur Emalin said that the Augurests would emerge triumphant, but a few Timeweavers would slip through the cracks, and the Augurests would have to remain vigilant for centuries after their initial conquest, awaiting the second uprising, making sure to slaughter every last one.

Saff struggled to process the magnitude. The prospect of a time-wielding kingpin was almost too hideous to comprehend.

"So the Bloodmoons are Timeweavers?" she asked, throat dry.

Levan shook his head. "My mother had a trace of it, but barely enough to roll back a few minutes, and even that would drain her for weeks. Rasso was hers. After she died, he stuck with me, though I don't have a single weaving muscle in my body. Not for lack of trying. My father was obsessed with learning the lost art, for a while, even though the Rezaran bloodline was on my mother's side. He still uses my mother's weaverwick wand in the vague hope a dormant power will eventually show itself."

Saff's mouth fell open. Levan's mother had been the notorious Lorissa Celadon. Her bloody ambition and ruthless genius had raised the Bloodmoons from a lowly street gang to the most feared criminal organization Vallin had ever seen. When she died, her husband, Lyrian, had taken the reins.

Lorissa *Rezaran.*

"Why are you telling me this?" Saff asked, breathless. "It's not common knowledge that you have Rezaran blood. It could see you hunted by Augurests the world over."

Levan's jaw clenched. "Because I see no reason to hide. If they want to hunt me, let them come. I fear no one. And as for why I told you so freely . . ." He tapped two fingers over his heart to symbolize the brand. "You can't share it any further."

Oh, but I can.

Aspar would salivate at the knowledge that the Bloodmoons were descendants of House Rezaran. As an Augurest, she supported the eradication of all Timeweavers. This revelation would not only solidify her motivations for bringing them down, but it would pay credence to the fourth prophecy she had devoted her life to.

How she would *love* to be the one to end the Timeweaver bloodline once and for all. Not only would she be named commissioner, but she would also fulfill her own religious mandate.

And as for Levan fearing no one . . .

Well. His killer was sitting right in front of him. He was wrong not to be afraid, and his arrogance would be his downfall.

"Eat your breakfast." Levan gestured to the pile of almond pastry cones and the mug of hot chocolate on her bedside table. "I know the first kill is rough, and the brand hurts like all hells, but you've wallowed enough. Time to earn your place."

"I thought finding Nalezen Zares was earning my place."

"You have to earn your place over and over again, like watering a plant. You can't feed it once and expect it to thrive forever."

"I knew you were a poetic sort."

For some reason, the quip landed. There was a flash of something childlike on Levan's face, and it was only then that Saffron noticed the black leather-bound book tucked beneath his arm. He stuffed it awkwardly inside his cloak, but not before Saff caught sight of the novel's title in embossed gold foil: *The Great Adventures of the Lost Dragonborn.*

All at once, Saffron's memory was yanked back fifteen years.

She stood in front of the dressmaker's mirror in her uncles' Cloakery, willing herself to speak. It had been over half a decade since her parents were killed, and grief was no longer a blade-sharp shock; rather a hollow shaft had opened inside her, emptiness pressing against all her vital organs.

And still she had not been able to find her words—which meant she had not cast a lick of magic in that time either.

Her uncles had been warned that if she didn't start casting soon, she'd have to be sent to a Ludder school on the outskirts of the city. The niece of Vallin's finest cloakiers would not be permitted to wear a cloak at all. There was an elegant sort of irony to it.

Say something, she had begged herself, staring at her halo of silver-blond curls. Her pale blue scholar's cloak was a luxurious, neatly pressed silk, and she couldn't bear the thought of losing it.

Say anything.

She could not remember what her voice even sounded like. The exact pitch had been lost to the dusty attic of time.

Watching her struggle, Uncle Mal had pulled something out of the top drawer.

"I picked something up for you last night, on my way past Torquil's Tomes. *The Great Adventures of the Lost Dragonborn.* This is the first book, but there are five more published, and the sixth is being released in the spring."

By spring, Saffron still had not spoken, but she had devoured all six of the available *Lost Dragonborn* tomes. The sixth book ended on a massive cliffhanger, and there was still a year until the last installment, and she was dying to discuss it with someone. She had burst into the living room where her uncles played chess, brandished the book in the air like a wand, and said, "Dragons are fucking *awesome.*"

The words had been hoarse, painful, rasping.

Freeing.

There had been a moment of stunned silence, in which Merin's pincered fingers hovered over a bishop. Give them their due, her uncles did not erupt in joy or surprise, did not make any great fanfare of the moment, but rather acted like she hadn't been silent for the better part of six years.

"Language, Saffron," Merin had admonished, peering over his monocle before going back to his chess game.

Now, in the Bloodmoon mansion, disbelief felled her for the second time in the span of a few minutes.

The kingpin's son was a *Lost Dragonborn* nerd.

The revelation glittered with possibility. She could use this shared ground to her advantage, establish a rapport with Levan so that eventually, he would trust her with the Bloodmoons' true motivations. He'd already shared with her his heritage. How much deeper could she go?

But before she could ask Levan about the book they both loved, he muttered, "I'll wait for you outside."

SAFFRON FOLLOWED LEVAN AND Rasso through the warded tunnels, discreetly studying the markings on the darkly lit walls. They told a story, albeit in the crude style of an ancient cave painting—the Divine Peaks of Kudano were filled with such art.

This sequence was as follows:

A figure walks through a forest.

A few steps later, they're skewered by a bladebull's furious horn.

The bull flees.

Another figure hunches over the corpse in grief.

From the folds of their cloak, they retrieve a miniature hourglass, like the one on Lyrian Celadon's desk.

They turn it upside down, so the sand flows in a different direction.

Then, a single word: *tempavicissan*.

The second figure disappears again, and the bull reappears.

The original figurc is unskewered.

The bull retreats.

The original figure is alone in the woods once more.

The hourglass-wielding figure approaches, takes the other figure by the hand, and leads them in another direction.

A simple depiction of timeweaving, Saff realized.

Heresy, according to the Augurests. But after what Levan had told Saff about his mother's bloodline, it made all the more sense.

"What do you know about loxlure?" Levan asked, snapping her attention away from the carvings.

"Loxlure?" It wasn't a familiar word, though she sensed that it should be, that her ignorance was an admission of failure.

"You mean the Silvercloaks don't have a big fat case file on it?"

"Not that I know of, but my clearance level wasn't high. They classify almost everything—streetwatchers and cadets walk around the city half-blindfolded, because the Order is so afraid of truth elixir."

"Interesting." Levan pursed his lips, the scar on the bottom puckering around the old wound.

"Why?" Saff asked, detective's instincts firing up. "What is loxlure?"

"Lox is a . . . substance. It comes from a rare kind of nightpoppy that only grows in northeastern Laudon. It's what gives blackcherry sours their color." A heavy pause. "And it causes all-consuming addiction."

Oh.

Saff's experience in the gamehouse made sudden and terrible sense. The way her fear had been eased by the drink, the way she'd immediately ordered another. The rich, almost erotic pleasure of it. The heightened euphoria while playing roulette. The bone aches and burrowing weakness when the effects wore off. And then, when she'd returned for Tenea, the slack-jawed, dead-eyed stares of the patrons.

She'd been right—it was more than a potion, which wouldn't affect her, and more than simple booze. It was a narcotic. And she was as vulnerable to those as anyone.

Was that the real reason she'd felt so rotten the last few days? Not feverish and dizzy and algae-like because of the brand, but because of lox withdrawal?

Saints. No wonder the citizens of Atherin couldn't stay away from the gamehouse. Despite the violence and death and binding debts, despite mutilated bodies hurled from the rooftops, despite the naked dancers in glass jars . . . the loxlure was simply too powerful to resist.

"Why are you telling me this?" she asked, pulse thrumming.

This was *major.*

"You're hardly going to be useful to us if you have no idea how the operation works."

"Which is how?"

"Our supplier from Laudon sails the lox along the Sleepless Sea and into Port Ouran—though we've lost several ships to pirates around Mersina over the last few years. Once the goods are safely in Vallish waters, our trader boats sail the freight east up the Corven and into the Royal Quay, where we've blackmailed several customs officers into not searching our holds. But there was a crate missing from our last shipment, so today we're going to interrogate the dock workers who handle our cargo."

Saff's blood fizzed. Potential evidence had been handed to her on a platter. There was no way the Grand Arbiter would be able to bury something like this. Charges would *have* to be brought. Aspar would be named commissioner, and Saff would be formally reinstated into the Silvercloaks with Quintan's Cross pinned to her lapel.

Yet she felt a little uneasy over how willingly Levan was sharing this information—and the information about his Rezaran bloodline. He really did have blind faith in the brand's dark power. He really did believe she couldn't relay this information without immediate and agonizing death. And this was a smart mage, rigorous and cynical. If he had faith in the brand, it was for good reason.

What if he was right?

What if even her strange immunity couldn't stop such dark magic?

What if she *was* trapped in the Bloodmoons?

19

...

The Missing Shipment

IN THE CHAOS AND CLAMOR OF THE DOCKS, LYRIAN WAS A QUIET, coiled serpent.

Standing between stacked wooden cargo crates, the kingpin was flanked by Segal and Vogolan, an expression of anticipation, of *hunger,* on his pale face. His scarlet cloak was pinned high in the hollow of his throat, his white widow's peak pronounced in the warm autumn sun. A swirling roulette ball hung around his neck on a chain—his eye into the gamehouse. Levan and Saff both towered over Lyrian, and yet his modest stature did not make him any less threatening. A dagger could be wielded far more precisely than a broadsword.

As they approached, Levan muttered something fast and low under his breath. "I say this because I have no particular desire to see you slaughtered. Do *not* fuck with my father. Don't crack your little jokes, don't argue for the sake of gaining control, don't put a single foot wrong. And for the love of hells, if he tells you to kill someone—do it."

Saff clenched her jaw so hard her teeth hurt.

Lyrian's gaze narrowed as she and Levan approached.

"We've been waiting." The kingpin's words were soft, but not kind.

"We're right on time," Levan responded coolly, without glancing at his watch.

The kingpin fixed his son with a look of such sudden and potent loathing that Saffron physically recoiled. The expression was gone almost as soon as it appeared, leaving behind only a pale vestige of displeasure, but it had been there nonetheless: an obliterating and unfiltered hatred.

Levan simply stared back, blandly, unmoved.

Every single interaction between father and son seemed to be a power struggle.

"Very well," Lyrian said, after several taut beats, and Saffron had the strange sense he was fighting some fierce internal battle. "Let us proceed."

The docks clanged with the bustle of trade, the calls of workers, the tinkling of bells, the snapping of banderoles. Over their heads, a crate hovered of its own accord, then floated away in the direction of a magnificent purple riverboat.

While the sun was high in the sky, the air was cool in the shadows between freight stacks. Following Lyrian, the Bloodmoons snaked silently through the maze of crates until they arrived at an old shipping container repurposed into an office, the name Kasan Melian etched neatly onto a wooden sign nailed to the door.

Lyrian entered without knocking, bracketed by Segal and Vogolan. Levan and Saff followed.

"Good day, Kasan." Lyrian's tone was pleasant, and somehow more unsettling than overt hostility.

Behind a squat wooden desk, Kasan Melian leapt to his feet. The merchant had deep olive skin, gold-rimmed glasses, and a densely lined forehead. He wore a royal-blue cloak, a gold cuff etched with thirteen dragons around his wrist—a follower of Draecism, then—and a petrified expression.

"S-sir?" he stuttered. "Sir. A pleasure, of course, but . . . I usually deal with Vogolan."

Lyrian strolled casually around the office, studying the dates and transactions pinned to the noticeboard, slowly leafing through a ledger on Kasan's desk. Subtle yet invasive shows of power, almost daring Kasan to protest. The noises of the dock were dulled, leaving only taut, threatening silence.

"There was a crate missing from our latest shipment," Lyrian eventually said. Every word was calm, precise, as though it had been measured on a set of scales. "I would like to know which of your workers pilfered it."

Kasan blanched, gripping the edge of his desk so hard that his dry, cracked knuckles turned bone white. "I don't know what you're talking about."

Lyrian pinched the bridge of his nose, his serenity fissuring somewhat. Saffron recognized the tic of impatience; Levan did the same.

"Nobody ever makes it simple, do they?" he said, then sighed. "Nobody answers my questions, nobody tells the truth. It's exhausting. Because you know I always win, and so why put off the inevitable? Fighting the inevitable is not bravery, but idiocy."

Kasan steeled his jaw. "I truly didn't know there was a missing—"

"When you took the contract, you assured us that you ran the tightest of ships." Lyrian had yet to draw his wand—another subtle show of strength. *To wield fear is to wield the greatest power of all.* "That your boat would never spring a leak."

"Sir, I can only apologize if supply went astray," said Kasan, banging a fist on the desk as though he was as incensed as the kingpin. "Whoever's responsible will be let go immediately."

Lyrian rubbed at his temples, as though this was giving him a headache. "Lox addiction is hardly difficult to spot. The sweats, the night terrors, the black tinge to the veins. You must know *exactly* who stole from the stash."

"I don't, I swear it, I—"

"Honesty is so hard to come by these days." Lyrian withdrew his wand at last. Segal and Vogolan raised theirs in unison. "And you know, I don't want to do these gruesome things to people. I have no innate bloodlust, believe it or not. But I will stop at nothing to protect my own." A thin curl of a smile. "Perhaps we aren't so different, after all."

"Sir, please—"

"Clear the desk," Lyrian said coldly.

With a swoosh of his wand and an inaudible mutter, Segal cleared the desk. Kasan took a step backward, hand floating to the gold cuff at his wrist as though his faith might protect him, somehow, but everyone in the room knew he was long past saving. He was outnumbered, and overpowered, and nothing short of dragon intervention would save him now.

Lyrian raised his wand, which Saff now knew to be his late wife's weaverwick. The garnet wood tremored slightly, as though it contained too much power for Lyrian to command.

"Sen ascevolo."

Kasan's body arched hideously as it was dropped onto the desk, all the wind slamming out of his lungs with an audible *ooft.*

A curl of a smile on Lyrian's face. "*Sen debilitan, nis cerebran.*"

Every inch of the merchant's body was paralyzed—except for his head, which shook frantically.

"Here's your first lesson, Filthcloak," Lyrian drawled to Saff. "Nothing gets you what you want faster than pain. Of course, fear is a more powerful tool long term, and in time you will learn to manipulate those threads. But for a quick fix, pain is king. Levan here is known for his, ah, *handiwork.* Segal has a penchant for kneecaps, while Vogolan likes teeth. In my youth, I used to enjoy removing minor organs. Appendixes, gallbladders. A kidney, if someone badly misbehaved. A painful procedure, without whiteroot or poppymist, as I'm sure you can imagine. I wonder what your signature will be?"

Saff's ribs felt like they were about to cave in.

You have to earn your place over and over again, like watering a plant. You can't feed it once and expect it to thrive forever.

"You seemed particularly compelled by the plight of Neatras's daughter. A cruel fate, indeed." Lyrian paused, and Saffron waited for an indication that the kingpin knew what she and Levan had done to free Tenea, but none came. "Perhaps eyes . . . yes. Eyes could work."

With the toe of his boot, Lyrian rustled through the detritus that had flown from Kasan's desk. "I could teach you the spell, of course, for removing an eye. But there's something so visceral, so satisfying about doing it the old-fashioned way." The glint of something sharp and silver caught his eye. He stabbed his wand at it. "*Sen convoqan.*"

The instrument leapt from the floor into his palm, and he held it out to Saffron.

A letteropener. Long, pointed, with two parallel grooves on the narrow handle.

"Carve out the eye, and I'll show you how to bind a person's consciousness to it. Then we'll end the body and leave the mind entombed."

Saffron's stomach roiled. She couldn't carve out a person's eye with a Saints-damned letteropener.

She had to think her way out of this.

As it had in the final assessment over a year ago, her mind skirted around the reality in front of her and went straight for the *why.* Lyrian claimed that he didn't want to commit such heinous deeds—he just wanted to reach the desired outcome as quickly as possible, to know who had pilfered the lox from the shipment.

In theory, anyway.

"Why can't we just use truth elixir?" Saff suggested blandly, as though her heart was not skittering like a snare drum inside her chest.

To her surprise, it was Kasan who answered her question.

"Because truth elixir does not spread panic the same way torture does." His voice quivered but did not break. "Because their empire does not run on information, but on fear. They don't just need loose lips, they need willing bodies. My mutilated corpse will keep my workers in line for years to come. Is that about right?"

Levan gave a flat nod, and Saffron knew then that it was a lost cause.

For several long, terrible moments, she stood rooted to the ground. Levan's eyes were fixed upon hers, burning with the same warning he'd leveled at her earlier: *And for the love of hells, if he tells you to kill someone—do it.*

She had to do this. She could not appear weak, uncompliant. She had to make it seem as though the brand had unyielding power over her.

She approached Kasan, her stomach a stone fist as she pressed the pointed metal to Kasan's face. He flinched away from it, a tear beading on his lower lashes, his whole body shaking.

Just get through this, Saffron told herself. *Get through this, and you can tell Aspar all about the loxlure, all about the Rezaran bloodline. Get through this, and you'll be one step closer to tearing the whole rotten empire down.*

Unless the Bloodmoons' unfaltering faith in the brand was justified, and she'd die horribly before she could ever open her mouth.

Kasan jutted his jaw high. Resolute, as though picturing the worker he was protecting.

The letteropener dug into the outer corner of his socket with a grotesque squelch, and he let out a scream so visceral Saffron felt it reverberate in her ribs, in the hollow chambers of her heart.

She kept waiting for her mind to detach itself from reality, the way it always did during moments of horrific violence, kept waiting to float out of her own body and watch the scene from afar, but she remained agonizingly rooted inside herself.

She drove the instrument in farther, working around the socket, trying very hard not to retch at the wet snap of tendons, the pop of fluid, the scream so raw it sawed through her torso. Finally, with a roar of world-ending hurt, the eyeball was severed at the root.

Trembling, she picked it up with her bare hand and passed it to Lyrian. Kasan's wails echoed around the deepest recesses of her psyche.

If she breathed, she would unravel, and so she did not breathe.

The kingpin pulled an empty roulette ball casing from his cloak pocket, placing the ruined eyeball inside and uttering a seething incantation. Kasan's soul drew from his body in a misty whorl of ocean blue—the color his gemstone would've been, if he'd been properly mourned—and seeped into the roulette ball. Lyrian swiftly issued a killing curse. The wailing stopped abruptly, leaving the air ringing with its absence.

Lyrian held the eye up to the light.

"Shoddy execution, Filthcloak. Nowhere close to a clean cut. And all those burst blood vessels." He *tsk*ed, then shook it like a snowglobe. "Levan, Segal, parade the corpse through the docks, then take it to the incinerator. Oh, and Vogolan?"

"Yes?"

In a flash, Lyrian raised his ring-decked palm and slapped Vogolan backhandedly across the cheek. The gold rings around his knuckles peeled Vogolan's skin open like ripe fruit, drawing streaks of poppy-red blood. "I'll handle all lox shipments going forward."

"Yes, sir." Vogolan's voice betrayed no shock or pain, but he had to be stung by it. Non-magical violence was considered highly derogatory. It said, without words, *You are not worth draining my well for.*

And then they were gone, Lyrian's cloak flapping behind him like a flag.

20

...

Esmoldan's Baths

THE REST OF THE DAY WAS SPENT PARADING KASAN'S MUTILATED corpse through the docks, then hauling the body to the incinerator to destroy all evidence of the event, which was a very normal and not at all miserable way to spend an afternoon.

As Saffron and Levan traipsed back to their respective chambers, she pulled her cloak tighter around herself. It reeked of the smoke, ash, and human remains chuffed out by the incinerator, and she could still hear the wet snap of Kasan's tendons, feel the gruesome squelch of the socket beneath her hands. She longed for another bath—to wash away the greasy shame coating her from head to toe—and yet she knew, somehow, that it would not help.

She was dirty now. She would be dirty forever.

They drew level with Levan's chambers, and as his hand went to the doorknob, Saffron remembered what she'd resolved to do.

She swallowed hard, allowing the smallest crack of emotion into her voice. "I don't know how you do this all day every day. The torturing, the killing. You must be frighteningly detached from your emotions."

"I don't do it all day every day," he answered flatly. "And my emotions are essentially scar tissue, at this point."

"I just don't understand what it's all *for*." She wanted to grab him by the lapels and shake the answer loose, but this would require a softer touch. "All the violence, the death, the addiction. The horrors inflicted on innocent people. You have all the ascens you'll ever need. You could retire now and never be poor again."

An impassive smile. "Don't Silvercloaks believe that some people are just born evil?"

"Some do. I don't. There's always a reason. A formative event that warped their worldview. Nobody is born bad. Did *Lost Dragonborn* never teach you that?"

A calculated reference to their common ground. A chisel hovering over the chink in his armor.

"You've read—?"

His eyes lit up almost imperceptibly, and for a split second, it was nearly possible to forget that this was the man who'd amputated and reattached a hand several times before her very eyes. He was just an awkward kid who loved a book.

"I lived and breathed it." Saffron tamped down the bittersweet memories of curling up on Mal's patchwork bedspread, head resting on his barrel-like chest as he read the story to her night after night. After the books had finally broken her spell of silence, he'd wanted to enjoy them with her too.

Levan looked as though he desperately wanted to follow this up with a thousand detailed questions, and then suddenly remembered who and where he was. When he spoke again, he'd lowered his pitch, as though trying to remind himself he was a grown man.

"*Lost Dragonborn* is just a story. You'll have to let go of childish concepts of good and evil if you're going to survive this life."

"'There is no good or evil, only evil and greater evil. And you still have to choose a side.'" As she quoted the villain from the series, Saffron rolled her eyes. "Got it."

There was a stiff silence as Levan's gaze flickered over her face. The intensity of it, the way he studied her like an ancient language when he was usually so averse to eye contact, sent warmth prickling up her neck.

"Do you know what I don't understand?" he asked, and the keen narrowing of his stare set Saffron's teeth on edge. "There was a moment in my father's study, before you were branded, in which you could have killed him. For a moment I thought I'd made an error in bringing you there, that the whole thing had been a ploy to get to him."

Saffron shrugged. "My well was empty, and I was vastly outnumbered. To kill him would've been to kill myself, and I don't want to die."

"But if it were me . . . We took your *family*."

"No need to remind me." Saff tapped two fingers to her brand, the way she'd seen him do. "In any case, I've lost my chance for revenge, haven't I?"

He pushed a dark wave of hair from his face, and something odd darted over his features. Was it . . . suspicion? Realization? As though he were just now figuring out that it *was* unlikely for her to be here, cooperating, bantering, without an ulterior motive?

"Do you still grieve them?" he asked, genuinely curious. "Your parents."

Saffron was surprised her *Lost Dragonborn* chisel had worked so quickly. Then again, she'd always been good at reading people. Finding their soft spots, pressing the advantage.

Still, the question wrought a sinking, plummeting feeling low in her belly. Grief wasn't something she wanted to discuss with the very people who'd caused it, yet this felt like an important moment in which to build rapport with the kingpin's son. A drawbridge lowered, a pot of tea shared.

"It feels like a brick lodged in my chest," she admitted. "I carry it with me everywhere, and I do so willingly, because it's all I have left of them. That brick proves that they existed, and that they made a mark, and that mark lives on in me. As long as I'm alive to mourn them, they are alive, in some way, too. And there's also . . . I don't know. Relief? Relief in knowing that the worst has already happened. That no other loss will ever feel as large or as heavy."

Levan nodded, slow, processing, and Saffron could've sworn she saw something like recognition on his face. Then, rather abruptly, he seemed to remember himself, and became at once very uncomfortable.

He pushed himself off the wall and opened the door to his chambers. "Goodnight."

"Levan, wait." She swallowed hard. "If I want to leave this place. Be alone in the outside world for a bit. Can I?"

Levan shrugged. "You're not a prisoner." He gestured to her heart. "The brand will know if you're planning anything."

HIS WORDS TROUBLED HER for hours.

She'd come into this assignment with the singular belief that the brand could not hurt her beyond the initial burn. That she was immune to magic, all magic, and though terrible things could and would happen undercover, she would still be able to operate outside of the bounds of the seared curse. She would not be bound to them, not *truly.*

Yet now that it was time to betray the Bloodmoons in earnest, doubt crept in.

They were unfalteringly trustful of the brand. And these were intelligent mages—Levan with his powerful transmutation and gift for ancient tongues, Lyrian with his frightening omniscience and impenetrable memory—who would likely need evidence before believing so wholeheartedly in a curse. True, Saffron had never met another mage like her, never found any reading material about magical immunity in the Academy's vast library. Her quirk was rare, possibly unique, and the Bloodmoons likely had not prepared for it.

But the way they had so brazenly shared their secrets within days of her arrival . . .

Was there a kind of magic that could bypass magical immunity?

That nobody, not even her, could escape?

As she left the compound through the warded tunnels, her pulse pounded in her throat like a Bokolani battle drum. The instrument from the Nomarean capital was so powerful that hearing its beat would send a surge of raw adrenaline through any listener's veins, compelling them to don their armor and march to the battlefield. That's how Saff felt now—as though her very heartbeat was driving her to bold and reckless action.

She half expected every footstep to be her last.

At what point would the brand act? Did it sense what she was about to do? Could it read her thoughts? Or was it only the action itself that would trigger her death? Would her heart stop the moment she opened her mouth to tell Aspar what she'd learned?

She spent the entire walk to Esmoldan's Baths coiled with tension—and convinced she was being followed.

It was early evening, and the streets shone with the kind of low golden light that drove artists to their easels. The slouching creamstone buildings were swathed in a honeyed glow, the twisting streets lined with fountains and forest-green shutters, the occasional peak of an obelisk or a purple temple dome towering at the end of each alley. Every time Saffron rounded a corner, she checked over her shoulder, but there was no flash of another scarlet cloak in the crowd, no shrouded figure emerging from the shadows.

There was a certain heightened thrum to the city, an uneven canter, although it was possible Saffron was just projecting. Outside the Merchants' Guild stood a Daejini delegation in long embroidered robes, muttering in a language of choppy waves.

"Oga dracaki ka sutinai. Inu Jakin-ori te-rukai."

"Dika-ki fayu inu wogu?"

"Nik sashin i dracaki-mai."

The only word Saffron picked out was *dracaki.*

Dragon.

Along Dubias Row marched a funeral procession dressed in mourning blue—for the fallen Whitewings, perhaps?—and the sun seemed to hang suspended over the horizon for several moments too long. Then, all at once, darkness fell like a curtain, the sky sprinkled with high, bright stars. Time in Ascenfall often had a slippery, unpredictable quality to it, as though the mages who'd repaired it after the Dreadreign had never quite managed to iron out all the kinks.

Passing Torquil's Tomes, the quadruple-storied bookstore on Sentry Street, Saffron saw an advertisement in the window for the Vallish Arts Festival. The headliners included the illustrator behind a popular pulp about fallowwolves, the cast of a stage adaptation of the beloved *Spectral Things* novel, and the writer of the newest Promise War epic.

There was a contest for the best costume and the best fan art, as well as a trivia quiz held at the Jaded Saint after hours.

With a curious twist of her heart, Saffron saw that Erling Tandall, the wizened author of the *Lost Dragonborn* books, was doing a signing. In another life, maybe Levan would spend his time at festivals like this one, clutching his well-worn book as he queued to meet his idol. Maybe they both would.

Esmoldan's Baths were housed in a grand pillared building, outside which stood creamstone statues of various historical figures in the nude. Parlin the Great had a characteristically large appendage, while Murias the Mighty, who had cast the very first wards around Atherin, appeared to be ogling the resplendent cock with little to no sense of decorum.

Saffron checked into the bathhouse at reception, noting her captain's name was already scrawled on the sign-in parchment. She entered the disrobing chamber, which had an ornate marble fountain ringed by little wooden galleries where bathers could sip at espresso or herbal tea after they'd bathed. There were only a few other mages in the chamber, and at the appearance of Saffron's scarlet cloak, they quickly drained their drinks and departed.

She shrugged off her cloak and other clothing, hanging the raiment on a small golden hook. She was about to see her commanding officer naked, and vice versa, which was almost definitely a recurring nightmare come true, and not something from which she expected to emotionally recover. Yet the thing that disturbed her was not Aspar seeing her pear-shaped breasts or her hair-tangled privates—it was the fact that her brand was out in the open. A hideous dark crust, like dried blood and melted wax. She was glad her cloak had cleared the chamber. At least now nobody beheld her ugly, soul-marring wound.

The main bathhouse had vaulted, mosaicked ceilings of dark blue and gold. Its walls were notched with shelves spilling over with green foliage—fern and ivy, palm and monstera, even some rare star-leafed plants said to be the favorite of Aterrari, the patron saint of earth-wielding. The space was dotted with enchanted goldencandles, which would neither burn down nor set fire to the greenery. The hall held one vast pool and several smaller pods tucked into the naves, and it was in one of these alcoves that Saff found her captain.

Naked, still, the low light flickering over every ridge of her skull.

"Evening," said Saff, setting her wand down on the ledge of the bath and lowering her body into the small pool of hot water adjacent to Aspar. She didn't opt for the same bath for two reasons: one, because she'd have to *lower her naked body right in front of her commanding officer,* and two, because if anyone else entered the bath chambers in pursuit of Saff, she had plausible deniability.

At the sound of Saff's voice, Aspar did not turn to face her, but said only, "You're alive. And branded."

"I'm alive. And branded."

This time, she was prepared for the vicious sting of fragranced bathwater against her brand, and she sucked the air through her teeth instead of screaming. Once she'd grown accustomed to the heat, magic gathered and swirled in her well, as she fought the urge to sigh into the sensation. Aspar too would be experiencing the divine sensation of pleasure turning into magic, but would never let it show on her face. The captain was so repressed that Levan looked like a gushing sycophant by comparison.

"How full is your well?" Aspar asked, as though reading Saffron's mind.

"Fairly. Both pleasure and pain."

"Draw a mattermantic shield around us."

Saffron picked up her wand from the ledge of the pool, then drew a circle in the steam.

"Ans clyptus."

A shimmering film of golden magic formed a ring around their two bodies.

Aspar lifted her own wand and pressed it against the shield, murmuring, "*Et aquies.*"

A silencing charm. The magic poured out of Aspar's wand, following the path of the mattermantic shield and mingling with the raw magic.

"Clever," Saffron admitted. Though a silencing charm wouldn't work on Saffron directly, this created a sort of muffling blanket around them. Other mages would still be able to hear them, but they'd have to strain to pick out individual words.

"Do you have intel?" Aspar asked briskly.

Straight down to business. Saff felt a needle of irritation that the captain had not asked how she was. Their time in the baths might be limited, but after everything Saff had endured . . . it rubbed her the wrong way.

Nonetheless, she *did* have information for Aspar—lots of it—although she decided not to share the mysterious quest for Nalezen Zares, and the fact she'd had to rope in Nissa. Saff hoped that if Nissa got her the information on time, she would escape this situation with her reputation unscathed.

Saffron took a deep breath, letting the steamy air fill her lungs for what might be the last time. Her pulse thrummed, and she hesitated.

Was she about to perish beneath the dark magic of the brand?

A test of her mettle, her resolve. There were not many causes for which she'd risk death, but this was one of them.

"The Bloodmoons are using loxlure to draw punters into their gamehouses," Saff started, and then paused, waiting for a hook of pain through her heart, for a choking sensation around her neck.

None came.

Every muscle in her body sank with relief. The mattermantic shield wavered as she relaxed, and she had to yank herself back into focus.

Then, her voice so low and urgent that the echo was a dim hum, she told Aspar everything she'd learned about the operation so far. When she mentioned Levan's Rezaran blood, the captain practically foamed at the mouth—it was evidence of Emalin's fourth prophecy, and for an Augurest as devout as she, it was akin to finding the Holy Grail. Saffron had to hasten the conversation onward, describing the imported loxlure and its hideous effects on the city.

"That's enough for you to bring them in, isn't it?" she finished, breathless. Sweat beaded at her temple from the heat of the baths and the effort of holding the mattermantic shield. "Supply of a banned substance on a broad scale—organized crime at its finest. If they're using lox in their drinks, it must be held on the premises. You can raid them."

"Not without a search warrant we can't. And we can't procure a warrant without—"

"Evidence."

There was always, always the burden of proof to contend with.

"And your word alone is not evidence. Not in the Grand Arbiter's eyes."

The Grand Arbiter's *corrupt* eyes. For Dematus to act against the Bloodmoons, even once turned, the evidence would have to be so airtight, so compelling, that *not* pursuing warrants or charges would end her career.

Aspar shifted in her pool. "Find out when the next lox shipment is due. We can arrange to be at the docks, since it's a public place. If we can intercept a large delivery, that'll be evidence enough to secure a warrant for the rest."

The captain climbed from the tiled seat built into the baths. Water slid down her pale, sagging body. Stretch marks and loose skin hung around her abdomen, and her tiger-striped breasts sank almost to her navel. Saffron wondered distantly whether she'd had children. She couldn't picture Aspar as a mother, and yet as a female authority figure, she was the closest thing Saffron had to one.

Wrapping a white cotton towel around herself, the captain issued her a look that might, from anyone else, constitute approval.

"Good work, Killoran. But we need more."

21

. . .

The Flight of the Raven

As SAFFRON TOOK THE MEANDERING ROUTE THROUGH MOONLIT Atherin, she thought of her parents, of their ramshackle home in Lunes, and of their favorite board game.

"Today, we're going to play something different," Joran had announced one Plenting eve, dropping an unfamiliar wooden box onto the low table in the living room.

Saffron, sitting cross-legged on the floor, had frowned. "But I like chess best."

Joran had smiled, opening the box and pulling out a large board folded into quarters. He'd spread it on the table to reveal an intricately painted map, with a series of squares charting a path from one side to the other. The trail went through forests and mountains and rivers, volcanic eruptions and flooded marshland, the board textured to reflect the terrain.

"It's called Flight of the Raven. Look how beautiful the artwork is."

Saffron had sighed dramatically, blowing an errant curl out of her face. "I don't want beauty. I want to win."

"Six years old and already so headstrong." Mellora had laughed, her eyes glazed with honeywine as she joined Saffron on the floor. "Never lose that, sweetling."

Joran had pulled three wood-carved ravens from the box, setting them all on the starting square. He'd tapped their feathered backs, and their initials appeared on each: *S*, *J*, and *M*. "The aim of the game is to maneuver your raven across the board so it can deliver a message to the king. Some squares require you to pull a Fate Card, and you might be pushed back due to dragonfire, or stumble on some good fortune and move forward on a tailwind. Whoever gets their raven to the king first wins."

"So there's no skill to it," Saffron had grumbled. "Just the roll of the dice and the words on the Fate Cards."

"No, you have resources you can allocate as you wish." Joran had dug out a series of other wooden miniatures. "Scouts who can fly ahead, a single-use golden feather to skip a square. And you'll have to choose when to descend from the sky to the land to pluck worms from the soil. Flying hungry will cost your raven in the long run."

"Besides," Mellora had chuckled, ruffling Saffron's wild silver-blond curls—a mirror of her own. "It's not always about outthinking your opponent. Sometimes it's about spending time with them."

"Sounds like something a loser would say," Saff muttered.

The game had gone on for an hour, and Saffron was in the lead until the very last moment. On the square before the King's Keep, she pulled a disastrous Fate Card that sent her back to the mountains to retrieve a dropped letter. She'd already wasted her golden feather earlier in the game, so Mellora swooped in and took the victory.

Saffron had thrown herself dramatically onto the couch, arms folded and forehead scrunched. "See? This is why I like chess best. You don't have to worry about bad luck. Whoever plays best wins."

Joran had nodded sagely, as though this was the lesson he'd wanted to impart all along. "And that's why games like Flight of the Raven better represent real life. Sometimes you can do everything right and it still won't work out. Sometimes it won't be fair, and you'll have to adjust accordingly. To plot a new course. The art of adaptation is one that will serve you well, my love."

The memory was warm, wine-scented, cast in golden light. A reminder of all Saffron had lost, and all she would do to even the score.

But it was also resonant, a bell tolling deep in her chest. This experience inside the Bloodmoons was not a neat, simple game of chess, but instead a Flight of the Raven. Every encounter she had was a Fate Card, a roll of the dice, and she just had to stay nimble. Adjust, adapt. Plot a new course.

Which is why, when she returned to the mansion to find Vogolan waiting in her bedroom, she did not panic.

At least, not at first.

Vogolan perched on the edge of her bedspread. The cut from Lyrian's backhanded slap across his cheek had already been magically healed, leaving no trace of its existence. His greasy gray hair was slicked back from his face, his slate-colored eyes sinister and knowing.

"Are we feeling nice and *clean,* Filthcloak?" he drawled.

Saints. Had he been following her, after all?

She'd been so careful, but the kingpin's right-hand mage was a Brewer. Did he have invisibility tincture in his arsenal? It was famously difficult to brew and required an array of rare and unruly ingredients. But with all the ascens in the world . . .

She was struck by the memory of Vogolan morphing from a curtain drape into a man. Had he somehow concealed himself in the baths?

At least Aspar had the foresight to cast a makeshift silencing shield.

"Erm, yes?" Saffron said, forcing herself to remain steady. "Why?"

"Had a nice little *bath,* have we?"

"I think we've established that I have."

A sickly grin spread over Vogolan's face. "By the time I entered the water, you were the only one there. And yet as I disrobed, I could've sworn I saw a familiar figure leaving the gallery. The *silverest* of Silvercloaks."

"Maybe you did," Saff said evenly. "But I was the only one in the baths."

Vogolan rose from the bed and strolled slowly over to where she stood in the doorway. "Are you telling me it was coincidence that Captain Elodora Aspar, the very woman who gave evidence against you at your trial, just so happened to be in the baths at the same time as you?"

"I have a loyalty brand." She swallowed hard, heart thudding, and forced herself to meet his hateful gaze. "If I'd done anything to betray the Bloodmoons, I'd quite literally be dead in the water."

A scoff, raspy and rough. "You know, Filthcloak, I'm not a religious man. I believe most things to which the pious ascribe divine meaning are simply random chance. Coincidence. Yet this *coincidence* is a stretch too far, even for me."

Saffron's mind rerouted, remapped, seeking the least treacherous patch of terrain.

"Fine, you caught me. I despise that woman for what she did to me." She spoke coolly, calmly, as the kingpin and his son did when discussing cold-blooded murder. "I went to kill her, if you must know. After slitting Neatras's throat, I realized it isn't that hard. But when I got there, Aspar had already left. Happy?"

A flimsy, unconvincing story. Aspar's death would have been the easiest murder to solve of all time—clear motive, a bathhouse entry parchment with both their names on it. But Saffron was thinking on her feet, and sometimes feet were clumsy.

"Delighted." Vogolan's breath reeked of stale tobacco tea. "Do you know what else makes me delighted?"

Saffron said nothing, only glared.

"Gelato."

The singular word, coupled with the self-satisfied sneer on his face, was enough to make her blood run cold.

He grinned grotesquely. "You see, our kingpin does so love banana cream pie gelato. And so I thought to myself, why don't I pay a visit to Papa Marriosan myself? Kill two ravens with one rock?"

No.

"Papa Marriosan works out of the Arollan Mile shop on Oparling afternoons, serving the customers himself. Such a humble, hardworking man, is he not? And so I swung by, for some banana cream pie."

Saffron couldn't move, couldn't breathe.

"Although . . . perhaps I should start at the beginning." Vogolan twiddled the edge of his gray moustache. "Earlier this morning, I found Auria Marriosan. Lovely little thing, isn't she? Such interesting scars. So innocent-looking, but such a bad temper, my my."

"What did you do?" Saffron asked coarsely, dread pooling in her gut.

"I only asked her how the search for Nalezen Zares was going. Just to coax her along, offer some gentle encouragement. To remind her of the stakes, as such. And the curious thing was, she had never heard the name before in her life. Not even under the influence of truth elixir."

Saints.

Saffron hadn't ever told Auria the name.

And now . . .

Vogolan's jaw twitched. "Which led me to think one of two things: either she was a remarkable liar . . . or *you* are. Perhaps you never asked for her help at all. Perhaps you invoked her name to buy yourself time—to weasel your way out of this mess before you ever had to get her involved."

Saffron shook her head fiercely. "No, that's not it. I couldn't find Auria that first night, so I asked a different contact. So that I'd get the information faster."

One tiny detail—the omission of a name—was unravelling everything.

Reroute, recalibrate, readapt.

Vogolan sighed emphatically. "I do find myself hoping that isn't true. Because that would make what I did to Papa Marriosan this afternoon rather unfortunate, indeed."

He searched every inch of her face, savoring her reaction. His expression was almost . . . *aroused.* He wanted to see her squirm, and she would not give him that gratification. Instead, she met his slimy satisfaction with squared shoulders and a hateful stare.

"I'm actually rather proud of it," he said silkily. "You do quickly run out of different ways to kill people, in this line of business, and when you do the same thing over and over again, it does grow tiresome. But gelato cones make fantastic weapons, when jammed so far into an eye socket that the brain weeps out the ears."

Somewhere deep in her belly, a wounded animal let out a roar.

Sweet Papa Marriosan, with his jovial laugh and his potbelly and his famous, glorious ice cream.

Dead because of her. Because of a single misstep.

Auria would never recover. Would she know that it had been Saff's fault? Would she connect those damning dots? She was one of the best detectives Atherin had ever seen. Of course she would see the bigger picture—and Saffron's role in it.

"Oh, and Filthcloak?" Vogolan growled, raising his wand. "Don't approach your former captain again without our consent. That is an order, and to refute that order would be a death sentence, as far as your brand is concerned." He lowered the tip to her forearm, a hungry, almost feral expression on his greasy face. "*Sen efractan.*"

The bones should have snapped in an instant.

Should have, had Saffron not been immune.

Reeling, she couldn't cast an illusion fast enough.

When nothing happened, a white bolt of fear snapped through Saffron, hot and fast.

Vogolan peered down at his wand, frowned, then repeated, "*Sen efractan.*"

Again, nothing happened.

"Invisible shield," she said calmly. "I cast it before I ever set foot in this room. But nice try."

Yet slowly, terribly, the pieces arranged themselves in Vogolan's mind. He looked up at her, a look of cold accusation in his pallid eyes, the truth of it all playing out over his sallow face.

"You're immune to magic," he drawled, pupils flashing with a satisfied glint. "That's why you willingly drank the truth elixir. That's why you so willingly offered yourself to the brand. You're still a Silver—"

"*Sen ammorten,*" Saffron said, and the killing spell landed true.

22

...

The King's Prophet

STARING AT VOGOLAN'S LIFELESS CORPSE—A CRUMPLE OF scarlet silk, grayish skin, and oily hair—Saffron waited for the guilt to crash through her, waited to feel even the slightest ebb of remorse, but it never came.

The world was a better place without Porrol Vogolan.

She was glad she had not hesitated.

And yet . . . what did it mean, that she had not even blinked? That the decision had been made between one heartbeat and the next? Had it been borne from necessity, to keep her fatal secret, or from anger—a desire to avenge Auria's grandfather?

Which motivation would be worse?

No matter. The simple fact was that it was done, and she felt nothing but relief.

And now she had a body to dispose of.

Not for the first time in recent days, she wished the *portari* charm hadn't been stripped out of every wand in the land. How simple it would be to transport them both out of the city, to head down to the coast and dump Vogolan over the cliffs of Sarosan into the Sleepless Sea. Or even just down to the incinerator, so that she could turn his ashes into a gemstone and hand it to the first lox-addicted mage she came across. Though she supposed that was precisely *why* the transportation spell had been outlawed to begin with. Corpses should not be so easy to hide.

Nor could she simply make the corpse disappear. One of the cardinal rules of magic was that something could not be turned to nothing. There was whatever Levan had done to usher Tenea's spirit *elsewhere,* but Saffron didn't understand that magic, let alone how to wield it.

She mentally rifled through her old stack of case files, trying to recall any particularly ingenious methods of corpse disposal, but none came to her. There was one serial killer who'd used waneweed to shrink his victims down to palm-size, but he did that *before* ending their lives. And besides, leaving the mansion to seek out waneweed would require leaving a dead body in her bedroom for anyone—namely Levan—to stumble upon.

Saffron pressed her eyes closed and did what she always did when she needed to channel brilliance: asked herself what Auria would do. Auria, with her encyclopedic knowledge of magic, with her love for rare spellwork and obscure charms whose uses had long become obsolete.

Auria.

Slowly, an idea came to her—drip by drip, then all at once.

She opened her eyes and raised her wand, aiming it at Vogolan's gut. "*Sen effigias.*"

She wasn't wholly sure whether the curse would work on a cadaver, but sure enough, Vogolan turned from flesh and blood to pure stone.

"*Et ascevolo,*" she incanted, lifting her wand up, guiding Vogolan's stone form to the high ceiling.

And then she let it drop.

He smashed into a few dozen pieces. Not quite small enough for her purposes, but enough to convince her that this would work. She just had to hope nobody in the servants' quarters below would hear the thumps and come running.

She repeated the levitation and the drop several more times, until Vogolan was rubble so fine that no human features could be identified. The chunks were larger than gravel, but not by much. Sweeping them into her old black cloak, Saffron stuffed the bundle into the trunk at the foot of her bed. Every time she ventured into the city, she'd take a few handfuls with her, scattering Vogolan all over Atherin.

Perhaps she'd frequent her old favorite gamehouse while she was at it. The adrenaline, the sense of victory, had flooded her veins, and suddenly all she could think about was the heady release of gambling. Of *winning*. Of how it felt to be so thoroughly outplaying your opponents that nothing short of tragedy could strike you down now.

As she lowered the lid of the trunk, a slow smile spread over her face.

THE NEXT MORNING, she approached her assignment with renewed vigor.

Her focus had narrowed, intensified, following Aspar's order. Uncovering details of the next lox shipment would be no mean feat, but when had anything ever been easy for Saffron? She was used to taking the undulating path through the mountains while everyone else meandered along the riverfront. She was used to adversity, to working twice as hard for twice as long. Thanks to her father, she was used to unfavorable rolls of the dice.

The first problem she had to address upon waking was that her magical well had been thoroughly depleted. The killing curse was infamous for its almighty drain, and all the subsequent spellwork she'd done to decimate the corpse had left her dry. Having decided to head into the city—to replenish her power with food and music and art and possibly a visit to a pleasurehouse—she shoved a few palmfuls of Vogolan rubble into her cloak pockets, stuffed her feet into her boots, and left her bedroom.

Fate had other ideas, however.

She passed Levan's chambers on the way down to the main atrium, and when she drew level with his door, she heard male murmurings behind it. He had company. Her detective's instincts prickled.

"*Ans vocamplican,*" she muttered—one of the first spells they'd perfected at the Academy.

Two male voices talked in muffled, almost sleepy tones.

"—I see a bloody uprising." The unfamiliar voice was as smooth as caramel. The words were a caress, despite their violent undertones. "The head of King Quintan on the Palace steps. Just as the pulps depicted."

"A Bloodmoon boot at his throat?" asked Levan.

"I don't know, darling. The prophecies are offered to me as gifts. I cannot maneuver them to my will."

"When is it happening? This bloody uprising?" There was a latent hunger in Levan's tone. "Can you discern a season?"

"Darkest winter, at a guess."

"How accurate a guess?"

A buttery laugh. "Oh, not very. I'm rather addled with honeywine. And there's no way of knowing what year."

"Fine."

Then came the distinct sound of a lingering kiss, followed by a subtle male groan.

"I *can't,* you magnificent being," murmured the stranger. "The king is expecting me any moment. Help me button up my doublet, won't you? My hands don't seem to be cooperating."

"You drink too much. It's not even noon."

"I don't think we should go down that path, darling. I still remember finding you in a pool of your own piss after a lox overd—"

"You're right. Let's not go down that path."

Something curdled in Saffron's stomach.

Levan had overdosed on lox?

Moreover, he was having an affair with a man she had discerned to be the King's Prophet?

She didn't know which was more shocking.

A few moments later, booted footsteps strode toward the door. Saffron dropped her *vocamplican* charm mere seconds before it swung open, raising her fist as though she had been about to knock.

The man on the other side of the threshold was exceedingly handsome. He was short and slight, with pale, freckled skin and dark red hair styled in perfect waves. Sure enough, he wore the recognizable navy doublet of House Arollan.

The King's Prophet.

He did not seem at all surprised or perturbed by Saffron's presence.

Had he known she would be there?

If so, what else did he know?

"You must be the fabled Silver." He offered her a hand covered in jeweled rings, and she shook it. "Harrow Claver. Truly *ensorcelled* to meet you."

"Saffron," she replied. "Claver is a Bellandrian name, is it not?" Saffron's father also hailed from Bellandry—from the northwestern town of Charlet, famous for pinewood liquors and romantic poets.

"Oh, yes." A playful grin spread across his handsome face. "I'm a traitor to my home country. And my new one. All crowns, in fact. Thrones, conceptually. I have issues with authority."

Levan appeared behind Harrow. His belt was undone, and he'd thrown on his black tunic so hastily that one side was raised above his hip, revealing a strip of pale, toned stomach—the very place she would eventually fire a killing spell. Saffron chastised herself for the flutter of *something* it sent through her traitorous body.

"So you're together?" she asked.

"*Hells,* no." Harrow clasped a hand to his chest as though mortally wounded by the suggestion. "I'll never be tied to one *vock*. And besides, darling Levan here will never take another life partner. Not after what happened to—"

"Goodbye, Harrow." Levan shoved Harrow over the threshold, and the prophet almost collided with Saffron.

"Oh, I see. I've served my purpose and now I'm dismissed?" Harrow *tsk*ed playfully. "Careful, darling. You wouldn't want me to *withhold* on you, would you?"

And with that he strode down the corridor, humming a jaunty little tune before disappearing down the grand staircase that swept into the atrium.

"Fucking the King's Prophet for information, are you?" Saffron smirked.

"The fucking is for pleasure. The information he gives freely."

Levan finished buckling his belt, and Saffron had to swallow quite hard to banish the grooves of his hips from her mind. *Saints,* she needed to get to a pleasurehouse, or she was in real danger of mounting any particularly phallic lampposts she saw streetside. Magic—and the lack thereof—made all her various *appetites* swell and pulse.

"Why are you here?" Levan asked, neither irritated nor pleased at her presence.

At the question, Saff opened her mouth in the hope that a plausible excuse would fall out, but she never got the chance. From somewhere inside the room came Lyrian's tinny voice through a wandtip.

"Et vocos, Levan Celadon."

Levan disappeared back inside to grab his wand—Saffron dimly realized that he didn't deem it necessary to be armed around her—then reappeared moments later. There was that scent again: leather and warm skin, lemon zest and peppermint leaves, plus the unmistakable underpinning of sex.

"Yes?" he spoke into the black elm tip, a single rough syllable.

"Vogolan's missing." Lyrian's tone was strained, furious, but also . . . afraid? "I think he's dead."

Saff ordered her face into a plain expression.

"And why do you think that?"

"I had a tracing charm on him and it dropped last night. Now I can't find him."

Saffron's mind reeled. How accurate was the tracing charm? Would Lyrian know his right-hand man had died in her chambers? Surely not, or he'd already have hunted her down.

A muscle worked in Levan's jaw. "Maybe he doesn't want to be found."

"It was you, wasn't it?" A searing snarl of an accusation. "You killed him. You've always hated him, ever since—"

"Let's talk about this face-to-face." Levan pinched the bridge of his nose. "Without an audience. *Et cludan.*"

The connection between their wands dropped.

"Is your father always this paranoid?" Saffron asked, grateful for her training, for how easy it felt to maintain aloofness. She'd always been the best at holding a polderdash face—Tiernan wore every emotion in the notches between his brows, while Auria's voice grew shrill under pressure, and Nissa was incapable of tamping down her anger.

Levan shrugged. "He's paranoid for a reason. A lot of people want to hurt him. And since Porrol Vogolan is his fiercest ally and closest confidant, wiping him off the map would be a brutal blow."

Saffron nodded sagely, disguising the flip in her stomach. "Thanks for the tip."

"It's not funny."

"Should I send a flower arrangement afterward?"

"It's not fun—"

"He strikes me as a magnolia man."

Levan sighed gruffly. "You're not as afraid of him as you should be."

"Would you like me to quake a little?" Saffron pointed at her boots. "*Ans quassan.*"

Her feet lurched and shuddered, giving her the appearance of riding on horseback, jostling chaotically in the saddle. Against all odds, Levan's lips quirked upward. Almost imperceptible, and immediately suppressed, but they quirked nonetheless.

Then the black elm wand in his hand crackled and hissed. "*Now,* Levan."

With a long-suffering sigh, Levan swept past Saffron without a backward glance.

Saffron looked around for a moment, stunned that in his distraction, Levan had left the door to his room wide open.

So much for *I control* everything.

This was his first lapse in said control—wrought by one of her father's ridiculous jokes, no less. Perhaps that had been the real reason for Joran Killoran's unrelenting jocularity: he was secretly running extremely dangerous undercover missions, frequently using humor and whimsy to slip between the cracks of suspicion. Or, alternatively and far more probably, he was just a clown.

In any case, Saffron's instincts ushered her inside the open doorway.

Levan's bedroom was bigger and brighter than Saffron's, and exponentially neater. Even the bedspreads on his four-poster bed—mounted on a raised dais at the back of the room—had been straightened with military precision. Is that what he'd been doing while Harrow introduced himself to Saff? Making his bed? Saff had to stifle a laugh.

Ever-burning goldencandles were studded around the walls, and the sill of the arched window was lined with plants she recognized from her mother's medicinal greenhouse—each of them neatly labeled with genus and watering instructions. The glass windowpanes were stained sapphire and emerald, depicting a grand dragon breathing yellow-gold fire.

There were books *everywhere,* not only covering rows upon rows of shelving built into the alcoves on either side of his bed, but also in carefully arranged stacks on the floor, ordered seemingly by genre and then subject and then author surname. A veritable library.

Saffron debated where to begin. Even if there was some kind of lox ledger to be found here, it would be like searching for a specific coin in a vault full of ascens.

Her eyes found a small antique writing desk in the corner of the room. It was a handsome thing, with spindled legs, several inkwells, and a glossed mahogany finish. A hexagonal gold teapot sat on the surface, the strings and tabs of three teabags dangling through the lid. He liked his tea *strong.*

Down one side of the desk there was a column of small drawers. Quickly and silently, Saffron crossed to the desk and opened the top drawer. It was full of blank parchment scrolls, lavishly feathered quills, and several pots of ink in various jewel tones. The next drawer down was segmented with little wooden compartments, each holding dozens of different sachets of tea. Herbal, fruit, and a burlap pouch of loose leaf that smelled strongly of clove and star anise. They were also arranged in alphabetical order, which was a very normal and not at all obsessive way to store tea.

The third drawer was locked fast.

The fourth drawer contained a single sleek notebook, whose pages would not open no matter how hard she pried.

A lox ledger? Something else that could be evidence?

Chewing her lip, Saffron wondered whether the password she'd heard the Bloodmoons utter countless times might charm the volume open.

"*Fair featherroot,*" she muttered, but nothing happened. Sighing, she tapped her wand on its plain black cover. "*Et exuan.*"

Again, nothing happened. *Exuan* was a spell used to strip an object of its enchantments, but Saffron had never quite cast it successfully. It was a simple uttering but required a *lot* of raw power—more than the sum total of the other enchantments layered on the object. And Saffron was already depleted from casting the killing spell—and breaking her victim into a thousand pieces. After several failed attempts, she shoved the ledger back into its drawer and left Levan's room before he found her snooping.

As she made her way into the city, scattering handfuls of Vogolan as she went, she thought of the prophecy Harrow had shared: a bloody uprising. And Levan's subsequent question: *A Bloodmoon boot at his throat?*

Was there something important to be gleaned from this conversation?

Something to do with the *why* of it all?

As she'd told Levan, she didn't believe that some people were just born violent, born greedy, born bloodthirsty. That some people wanted power for power's sake, wealth for wealth's sake. Though she did understand that some people had so sorely missed these things as a child, and spent the rest of their lives trying to rebalance the scales.

But Aspar believed there was a deeper reason beneath the Bloodmoons' drive for power.

The head of King Quintan on the Palace steps. Just as the pulps depicted.

Did the Bloodmoons have their sights set on the crown?

23

...

Lyrian's Conclave

IT WAS TWO MORE DAYS BEFORE VOGOLAN'S DEATH CAME BACK to bite her.

Saffron spent that time attempting to learn when and where the next lox shipment was going to happen. She bought an expensive invisibility tincture from Atherin's finest apothecary—after visiting the bank to draw from her amassed gambling wealth, since the Bloodmoons did not exactly pay a salary—and roamed the mansion in the vague hope of overhearing something compelling.

Nothing.

When Segal summoned Levan to Lyrian's office to discuss the influx of recent debtors in the gamehouse, Saffron hung at his heel and raked her gaze over the kingpin's desk, aiming to identify a loose piece of parchment that might betray a time or date for the next shipment.

Nothing.

She tried to coax the information out of Levan on a trip to the Cherrymarket for potion supplies—Aspar had been there under the guise of her familiar, Bones the cat—but Levan had remained vague, and Saff didn't want to push too hard in case he grew suspicious of her intentions. Or the pissant of a feline on their tail.

Still nothing.

Speaking of Levan, she spent many hours memorizing the pattern of his movements, building a picture of his role in the Bloodmoons so that she might find the natural holes in it.

Each of his days followed the same blueprint. His arrival at her chambers with breakfast and hot chocolate was as regular and reliable as clockwork—perhaps more so, in a world where time was not always as steadfast as it ought to be. Outside of their interactions, he oversaw several operations, keeping tabs on the gamehouses and monitoring the docks. He also disappeared for vast swaths of the day, reappearing with a sheen of sweat on his forehead and a raggedness to his breathing, and though Saffron was none the wiser as to what he got up to during these junctures, there was a fair chance the King's Prophet was involved.

In his absence, Saffron took regular solitary trips into the city, heading down to the riverfront and scattering Vogolan's remains into the water piece by piece until nothing incriminating remained in her chambers.

Soon, the time to meet Nissa at the Jaded Saint was upon them.

However, Saff and Levan didn't even make it to the warded tunnels before their wand tips glowed green simultaneously. Levan paled slightly, before explaining to Saff that this was his father's means of widespread communication to the Bloodmoons in his employ. It loosely meant "Proceed to my office at haste, lest I decapitate you for your tardiness." Though she didn't say as much, Saffron felt uneasy that the kingpin was able to commandeer her wand in such a manner. If he could make it glow green, what else could he do?

"Do you know what this summons is about?" Saffron asked Levan, as they marched back up the sweeping ascenite staircase.

Though deep down, she already knew.

"Vogolan, I'd imagine. Still no sign of him."

Saffron reluctantly followed, afraid to keep Nissa waiting. What if, when Saffron didn't show up on time, her former lover came looking, terrified that something horrible had befallen her? The idea of Nissa walking willingly into Celadon Gamehouse was a disquieting one.

Not only was Nissa hotheaded and impulsive, but she also had an addictive personality. She'd become hooked on achullah from her very first smoke, so Saints knew how deep loxlure could sink its claws.

All thoughts of Nissa vanished, however, as they entered Lyrian's fire-lit office.

The space was rammed full of scarlet cloaks, with barely enough room for her and Levan to stand. Shoving past Bloodmoons of all heights and ages, they pressed against the rear black wall where Saffron had been branded. Rasso let out a yelp as an ungainly mage stepped on his paw with a careless foot, and Levan scooped the fallowwolf up into his arms, as though Rasso weighed nothing. Rasso licked his cheek gratefully, and despite the tension of the situation, Levan smiled.

It was the same kind of boyish smile as when she'd asked him about *Lost Dragonborn:* a pure, fleeting joy before he remembered who and where he was.

Almost without forethought, Saff reached out a hand and stroked Rasso's ridged head. The fur was soft and supple, and rather than growling in warning, the fearsome animal twisted its head back and licked her palm. She felt as though a formidable deity had blessed her, and partially regretted turning Vogolan's heart to stone, since the fallowwolf might have liked to eat it.

As Saff scratched a spot behind Rasso's ears, Levan looked over at her, surprise darting across his face. Was he shocked that she'd willingly pet an animal who had fairly recently ripped the throat out of a Whitewing? Or was he stunned that a beast as ferocious as Rasso appeared to have warmed to her so fast?

Either way, Rasso's affection was a welcome distraction from what might be about to happen. She reminded herself that there was no way the kingpin knew she'd killed Vogolan, otherwise she'd already be dead. She just had to don her mask of detachment and get through this conclave without drawing undue attention.

Another smattering of Bloodmoons filtered into the room, including a haggard, wart-nosed woman shaped like a barrel. The double doors slammed shut so hard that the whole room rattled.

At once, the low mutterings fell into taut, hesitant silence.

Behind his desk, Lyrian spoke coldly, quietly, clearly. "I believe that one of my dearest and longest-standing servants has been murdered."

"Murdered?" croaked the ancient crone with the wart-nose.

"The tracing charm upon him dropped two nights ago. He was somewhere in the mansion, and then suddenly he was not. One of you murdered him. I intend to find out who."

"Or he used the *portari* gate," suggested a tall, elegant mage with a twirly moustache and a monocle. His dark skin had the distinctive purplish undertone of the Nomareans. He leaned his weight on a gilded cane, a black marble macaw perched atop the handle. "Often tracing charms drop off during transportation."

The Bloodmoons had a working *portari* gate?

Saffron mentally filed this revelation away. She was almost positive Aspar didn't know about it.

Lyrian shook his head fiercely. "No. I have a trusted set of eyes"—his gaze went to the bowl of roulette balls on his desk—"on the gate at all times. Vogolan never left this building. He must be dead. *Killed*."

"You think one of us could do this?" Segal all but grunted. He looked pale, with something resembling grief on his blotchy face. "Despite the brands?"

"It took place inside the wards, thus only a Bloodmoon could have done it. As for how it could have escaped the brand's wrath . . . well. The full picture will emerge in due course. You will each come to me in turn to drink truth elixir. There's enough left in Vogolan's stash to go around."

His tone was threaded with emotion, but rather than humanizing him, it only made him seem more dangerous, more prone to sudden and devastating action. He gestured to the row of pale tincture vials lined up on his desk, and then his gaze found Saffron. Her guts were clenched by an invisible fist.

"Perhaps our resident rat would like to go first," Lyrian said, the calm words undercut by a low, dark hatred. He thought it was her, but he didn't *know*. And he was not about to find out.

As Saffron stepped toward the desk, she could've sworn Levan's stance tensed, as though bracing for impact. Did he believe she was guilty? Or did he still trust wholeheartedly in the brand?

Feeling the sear of a hundred eyes burning into her back, Saffron tried not to hear the sharp intake of collective breath as she lifted the vial to her lips. She gave Lyrian a confident, unworried look and then drank.

The elixir tasted sickly sweet and vaguely acrid, like burnt sugar.

"Did you murder Porrol Vogolan?" Lyrian asked, eyes gleaming with the need for revenge. His irises were the color of desert sand—his mother had been Eqoran, Saff remembered from his case file.

"I did not," said Saffron evenly, wondering why she had ever resented her magical immunity. She was beginning to see *why* her father had always insisted it was such a gift.

There was a scattered muttering around the room.

Lyrian looked entirely wrong-footed. "I see. And do you know anything about the murder of Porrol Vogolan?"

"I do not."

The kingpin stared at her, confused and perhaps, she thought, a little afraid. Because if the new recruit had not betrayed him, it meant that someone far closer had. Not a pleasant proposition, for someone who considered themselves all-seeing, all-knowing.

Satisfaction glittered between Saffron's ribs. She was contributing to the rocking of Lyrian Celadon's worldview, cracking the once solid ground beneath his feet. And she was enjoying it.

"Are you certain?" he asked, and it was such an innocuous question, to the outside ear, but Saffron relished in his newfound uncertainty. He was doubting the elixir. He was doubting everything.

She tilted her chin high and nodded. "I'm certain."

A long, pregnant pause, in which she met his gaze without blinking.

Then, finally, "Very well. Segal."

Saffron stepped back from the desk as Segal stepped obligingly forward, stuffing his wand into his cloak pocket and picking up a vial of truth elixir. He swallowed it in one.

Next to Saffron, Levan's posture eased, the relief palpable in the negative space between them. It seemed he had not wanted Saffron to have been responsible for Vogolan's murder—likely because he didn't want to lose such a fruitful resource. She was his best chance of finding Zares, after all. Whatever that meant to him.

Lyrian leaned over his desk toward Segal, resting on his knuckles like an ape. "Did you murder Porrol Vogolan?"

"I did not," said Segal clearly.

"Do you know anything about the murder of Porrol Vogolan?"

The fire crackled and spat. "I do not."

A nod from the kingpin. "Zirlit, step forward."

The tall Nomarean mage with the monocle and macaw cane stepped forward.

One by one, every Bloodmoon in the room stepped forward and drank the truth elixir until the only person left was Levan. There was a tense beat, as everyone waited to see whether the kingpin would question his own son.

Lyrian did not hesitate. "Levan, step forward."

Levan lowered Rasso to the floor as he crossed to the desk, then took the last remaining vial and drank.

"Did you murder Porrol Vogolan?"

He seemed afraid of the answer.

You've always hated him, he'd said when he first confided in Levan. Why? What was the history there?

"I did not," said Levan in a low voice.

"Do you know anything about the murder of Porrol Vogolan?"

The room held its breath.

"I do not."

A tendon flexed in the kingpin's jaw. "Very well." The three syllables crunched out like grinding bone. "You're all dismissed. But rest assured, this is not the last you will hear of Porrol Vogolan's death. Segal, fetch me the servants. It's time we interrogated them." He hooked a finger toward Saffron. "Filthcloak. A word."

All the other Bloodmoons filtered out until only Saffron, Levan, and Lyrian remained in the office. The kingpin kept looking over his shoulder, as though to find Vogolan, before he remembered what had happened and a brief, bright pain flashed across his face.

Good, thought Saff bitterly. *This is the same pain you so casually inflict on countless families. I hope it swallows you whole. I hope you never recover. I hope you're sad until your dying breath.*

"Levan," said the kingpin, waving a hand. His rings caught the firelight. "You may go."

"What she hears, I hear," Levan replied gruffly.

"Fine." Lyrian sank into his wing-backed chair, keen eyes still trained on Saffron. "There are rumors that the Silvercloaks have developed a charm capable of tracing a spell's origin back to the wand that cast it. You have an informant in the Order, do you not?"

"I do." Saff kept her answer intentionally vague. "But that charm is under lock and key—or at least, it was when I left. Forensics say it's too unreliable to be implemented yet, and my informant doesn't have the clearance to access it."

"Get it for me," he said coolly, as though he hadn't heard her.

Saff shook her head. She couldn't ask Nissa to do that. Slipping her information was one thing. Stealing a charm was quite another.

"I don't think she'll be able to breach—"

"Not my concern. Get me the charm." A hard, leering smile. "You know what we do to sources who cease to be useful."

"Yes, sir," she said, but she couldn't ask Nissa to do this.

She couldn't *not* ask Nissa to do this.

Panic grabbed her by the ribs and rattled them like the bars of a cage. The collar was ever tightening around her neck. It was one thing to endanger her own life, but to so brazenly risk someone who meant so much to her . . .

As she and Levan exited the office, she bridled her breathing as best she could, but he still picked up on her disquiet.

"Are you alright?" he asked.

"Wonderful," she muttered, only just resisting the urge to kick at the nearest wall. "I love living with the knowledge that one wrong turn down the wrong alley on the wrong night has put everyone I've ever loved in jeopardy. I love knowing that one wrong move could mean execution, for me or for them. I love torturing and killing, I love bending my knee to your tyrant father." She uttered all of this without pausing for breathing, her lungs tight and throbbing. "And I love knowing that there's no way out."

Of course, this last part wasn't true—she had a very clear way out.

But as for the rest . . . the dread clawing up her throat was real, the phantom collar around her neck suffocating, unyielding, an almost physical force.

The threads tying her to the people she loved felt like garrotes.

I'm sorry, Nissa. I'm so sorry.

Levan said nothing, but as they entered the warded tunnels, he laid a gentle palm on her shoulder. The touch sent a curious frisson through her, both warm and shimmeringly cold, and he tugged slightly, willing her to stop marching for a second. She did, but she couldn't meet his eye, couldn't let him see the tears she was only just holding back.

"I'm sorry it came to this," he said. "You were just in the wrong place at the wrong time."

Saffron scoffed. "Why do you care?"

A muscle feathered in his jaw. "Because I know what it's like to feel like every choice you make is the wrong one. To understand that the world can come crumbling down with a single wrong move. My apology might not change anything, true. But you're not alone, Silver. And if you're anything like me, which I think you are, then that means something."

Saff's breath caught in her throat, surprised by his outpouring.

It seemed so . . . *genuine.* More genuine than anything he'd ever said to her before. The careful mask he always wore had dropped, and his expression was a little pained, as though embarrassed by his own unabashed honesty. His piercing blue eyes had crinkled at the corners, and there was a kind of urgency to his gaze, so at odds with his usual aloofness. Soft lanternlight danced over his face, and in that moment, he looked so *real.* There was a beauty to him that even Saffron, with all her worldly hatred for the Bloodmoons, could not deny. Could not tear her gaze away from.

But why was he so openly—

Of course.

He was under the influence of truth elixir. It'd be in his system for the next six hours.

The kingpin had just handed her one hell of an advantage.

24

...

The Enchanted Necklace

THE NIGHT WAS BITTEN WITH A CRISPER CHILL THAN THE previous week. The inky sky was flecked with stars and the pleasure-houses were in full swing, the streets ringing with moans and music, clinking glasses and pops of laughter against a backdrop of jewel-toned awnings and gilded obelisks. Woodsmoke hung on the air, and Saffron tried not to think of the incinerator, of the spark and *whoosh* Kasan's body made as it caught.

Her mind focused instead on all the things she might ask Levan while he could not help but tell her the truth. She couldn't ask outright about the lox shipment schedule—it would be far too suspicious—but she *could* chip away with seemingly innocuous conversation.

"Why do we go everywhere on foot?" Saffron asked, easing into matters. "Since there's a *portari* gate at our disposal."

They passed an Augurest temple, where evening worship was in full swing. A low litany of chanting floated up through the domed purple ceiling, and Levan glanced at the eye-shaped building with thinly veiled loathing. He had Timeweaver blood, after all, and the Augurests were praying for his eradication.

"My father's insistence. He doesn't trust that the gates aren't being watched by the Silvercloaks. We only use it when we absolutely have to."

Saffron didn't think the Silvercloaks *were* watching. Aspar surely would've briefed her on the unregulated gate, if so, classification level be damned.

"Your father also said you hated Vogolan," she said carefully, picturing the enormous case file she would eventually drop onto Aspar's desk with a satisfied thud. "Why?"

Levan stared straight ahead. The towering marble and creamstone of Arollan Palace stood at the end of the Mile, lit from below and glowing pale in the moonlight. Crenels stood out like teeth against the night. A row of flags sat upright in the breeze: one rich purple for Vallin, one a gold chalice and laurel wreath against a burgundy backdrop for the patron saints, and one navy blue with a crown of silver stars for House Arollan.

At last, Levan replied, "He killed someone very important to me."

Saffron's heart skipped. "Your mother?"

Nobody outside the Bloodmoons knew how Lorissa Celadon had died.

"No." The syllable was a hammer striking an anvil. A warning edge to it, as if to say *If you keep pushing this, you won't survive long enough to hear the truth.*

She tried a gentler tack. "To me, Vogolan seems evil just for evil's sake." She was careful to use the present tense—she shouldn't know for certain that he was dead.

"Yes," he agreed, a thin line of steel in the word.

The silence between them hovered on a blade edge. Saff knew she had to press this advantage—how often would she see Levan even the slightest bit vulnerable?—but it felt treacherous. She couldn't ask anything that would make her seem like a detective.

Yet they only had a few minutes until they reached the Jaded Saint, and by the time Saff reemerged from her meeting with Nissa, the elixir would be nowhere near as potent. His body would've already started to flush it out.

Oh, what the hells.

"Why are the Bloodmoons doing all of this?" The words were jagged, rushed. "What's the end goal for all this torture and killing and amassing of wealth?"

The strangest thing happened, then. Levan made a sort of grunting noise, as though trying to strangle the words before they could make it out of his throat. His fists clenched at his sides, and a muscle twitched in his squared jaw.

He was fighting the truth elixir.

And he was *winning*.

Which had to mean there was something deeper to the Bloodmoons' motivations. It was not just simple power, or he'd say as much. Had her earlier hunch been right? Did they have their eyes on the weakened Arollan throne?

Yet Saffron could barely think about that right now, because Levan was *fighting the truth elixir and winning.*

Just how powerful was this mage?

Fear curdled in her belly at the thought.

"I think it's time," Levan spat out, through gritted teeth, "that you stop asking questions."

Saffron dug a thumbnail into her palm, inwardly chastising herself. She had gone straight in with an axe when a subtler hand would've yielded more fruit. Then again, if Levan was powerful enough to choke out the truth elixir . . . would she have gleaned anything worthwhile? She should've prioritized rapport-building, should've tried to establish another level of closeness between them, should've responded more warmly to what he'd said back in the warded tunnels: *You're not alone, Silver. And if you're anything like me, which I think you are, then that means something.*

Was she losing her touch, her killer instincts, her nose for a good gamble versus a bad one? Or did the kingpin's son rattle her, somehow?

They walked in jagged silence until they passed a section of creamstone wall folded in on itself like a pocket, creating not a pleasure nook but a resting spot for a weary passerby. On the bench—tiled with blue and green and glittering star white—lay a mage in clear distress. She was barely conscious, moaning like a dying animal. Bones jutted through her thin, clammy skin. Sweat pooled above her top lip and in the nook between her bladed collarbones.

Even in the dim light, her veins clearly ran black. They spidered over her white skin like spilled ink.

Muscle memory kicking in from her years on the streetwatch, Saff crossed to the woman, laying the back of her hand against a glistening forehead. It was like a furnace. She knelt to the ground beside the mage and spoke low and clear.

"Do you need help, sweetling?"

Sweetling: a southern term of endearment her mother always used with patients. It made Saffron's heart swell to use it.

The woman groaned, eyes fluttering, limbs jerking.

Levan stopped to watch Saffron but did not kneel beside her. His face had darkened; he seemed lost in the shadowy corridors of his mind.

Saff gritted her teeth. "Does this look like lox to you?"

Levan nodded stiffly. "Overdose."

Saffron remembered something Harrow had said: *I still remember finding you in a pool of your own piss after a lox overdose.*

Harrow had found Levan like this.

"How do we help her?" Saffron asked, clutching the woman's hand in hers. It was ice cold, unlike the fevered forehead.

"We can't," Levan muttered, looking away. "That's the vicious thing about lox. Once it's in your system, no magic can pull it back out. She just has to wait and hope. And we're already late."

"We can't leave her here," Saffron argued, feeling the righteous, principled courage of her mother beating in her own chest. "We should call a Healer."

"This is not something that can be healed."

"Maybe not, but she still deserves a warm bed and someone to care for her."

Levan looked at his leather-banded wristwatch, then at the moon hanging above the city. With a reluctant sigh, he brought his wand to his lips. "*Et vocos, Karal Kelassan.*"

It took a few moments for the response to come. "Hello?" The voice was bleary with sleep.

"It's Levan. I have someone for you. Lox."

The sound of a bedspread being shoved off a body. "Where?"

Levan didn't even have to look up at the street sign. "Lancen Place. By the apothecary with the yellow awning."

"On my way."

"Is Kelassan a Bloodmoon?" Saffron asked, guts twisting at the thought of involving this woman with the scarlet cloaks.

"No. He helped me when I . . . was sick." A grinding of his teeth, an aversion of the gaze. "We should go. Your contact has already been waiting too long."

Saffron nodded, squeezing the woman's frigid hand. "Help is coming, sweetling."

The lox-addled mage only moaned in response, but a moan meant she was still alive.

"Will she live?" Saff asked quietly, once they were out of earshot. "Or is she too far gone?"

"I don't know," Levan admitted.

"That's what happened to you—when you were sick?" She framed this question not as an accusation but as a gentle nudge toward the truth—one that implied she already knew the answer. The simplest way to slip the knowledge Harrow had gifted her onto the public record between her and Levan.

Levan looked up at the sky, the narrow moon draping pale light over the hard lines of his face. "Indeed. Lox nearly killed me."

Something like sadness sank into Saffron's lungs, but it quickly dissipated. "And yet you subject countless others to the same fate. How can it not make you sick? When you think about what lox is doing to the city?"

"Lox wasn't my idea," he replied evenly, but it had to trouble him.

"You also didn't stop it." She chose her next words carefully. "I don't get it, Levan. Unlike Vogolan, you seem to need a reason for the evil in order to make peace with it. So why—"

"You play fast and loose with the word *evil*."

"How else would you describe it?"

"Well, would you use the word *evil* to describe what the Vallish soldiers did on the battlefield during the War of Eight Mountains? They killed. Slaughtered." When she did not respond, he added,

"Would you use the word *evil* to describe Aymar in *Lost Dragonborn*? He takes lives for the greater good."

They slipped from Lancen Place onto Arollan Mile. "And you believe you do the same?"

"Most of the time. There are missteps. The Brewer in the alley, the night we met—that was a misstep."

"And the Whitewings?"

"Only ever killed in retaliation."

This didn't ring entirely true. She thought of what he'd said to her that night in the alley: *If I find out this is all a trick, I will not kill you. I will hunt down everyone you have ever loved and bleed them dry in front of you. And when you beg me to kill you, I won't. I will force you to live with the pain until your heart eventually dies in your chest. And I will* enjoy *it.*

She knew the threats were not empty, but when she looked back on them, she thought there might have been an element of performance to them. He'd just been trying to scare her, to keep her in line, but the pleasure he claimed he'd derive from destroying her . . . that was wholly at odds with the mage she was coming to know. He didn't seem to derive any satisfaction from fear or violence, the way his father did. He just believed the end justified the means—whatever that *end* may be.

And wasn't she doing the exact same thing? Hadn't she killed Neatras and maimed Kasan in the pursuit of her own goals?

"Are you going to force your contact's hand?" Levan asked, changing the subject somewhat. "Over the tracing charm my father asked for."

Saffron had almost forgotten what Lyrian had ordered her to do.

She grimaced. "I suppose I'll have to. Your father will torture or execute my loved ones if I don't."

Just then, her wand tip crackled, and her uncle Mal's familiar voice sang through the tip. "*Et vocos, Saffron Killoran.*"

Saff stared down at her wand, cursing the woeful timing. He'd tried to reach her half a dozen times since her release from Duncarzus, and she still hadn't mustered the courage to respond.

How could she? How could she speak to the sweet, kind mage who raised her when it would only put him more at risk?

"Saffy, my love, sometimes I feel like I'm talking to a brick wall. Al-

though that stretch of creamstone in the alley behind the Cloakery certainly has better conversation. Don't tell me you've gone mute again? Because frankly, I don't have another Lost Dragonborn *up my sleeve."*

Levan watched her grapple with the emotions, but he didn't ask her about the significance of *Lost Dragonborn,* or what her uncle meant by *mute.*

When Mal tried several more times before finally giving up, the kingpin's son said, "Your uncles raised you?"

Saff nodded numbly.

"What were your parents like?"

Once again, Saffron did not want to taint her parents' memories by sharing them with a Bloodmoon. And yet she was also supposed to be under the influence of truth elixir, and so she'd have to answer.

"My mother was a Healer. And she was very, very good at it. She developed a hornpox vaccination that cured a savage outbreak when I was three or four. King Quintan himself nominated her for the Vallish Distinction Prize. She had dozens of job offers after that, mostly in the capital, but she refused them all. She believed rural villages were just as deserving of excellent care." A wistful smile twisted her lips. "She could also *drink.* She loved honeywine. The smell always reminds me of her."

And your terrible family took her from me.

"What about your father?"

A sort of sighing feeling sunk into Saffron's chest, heavy and solid. "A highly gifted Enchanter, but he never had particularly grand ambitions. He used to spend his days pottering around our house, charming it in new and increasingly absurd ways for when I got home from school."

Something reared in Saffron's memory—something she hadn't been able to quite shake.

Aspar, on that fateful night of the final assessment.

Once upon a time, I owed your father a great debt of gratitude.

Would she ever find out what that had meant?

Saffron's hand went once again to the wooden pendant hanging around her neck.

"Our front door changed color depending upon who knocked. One of my father's favorite enchantments. Sky blue for an acquaintance, heart red for a lover present, past, or future. Clover green for an enemy, plum for an old friend. Vibrant orange for someone trustworthy, pale pink for a blossoming relationship. Mustard yellow for family and, erm, traveling salesmen. The best door in the world. This pendant is all that remains of it, and of them."

The two jewels, studded into the wood. Emerald and purple sapphire.

"I still don't quite understand how he wove that spell—how the magic could understand human relationships well enough to reflect them back on the beholder. But the door was damaged on the night they died, and the enchantment slipped out of it. I wish more than anything it still carried the magic. It would feel like my dad was with me, in some way. And it would show me exactly who I could and couldn't trust."

Levan stopped walking for a moment.

"Can I?" He gestured to the pendant.

Saffron nodded, unsure why her breath froze in her throat as his hand went to the necklace, holding it up to the nearest streetlamp. A frowned notched between his brows.

"I think I can re-create the enchantment. If you want me to."

Something surged in Saffron's heart. "How?"

"I remember something similar from an ancient book of enchantments in the mansion library. The volume is six hundred years old—from when House Portaran reigned. They were gifted Enchanters too, and wanted to spread their knowledge to all the people of Vallin."

"Do you remember *everything* you read?"

He shrugged, a little bashful. "The pages remain in my head, like a personal library I can peruse at any moment. Do you want me to try?" He gestured to the pendant, and the softness of his words took her aback. "I understand if not. If the spell feels sacred."

Sacred was the right word.

"Why would you do that for me?" she asked.

"To see if I can," he said evenly, still composed despite his lowered defenses. "It's very interesting magic."

Saffron gave him a wry smile. "Is that the only reason?"

Levan's eyes bore into hers so intensely it sent a shiver down her spine. "Fine. I meant what I said earlier. You were just in the wrong place at the wrong time, and now you're caught up in all of this without deserving to be. My apology doesn't mean much, but I can tell this does."

The words flowed easily, coaxed out of him by the truth elixir. Not worth choking back.

And so Saffron replied, rather coarsely, "Alright."

Levan withdrew his wand, laying the tip on the smooth oval, then furrowed his brow even deeper in concentration. He uttered a string of low, urgent enchantments all rolled into one, so quickly and expertly that Saffron could not even begin to parse them into separate commands. At the sound of the style of magic—so familiar, and yet she hadn't heard it for decades—her heart ached like a wound, deeper and more primal than her prickling brand.

Slowly, beneath the assertive pulse of Levan's wand, the wooden oval came back to life, flaring into a rainbow spectrum of colors before settling into a select few.

Some patches were a pale floral pink, while others were vibrant orange. There was a blotch of clover green, and right down the middle, cleaving the oval in two, was a streak of heart red.

Levan frowned down at it. "I'm not sure I did it right. It should only be one block color, shouldn't it?"

Saffron nodded, but she could barely speak.

The hues were so perfect, so precise. It was an arrow through her chest.

"I think you did it *better*," she whispered, a betrayal of her father. "His chose only the most dominant relationship dynamic. Yours seems to highlight all present ones."

Clover green for an enemy.

Vibrant orange for someone trustworthy.

Pale pink for a blossoming relationship.

Heart red for a lover present, past, or future.

As Levan slotted those pieces into place, his gaze lifted from the necklace to her face, and a mottling of color spread above his collar. He exhaled slowly, searching her eyes for some clue as to how *she* felt about these conflicting connotations. In truth she was hot and cold all at once, both horrified and bewildered.

The prophecy came back to her unbidden: her lips on his, a firm palm in the small of her back.

A moan of pleasure. A wand pressed to his stomach. The killing curse.

Was there going to be something more to their relationship?

No. She wouldn't allow that.

She had been letting herself get closer to him because it's what the mission required—but the pendant mistook that closeness for something else. For a blossoming relationship. For a future lover.

Surely that was all it was. An error in the spellwork.

Levan cleared his throat and turned away.

"We should go," he muttered, rearranging his cloak before striding off in the direction of the Jaded Saint.

25

...

The Valiant Sword

VIOLIN MUSIC RANG OUT INTO THE STREET. THE PAVEMENT tables of the Jaded Saint were full of young mages doing raucous lines of lemon shots, and from their light-blue scholar cloaks and the collection of matching monocles, Saff suspected they were students from the University of Atherin.

She shrugged off her cloak and passed it to Levan. "Will you—?"

"Wait here. Yes."

Swallowing the pitted stone of dread in her throat, Saffron entered the tavern. She spotted Nissa tucked into a quiet corner, her black hair a glossy sheet and her lips painted ruby red. The table was lined with empty tumblers—by the looks of things, Nissa had been drinking a *lot* while she waited. She'd also sparked up a hand-rolled achullah, despite the many placards stating they were forbidden inside the vine-strung tavern due to fire risk.

At the sight of Saff, her bronze eyes lit up and she stubbed the achullah out into an old glass.

"You're still alive," Nissa slurred, as Saff took a seat beside her.

"I'm still alive. And I'm so sorry for dragging you into this."

"As far as I remember, I dragged myself into it. Please do not imply that you have the power to make me do something against my will. My will is iron."

Saff snorted. "Iron can be struck into shape if the forge is hot enough."

"Fine. My will is coal. Black and ugly and misshapen."

"But coal—"

"Oh, shut the fuck up." Nissa's brandy-slackened lips twisted into a half smile, half grimace. "Metaphors aren't my thing. Let's just say I'm a stubborn wretch and be done with it."

It was only then that Saff noticed how unwell Nissa looked. There were dark smudges beneath her golden eyes, and a sort of sickly green pallor to her usually warm brown skin.

"Are you alright?" Saffron asked, resisting the urge to reach out and touch Nissa's forearm.

Nissa grunted. "Crescent moon."

Of course. Nissa's monthly blood cycles, which always fell on the crescent moon, caused her immense pain. Searing, clenching agony around her lower belly, radiating around to her back. Nausea, vomiting, and a sharp nosedive in mood. The Healers thought it'd be very difficult for her to conceive a child, which Nissa was largely delighted about, but she could still do without the debilitating symptoms.

"Still holding out on Paliran's tincture?" Saff asked.

Nissa's expression darkened. "I've told you, I'm not touching whiteroot. No matter how bad it gets. You know how addictive my personality is. I'll be begging in the gutters within the month if I go near the stuff. And anyway, the pain is what makes my wielding so powerful. I don't want to lose my edge."

Flawed logic Saffron had heard one too many times. Her mother had suffered badly with anxiety, but since she was convinced that it made her a more vigilant Healer, she refused all medicinal and psychological aid. But Saff knew better than to argue with Nissa, to insist that living in pain was no way to live at all.

Nor should she offer any sympathy. Even at the height of their relationship, Nissa hadn't wanted Saffron's comfort. She'd just wanted to be left alone in the pain cave until it was finally time to emerge. And so they would proceed as normal, pretending Nissa was not a shadow of her usual self.

Saff looked around the bar, squinting through the hazy spores and the dim light. "No Auria and Tiernan?"

"Night shift." Nissa didn't meet Saff's eye, and Saff suspected her former friends simply did not want to be seen with her. Despite everything that had happened, their rejection still stung. "How have things been?"

Saffron grimaced. "Well, they made me carve out an innocent man's eyeball with a letteropener, so not great."

"Hells, Killor. You know I enjoy a bit of sadism, but that's . . ."

"I know. Do you have anything on Nalezen Zares?"

Nissa nodded briskly. "She's a necromancer and known criminal. Detective Jebat has been building a case against her for some time but hasn't gotten enough evidence to stick the charge. Essentially Zares seduces mages in bars, brings them back to her apartment, and executes them just so she can practice bringing them back to life. Well, *practice* is the more charitable theory. Jebat reckons it's a fetish of hers."

Saff tried not to blanch. The Bloodmoons had been looking for a necromancer twenty-one years ago, on the night Saff's parents were killed.

Never mind that raising the dead went against nature. Never mind that the Risen never *truly* rose. Something essential in their spirit would be forever lost. Hundreds of years ago, the state would have put the Risen to death once more, struck them with a Crown-sanctioned killing spell in a jeering town square. Now they were simply cuffed with deminite, to minimize the damage their corrupt souls could do, and at the first sign of trouble, they'd be hauled off to Duncarzus for life—the harshest punishment decreed by judge and jury since the Grand Arbiter had abolished the death penalty.

And so not only was Zares committing a series of unlawful acts, she was also condemning her victims to a lifetime of damnation. All for a *fetish*.

"Grim," Saff muttered. "Any idea of her whereabouts?"

"Last seen wreaking havoc in the Valiant Sword. A tavern in Port Ouran, by the King's Canal."

Saff nodded gratefully. Tiredness weighed her down, her bones made of molasses. She longed to sink into a hot bath and never resurface. "Thank you."

Nissa studied her face as the bard plucked a bum note on his lute, and an old man jeered his disapproval. "There's something else, isn't there?"

"You don't have to do it," Saff muttered. "You can walk away from this now."

"But you can't."

"No, I can't."

"And they'll make your life hell if I don't." Nissa pressed her lips into a flat line. Her lipstick was smudged at the corner, and her eyes were fuzzy with liquor and pain. Sweat poured down her temples in slick runnels. "So it's hardly a choice, is it?"

Saff sighed. "The spell-tracing charm. The one forensics have been working on for years. Any significant progress?"

An uncertain beat. "Aspar hasn't mentioned it in an age, so I suppose not. At her last update, the spell would get distracted while following a trace back to the original wand, and latch onto the shiniest, most exciting one instead. It has a particular penchant for elm."

Nissa gestured to her own black elm wand, and Saff realized for the first time it was carved from the same wood as Levan's. *I clearly have a type,* she thought, before internally recoiling from the idea. She did *not* feel that way toward the kingpin's son, no matter what her newly enchanted pendant might think.

"Why?" Nissa nudged.

"I need you to get it for me."

Saffron wasn't sure how dangerous this play was. There was a chance the tracing charm wouldn't work on her, since she was magic immune, but could the same be said for her wand? Would it be able to trace the *ammorten* curse that slew Vogolan back to her own knobbly beech?

And yet as she so often was, she was backed into a corner. No other options, no less perilous paths. If she didn't procure the charm, Lyrian would strike fast and hard.

"The charm? *How?*" Nissa replied, aghast. "It's under—"

"Lock and key. I know."

"Who wants it?" Nissa picked up the nearest tumbler and examined it for any lingering flamebrandy. There was none, so she caught a young, handsome bartender's attention across the room and held up two fingers. They had deep Eqoran skin and long glossy hair like Nissa's. At Nissa's summons, they smiled at her flirtatiously and nodded.

"The kingpin. One of his top men was murdered."

The fewer people who knew it was at Saffron's hand, the better. Even people she could trust. Because though Nissa was hardened against torture, the same could not be said for truth elixir. Saffron was the only mage she knew of who could resist that.

Until Levan, of course. She'd yet to unpack how he'd managed to overpower it.

The handsome bartender brought the two flamebrandies over, setting them down on the table alongside a small scrap of parchment. The note read: *et vocos Rababi Äin.* An invitation to call them.

"*Hells,*" muttered Nissa. She was a few years older than Saff, having just turned thirty, and there were the beginnings of crinkles around her eyes. A shallow notch between her brows. The last few weeks had aged her, and Saff felt equal parts guilty and touched. "I'll try my best, but I'm not promising anything." Something glittered in those dragonesque eyes as she glanced from Saff to the note and back again. "Meet you here same time next week? Leaked intel and a quick fuck?"

Saffron laughed. "I thought you didn't want to be *distracted* by me." She threw mocking air quotes around the word, before mimicking Nissa's own words: "*The best Silvercloaks cut off sentimentality at the root.*"

Nissa shrugged. "Fucking isn't sentimental. Don't let it go to your head. It's just that all the danger is making me more attracted to you."

Saffron's heart darkened. "Trust me, if you saw the brand up close, you would not want to fuck me." It throbbed in response, like a second heartbeat, even though she'd applied salve mere hours earlier.

A curious smile. "For what it's worth, I'll always want to fuck you." Nissa stood up, leaned in, and kissed Saff on the cheek, a warm, tingling kiss that lingered a second longer than it should have. A kiss that suggested she wanted more than just to fuck. "I'll try to have the charm for you next week."

Then Nissa was gone, and Saff was left alone to finish her flame-brandy. It scorched down her gullet like molten candle wax. Which, incidentally, reminded her of Nissa's bedroom. Sadism, indeed.

As Saff got up to leave, another familiar face entered the Jaded Saint, scanning the room as if to find someone.

Tiernan.

He was dressed in his silver cloak, proudly pinned at his throat with the sapphire brooch Saffron had dreamed of for so long. His curls were a mess atop his head, and he squinted despite his thick-rimmed glasses. When his gaze found Saff, his shoulders sagged with relief.

She pushed through the throngs of intoxicated bodies and smiled reassuringly at him.

"Saff," he said, throwing his arms around her. He was a couple of inches shorter than her, and his hair tickled her cheek. "Thank the Saints."

"Everything alright?" she asked carefully, pulling away, keeping her guard up.

"I'm so sorry about last week." He rushed the words out so fast they crashed into one another. "I've stewed on it for seven straight days, and . . . god, I was a *vock*." Saff laughed; *vock* was a crude Bellandrian word for a male appendage. "I understand, you know. The reason you lied about your accreditation . . . I'd do anything to make my parents proud." He raked his hand through his messy hair. "You were just doing the same, weren't you? And it's even harder for you because they're gone. And I'm *sorry*."

Something frozen thawed slightly in Saff's chest. "I forgive you."

"Are you alright? That should have been my first and only question."

"I will be," Saff said, though the answer didn't feel particularly robust.

She'd never felt able to share her darker emotions with Tiernan or Auria; she didn't want to taint them, overwhelm them. And yet she had so easily confided in Levan about the brick of grief in her chest—and the terrible, traitorous relief that followed her parents' death. Perhaps there was a darkness in him that called to a darkness in her.

Clearing her throat, she asked, "Is Auria still . . . ?"

Angry? Ashamed of me?

Mourning her grandfather?

"She needs a bit more time, I think. I'm sorry."

Saff wanted so badly to ask about Papa Marriosan, but she couldn't let Tiernan know that *she* knew. It was far too damning.

Tiernan gnawed at his bottom lip, still visibly in self-loathing turmoil. "You're a good person, Saff. I hope you know that."

The image of Kasan's empty eye socket came to her, but she said nothing to refute the idea.

"Can I buy you a drink?" Tiernan asked, a hopeful note in his voice.

Saff shook her head. "I have to go. But thank you for coming. It means more than I can say."

"Of course. Take care of yourself, Saff."

Levan was waiting for her across the street, leaning back against a shopfront with one foot pressed flat against the wall. Beside him, Rasso was enjoying a staring match with an underripe lemon that had fallen from a nearby tree and rolled into the moonlit gutter. The fallowwolf's ears were folded over, as if to block out the noise of the taverns.

At the sight of Saffron, Levan stepped forward.

"Well?" The word was urgent, laced with equal parts hope and desperation. By his side, his hand clenched into a fist, but the gesture wasn't threatening, just . . . determined.

Determined to find this necromancer.

Who was he trying to bring back to life? Necromancers could only work with fresh corpses, and he'd been trying to find Zares for weeks. Maybe longer.

Harrow Claver's curtailed words played over and over again on a loop.

Darling Levan will never take another life partner. Not after what happened to . . .

The kingpin's son had loved and lost someone. That much was clear.

And then the revelation from earlier this evening, when she'd asked why he hated Vogolan.

He killed someone very important to me.

The pieces slotted together.

She thought about the night she had first met Levan, how utterly dead behind the eyes he'd seemed. Like all the light had gone from his life. And she supposed that it had. He'd lost his mother as a child, and the person he loved as an adult. His despair had been so deep and dark that he'd run straight into lox's gnarled, suffocating arms.

There had been glimmers of internal life since, she thought. Brief flares of emotion before he smothered them.

Was Levan's loss recent enough that finding a necromancer was worthwhile, potentially fruitful? Saff recalled a book her mother owned on the maligned art. One moon cycle was around the longest a body could lie dead for before a necromancer revived it, and even then it would require extremely complex and power-draining magic to preserve the corpse as well as it needed to be preserved.

When had his life partner died?

"Silver?"

He took several more steps toward her, close enough that she could feel his breath on her face. Hunger burned in his eyes, so potent her heart stumbled and faltered. She knew now, after being around him for seven days, that his gaze was not something he gave easily, casually. She had something he wanted, and that *want* coursed between them like a current.

In that moment—that brief and fleeting moment—she had the power.

The control.

There was a curious sense of tension in all the places their bodies ran parallel but did not touch, and for several beats, it seemed he might reach out to her, close the gap through sheer impatience, through a deep, penetrating desperation for the contents of her mind. Some primal part of her wondered what it would be like if he did. She wondered how she might respond, how she might run a palm over his chest in search of an old, pitted brand scar. How she might seek power another way.

But she couldn't—or *wouldn't.*

This assignment was her life's purpose. She would not set fire to it just to heed a base impulse.

Besides, he was not hungry for her. He was hungry for what she knew.

She took a deep breath, a little afraid of what she might be handing him on a platter.

"I know where you can find Nalezen Zares."

26

. . .

The Scholar's Twinkle

THE NEXT MORNING, THEY TRAVELED TO PORT OURAN BY WATER. The Bloodmoon riverboat was a handsome scarlet vessel with two tiered decks, dozens of cabins, and a paddlewheel of solid ascenite. It was almost twice as large as the trader boats that meandered up and down the Corven, and a row of three Bloodmoon banderoles—pale gold with a crimson crescent moon—snapped in the breeze.

A small crew of Wielders powered the riverboat, and once the Bloodmoons and the fallowwolf had embarked, they set sail. Segal grunted his goodbyes and disappeared into a back cabin to sleep off a hangover—he hadn't taken his good friend Vogolan's departure very well—while Levan, Saffron, and an unfamiliar mage took to the uppermost deck, far away from the listening ears in the wheelhouse.

The sky over Atherin was a moody smudged gray, but the city still looked beautiful as it passed: cherryblossom and market stalls, purple domes and towering pillars, marble columns and gold obelisks and wooden shutters of ocean blue and emerald green. The two banks of the river—Sun Bank and Moon Bank—were lined with pavement cafés and art galleries and street orchestras, and the famous Seven Bridges of Atherin arched over the water.

Saffron savored the wind in her hair, the crystalline scent of the water, the clarion bells of passing vessels. She felt freer than she had in weeks. *Months.* She hadn't spent much time on the water—hell, she'd never even seen the ocean—but the feel of it soothed her almost immediately, like a beloved blanket, a mother's embrace. Perhaps she'd been a pirate in a past life.

Levan stood at the bow of the riverboat, elbows leaning on a white railing, the corded muscles of his broad back rippling through his cloak. Rasso snoozed beneath a crimson awning. Saffron sat near the fallowwolf on a cushioned bench, and the unfamiliar mage took a seat beside her. He had wrinkled brown skin, a long gray beard down to his waist, and half-moon spectacles rimmed with gold—more like a Royal Scholar than a Bloodmoon.

"You must be Saffron Silvercloak." His words were lightly accented with the lyrical lull of the Eqoran desert.

"*Q'taem,*" she affirmed, drawing on what little Eqoran she'd picked up from Nissa. She gave him a wry smile. "But Silvercloak isn't my family name, believe it or not."

He laughed more raucously than the situation demanded. "*Taqin.*" True. He extended a weathered hand, and Saffron shook it. The skin on his palm was dry and wrinkled. "Miret Tomazin. A pleasure."

There was a kindly energy to Miret, but Saffron knew from her endless study of case files that it was often the quietest, most unassuming people who were the deadliest.

"I haven't seen you around before," she said casually, kicking her boots up on the bench opposite. "Not even at Lyrian's little conclave. After Vogolan's disappearance." She was careful not to say *death.*

Miret removed his glasses and polished the lenses on the hem of his cloak. "Alas, no. I keep to myself in the library, reading every tome cover to cover. So that if anyone comes in search of knowledge, I know exactly where to direct them." A playful smile. "When one is blessed with such flawless intelligence, one must put it to good use, but it's a time-consuming endeavor. And I daresay I'm not getting any younger. Lyrian knows I'd hardly have the superfluous energy to immolate poor Vogolan."

Saffron frowned. "So why are you on a riverboat in search of a necromancer?"

Miret replaced his glasses on his crooked nose, a twinkle in his brown eyes. "Curiosity, my dear child."

But from the way he glanced at Levan's back—with something oddly paternal in his eyes—Saffron sensed there was something more. She thought of the countless books in Levan's room, his panoramic memory of everything he'd read, and suspected he'd probably spent a good amount of time in the library with Miret Tomazin. With a father like Lyrian, it would be little wonder if the two had developed a bond.

They sailed down a narrow stretch of river, the water flanked on either side by tall, towering trees that kissed in the center. Havendoves nested in the branches, cooing wistfully, and it reminded Saffron of Lunes; her home village was packed to the rafters with the melancholic birds.

"Do you know *why* Levan's so intent on finding a necromancer?" she asked Miret, not truly expecting an answer.

He smiled wryly. "That is not for me to divulge."

So he did know. "Are the two of you close?"

"Ever since his mother passed. The death had a profound effect on his sensibilities, and he developed . . . compulsions, of sorts. A rigorously ordered way of doing things, every action packed with rituals and mutterings. At one time he was obsessed with writing down every sentence ever spoken to him, as though recording the words would make them real, somehow. The only thing to break through it all was the *Lost Dragonborn* series."

Saffron had the acutely shameful feeling that Miret should not be telling her this. It was too private, too personal, and yet he recited the information with an academic distance. It was exactly the kind of intel she was here to collect, the kind of intel that would bring the Silvercloaks' case file on the Bloodmoons to life, and yet it felt oddly uncomfortable to stare right into the traumatized heart of Levan Celadon.

Still, the revelation struck Saffron deeply, resonantly. The thought of young Levan, riddled with grief-fueled compulsions, caused a curious clenching sensation in her chest. Her young mind had also splintered from the loss of her parents—leaving her mute for the better part of six years—and the same book had brought them back from the edge.

Levan's pain was her pain. The same texture, the same shape.

The same emotional wound, carved as children, scarring into adulthood.

The same cleft in their hearts that would never smooth.

Almost without thinking—a rarity for Saffron—she rose to her feet. The boat glided over a harsh current, and she canted sideways before regaining her composure. She strode over to Levan, resting her forearms on the railing beside him. His hands were clasped together, broad and firm but somehow elegant. A few scarred nicks on the knuckles, wounds he could easily have healed clean and yet had chosen not to.

They were not the hands of a killer, and yet they were.

His forefinger tapped out a repetitive rhythm on the railing. A remnant of the compulsions? She thought of his alphabetized teabags and neatly labeled plants, the way he followed a regimented daily schedule without a minute of deviation, and wondered.

"Why are we chasing a necromancer, Levan?" Her words were gentle but firm.

A faded-green trader boat passed them on the water, giving them an unnecessarily wide berth. Levan said nothing, as expected.

"Harrow said you lost someone you were romantically involved with," she added, hoping to draw out some semblance of emotion from him, because emotion created cracks, and cracks could be broken wide.

"Don't," he warned, gaze fixed straight ahead.

"You want to revive them? The partner you lost?"

"Don't."

The word was a knife tip, but that was good. Bladed words were usually emotional ones.

Saff swallowed. "Sometimes I think there's nothing I wouldn't do to bring my parents back to me."

A pulsing silence. Then, "Even torture and kill?"

"I've already tortured and killed *without* the promise of a family reunion." She couldn't keep the bitterness from her voice. "What does that say about me?"

A sigh. "What did Miret tell you?"

"What do you mean?"

"I saw you talking. Heard the word *necromancer.*"

"He told me nothing," Saff said carefully. "Said it wasn't his place."

"Good."

"He obviously cares about you."

Levan stiffened. "Yes."

"It's alright to admit you care about him too."

"No, it's not. You should never admit who means something to you. Look at your uncles, your old friends. They're being used against you." A sharp exhale. "Shut yourself off, Silver. It's safer."

"If your lost love is already gone, they can no longer be used against you. So what's the harm in telling me about them?"

A subtle test. If he was planning to bring them back, this logic didn't track.

He didn't reply, but nor did he actively chastise her for asking. Progress.

She rested a hand on his forearm, and he flinched as though he'd been struck. But when she didn't pull away, he relaxed into it. For some reason, she was surprised how warm his body felt beneath his cloak sleeve. What had she expected? That he was literally cold-blooded?

Time to drive the chisel all the way in. "I just want to understand you better. To remind myself that my captor is human."

The moment ruptured like a membrane. He wrenched his arm away, storm clouds drawing in behind his eyes. "I'm not your captor. *You* asked to be branded. *You* insisted you were useful to us."

"To save my skin," Saff retorted hotly, meeting his anger with her own—it was always simmering beneath the surface, waiting to be spent. "You'd have killed me otherwise."

"You're right." Something flared behind his blue eyes, usually so devoid of feeling. "I suppose I'm not human, after all."

He stormed away, toward the inner cabins, leaving Rasso staring languidly behind him. The fallowwolf didn't follow, but instead sighed, rolled onto his back, and fell asleep once more. Nearby, Miret's arms were folded across his chest, his mouth hanging open slightly in slumber.

Staring after the kingpin's son, Saffron couldn't quite comprehend Levan's overblown reaction. He was usually so controlled, so closed off. Why should it matter to him whether she thought of him as a captor? As human? His focus seemed wholeheartedly on finding this necromancer—and presumably bringing his lost love back to life. Saffron was a means to an end. The way she thought of him should be an utter irrelevance. Still, she felt a curious thrill that she'd managed to evoke such a strong response. Her efforts to get under his skin were working.

Wrenching her focus back toward the larger mission, Saffron decided to use the slumbering passengers to her advantage.

"*Et aquies,*" she muttered, tapping each of her boots in turn. A basic silencing charm.

Creeping across the deck, past Rasso and Miret, Saffron ducked beneath the wraparound scarlet awning and inside the upper level of the riverboat. The air inside the peg-straight corridor was cool and salty and a little stale, like brine and old coffee and dusty manila files. The latter reminded Saff of the back rooms at the Academy, where she, Auria, and Tiernan had spent hours poring over obscure and impossible vanishment cases. Rather than knocking the wind out of her, the memory was fortifying. The light at the end of a long, dark tunnel. She would get back there. Not only would she no longer be ostracized, but she'd also be actively celebrated for what she had done.

All the doors lining both sides of the corridor were closed. There were twelve in total, and she knew one would reveal a snoozing Segal, and one a livid Levan. The first handle Saff tried was locked, as was the second. Another was an empty cabin with two stiffly made bunks. There was a faded maroon mark on one bedspread, as though someone had bled to death and even magical cleaning charms couldn't get the stain out.

The next room was also a cabin, but this one contained Segal's sleeping form on a bottom bunk. At the sound of the door opening, he sat bolt upright, thunking his head off the slats of the bunk above. He screwed his eyes shut and swore rather profoundly, allowing Saffron to sneak away without being seen.

Three more doors. Two cabins, and then finally an office.

It was small, neatly ordered, lined with floating shelves. Through a wide porthole, dappled light spilled onto the floorboards, illuminating a squat desk, a rickety chair, and little in the way of reading material—just a dried-up inkwell, an empty coffee press, and a single drawer with a gold keyhole. Saff tried to open it with the *aperturan* charm, then the *fair featherroot* password, but the lock wouldn't budge.

The shelves bolted to the walls each held a row of plain black notebooks, with red reading ribbons and year dates embossed on the spine. As she pulled the oldest-dated volume down, the air fuzzed with dust motes. The notebook fell open in her palm, and a thrill bolted through her.

A ledger.

From ten years ago, but a ledger nonetheless.

A ledger detailing every shipment of loxlure the Bloodmoons had orchestrated.

The early dates were sporadic, the quantities tiny, hidden amongst vast quantities of other legitimate supplies. But they were there nonetheless. Saff sucked in a mouthful of dusty air.

The Bloodmoons had been smuggling lox into the city for over ten years.

She replaced the ledger with a shaking hand, then ran a fingertip over every spine until she found the most recent date. The previous calendar year. As she leafed through the latest notebook, she discerned a clear pattern. The Bloodmoons received weekly shipments every Elming from Port Ouran—originating in Laudon and the other Eastern Republics—but not all of them contained lox. Three shipments a month were clean, involving only routine spell ingredients and other luxuries. Silks and cottons, parchment and inks, rare mountain ash and refined soil from the Valley of the Seers in the heart of Esvaine.

Only one shipment a month carried lox, albeit in a vast quantity.

Clever, Saff thought. If the Silvercloaks tried to raid a shipment at random, there was only a twenty-five percent chance they'd get lucky.

If they failed, they wouldn't be able to raid another without a proper warrant, or the Grand Arbiter would have their heads.

As for which shipment contained the lox, it cycled according to a basic monthly pattern—hugging closely to the moon's own cycles, since each of the thirteen calendar months was also a lunar period. (The months were named for the thirteen founding dragons, and as a mark of respect, they were the same in every language.) In Mónyriel the shipment would arrive on the first Elming, in Áqiriel the second, in Gláciel the third, in Magnáriel the fourth, and then it would rotate another two times throughout the year. In Nyrápiel, the thirteenth month, it seemed to land on a random date. All shipments arrived at darknight, when the docks were relatively deserted.

It was early Sabáriel, which meant the next lox shipment would fall on the second Elming.

In three days' time.

Euphoria flooded Saff's veins, rich and vibrant.

She was going to do it. She was going to get this information to Aspar, and the Bloodmoons would be successfully raided, and the vast quantities of lox would be more than enough to bring both a charge *and* a conviction.

Sinking into the desk chair, she hugged the ledger to her chest, and a coarse voice echoed in the doorway.

"What *are* you doing, Filthcloak?"

Her back was to the door, but she didn't have to turn around to know who had caught her.

Segal.

27

...

Nalezen Zares

TAPPING THE TIP OF HER WAND TO THE LEDGER, HER BACK still to the door, Saffron whispered under her breath, "*Et lusio Lost Dragonborn.*"

The illusion shrouded the ledger in a faded indigo clothbound cover. She hadn't been specific enough, and there was no volume number on the spine, but she hoped Segal wasn't enough of a fan to notice. She turned to face him.

The smile on his face was as crude as it was smug.

He was *delighted* to have caught her.

A quiet fury unfurled inside her, like a porcupine unrolling its barbs. This man had slaughtered her parents, and even though some distant part of her understood that he had been following orders, she couldn't rationalize away her hatred of him. Her impulses twitched, longing to slay him as she had slain Vogolan.

Because truthfully, it was troubling how easy it had been to kill the kingpin's right-hand man, how difficult it was for them to trace it back to her. How little remorse she felt in the aftermath. Only a vague, abstract guilt—a shadow, an afterimage, a distant vestige of shame but not shame itself.

How good would it feel to avenge her parents this very moment?

But she didn't. She simply stood from the chair and held up the fake novel.

"Trying to read in peace."

A beat of suspicion. "And you couldn't do that on the deck?"

"Miret was snoring."

His eyes narrowed. "There's sensitive information in this room."

Saff made a show of looking around, as though seeing where she was for the first time. "Is there?"

"You expect me to believe a *former* Silvercloak is so unaware of her surroundings that she missed the row of shipment ledgers?"

She gave him a twisted smile. "Surely the brand would kill me for snooping."

Segal leaned against the doorframe, blocking the only exit. One half of his bulbous face was red and wrinkled from the way he'd slept on the bunk. "Something doesn't sit right with me, Filthcloak. Your parents died at our hand, and yet here you are. Working missions. Lurking amongst ledgers. Now tell me, Saffron Killoran, why would the daughter of two murdered mages willingly walk into the den of the monsters who killed them?"

The lie came to her from thin air. "I got hooked on loxlure in Duncarzus. One of your scarlets supplies the prison. When I was released, I just . . . followed the scent. All the way to the gamehouse. The need overrode everything else."

As all the best lies were, it was rooted in truth. The Bloodmoons *did* supply Duncarzus—Saffron had overheard them discussing it the previous night. Half the guards were in on the smuggling, and paid handsomely for it too. After all, some of the best gamehouse patrons were vulnerable ex-cons with nowhere better to go. The Bloodmoons hooked them fast and early, the moment they were hauled through those gates in deminite chains, and by the time they were free . . . their feet would find the gamehouse before their heads caught up.

Segal studied her for signs of deceit. "A neat little story."

"Feed me truth elixir, then."

"Or I'll cut you open and see how black you bleed."

Saff proffered her forearm, feigning casualness, when her body was straining at the effort of holding the ledger illusion. She fought to keep the tremor from her hand. "You're most welcome to. But I've been clean for weeks. I'm in the monsters' den, after all. I have to keep my wits about me."

Before Segal could respond, a hulking silhouette appeared behind him, head and shoulders taller than the squat brute.

Levan.

"What's going on?" His teeth were gritted, his cold eyes hardened even more than usual—and pointedly averting Saffron's own gaze.

Segal scoffed. "The Filthcloak was snooping through the ledgers."

"I was just trying to read *Lost Dragonborn* in peace." Saff held up the book, but her pulse faltered for a second. Levan wouldn't be as easily fooled by the illusion.

Sure enough, he frowned at the indigo spine. "What edition is that?"

"I'm not sure. It belonged to my uncle."

"Can I see?"

As she handed him the enchanted ledger, she prayed to Naenari, the patron saint of enchanting, that it would hold up under scrutiny. All those hours of practice with her father could not have been in vain.

He flipped through the pages, and Saffron held her breath. He paused over the elaborate world map and the meticulously ordered glossary, then handed it back to Saff, expression impenetrable. Perspiration beaded at her temple. Her well must be emptier than she thought.

In the dim light of the hallway, Levan's under-eyes were shadowed. Eventually he turned to Segal and muttered, "Don't call her *Filthcloak*."

An entertained smile spread across Segal's face. "Whatever you say."

PORT OURAN WAS A city latticed by canals, gondolas floating between rows of tall, wonky townhouses painted golden yellow and burnt orange and pinkish red. The low bridges over the canals were hewn into floral friezes, and a brisk wind threaded through the narrow streets. The city stood vigil at the side of the Malsea, and a clamorous marina rang bellsong through the neighboring districts. The whole place smelled of salt and brine, damp wood and aged stone.

The Valiant Sword was a dingy tavern on the northern edge of the city. Its sea-green awning was rotted at the edges, the terra-cotta planters were filled with dead flowers, and much of the blue paint had flaked away from the white sign, so it read *The Vant Sod.* It would require a simple charm or an ordinary paintbrush to mend, but the owner was either a Ludder or simply did not care.

Upturned barrels on the street served as tables, next to a blackboard saying *Strictly No Brewers!!!!* in faded chalk. There had been a spate of drink-spiking a few years ago, in which errant Brewers laced beverages with a dancing tincture that inspired the consumer to waltz uncontrollably for hours on end, resulting in a lot of unnecessary property damage.

"Wait here," Levan ordered their gondolier as he disembarked, the sudden absence of his hulking weight causing the vessel to tilt severely. "And you, Miret."

Miret smiled and gave a mock salute, then leaned back in the gondola, interlacing his fingers behind his head.

"Don't fall asleep," Levan said, with the sort of tone one might use to chastise a misbehaving grandfather.

Miret yawned and closed his eyes. "Wouldn't dream of it."

From the pavement, Levan offered Saffron a hand out of the boat—a truce, after their locked horns on the deck. As their palms met, Saff's stomach dipped. She looked down at her newly animated wooden pendant, and found the same colors as before: pale pink, vibrant orange, clover green, and heart red.

The orange and green, contradicted each other.

How could he be both trustworthy and an enemy?

Don't call her Filthcloak.

She thought of the prophecy, and of the *want* she felt outside the Jaded Saint the previous night, and sensed that they were marching closer to their fate. She wondered if that final moment would spring from nowhere, or would feel like a long, slow crescendo. Wondered which would be worse.

Segal followed them ashore, and the three of them entered the

Vant Sod, whose interior was even shabbier than its facade. There were a few tables of solitary drinkers inside, as well as a group of old mages in blood-orange Wielder cloaks sharing a trough of greasy seafood. As the Bloodmoons arrived, all eyes turned to stare. The Wielders looked to one another, silently communicating their fear, then hastily chucked a few palmfuls of ascens on the table before scarpering.

Levan approached the bar, and the barkeep blanched.

"We're looking for Nalezen Zares," Levan said curtly.

"Always knew that *stult* would bring trouble to our door." The barkeep grunted his dissatisfaction. "Lives across the street. Number twenty-eight, with the mourncrow knocker."

They crossed the canal over a floral-friezed bridge and came to Zares's door.

The mourncrow knocker was made of scuffed brass, but it still sent a belt-whip of emotion through Saffron. Spotted in the wild, mourncrow sightings meant one would dream of lost loved ones that evening. She had spent so many days after her parents' deaths stalking the unfamiliar streets of Atherin, trying to find a single damned bird, because seeing her mother and father in her dreams was better than not seeing them at all.

Levan raised a hand and tapped the brass knocker, and with a breathless yank, Saffron was mentally transported back to that fateful night in Lunes.

Ink-dark wood. A thin gasp.

Her mother laying down the goblet of honeywine with a trembling hand.

"Saff, you have to hide."

"But Mama. Who is it? I've never seen the door black before."

"Please," her father is saying, hoarse. "Please, Saffy."

Another knock. A towering fear in Saffron's heart.

"Saffron, we love you. We'll see you soon."

She was on the other side of the door now.

She was the knock the whole world feared.

There was the sound of footsteps approaching from inside the house, a brief pause, and then the sound of decidedly more hurried footsteps disappearing again.

"*Sen aperturan,*" Segal hissed at the door, and it blasted clean off its hinges.

As Levan raised his wand and crossed the threshold, there was a sickening squelch, and he became ensnared in a kind of invisible membrane. Pulling himself free, his face and hands—the only bare skin on his body—mottled like a bruise before erupting in a grotesque crosshatch of welts.

Levan grunted roughly, tapping his wand to the affected areas and muttering *ans mederan*. The welts healed in an instant, and he sprinted down the hallway as though nothing had deterred him.

Saff could barely disguise her astonishment.

He was as powerful a Healer as he was an Enchanter. And with a memory as vast and exhaustive as his, she had to assume he'd mastered brewing too. A mage with three classes was almost unheard of—Auria was the only other Saff had ever met.

Rasso clambered over the discarded pane of wood into the dank corridor and hared after their target.

"*Sen ammorten,*" came a female cry from a room at the end of the corridor.

A male grunt. A lupine growl.

Had Levan dodged the killing curse? Had Rasso?

Segal burst into the room behind him. Saff conjured a mattermantic spellshield and followed, creeping through the doorway with a cold, misty dread settling in her lungs. Her arm quavered beneath the effort of holding the enchantment—she was already depleted from the illusionwork on the boat—and she knew she'd have to exact some pain on herself if she wanted to ameliorate her remaining power.

The aubergine-colored kitchen had a solid ascenite island in the center—though the townhouse was narrow from the outside, it had been internally enchanted to create a capacious area. Saff stared in bemusement at the island. How had a lowly necromancer like Zares, who drank in an establishment like the Vant Sod, garnered enough wealth to afford such a mammoth block of ascenite? Did she sell her unlawful services to weeping widows desperate to revive their loved ones?

Zares ducked behind the farthest side of the island, while Levan crouched on the floor beside Rasso, wand outstretched. Tiny flames flickered in a set of sconces bolted to the walls, the fire white-hot and strange. Three velvines perched atop the oak rafters, watching the scene with utter disinterest. A total lack of loyalty to their necromancing mistress.

"*Sen effigias,*" Levan snarled—clearly trying to take Zares alive—but the spell chinked the side of the island instead of meeting its mark.

Silently, Levan gestured behind him for Segal to wrap one way around the island while he went the other.

Segal crept around the edge, but was ensnared by another invisible membrane. This one was harder to wrench free from—or maybe he just lacked Levan's raw strength—and Segal dropped his wand in an instant, making fraught gulping sounds.

Zares leapt to her feet.

She was around fifty or sixty, with long, straggly gray hair and feral blue eyes. Her olive skin was the faded leather of an old purse, and her cloak hung off her skeletal frame.

"*Az-ammorti,*" the necromancer bellowed—the killing curse used by Eqorans and the Mersini alike.

The forked spell struck Segal square in the chest.

He did not fall to the ground, but instead hung suspended in the membrane, like a dead spider dangling from a web.

"*Az-ammorti,*" Zares shouted once more, and this time the curse darted directly at Saff's face. She dropped to the ground, because although the spell could not kill her, she could not let Levan *know* it couldn't kill her.

"*Sen effigias,*" Levan snarled, aiming his wand up at Zares from his crouch on the floor.

Zares ducked back behind the island.

"*Az-iruani,*" she yelled, voice rasping and desperate, and a chandelier tore loose from the ceiling above Levan's head. He hurled his body on top of Rasso, taking the blow to his back with a guttural *ooft.*

Glass shattered everywhere, and Saff grabbed a shard that skittered to her feet. Dragging it across her forearm, she cringed as pain surged toward the cut, as blood welled in the peeled skin, her flesh parting like ripe fruit. She'd gone too deep, and magic could not heal it, but the final vestiges of power in her well deepened and brightened.

Zares had ducked behind the island once more, and Saffron didn't have a clear shot.

Time to lure her out.

"*Sen lusio dulipsan,*" she whispered, and the illusion sprang from her wand.

Guiding the illusion with her wand tip, Saffron sent her mirrored self around the island. Levan saw the illusion, and the briefest flash of panic flared on his face. Then he seemed to remember Saffron's skillset, and with a quick glance back at her, the curious fear melted away again.

Zares, however, was not so privy to Saffron's tricks.

She stuck her head out around the island, hissing, "*Az-ammorti.*"

The curse struck the illusion—and passed through its insubstantial chest.

Straight at Levan.

"*Sen praegelos,*" Saff bellowed, the illusion dropping, the forked lightning still firing.

Time froze solid.

All except for her . . .

. . . and Rasso.

28

. . .

The Necromancer's Brand

THE SILVER FALLOWWOLF DRAGGED ITS SLENDER BODY FROM beneath Levan's protective grip, fixing a pair of stark white eyes on Saffron. Emotion welled in the pale irises, as though the beast was seeing her for the first time.

Saff recalled what Aspar had said.

Praegelos *is an abomination. Too reminiscent of timeweaving.*

Did it remind Rasso of Lorissa, his long-lost mistress?

The fallowwolf approached her silkily, raising itself onto hind legs and resting a front paw on each of her collarbones. Another soulful gaze, and then a rough pink tongue licked her cheek.

Everything else remained frozen.

This moment was theirs alone.

And this time, unlike in the final assessment, the charm did not feel anywhere near as onerous to hold up. It was as though she had . . . support beams. A light, lifted feeling, as though she were carrying feathers instead of bricks. A gift from the fallowwolf—and from the giant block of ascenite at the center of the room.

But she knew it could not last forever, not when her well was already so low. She ruffled Rasso's sweet ears, lowered him back to the ground, and quickly crossed to Levan. His body was hunched atop a faded rug embroidered with a map of Mersina, the infamous isle of merchants, mercenaries, and mendicants. Saff grabbed one side of the rug and hauled it across the floor—not easy, given Levan's bulk—so that when time resumed, Levan would not be in the firing line of the killing curse.

Rasso watched intently, head cocked, eyes bright.

Trembling from the exertion of holding time still, she wrapped around the island to where Zares stood in a semi-crouch, face still twisted from the casting of the spell. She wanted to use *effigias,* to turn her to stone, but she wouldn't be able to cast another spell while holding time still.

She looked around for something, anything, she might use to tie Zares up. Her gaze landed on the ascenite island—and the dull gray manacles bolted to the surface, one at each corner. The material seemed to absorb light, absorb energy, its surface darkening and then lightening in slow fading sweeps.

Deminite.

How the necromancer restrained her victims.

Using brute strength instead of magic, Saff hauled Zares's gaunt body onto the counter, wrestling her stiff wrists into the top two corners, her dirt-streaked ankles into the bottom cuffs. She removed Zares's grubby walnut wand from her claw-fingered hand, because while it wouldn't be much use with deminite shackles, it was good Silvercloak practice to disarm captures.

The wound on Saffron's arm dripped scarlet all over the star-shaped tiles, but adrenaline numbed the sting. Later she'd have to stitch it up with an old-fashioned needle and thread.

She surveyed the room one last time. Segal was still suspended in the deadly membrane, entirely lifeless, but his demise didn't bring the sense of victory she thought it would. Because while the man who'd killed her parents was dead, the man who *really* killed her parents was not. And so she felt nothing. Not vindication, not revulsion. Not even a vague sense of justice. Just a dull ebb of pride that she had wrested back control of this situation, where two hulking Bloodmoons had failed.

She glanced at Rasso, who stood by her feet like a loyal servant, and nodded.

The *praegelos* charm dropped.

Levan crumpled to the ground. The killing curse splintered the back wall instead of his head. On the countertop, Zares let out a roar of frustration, confusion spreading over her face. She had been winning, and then, between one breath and the next, she wasn't.

There was a split second in which Levan stared up at Saff, gaze ripe with surprise and something like awe, before he climbed hastily to his feet, shaking off the shock. He strode over to where Zares was pinned helplessly to the island.

"Necromancer." His voice was silk-smooth, as though he hadn't almost been overpowered, as though the chandelier hadn't almost shattered his spine. As though his colleague did not hang suspended three feet to his left, all the life sucked clean from his lungs.

Zares spat at Levan's face, but he tilted his head and the globule missed its mark.

"We have someone we'd like you to bring back," he said blandly.

"I'd rather die," snarled Zares, her voice accented, grains of sand between each syllable.

Levan ran a palm over the smooth ascenite island. "So this is where it happens. Where you bring your victims to kill and revive, over and over again." He tapped the manacles. "Deminite. Very clever. Prevents any sort of struggle. Particularly if you have the misfortune of accidentally abducting a Compeller."

Compellers often didn't require wands to cast their magic. Only deminite could tamp down their raw power.

Zares glared at Levan hatefully. She thrashed her head back, and her skull cracked on the ascenite, but if she was trying to knock herself unconscious, she failed.

Levan pressed the tip of his wand to her exposed wrist. "We're going to exercise a little *persuasion* upon you, and then you're going to revive Segal."

Saff's stomach lurched.

Zares was about to lose her hands.

And Segal was about to become Risen.

"I cannot revive in manacles," snapped Zares. She stared straight up at the ceiling, cracked and crumbling where the chandelier had wrenched loose. "And if you give me back my wand, I'll kill you. You will not win, Bloodmoon."

"I always win, necromancer. *Sen perruntas.*"

The hand fell from her wrist, all the tension leaving its snarled fingers. Zares screamed like a beast at the abattoir. She thrashed her handless arm against the counter, magic already knitting the stump closed.

"Ans annetan."

The wound reopened with a bloody spurt, and the limp hand stitched itself back onto the stump.

Segal still dangled lifelessly from the ceiling, suspended in an invisible membrane like a moth preserved in amber.

This is a scene straight out of hell, Saff thought, grateful for the many years of hardening on the streetwatch. There was the echo of horror somewhere deep in her psyche, but not the full force of it, and she understood why the Academy mandated the five years for all candidates. She might not have emotionally survived situations like this otherwise.

Levan repeated the process three more times, until Zares whimpered like a child. Saffron could not reconcile how cold and callous he was, how at odds it was with the quiet, studious child she knew was at the heart of him.

"Will you cooperate now?" Levan asked, as though this was all very boring.

"*Za't,*" sobbed Zares.

Yes.

Levan unclasped the manacles one by one, then magically bent Zares at the waist so she sat bolt upright. Levan pointed his wand at one of the flickering sconces bolted to the wall.

"Don incendras."

The white-hot flame leapt toward his wand in a strand of brilliant light, and he guided it to Zares, scorching a black hole through her filthy brown tunic.

She screamed a wholly new scream.

Saffron stared in disbelief.

Not only was he a gifted Healer, not only was he the finest Enchanter she'd seen in years, not only could he transmute one object into another . . . he could also *wield.*

The elements were temperamental, disobedient, incredibly draining on the magical well. And he'd just manipulated fire as though it were nothing.

Four mage classes.

Unheard of.

How did he have so much *power*? The hoards of ascenite? Or something more?

Saffron thought of pleasure and of pain—the twin pillars that held up the magical world—and she wondered.

When the flame burned through the fabric to Zares's bare skin, Levan began to chant.

"Ver fidan, nis perruntas. Ver fidan, nis perruntas. Ver fidan, nis perruntas."

He was branding her, but it was different. Lyrian had repeated *ver fidan, nis morten,* which Saff had interpreted as a sort of conditional curse. If you betray, then you'll die. But *perruntas* was not death—it was a severance. If Zares tried to betray Levan or the Bloodmoons—attempted to shoot a killing curse at his chest instead of reviving Segal—her hand would cleave clean away from her wrist.

I always win, necromancer.

Saff's own dark crust pulsed in sympathy, the skin around it tight and stinging, its roots burrowing deep into her bones.

When the brand was done, Zares left panting raggedly, Levan handed back her wand. Saffron admired the necromancer for not passing out, feeling a strange kind of shame that she *had.*

A solitary tear darted down the necromancer's sallow cheek. She seemed to know, without really *knowing,* what the brand meant. She raised her wand to Segal.

"Hal-exaat."

The membrane holding Segal in the air evaporated, and his lifeless body slumped to the ground.

"Hal-avissa. Hal-avissa. Hal-avissa."

In that moment, Saff was six years old, quiet, afraid, watching her mother try to revive her father through a keyhole.

Her chest heaved with sadness, so fresh and brilliant it might have been yesterday. She remembered the moment her hand had gone to the doorknob almost of its own accord. A primal instinct to run toward the people she loved most in the world. To seek her parents' comfort in the worst moment of her existence.

How could something as pure and bright as a child's adoration bring everything crashing down?

How had it led her *here*?

Levan's mumbled apology from the previous night came back to her: *I know what it's like to feel like every choice you make is the wrong one. To understand that the world can come crumbling down with a single wrong move.*

She felt the words in her bones.

"Hal-avissa. Hal-avissa. Hal-avissa."

Slowly, slowly, and then all at once, Segal groaned back to life, smacking his lips as though awaking parched from a dreadful hangover.

The room hung suspended on a breath.

Saffron had never met a maligned Risen before. For most, the idea of the undead was confined to storybooks, but the defining moment of Saffron's life was watching as her mother attempted to raise her father. Joran had hung momentarily on the cusp, but both parents had been slain before he ever passed back through the veil between *there* and *here.*

Segal blearily surveyed the blood-splattered room, an uncanny blankness to his expression. There was a sort of milky, glassy quality to his gaze, its color faded and wan. Stooping to retrieve his wand from the floor, his movements were lurching, almost spasmodic. Unease slithered just beneath the surface of Saffron's skin.

Hauling himself upright with immense effort, Segal strode toward the doorway where Saffron still stood, his gait somehow both too slow and too fast, too heavy in the heel, a sort of disconnect between his upper and lower body.

When he spoke, his words were long and loping, as though his tongue wanted to swallow them.

"Move out of the way, Filth—"

Levan was on him in an instant, grabbing a fistful of collar and slamming his recently revived henchman against the wall. Segal was not a small man, and yet his feet were lifted off the floor by Levan's sheer raw strength. Still his gaze remained pale, almost unseeing, as the kingpin's son pushed against his throat.

"We'd both be dead right now if it wasn't for her." Levan's tone was dangerous, every vein in his neck bulging to the surface. "Do. Not. Call. Her. Filthcloak."

He dropped Segal inelegantly to the ground. Saff stepped out of the way, and Segal left the room, still uncannily blank, still *wrong*, somehow. He had not done anything out of character, anything to suggest his spirit had been fundamentally lost, yet he still sent a shiver down Saffron's spine.

Levan glared after him, then, instead of meeting Saff's questioning gaze, he rearranged his cloak and looked back at Zares, who glared loathingly through her tears of pain.

"Shall we?"

29

. . .

An Unexpected Invitation

BACK ON THE RIVERBOAT, LEVAN ASKED TO SPEAK TO SAFF in a small office at the stern of the ship.

Rasso followed at her heels. The fallowwolf hadn't left her side since the *praegelos* charm, and kept nuzzling his face against her thigh. On the gondola, he'd curled up in her lap, and Levan had eyed them jealously when he thought Saff wasn't looking.

The beast's newfound affection filled Saffron with an unexpected warmth—there was something primal, comforting, about a soft body pressed against your own—but also a kind of latent unease. This was Lorissa Celadon's pet, and now he doted on *her.* Any connection to the dead queenpin felt damning, somehow. It was the same way she'd felt upon learning of Lyrian's knack for illusions. She did not appreciate the reminders that the Bloodmoon founders were people, just like her.

The riverboat office very clearly belonged to Levan. There were books and plants and little dragon statuettes everywhere, as well as a large sepia map of Ascenfall hanging on the wall. Gold drawing pins were pressed into a seemingly sporadic selection of locations: the southern tip of Mersina, a valley in Laudon, the craggy heart of Nomaden. Shishai and Soral and Suva, even a speck-sized island in the Ashen Narrows.

Levan stood and faced the map, his back to Saffron, hands balled up at his sides. Saffron's own were clasped behind her back—she'd stanched the bleeding of her forearm with a torn strip of her cloak, but she didn't want Levan to spot the dark tide marks of dried maroon on her sleeve. He'd only offer to heal her, and she could not let him know that she was immune to such things.

"Thank you," he said, soft and measured, and she didn't have to ask for what.

The impish idiocy she'd inherited from her father suggested that she goad him, that she mock the way he'd needed a knight in shining cloak, but she suppressed the urge, learning from past mistakes. She had the distinct sense that this conversation could be an important one in her relationship with Levan—in getting him to open up, in getting him to trust her. Taking the almighty piss would not help matters.

"That charm you used," he said quietly. "*Praegelos*? Where did you learn it?"

"My mother," Saff said carefully.

"And when she cast it, she was able to continue roaming through space even when time itself was frozen?"

Ah. The detail Aspar had snagged upon.

Saffron had concluded that this curious quirk was a consequence of her magical immunity—when enchanted, even the stalwart forces of time and space did not impact her the way they ought to—yet this too must remain a secret from the Bloodmoons. Saffron was weaving a complicated web for herself, and she had to make sure she never became trapped by it.

"Yes. My mother used *praegelos* to buy herself time with trauma patients." The lie came easily, confidently. "To treat them before their condition worsened."

His hand curled and uncurled at his hip. "Can you teach me?"

Saints. It wouldn't work the same for Levan. It would only freeze time; he wouldn't be able to move through it.

"What is there to teach?" Saff muttered evasively. "You say the words and time stops."

"You know as well as I do there's more to casting than that. Magic is directional, but time is everywhere. Where do you aim your wand?"

Saffron said nothing; almost always the safest choice.

"You don't want to teach me," Levan said mildly, still with his back to her. "You think I'll use it against you."

Instead of answering directly, Saff did what she did best: rerouted.

"My old captain had a theory," she started, "that the Bloodmoons had developed a spell or device to siphon pain's potency away from the victim. So that you could inflict torture and reap the benefit for yourself, instead of giving the victim a potentially lifesaving power boost. But I've never seen you use such a thing, and Zares seemed like the perfect opportunity."

Levan shrugged, but it was careful, stiff. "Pain is not something I've ever found myself to be lacking."

A strange thing to say. She'd never seen him especially injured, and earlier he'd healed those ghastly welts with little to no effort.

"Are you saying such a device or spell does exist, and you choose not to use it?"

He used her own trick against her, dodging the question.

"Why *did* you save me?" Levan's words were precise, puncturing. "From Zares's curse. We've already established that inaction does not trigger the brand. You could've let me die, and no ill would have befallen you. So why didn't you?"

Saff found that she did not have a good answer, and so once again she did not offer one.

Levan finally swiveled on his heel, and Saff was surprised by the expression on his face. He almost looked angry. "Why did you save me, Silver?"

"I don't know," she said, and it was the truth.

Because it wasn't just that the mission required her to take him alive. It was something innate, the same instincts that drove her to kill Vogolan before the thought had even fully formed. And it troubled her, that these instincts had now overridden her careful strategizing not once but twice.

Levan tapped out the familiar rhythm on his knuckles. "After what you said before, that I wasn't human, I—"

"I didn't say that," she snapped. "I said the exact opposite, in fact.

That I wanted to remind myself that you *are* human. A reminder means to reiterate something already known."

Although after what she'd seen him do to Zares, she wasn't quite so sure. His ability to compartmentalize cruelty was . . . monstrous. And yet didn't she do the exact same thing, albeit for different reasons?

Levan sighed. "You're rather pedantic."

"And you're rather belligerent."

He shook his head, hair falling around his face in dark brown waves. "Why did you save me?" he asked again, and this time it was soft, almost pleading. She got the sense that he badly needed to understand this.

And yet Saffron herself did not understand. Not one bit.

Saff gazed over Levan's shoulder at the map of the continent, lost in thought. "You know in the climax of *Lost Dragonborn,* when Aymar saves the villainous wyvern who tried to kill him at the Battle of Tearfall? And Baudry asks Aymar why, and he can't answer, but deep in his chest he feels this kind of golden strand of light. An inherent goodness. It seems oversimplistic to say he did it because it was right, but it's true. He did it because it was right. Same with saving you. With stopping to help the lox addict in Atherin. With sneaking out to end Tenea's suffering. These things are just . . . ingrained in me. From my parents, I think. They were good to their bones."

Levan looked as though he was turning this over in his mind, like tilling a garden before letting the idea plant its seed. "So how do you reconcile that with what you did to Neatras? To Kasan?"

Saff's insides clenched. "I don't. Life is rarely that simple."

Levan perched on the edge of the desk, laying down his wand and instead picking up a dragon statuette. It was forest green with bronzed ridges. "Who was your favorite character in *Lost Dragon*—"

"Baudry Abard," Saff said confidently. This conversation was safe ground. It was not severed hands and bodies hanging like moths preserved in amber.

"The wise old mentor." Levan smiled, and Saffron was astonished to see he had dimples. It was almost comically incongruous with the man she knew. "Why do you think I've warmed so much to Miret over the years?"

"He does feel like a Baudry figure." Saff paused before adding, "Did you know that Erling Tandall is at the Vallish Arts Festival next weekend?"

He looked up at her, surprised. "I thought Tandall didn't do public events anymore. I heard he has the fading disease."

"The sign outside Torquil's Tomes professed rather proudly that he'd be there."

Something passed over Levan's stubbled face. "Do you want to . . . never mind."

Saff's chest twinged. "Do I want to what?"

"Go with me." He rubbed the back of his neck with his palm, looking bashful, of all things. "To the festival. On the night I enchanted your necklace, your uncle mentioned that you liked . . . actually, never mind. Forget it. Please. If I could timeweave, I would undo these last few seconds."

Was he . . . *babbling*?

In the tightly wound spool that was his self-control, there emerged the very tip of a loose thread, begging to be pulled.

The realization exhilarated Saff in more ways than one.

On a Silvercloak level, the invitation felt like the first step toward uncovering his true motive. It felt like something grand and inevitable, a cart rattling along the predetermined tracks of the prophecy. A sense of fate rushing to meet her.

And on a human level . . . it was a fundamentally compelling thing, to relate to someone, to see your passions and your flaws reflected in them. Not just *Lost Dragonborn,* but that traumatized quietude, that stubborn streak, that questionable moral code, that unfaltering determination in pursuit of a goal. A tendency to bury feelings deep, deep down. A kind of jaded, cynical worldview, born from both childhood tragedy and the kinds of lives they led. She had never met someone whose emotional contours cleaved so closely to her own.

Her uncles—so wildly different from each other—had always told her that opposites attract.

So why did her similarities with Levan feel so intimate?

Enough, she scolded herself. *Enough of the murky emotions. What's the right strategic play here?*

It was obvious. She should go with him to the festival, if only to lower his defenses enough to slip behind them.

Saffron made a show of considering the proposal: a notched frown, a finger tapping her bottom lip. "Two conditions."

Levan looked up, surprised. "Which are?"

"Number one, we don't wear scarlet cloaks. I don't want to spoil it for all the other fans. They'll run in the opposite direction if they see us."

"Fine. Number two?"

"You answer one question truthfully."

He smirked. "I thought you'd gotten all the invasive questions out of your system when I was addled with truth elixir." Levan studied her with interest, the same way she imagined him searching for an obscure word's meaning in the *Lost Dragonborn* glossary. "But go ahead."

Saffron had many to choose from.

Why do you need a necromancer?

Who did you love and lose?

How did your mother die?

What does your father *want*?

But she found that none of these were what needled at her most. What needled at her most was *him.* How he could be so ruthless, so cruel, without breaking a sweat. Did it come from his own whims and desires, or from the brand? Was Lyrian pulling the puppet strings? Did Levan hunger for violence, or was he fulfilling a fate dealt to him at birth?

Eventually, she settled on, "Do you want to be a Bloodmoon? Do you truly want this life? Or are you only here because of the brand?"

He gave her a pointed, displeased look. "That's three questions."

Saff snorted. "And *I'm* pedantic?"

"We both are. It's why we get along."

"Alright, let me rephrase. Do you have a choice but to be a Bloodmoon?"

His expression darkened. "That's not something I often think about."

Saff used her tried-and-tested technique: she said nothing, in the hopes he would fill the silence.

"No, I suppose I don't have a choice," he said finally. "But even if I did, I would still choose my family."

Another notch in the similarity column.

Everything Saff had ever done, good or bad or downright heinous, had been for hers.

The riverboat canted suddenly over a current, and she threw out an arm to steady herself. She felt a little faint then, and leaned back against the wall for support, her vision vignetting at the edges. Now that the adrenaline of the encounter with the necromancer had faded, the effects of her overcasting hit her at full force. A light tremble started at her fingertips and spread to her shoulders. She pressed her eyes shut, trying to right herself.

"Are you alright?" Levan asked, and it was far less wooden than the first time he'd asked her that, hours after she'd been branded. A soft emphasis on the final syllable.

"Just depleted. I cast too much. I'll have to refill once we're back."

He sighed. "Me too."

There was a strangely loaded pause, in which they considered what each other might do in the pursuit of pleasure. Her breath hitched slightly as their gazes met, and there was a sort of crackle, a spark, a scintilla of *something* that Saffron did not trust. His cerulean eyes, no longer so flat and lifeless, raked over her halo of silver-blond curls, down to the place where they ended at her waist.

For a few beats, the truth of who and what they were fell away. A fading mist, a dropped drawbridge, the vines around their ankles melting into the earth.

In that moment, they were just two mages in need of power.

Feed me, said the empty well inside her, *feed me now, because it will feel so good.*

She tried to shake away the troubling instinct, but once she finally allowed herself to imagine what she and Levan could do in the name of pleasure, she had immense trouble unimagining it.

Levan clearly waged the same internal war—and lost.

And she sensed that he did not often lose the battle against his own mind.

He pushed off the desk and crossed the room to where she stood. Breath failed her. He was so *close*. She felt his body's heat, smelled the leather of his belt and the lemon-mint of his soap. She remembered the sight of him rebuckling his belt over his hard, pale stomach after his dalliance with Harrow, and everything in her tightened.

Slowly, so slowly, he tucked a stray curl behind her ear, his touch so gentle it sent a shiver down her spine, then cupped her jaw in both hands. Pleasure trickled into her well, down her spine, deep into her belly, so much more powerful than a mere stroke along the cheekbone should be, and with it came a fresh pouring of magic.

He looked at her as though she had saved him, which she had, and as though she would be the death of him, which she would.

"Thank you," he said again, and there was a simplicity, a purity to the words.

"For saving your life?" she murmured, her voice strangled, uncertain, and she was thinking about the vast complexity of him, but also about what it might feel like if she gave into this temptation.

"For reminding me I'm human."

His cerulean eyes *glittered.* For a long, taut moment, she thought he was going to kiss her. They both needed pleasure, after all, and kissing was a convenient place to find it.

Her heart stilled in her chest.

Was this the prophesied moment? Her wand was in her hand, and because of the way his body was pressed against hers, it could very well be the moment she foresaw with that relic wand.

No. It couldn't be. She'd just saved his life.

Why would she murder him less than an hour later?

Saints. Those eyes looked brand-new. As though she was seeing an intimate, forbidden part of him.

She found herself caught up in the intensity of his gaze, surprised by the stirring of emotion in her chest. Her hand went absently to the pendant resting on her clavicle. Everything was muddled and confused, as though someone had turned her upside down and shaken her like a snowglobe.

She should not feel what she was feeling.

She should not find him so beautiful.

She should not long to grasp the invisible string that bound them together and pull with all her might.

The moment sprawled out a beat too long, and Levan misread the frantic parsing flicker of her eyes as fear, dropping his feather grip on her chin. Her skin felt cold with the absence of his hands, and there was an unbearable tingling speckled over the surface of her skin. Her ridiculous animal body urged her forward, urged her to lace her fingers through his hair, to—

Stop, she snarled at herself, and she pulled back at the last moment.

Disappointment played out over Levan's face—and too in her own stomach.

He gave her one final look of pained gratitude and left the room.

Saffron felt dizzy, disoriented, intoxicated. A little like she'd felt after inadvertently taking lox. Bright and new.

But the swelling behind her ribs was bittersweet. According to the ledger she'd found that morning, the lox shipment was happening several days before the festival. Either Levan would be in Duncarzus by then, or he'd know beyond all doubt that she was leaking information to the Silvercloaks and eviscerate her accordingly.

No matter what happened, they would not be meeting Erling Tandall together.

Maybe in another world, another timeline. But not this one.

She had to pull herself together.

When she was sure Levan was gone, she brought her wand tip to her mouth, hands shaking from overcasting and overfeeling.

"Et vocos, Elodora Aspar."

A short pause, then her captain's crisp voice. "Aspar."

"Dragontail."

The word was an enchantment, a curse, a promise, a death sentence.

Another pause. A shuffling sound. "Rising."

They could speak.

"The next lox shipment arrives on Elming, around darknight," Saffron whispered, only just loud enough for Aspar to hear. Her heart thundered against her rib cage. "At the docks on Sun Bank."

Aspar inhaled sharply, and when she spoke again, it was tinged with something like respect.

"We'll be there."

PART FOUR

—

TRAITOR

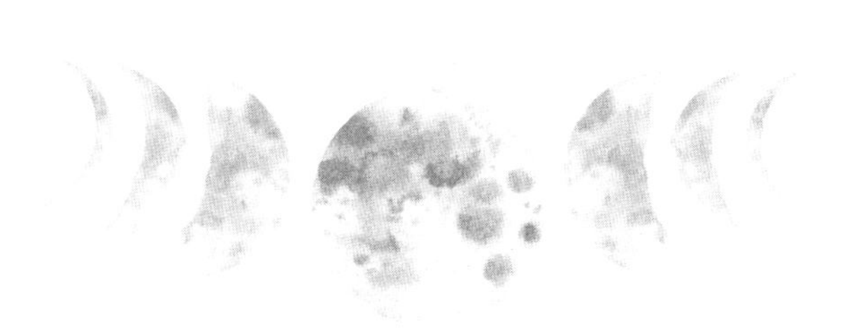

30

. . .

Fate's Bounty

THE DAY OF THE RAID CAME AT ONCE TOO SLOW AND TOO FAST.

Levan spent the most of his time after returning from Port Ouran in Nalezen Zares's cell, subjecting the necromancer to Saints knew what, but he was adamant that he didn't want Saffron to be alone and unguarded. Nor, for some reason, did he want her to witness what he was doing to Zares. Perhaps he wanted to preserve the sanctity of the charged moments they had shared on the boat, or perhaps he simply performed better without an audience.

He also seemed newly concerned that she was not safe in the mansion—whether because of Segal's sinister new status as a Risen, or because of the kingpin's fierce and unpredictable anger over Vogolan's death, Saffron was not sure. Regardless, Levan conjured a series of protective wards around her bedroom, the bath chambers, and the library, so that Saffron might rest and soak and read in peace. She was free to come and go through the wards as she pleased, he was quick to explain, but if she needed somewhere to feel at ease, she had it.

At first her pride had bucked indignantly. She was a Silvercloak, trained in the art of self-defense. She was built for this—she did not need his wards.

Yet something about the act warmed her. Something had shifted in him since that first night in the alley. It wasn't just that he trusted her, now that she'd saved his life—it was also that he *cared.*

Saffron was getting under his skin. That much was good.

It was not so good that he was beginning to get under hers.

They were moving toward the prophecy, that much was certain. Their cart rattled merrily, dangerously, along predetermined tracks. And yet Saffron was grappling with it more than she ought to be. She found herself wishing the cart would slow down, so that she'd have more time to peel back Levan's layers, to find the truth at the very core of him.

For the mission, she told herself.

Liar, said her heart.

She spent her remaining time before the raid in Miret's library, reading everything she could find on necromancy—as though absorbing every single word of theory would somehow unlock the truth of who Levan was planning to bring back. She was angry with herself for asking him such a woolly question back on the boat. Why had it felt, in the moment, more important to understand his psychology than his goals? In any case, his answer had given her nothing, and she had no idea when he'd next let down his guard.

Over those quiet days, she also devoted a substantial amount of time to replenishing her well in case the raid went south. She devoured a frankly irresponsible quantity of pastries and hot cocoa, relishing in the feeling of her body's edges softening once more. She took rose-scented baths surrounded by riotous greenery, raked her gaze over every painting and mural she could find in the mansion. In bed, and in the baths, and sometimes even in the library, her hand found the peak of her pleasure—the pleasure that bloomed beneath the memory of Nissa's forked tongue, and the thought of Levan's firm stomach above his leather belt—and coaxed it to new heights.

She longed to pursue said pleasure with another body, another mage—not just to fill her well, not just to feel *good,* but to feel in control, to wield some kind of power in a world where she often held none. And yet she couldn't bring herself to frequent a pleasurehouse, because what if her lover became another pawn in the Bloodmoons' game? What if proximity to her was becoming more and more fatal?

She couldn't put another life at risk, and so her own hand would have to suffice.

The gamehouse's thrills called to her like a siren, but she refused to answer. She knew lox was a false god to pray to. She knew that such pleasure was not real or lasting, that it would be disastrous to spend another week feverish and dizzy from its aftereffects. And she did not trust herself to play polderdash without caving to the lure of the black-cherry sours.

Still, the reckless side of her—the side that Levan lured to the surface—craved the release of gambling. It didn't make logical sense, that someone as patient and calculating as her could want such a thing, but if her time on the streetwatch had taught her anything, it was that people were inherently contradictory. The killer was a great mother. The arsonist did volunteer work. The innocent victim was a compulsive liar.

The kingpin's indomitable son was a lox addict.

Saff could not stop thinking about how Harrow had found Levan near ruin from an overdose. It frightened her, that someone so strong, so in control of himself, could fall victim to it.

What hope did the rest of the city have?

It was a steadying, validating thought. After this raid, she would be celebrated for saving innocents—not just from the Bloodmoons, but from the dark, addictive claws of loxlure.

Would tonight be the night the prophecy finally came to pass?

It had to be. Because if all went well, this was the last time Levan would ever be free again, the last time either of them would ever wear their scarlet cloaks. Which meant she was mere hours away from kissing him—and killing him.

How wrong would all of this have to go for her to kill him?

Surely taking him alive was the best way.

Surely.

On Elming evening, Saff was lying on her bed, struggling to concentrate on a *Lost Dragonborn* spinoff, when there came a knock on her door.

Levan stood on the other side, his jaw shadowed with stubble, his eyes tired and more lined than usual. At the sight of him, something dipped in Saff's stomach. She remembered the moment he'd tucked her hair behind her ear, ran his finger along her jaw, looked at her with life in his eyes for the first time since she'd met him. The feeling in her belly was akin to hunger, to nerves, but the good kind of both of those things. A slight rumbling as you're lifting a pastry to your lips.

But she had to remind herself who and what they both were.

What she was about to do.

"Are you ready to go?" he asked, oblivious to her wandering thoughts.

"Where?" she asked, though of course she already knew.

"The docks." He shifted, and Saff caught a scent of the potent clove-anise tea she'd found in his desk drawer.

"More needless torture?"

"A shipment." She couldn't parse his tone. It wasn't *flat,* exactly, but it was stilted, jaded. "Need to make sure the operation doesn't spring any more leaks. None of us want a repeat of Kasan."

Saff nodded. "You look tired."

He shrugged. "I ran ten miles this afternoon, then did combat training with Miret. He's a lithe old bastard." He rubbed at his shoulder, as though a bruise was forming there. "We meet at the same time every day. Keeps us both sharp."

The same time every day. Those compulsions might not be as potent as they once were—unless he kept his most obsessive rituals to himself—but he still made sure never to stray from his strict routine.

She raised her brow. "Why do you need combat training? Can't you just sever all your enemy's extremities?"

"You never know when you'll be caught without your wand."

Saff snorted. "You sound like my old commanding officer. Ma'am, yes, ma'am."

Judging by the hard look on his face, the joke did not land.

She pulled her cloak tightly around herself. It was starting to smell like her, and that was perturbing. She didn't want it to become an extension of herself. She wanted it to be an ill-fitting impostor cloak.

"So is that all you do in the Bloodmoons?" she asked, knowing this could be her last opportunity to gather intel. "Train and brood?"

"No, I oversee a lot of operations. The gamehouses, recruitment, discipline." The latter sent a shiver down Saffron's spine. "But finding a necromancer has been my priority for a while."

She stuffed her feet into her leather boots. "I note you don't object to the accusation that you brood."

The corner of his lips quirked at last. "I may be prone to such things."

She followed Levan from the room, pulse uneven despite her best efforts to keep it in check.

Everything came down to tonight.

"How's it going with Zares?" she asked, as they descended the ascenite staircase and strode toward the warded tunnels. The vast chandelier cast fractal shards of broken light all over the black marble atrium, and there was the distant sound of piano music playing in the minor key.

"Not well. She's resisting my usual tricks. Her hands have spent more time off than on."

As they slipped into the warded tunnels, Levan's gaze drifted to the timeweaving carvings, a misty expression on his face.

"Then I suppose you need a Compeller," Saff suggested.

"We brought one in, but it didn't work. The sheer force of will, the innate desire, has to come from her. Compelling alone isn't powerful enough to wake the dead." There was a sort of reverence to his tone when he talked about magic, similar to Auria's fascination with the intricacies of it, but with a darker underpinning. As though Levan loved and feared it in equal measure.

But that wasn't what Saff's brain snagged on. "You have a Compeller working in the Bloodmoons?"

"They're not in a scarlet cloak, but they're in our back pocket."

"Like Harrow."

"Are you making a joke about back pockets? I thought you were above crude innuendo."

Saffron couldn't help the spluttering laughter. "Certainly not. I practically invented it."

Levan looked over at her with a kind of bemused smirk. "You're different than how I thought you would be. Different than the night we first met."

"It's hard to be your true self when killing curses are being fired at you. Although it would be very Killoran of me for my final words to be a *vock* joke."

A thought darted behind his eyes, and the subtle mirth on his face withered and died. He fixed his gaze straight ahead once more, resuming his guarded facade. "I've already warned Segal, but don't mention anything about Zares to my father. He doesn't know we've brought her in already. He can be overzealous, and I don't want him to end up killing her before she can do what she needs to do."

"What's my silence worth to you?"

A careful beat, another tentative smile. "Marriosan's gelato before we meet Erling Tandall?"

"Deal," Saffron said, but the fleeting joy soured almost instantly.

Papa Marriosan was dead. The shop would be closed in mourning. Levan obviously didn't know what Vogolan had done hours before his death.

Besides—if everything went according to plan, Levan would end this night in deminite shackles.

Why did the thought leave her feeling so . . . *sad*?

Perhaps it was because she saw so much of herself in him. He was a killer, a torturer, yes. But the evil didn't seem core-deep to Saff—not in the way Vogolan was cruel for cruelty's sake. It was a product of his environment, his twisted upbringing. The result of what she suspected was a crude and terrible brand on his chest.

No, I suppose I don't have a choice.

Levan could have been something else entirely. His mind was brilliant, his power more potent than anyone she'd ever met. What could he have done with his life instead? That was what felt sad. The waste of it all.

But it wasn't the only sad thing. There was the thought of him squirming beneath a hot poker, branded at the hand of a person he should have been able to trust. Had that happened before or after the years of grief-induced compulsions? Before or after he had found solace in the story of Aymar and Baudry?

She was leading him to his shackled fate, and she hated that she was.

"Levan," she whispered, stopping abruptly. Her hand went to the wooden pendant around her neck.

"Yes?" He halted a few footsteps ahead, swinging to face her.

They looked at each other then. Truly looked. It started as a subtle frown, a beat of confusion, and then melted into something richer, something simmering and ephemeral.

All the desire Saffron had suppressed since first meeting him rose to the surface of her skin, and she drank in all the beautiful lines of him. All the muscles in her lower belly tightened, the blood in her veins quickening and pulsing, and something warm cracked open in her chest.

The cresting lust was followed by a surge of existential recklessness, a feeling of *we might be walking to our deaths,* the sudden and undeniable realization that there was no sense in fighting this *thing* between them, because it was always fated to happen, and who was she to deny fate its bounty?

She closed the space between them, mirroring what he had done to her, running her hands through the soft hair at his temples, tracing a finger along his jaw. Cupping his chin, brushing her lips tenderly against his, like satin against a bare thigh, like a breeze caressing the blossom trees, like a soft shiver and a sharp jolt all at once.

He pulled away for the briefest of seconds, eyes alight, so excruciatingly hopeful.

Saffron's lungs inflated like wings.

And then their lips met again, firmer now, a desperation to it. Their tongues touched tentatively, and it felt so intimate, so vulnerable. He tasted of clove tea and warm skin, and as she pressed her body against his, as she felt the warm, hard planes of him, he sighed into her.

The sound tugged at her deep below the navel, like a knot of hunger.

It was like no kiss she had ever experienced, all of reality falling away behind them.

The crackle, the spark, the scintilla, a *rightness,* a slotting together of two fated pieces, two equals, two halves of one whole.

Kissing him was a . . . test, of sorts. She knew it was destined to happen eventually, and she wanted to see if she'd feel the urge to dig her wand into his stomach and cast a killing spell, to see if they were nearing their awful, inevitable end.

But all she felt was *him.*

His palm at the small of her back, pushing her even more firmly into him, both cold and warm and sharp and sweet and rich, euphoria unspooling in her heart. She wanted *more,* all of him, everywhere. His teeth grazed her lower lip and—

Wrong, her brain hissed, and filled with self-loathing. *This is wrong, he's a murderer, he's a torturer, he's—*

—the man you're fated to kill.

So why did kissing him feel so Saints-damned *good*?

But she couldn't dishonor her parents' memories like this. She pictured herself at six years old, grumpily playing Flight of the Raven with a twinkle-eyed father and honeywine-scented mother who adored the bones of her, and then she pictured herself watching through a keyhole as two scarlet cloaks slayed them where they stood, and she knew that she could not do this. To herself, or to them.

She tore herself away, shaking her head.

Rejection, or something similar, passed over Levan's face as she withdrew. As though he knew exactly what was going through her head. As though he was picturing the very same scenes. Remorse pressed his lips together in a sad, straight line, and she could almost hear his heart sink in his chest.

The silence between them was endless and aching.

"We have to go," he muttered eventually, running a hand through his hair, not meeting her eye.

And then they were walking again, leading each other to mutual ruin, neither of them breathing in quite the same way they had before.

31

...

Kingpin's Instinct

THEY MET LYRIAN IN A NARROW ALLEY, SCARLET CLOAK PINNED at his throat, garnet wand gripped tightly in his palm. With him was a milky-eyed Segal and a mage Saff didn't recognize.

"Evening," said Lyrian, gesturing to the unfamiliar mage. "This is Aviruna Castian, the strongest Wielder I've ever known." A pointed look at Levan, who did not react to the words. "She'll be accompanying us this evening, should we need to bend the river to our will."

Aviruna was a coltish woman with short white-blond hair sticking up in clumsy tufts, pale skin with acne scarring, and earthen brown eyes lined with thick black kohl. Three stars were tattooed below each waterline. Crow's-feet deepened at the corners; she looked to be in her forties.

"Evening," she said, her expression a little glazed, a little imprecise, as though she had recently slammed back a blackcherry sour. Sure enough, her lips were stained dark, and her limbs hung too loose from her body. She did not ask Saffron's name, and nobody introduced her.

They set off for the docks, and it felt like walking to the gallows.

It was around half an hour to darknight, and Atherin was flecked with rain so fine it blurred the streetlamps, a silvery mist drifting down the streets in thin whorls. Aviruna waved her wand and muttered a few incantations, and the drizzle began to flow around them instead of onto them. Saffron's hair stayed dry, her cloak warm against the brisk night air. This was how it felt to be a Bloodmoon in general—everyone, everything, even the elements, gave you a wide berth. Fear was a powerful repellent, and its wielders could move through the world with ease.

Still, Saffron thought it was a risky endeavor to move so many valuable players at once. What would happen if Lyrian and Levan both perished on this routine mission? Perhaps they had grown complacent in recent years, assuming nobody would try to take on a band of Bloodmoons, assuming the Silvercloaks were forced to keep a safe distance, thanks to the corrupt Grand Arbiter.

While they walked, Saffron was painfully aware of Levan's every movement, his every breath. Her lips still tingled with the imprint of his kiss, and her tongue still tasted the clove tea. She loathed herself for losing control, for falling into the arms of everything she hated. Although such was the nature of dangerous things: gambling, loxlure, whiteroot, flamebrandy. The wrongness was the entirety of the appeal.

Yet, part of her wished the circumstances were different. That they had met at university and bonded over their scholarship, their shared grief, their love of *Lost Dragonborn.* That his potent magic could be something fierce and bright, not sinister and terrifying.

But fate was rarely so kind. Saffron knew that better than anyone.

As they neared the quay, Saffron spotted several familiar faces in plain cloaks. Detectives Alcabal and Jebat sat on a marble bench, laughing uproariously and passing a flask between them, pretending to be drunk as dormice. Detectives Qubayan, Dallar, and Ronnow stood on various street corners, checking their pocketwatches and reading pulp magazines as though waiting for a friend to arrive.

Too many, Saff thought. *They've sent too many. It's too obvious.*

But Levan wasn't looking at the undercover Silvercloaks. He was looking at *her.* Their eyes met, and something sharp and bright and complex passed between them.

He was about to suffer so immensely at her hands.

The cluster of Bloodmoons reached the quay and strolled along the paved dock. The Wielder crew who'd worked the Port Ouran mission sat with their legs dangling over the edge, passing a poorly rolled achullah between them.

Aspar's familiar, Bones, perched atop a mooring bollard, innocently licking her paw.

The sight of the cat brought it home.

This was finally happening.

"Something doesn't feel right," muttered Lyrian, looking around with an air of paranoia.

Levan's gaze snapped to his father. "What do you mean?"

Behind him, Bones stopped licking her paw.

"I thought the same," Castian said, pursing her lips. "I ran dozens of these shipments with Vogolan and something just feels . . . different."

"Different how?" Levan's tone was urgent, *knowing,* as though he'd felt the same himself but couldn't quite put his finger on why.

The drizzle still fell around them, the sound muffled by the repelling enchantment.

Castian tapped her wand to her lip, more sober than she was a few moments ago. "More people around than usual. The docks are usually deserted at this time of night."

She pointed to two figures leaning against a large shipping container, muttering in low voices. Saff's stomach twisted. Detectives Alirrol and Fevilan were not doing a particularly good job of feigning nonchalance. Their bodies were tightly drawn, their gazes darting.

Levan glared at the two interlopers, then muttered, "Excuse me."

He strode off in the opposite direction.

"Where are you—Levan?" Lyrian snarled.

But the moment Levan hit the shadows, he melted into the darkness.

Saff stared after him, bowels in turmoil.

What had he just figured out? What was he going to do?

"Ten minutes until the boat docks," said Lyrian crisply, the edges of his voice even harder since Vogolan's death. "Segal, search the quay." He dug a vial of clear liquid from his cloak pocket. "One of Vogolan's last fading tinctures. Stick to the shadows. Listen in to conversations. If anything feels truly wrong, we scarper."

Segal drank the tincture, and his contours faded to a vague smudge. True invisibility was incredibly difficult to brew, but in the inky night, this was close enough. He slunk away in the direction they came.

As they waited for the boat to arrive, Lyrian and Aviruna muttered in low voices. Saff was too jittery to pick up most of it, but they seemed to be discussing the Whitewings. Saff knew she should be concentrating on what might be the final piece of intel she gleaned from this operation, but her mind corkscrewed violently over where exactly Levan had disappeared to.

With a brain as ruthlessly efficient as his, was there a chance he'd figured everything out? The thought choked all the breath from her lungs.

Several agonizing minutes later, Levan reappeared, slightly out of breath. His crimson cloak was rumpled, and he hastily rearranged it. Saff stared inquiringly at him, but he actively averted his gaze.

Soon, a well-lit trader boat glided against the fenders on the edge of the dock, its Bloodmoon banderole hanging sodden and limp. A mage stood on the upper deck, manipulating the mooring ropes with her wand so that they looped in midair and tossed themselves over the bollards.

Bones made no effort to move, even when a rope almost lassoed her throat, even when the mage on the boat hissed at her.

"Let's go," muttered Lyrian, starting toward the vessel.

"We shouldn't board the boat," Levan said, gaze raking over the docks. "Castian says something doesn't feel right. We should stand back. Watch but not interfere."

Lyrian glared at his son, as though he'd suggested razing the entire city of Kylgard. "We need to oversee the offloading of every single pallet. Make sure none of these *vocks* ever steal from us again."

As the kingpin turned back to the vessel, Levan grabbed his arm to stop him, and Lyrian shot him a look so vitriolic it took Saff by surprise.

"You're not the kingpin, son. I am." Lyrian's voice was a low, malicious hiss, so far from its usual marble coolness. "Remember yourself."

Levan dropped his grip, cheeks pinkening with anger.

"Where did you go?" Saff whispered to Levan as they reluctantly followed Lyrian and Castian to the gangway.

Levan fixed her with a hard stare that made her feel like he knew everything. A stare that filled her with a cold, viscous dread.

Castian's attention had sharpened, and Segal was searching the perimeter for disturbances. Levan was riled, rattled, extremely alert. Lyrian was a coiled snake ready to pounce. The very air was charged with tension so palpable it could be sliced with a blade.

This wasn't how it was supposed to go. They weren't supposed to suspect a thing. Catching them off-guard was the best way to take them alive.

Yet Saffron was powerless to do anything but board the boat.

The cargo hold was in the hull of the vessel, and Lyrian stood vigil on the deck above, staring down at the pallets as they were unloaded. He interlaced his fingers and rested his forearms on the wrought-iron railings.

Castian stalked the deck, checking the small compartments beneath the cushioned seating benches as though traitors lurked in every nook and cranny. Crew workers scurried below, levitating and maneuvering cargo pallets with enchantments so that they floated into an open shipping container a few hundred yards away.

Levan stood at the prow of the boat, staring upriver. He was rigid as a soldier, and Saffron found herself afraid to approach him, afraid to provoke a premature confrontation.

A half-faded figure on the docks sprinted back toward the vessel, waving one arm in the air, footsteps hollow and loud as they thumped across the forecourt.

Segal, wordlessly trying to tell them something, blank eyes pinned wide and white.

But before he reached the boat, three mages in pale green cloaks materialized next to Bones's perch on the bollard. Segal ducked behind a stack of crates at the last minute, blending into the shadows as best he could.

How did the green cloaks get there? Invisibility tincture? It certainly couldn't have been *portari.*

In any case, Saffron didn't recognize them—they were not Silvercloaks.

"Good evening, folks," said a tall mage with neat strawberry-blond hair. "Mind if we take a look inside your hold?"

Understanding struck Saff.

Customs officers.

They had sent *customs officers* into this death trap of a situation. A sneaky bid to work around the warrant situation. The Grand Arbiter might not have granted one for the Silvercloaks, but customs officers were well within their rights to perform randomized checks on trader boats.

Realistically, there was no way the Bloodmoons would let a routine search happen, and the moment they became hostile, the moment things escalated, the customs crew could legally call for reinforcements.

Aspar was clever. Ruthless, but clever.

Lyrian narrowed his eyes. "On what grounds?"

"Routine check," said a round-faced mage with owlish glasses and a dark, whiskery beard on his full cheeks. He wore a shaven head and Augur tattoos, which Saff knew would only inflame the situation. Probably why Aspar, in all her savagery, requested him for the job. "The banned import and export lists have been recently expanded, and we just want to make sure traders are following the law."

Lyrian lowered his voice into a low, quiet seethe. "Perhaps in the dim light you can't see the Bloodmoon flag flying above this vessel."

The willowy mage with the posh accent stepped forward, drawing her wand. "Are you trying to intimidate us?"

"Oh, no. I'm trying to *threaten* you." Lyrian laughed, and it was a cruel, rattling sound. "Apologies if that wasn't clear. Step back, or we'll slaughter you right here and now. We'll dump your bodies so far upriver that your families will never find you. They'll spend the rest of their miserable lives wondering how you vanished without a trace."

Lyrian was playing right into Aspar's plan.

Needless escalation. Fair cause to bring in reinforcements.

Saffron's blood roared in her ears. Every sound and sight and smell was sharpened on the whetstone of fear—a fear she'd thought herself immune to, by now.

Levan stared at his father, every muscle in his body pulled taut. "Just let them search the hold. They won't find anything. Do you hear me?" There was a light insistence on this last question. "They won't find—"

"No." Lyrian's wand sparked with raw energy. "It's the principle of it. We bend to them now, over some petty customs law, and then what? Then they know we're weak, malleable, and they treat us as such."

"They. Won't. Find. Anything." Levan forced the words through gritted teeth. "Swallow your pride. Don't make a scene—"

Lyrian finally registered Levan's meaning, and his face smoothed over. "Alright. Search the boat."

The three customs officers stepped toward the hold, and then Lyrian's whims swung violently in the opposite direction, as though he had lost some furious internal battle.

He raised his wand, face twisted and crude as a gargoyle.

"Sen ammorten. Sen ammorten. Sen ammorten."

The three customs officers fell dead.

Someone screamed, and it echoed off the corrugated edges of the shipping containers.

A white crack of lightning forked the sky, illuminating the quay with a spectral paleness.

And then the world descended into chaos.

32

. . .

A Cruel Illusion

THE SILVERCLOAKS COALESCED ON THE QUAY, EVERY WAND RAISED toward the boat as though worshipping some sadistic god.

Bones transformed from cat to captain, conjuring repeated forks of lightning from the dark velvet sky. Behind Aspar, crates and shipping containers and coils of rope smoldered and erupted into flames.

Flames she could now use against them.

The crew workers on the dock scattered and scurried like ants, but there was no safe place to go.

"Sen ammorten. Sen ammorten. Sen ammorten."

Something in Lyrian had splintered. He shot hard-eyed killing curses at the dock, indiscriminate, unhinged. Segal was somewhere in the fold, but the kingpin didn't seem to care whether he hit one of his longest-serving allies.

He wanted ruin, and he was going to get it.

A Bloodmoon crew worker was struck and fell dead, ankle snapping in the fall.

Lyrian still did not stop.

Levan stared at his father in shock, *hatred,* but he did not move to stop the anarchy.

The Silvercloaks seemed to be awaiting a command. A vast, shimmering wall of magic separated them from Lyrian's curses: a matter-mantic shield. Detective Dallar's brow glistened with effort. It would not hold for long.

"*Don aquiss!*" yelled Castian, hauling a great wave from the river and sending it cascading toward the Silvercloaks.

As the water was torn from the river, the boat juddered and tilted violently, its hull scraping along something hard and rocky. Saffron pitched sideways, steadying herself before she hit the deck.

Dallar's protective barrier fell to the wave. The fresh bodies of the customs officers were washed away toward fiery containers, flames licking toward the dark sky like grotesque tongues. Several Silvercloaks—including Nissa and Auria—were wiped out before Aspar halted the rest of the wave in midair, the wall of water suspended into something solid and wrong.

A string of *effigias* charms shot up at the deck from Detectives Alirrol and Fevilan.

Saff ducked just in time.

Hunched on the wooden deck, she conjured her own shaky matter-mantic shield and threw it over herself and Rasso. The fallowwolf, far from the fierce predator she knew he was, cowered behind a bench, shaking from the roar of thunder. He pressed his body into her torso, whimpering in her ear.

"It's alright," she whispered to him. Possibly the worst lie she had ever told, and his doleful eyes told her he knew it too.

What would happen to the beast when every human he'd ever known was arrested? Perhaps he'd stick with Saff. The idea warmed her for a second, until she realized Aspar would never allow a creature so intrinsically linked to timeweaving into the Academy.

Fallowwolf aside, Saff just had to stay calm and survive the battle. She urged herself to keep her head down, to let the Silvercloaks take the Bloodmoons, to pray to a court of Saints she barely believed in that none of her friends fell victim to Lyrian's errant curses.

But . . . *no.*

She couldn't take that risk. She couldn't let Auria or Nissa die. She could not leave this in the hands of the Saints.

She had to disarm Lyrian, to neutralize his threat.

Another thunderclap, and Saff pressed her eyes shut against the blinding flare of light.

Think.

Think.

Thinking is your superpower.

How could she get to Lyrian without raising suspicion? If Levan or Castian saw her surreptitiously fighting *for* the Silvercloaks, and the raid didn't go to plan . . . they would know beyond all doubt she was a traitor. That the loyalty brand hadn't worked.

Hells, they'd likely know anyway.

Saffron lowered her shield as an *effigias* curse sailed over her head. With another whip-crack of lightning, a second docked boat caught ablaze. There was an echoing roar of anguish, but from who or where she could not discern.

From her position crouched on the ground, she had a clear line of vision toward Lyrian's stomping boots.

Footsteps stormed up the gangway, echoing beneath her in the hold.

"*Sen ammorten,*" Lyrian incanted, over and over, a wildness to the words now, burning indiscriminately as brushfire, even though his own son was somewhere in the fray, and Saffron understood why he was the top of the hierarchy, why he'd been impossible to topple for so long—because there was nobody he would not kill to ensure his own survival. There were no threads to tug that would weaken his will.

The boat rocked violently as Castian continued to wield river water, hurling it down the gangways and surely flooding the hold. Aspar's counter charms roared from ground level.

Crack came the lightning.

With a heaving snap, the boat tore itself clean from its mooring, gliding downriver back toward Port Ouran. A few moments later, it was brutally hauled back to the dock by some invisible force. Saffron fought to keep her dinner in her stomach.

Where was Levan?

And why did she *care*?

A wooden keg burst nearby, sending thick, sweet honeywine spreading all over the deck, sticky and cloying. The smell reminded Saffron of her mother, and her mother reminded her of . . .

Praegelos.

Was there something she could do with the *praegelos* charm?

It had worked back in Nalezen Zares's house. If she could freeze time for a moment . . .

How would that help? She couldn't very well restrain the Bloodmoons herself, in case it didn't work and she somehow had to maintain her innocence.

Her father's magic, on the other hand . . .

Maybe there *was* a thread of Lyrian's that could still be plucked.

She conjured an image from an old, dusty file she had perused endlessly during her time at the Academy. She called to mind every precise stroke of the myriad artist sketches, the parchment worn and thin, the charcoal pencils sharp and stringent. Every detail just so.

"*Et lusio Lorissa Rezaran,*" she muttered, grateful for her full magical well.

An illusion of the long dead queenpin sprung to life.

Lorissa was as tall as Levan, but spire-thin where he was broad. Chestnut hair plaited in a thick braid down her back, her face an orphic white against the bloody scarlet of her cloak. There was an awful blankness to her gaze—she wouldn't fool anyone for long—but hopefully it would be enough to stun the kingpin for a moment or two, to make him believe, if only for a moment, that she had Risen. The mirage might spook him enough to stop errant killing curses from finding their marks.

Directing the illusion with the tip of her wand, Saffron glided Lorissa over the deck and into Lyrian's line of sight.

He staggered back at the sight of her, his wand clattering to the deck.

Thunder bellowed overhead, and there was a shrill scream on the docks. Smoke fogged the air, but not so much that Saffron couldn't see the look on Lyrian's face, falling somewhere between horror and hope.

A firm hand grabbed her by the upper arm and hauled her upward.

Levan. His face contorted with fury and . . . something else.

Saints. Had he seen the illusion?

Surely not. Surely the sight of his dead mother would've felled him where he stood.

As he dragged her up from the ground, she lifted Rasso with her, pressing his cowering face into her chest.

A visible ache darted over Levan's face at the sight of them, and then he muttered, "Conjure a shield."

She dropped the illusion and incanted, "*Ans clyptus.*"

The spellshield leapt into a glimmering sheet of raw magic.

Saff took a split second to look around. The sky was torn apart with lightning and ash and flames and immense towers of water that refused to fall. The boat's deck was shredded by spell starbursts, its wood splintered and hanging apart. A strong smell of burnt coffee hung on the air, as though a pallet had caught fire somewhere in the hold.

Levan ushered Saffron and Rasso inside the top deck of the boat. The layout was similar to the boat they'd taken to Port Ouran, only smaller, and with fewer sleeping quarters. The lanterns bolted to the corridor walls flickered and blinked with every thunderclap, as though cowering from the din of the docks.

Saff peered back toward the deck, where the kingpin's gaze swung wildly from port to starboard, eyes peeled wide, as though he'd seen a ghost. His lips mouthed the word *Lorissa,* but no sound came out. Standing bolt upright amidst the countless flying curses, she had no idea how the kingpin hadn't been struck by *effigias* yet.

Perhaps Levan had conjured a ward or shield around him—it would explain why he'd needed Saffron to conjure *clyptus.*

"Your father . . ."

"I'm going back for him and Aviruna," he said through gritted teeth, and it was clear he was holding *something*. "I had to get you and Rasso out first."

Was he trying to repay some perceived debt from Zares's house? Is that where this misplaced trust came from? Or did he genuinely care?

Emotions warred in Saffron's mind. She didn't *want* to escape this situation. She wanted to watch as every last Bloodmoon was arrested and hauled off to Duncarzus. And yet some ridiculous, traitorous part of her was touched that Levan had put her above his own flesh and blood.

The enchanted necklace weighed heavy against her clavicle.

They ducked into a cabin containing a narrow bunk bed and a small desk. The porthole had been smashed in the furor, the floorboards lit-tered with shards of glass. Levan took up half the cabin with his hulking frame, his lemon-mint smell, the tang of something metallic.

Saff pressed herself behind the bunk, so she couldn't be struck with stray spells through the open porthole, and reassuringly stroked Rasso's fur, sticky with honeywine.

"Wait here for now," Levan ordered. "I think we're overpowering them, but they've scattered."

Saints.

This was all going wrong.

"Once I've got my father and Aviruna, I'll use *portari* to get us away from the docks."

Saffron stared at him. "But *portari* is outlawed in—"

"I have an imported wand from Bellandry." His voice was terse, hurried. "It hasn't had the spell stripped out of it."

Oh. "Is that how you—"

"I'll explain later." He held the door open a sliver and peered out into the corridor, every inch of him alert, precisely poised, like an archer atop the battlements of a besieged city. "Look after Rasso. And if someone comes, Silver . . ." His face softened almost imperceptibly. "You don't have to kill. I know they were your friends. Just neutralize them and wait for me."

Levan slipped into the corridor, met immediately with a female roar of, "*Sen effigias.*"

The voice was so shrill, so piercing, that Saff didn't recognize it. Fear had a funny way of strangling pitches. The spell must have struck the wall instead of Levan, because the cabin-side splintered from the impact.

"*Sen ammorten,*" came Levan's unflinching response, and a body hit the deck.

Horror tied a knot around Saff's heart.

Who was that?

Who just died at Levan's hand?

Echoing from far below in the hold, three overlapping voices sent a lance of despair through her.

"There's no lox!"

"Why is there no lox?"

"*. . . bad information . . .*"

Oh, hells. Had she been wrong about the pattern?

But no, she couldn't have been. Lyrian's very presence here proved they'd been expecting a shipment of the substance. Her information wasn't bad. It had just been undermined.

She ran back over the evening in her whirring head. Levan had disappeared as soon as Aviruna said something wasn't right. And his wand worked beyond the laws of the land. Had he used *portari* to magic himself into the boat's hold? Had he offloaded the lox into the river, or stashed it elsewhere? No wonder he'd been so rumpled and breathless when he returned.

Either way, the raid was a failure. The Silvercloaks might be able to bring Lyrian in on murder charges, but the organizational bust they'd hoped for hadn't worked.

Saff was still trapped in the Bloodmoons.

And they would undoubtedly kill her for what she'd done.

Yet . . . why had Levan saved her first? Surely he must have figured out by now that she'd leaked the shipment information to her former colleagues.

There were so many whys and not enough time.

Because there was a body on the other side of the wall.

And Saff had to know.

She *had* to know.

"Stay here, sweetling. I'm not going anywhere," she whispered to Rasso, ruffling his cowering ears.

Rasso whimpered, burying his face in the bedsheets of the bottom bunk.

Saff tiptoed toward the corridor, unsure why she even bothered—nobody would hear her over the cacophony of wielded elements and torn wood and fractured yells. When she didn't hear any footsteps on the other side of the door, she opened it.

A female body lay motionless on the floor, curled around herself like a newborn babe.

A silken sheet of black hair covered her face, but Saff would know that outline anywhere.

Nissa.

33

...

Seriqua

NISSA COULD NOT BE DEAD.

The flame-wielding part-dragon, so full of fire and life and spite and love, simply could not be dead.

Saffron fell to her knees at Nissa's side, a sob tearing from her throat. There was the patter of lupine footsteps, the clack of claws on floorboards, and then Rasso was by her side, nuzzling his face into her thigh.

She had kissed Levan, and then he had done *this.*

He had murdered one of her closest friends.

One of her greatest loves.

Tears flowed thick and hot down Saff's cheeks. This was all her fault.

She had called this raid.

If she hadn't done that—

—if she hadn't involved Nissa—

—if she hadn't accepted this mission in the first place—

—if she hadn't lied her way into the Silvercloaks—

—if she hadn't turned that doorknob—

—her thoughts tracked back and back and back through time, obsessing over every single decision that had led her here, to this moment, kneeling by Nissa's lifeless corpse.

There were so many ways this might not have happened, and only one way it did.

Because of Saffron.

The thunder was as distant to her as the rolling forest of Bellandry, as the scorched desert of Eqora, as the icy tundra of Nyrøth. Every shout and wail was muffled, as though sounding from another realm.

Nissa was *gone.*

Grief slammed into Saffron's chest like a fist, a solid, physical pain.

The sensation caused the magic in her well to swirl and darken, to become more glittering, more potent. This had happened in the aftermath of her parents' deaths—the loss was so acute that she felt it all over her body, and to feel it all over her body was to be in *agony.* Had she been able to utter a single word in that time, her magic would have been raw and devastating, impossible for a young child to control. Perhaps some part of her knew that. Perhaps some part of her stayed silent in self-preservation.

Perhaps such grief was the reason for Levan's terrifying strength.

Pain is not something I've ever found myself to be lacking.

Lifting a trembling hand, Saffron swept Nissa's sleek hair from her face. Though her eyes were closed, her cheeks still held with the warmth of life. The ruby lips, the gold stud on the bow, the column of runes up her neck, all so *Nissa,* so spirited and strong, she couldn't be *gone.* The shell of her body could not be empty.

But then—

—something.

A movement. A flutter. A hitching breath.

In Saffron's chest, hope kicked off the ground. Took flight.

She wasn't dead.

How wasn't she dead?

Levan's magic was the most powerful Saffron had ever seen. A killing curse from him should've crumpled Nissa's lungs in an instant.

Saffron searched the body for answers. Nissa's silver sleeve was slick with blood, her blisblade lying on the wooden floorboards beside her, its edge shining scarlet. Her well had obviously been running dry. Perhaps the split second in which she'd tried to replenish had cost her everything.

She loosed another breath. Ragged, shallow, but a breath nonetheless.

How was she still alive?

Unless . . .

Pulse thudding, Saffron tore open the front of Nissa's cloak, exposing her undershirt. The garment was made from a gleaming fabric Saff had only seen once before, on an Eqoran soldier who'd stopped at her mother's doorstep with a grievous injury. It was called *seriqua,* Saff remembered, and it was strong enough to take some of the lethal force out of a killing curse.

Saff yanked the vest down below Nissa's razor-sharp collarbone.

There, just above her heart, was the undeniable starburst of the *ammorten* spell. Faded like an old wound, but there nonetheless.

Nissa teetered on the knife-edge of life and death.

Saffron rolled up her cloak sleeves, held the tip of her knobbly beech wand to Nissa's curse mark.

"Ans mederan, ans mederan, ans mederan."

Heal. Heal. Heal.

But nothing happened. Saffron had never held any affinity for the work her mother had found so natural, and yet some part of her had thought—hoped, wished, beyond all reason—that sheer desperation would bend the magic to her will. That the grief and pain swirling in her well had lent her whole new power.

"Ans mederan, ans mederan, ans mederan."

Still nothing.

She tried again and again and again to rouse Nissa, dogged, almost frenzied, feeling the strength leech from her with every attempt. Somewhere in the distance was the bellow of thunder and water and fire, but none of it louder than the fact Nissa was *dying.*

Her chest rose and fell, but unevenly, unconvincingly.

On the brink, the precipice.

A wind gusted through the corridor, its direction and force so unnatural that it had to have been wielded, knocking Saffron backward so hard that her head slammed against the floor. Her vision starred. The gale carried with it a peculiar scent—like pepper and ash and rotten rose petals.

Sharp, hacking coughs erupted over the deck. Coughs, thuds, retching noises.

Large figures appeared at the end of the corridor. Levan stood upright, levitating the prone bodies of Lyrian and Castian along the hallway. Alive, but retching so violently they couldn't stand. Levan was coughing, staggering, gripping the walls and doorframes for support.

The smell stung the back of Saff's throat, singed the hairs in her nose, but it didn't force the air from her lungs the same way.

Which meant it had to be magical.

She forced a string of violent coughs to keep cover.

"We h-have to go," Levan gasped between hacking his guts up. "They h-have some k-kind of airborne weap—" The final word was severed with another vicious retch.

"Nissa's still breathing," Saff said in a rush. "Special undergarment. Please bring her back from the brink, Levan. Please."

He shook his head violently. "N-no time."

Castian fainted, her whole body convulsing around her middle, and Lyrian wasn't far behind.

"*Please.*" Tears spilled freely down Saff's face. She faked another cough, pretending to be dizzy. "I don't want to beg you, but I will."

"Get. Us. *Out,*" Lyrian hissed, thumping a palm on the floorboards, his face purple from lack of oxygen, before promptly falling unconscious.

Levan glanced over his shoulder, pitching dangerously as he did.

Auria and Aspar boarded the deck of the boat, wearing strange black masks over their noses and mouths. An endless whorl of fine purple mist curled and cascaded from Auria's wand.

An airborne weapon.

At the thought, a sharp chill scraped down Saffron's neck.

"Levan, please." Saff grabbed fistfuls of Nissa's cloak in her hands. "I love her. I love her so much."

Levan's gaze went first to the pendant around her neck, which shone an unmistakable heart red, then burned straight through to Saffron's very core, right into the wounded child at the heart of her. He seemed to see all the broken, shattered parts, how she'd glued them back together into something loosely resembling a person. He seemed to understand what irrevocable harm another breakage would do.

After a splintered moment of indecision, he dropped to his knees.

At first Saff thought he'd passed out, that it was over, that Auria and Aspar would take them all in despite the lack of lox, that Nissa would succumb to the lure of death, but . . . no. Levan was still very much alert.

Dizzily, he rested his wand on Nissa's curse mark and said, "*Ans mederan.*"

Levan's healing words sent a peal of grief through her chest. They always reminded her of her mother—and of her parents' final moments.

That sacred incantation coming from someone like *him* felt like a sick joke from the Saints. He had an unexpected mastery of enchantments, like her father, and yet he could heal as easily as he could breathe, like her mother. He read *Lost Dragonborn* like Mal, and pored over ancient languages like Merin, and kept his emotions tightly guarded like Nissa. It was like he'd been specifically designed by some cruel deity to torment her.

From a mage as powerful as Levan, one healing spell was all it took.

Nissa's back arched as though she'd been struck by Aspar's lightning, and she gasped an unsaintly amount of air into her lungs. Her bronze eyes peeled open, shining and *furious,* as though embers burned behind them.

For a second, Saffron hated Levan for how easily he'd done something so miraculous, for how much power he had at his fingertips, for the fact he did not choose to use that power for good. He used it to sever hands and torture necromancers.

"Killor?" Nissa was still dazed, but her voice was remarkably clear.

"H-hold on," Levan said weakly to Saffron, after another hideous coughing fit had shaken through his lungs. One of his palms clasped the wrists of his father and Castian, and he extended the hand that still held his wand.

Behind him, Auria and Aspar stormed across the outer deck.

They had mere moments to *portari* out of here.

"Killor," Nissa repeated, coughs wracking her own weakened lungs. She grabbed Saffron's wrist hard enough to bruise. "The tracing charm. It's *novissan vestigas.* Works around half the time."

Auria and Aspar entered the mouth of the corridor, each with a velvine perched upon their shoulders. The felines' eyes flared purple as they purred fresh pleasure into their mages. Aspar's palm bled; she clutched a blisblade in one hand and her wand in the other.

Auria's eyes found Saff's, and she recoiled with shock at the sight of her old friend in a scarlet cloak.

Saffron pressed her lips to Nissa's forehead. Raw emotion spilled from her like blood from a wound. The grief of her death, the relief of her resurrection, the unrelenting fear of what was about to happen to them all.

Levan's hand closed around hers, warm and fierce and terrible. She let go of Nissa and grabbed Rasso by the scruff.

"Et portari, Cryptmouth Tunnel."

The world folded itself around them, and everything went white.

THE NEXT THING SAFFRON knew, they were on their knees in the warded tunnels. It felt a little like regaining consciousness after fainting: a gap in awareness, a distinct disorientation, a sickening swoop in the stomach and the vision.

The other three Bloodmoons, all now conscious, were hacking up their lungs, sucking in deep lungfuls of unpoisoned air. Saffron couldn't even bring herself to pretend. She could barely see, hear, think.

They must know she had betrayed them.

She wouldn't be killed. The prophecy showed as much.

But the same could not be said for Mal and Merin.

A frightened animal clambered up her throat, the fear writhing and alive. She clung to Rasso, who was panting by her side. The tears over Nissa's almost-death were already drying on her face, leaving behind a salted crust.

Perhaps if she didn't move, didn't breathe, she could stay suspended in this liminal moment. Perhaps she could—

"What in all the *hells* just happened?" snarled Lyrian, the vitriol in his voice caustic and pure.

Castian lay flat on her back, red-rimmed eyes pressed shut. "We were raided," she hissed in dizzy disbelief. "Segal's still there. How did the cloaks know about the shipment?"

Levan sat up gingerly, leaning his back against the cold stone wall. His body did not tremble or shake, the way most mage's would after expending so much raw power. "You said something didn't feel right, so I reached out to my rat in the Silvercloaks. They confirmed a squad was moving against us. I got to the lox just in time. Stashed it up near Novarin."

Saff reeled from the cascade of revelations. First, that Levan was powerful enough to *portari* all the way to Novarin, which was hundreds of miles away.

But that was hardly the most pressing concern.

He had a *rat* in the Silvercloaks.

Did he mean the Grand Arbiter? Would Dematus have been privy to the plans for the raid? Surely Aspar wouldn't have told Dematus what they were doing ahead of time, knowing the Grand Arbiter was dirty. Unless Dematus herself had tendrils snaking into the ranks of Silvercloaks . . .

Detective Fevilan, a powerful Enchanter with a drink problem, had been disciplined earlier in the year for accidentally leaving a Bloodmoon case file in a tavern after a shift. Perhaps it was no accident, after all.

Another thought needled at Saffron, but she was afraid to look at it head-on.

Was there a darker reason Nissa was so willing to help Saffron? To find Nalezen Zares, to steal the tracing charm?

A darker reason Levan was willing to haul her from the brink of death?

A darker reason he'd so quickly executed her to begin with—to cover his tracks?

"I need to be able to *portari*," Lyrian snarled at his son. "Laws be damned."

"I've explained it to you a thousand times," Levan replied, jaw gritted. "If you didn't insist on using the weaverwick wand, I could have one with *portari* imported from Bellandry."

"Mare-shit." Lyrian clambered to his feet, woozy and stumbling, and jabbed his crooked finger down at Levan. "You knew there was a raid, and you let me get on that boat. Did you *want* to see me killed? Is that it? Are you so desperate to be kingpin that you'd see me slain? Give me one good reason I shouldn't execute you right—"

"The docks were crawling with Silvercloaks," Levan said, his tone disaffected, but he couldn't hide the sheen of sweat at this temples. He raked a hand through his dark waves, mussing them into twirled tufts. "If they heard me warn you, they'd know they had a rat in their midst."

Lyrian swung a loose fist at his son, and Levan caught it blandly in his palm.

Combat training, indeed.

"How was I to know you'd start killing people left and right?" Levan dropped the fist. "If you'd just let them search the hold, let them find nothing, they'd have been forced to get off our backs. They wouldn't have been able to search us again for at least a year, per customs law."

"*You*—"

"They can arrest you now." Levan stared coldly at his father. "Whenever they want. I don't know if they will, because they likely want to stick an organized crime charge, not petty murder. But you can no longer leave the bounds of the wards. They won't be able to breach them without a warrant from Dematus, and I'll make sure that doesn't happen."

Saffron waited with bated breath for the inevitable next part.

"All of this is incidental," Lyrian hissed, swinging on his heel. "Because the real question is how the *hells* they knew we were expecting lox tonight. And I'm not buying the routine search shit, because there were dozens of Filthcloaks waiting in the wings. That wasn't a routine search. That was a planned takedown." He glared at Saffron like she was a pail of animal filth. "I smell a rat."

"You branded me with your own two hands," Saffron retorted, although she felt a stomach-swoop of nerves as she invoked the brand once more. If there was any time the kingpin might abandon his belief in the spellwork, it was now. And yet what else could she do or say? "If I had anything to do with this, I'd have been struck dead on those docks."

Lyrian sank to his haunches. Spittle gathered at the corners of his thin, cruel mouth. As he had on that first night, he jabbed the tip of his wand in the hollow beneath her chin, forcing her face upward in a way that made it difficult to swallow.

"Listen to me, Filthcloak. If this was you—and believe me, we will learn the truth—I'll slaughter everything and everyone you've ever held dear." He stood unevenly, but there was nothing weak in his vicious glare. "Levan, find Segal. Aviruna, take Killoran to the cells. Rough her up a little. Then she and I can have a little talk."

34

...

The Golden Hourglass

THE CELL WAS A COLD, BARE SPACE MADE ENTIRELY OF CREAM-stone. No chair or bed, no tap for drinking, just a hole in the ground for various ablutions.

Saff shivered as Rasso trotted in beside her. When Levan had tried to take him on the quest to find Segal, the beast had growled and bared his vicious teeth. Thanks to *praegelos,* he had bonded to Saffron, and Saffron could only be grateful for the ally—even if Levan was wounded by the betrayal.

Levan. At the thought of him, emotions stirred up like a forest floor in a gale. Emotions so contradictory and infuriating that she couldn't separate them, couldn't examine them individually. There was the way it felt to kiss him, and the way it felt to crouch over Nissa's body knowing he'd killed her. The way it felt when he asked her to go to the arts festival with him, and the way it felt to watch him sever Nalezen Zares's hand.

The way it *felt,* all of it, when she was not used to feeling these things so deeply.

"Aren't you going to rough me up a little?" Saffron asked Castian, her sardonic tone unfaltering even when her heart felt weak.

Castian ruffled Saff's hair with a small flicker of wielded breeze. "I'm one of those freaks who believes in innocent until proven guilty. Don't get me wrong—if it emerges that you did this, I'll gladly obliterate you. But not before."

"Very noble."

Sarcasm, but Castian took it literally. "The only way you can survive in the Bloodmoons, emotionally." Her skin was clammy, her movements twitchy, pained. She was going into withdrawal. "Retaining some kind of moral code, no matter how dark things get. If you survive this, I suggest you do the same."

Saff rolled her eyes, absently petting Rasso's head. "It's hard to *retain a moral code* when the kingpin is threatening to brutally murder your family."

"Believe me, I know." There was a hollow, haunted look to her star-lined eyes. "But the kingpin is not always here. What you do in his absence matters."

Saff twirled her wand between her fingers. "Speaking of which, aren't you going to confiscate this?"

Aviruna smiled thinly. "Strangely enough, his majesty forgot to give me that order."

The door shut behind her, and Saff heard a deadbolt slide across the outside.

She still had her wand, but even if she could muster the strength to magic her way out of this cell, she knew deep down it was where she had to be. Because the Silvercloaks had failed to bring down the Bloodmoons, and that meant the assignment was far from over.

In that moment, lost and alone and afraid, Saffron—for the first time in a long time—did not have a plan. She did not know how she was going to salvage this, could not see the reroute, the clever sidestep, the winding mountain path. Even if a miracle occurred and Lyrian let her live, she knew another raid would be borderline impossible without a warrant. For a warrant, they'd need evidence, and how would she get within touching distance of such a thing now?

For the time being, she had been outplayed by Levan. By his cunning, by his raw power, by those tendrils of control he and his father had wrapped around the whole of the city.

I control everything.

I always win.

TWENTY MINUTES LATER, OR maybe four hundred, Aviruna escorted Saffron to Lyrian's office. The clammy pallor of Aviruna's skin had made way for a relaxed grin, a looseness to her limbs, and the smell of blackcherry had only intensified.

Every step up the corridor felt like a march toward the hanging tree.

Aviruna knocked on the kingpin's door, and it swung open.

At Saffron's heel, Rasso was stiff, alert, white eyes wide and searing. When the fallowwolf saw Lyrian standing by the fire, he let out a low, threatening growl. It surprised Saffron—Rasso had belonged to the kingpin's late wife for decades, while she had only known the beast for a couple of weeks. How swiftly the loyalties of magical creatures could shift in times of ruin, as the dragons had deserted the Rezarans all those centuries ago.

"Good luck," whispered Aviruna in Saffron's ear, and then she was gone, and it was only Saffron, Lyrian, and Rasso.

Her wooden pendant glowed a pure, poisonous green.

Saff searched the room for any signs that Mal and Merin were held hostage, but she didn't find any evidence of struggle, no telltale scents of silk dye and spiced cookies.

Lyrian stared into the flames of the stifling fire, as though trying to read his fortune in the embers. His hands were clasped behind his back, wand protruding between snarled fingers. It was an arrogant pose, as though he did not believe for a moment that Saffron would dare attack him. Unless, somehow, impossibly, he still held faith in the brand.

"Are we going to go through the farce of pretending you weren't behind this? Or are you just going to confess and let us be done with it? I can have Levan *portari* your uncles here in an instant. It'll all be over very quickly."

"I wasn't behind this." Saffron only narrowly resisted the urge to fire a killing curse into his exposed back. "And fair trial is not a farce."

He turned to face her, the light of the hearth casting a sharp shadow on one side of his hooked nose. "Fair trial? Does this look like a fucking courtroom to you?"

The seething hatred in his eyes was almost too powerful to look at head-on—so different from the cold, blank apathy of that first night. What was it about Saffron that unraveled something in these dark mages? Was it her refusal to cower and beg? Or was it what she represented?

Lyrian tucked a hand inside his cloak, and Saff caught a glimpse of Vogolan's old tincture belt. The kingpin pulled out a vial of truth elixir and handed it wordlessly to Saff. She drank obediently, the now familiar syrup-sweet taste leaving a thick fur on her tongue.

"Did you leak the shipment information to the Silvercloaks?" Lyrian asked stiffly.

"No."

"It was *you*. It had to be." He searched her face. "You know, I have all the ideas for how to torture the truth out of you. I could tear the scab from your brand, for instance. It would hurt like hells, and you'd doubtlessly be honest then." A heavy sigh, weighed down with exhaustion. "But I don't *want* to. The older I get, the less bloodlust I have. The less I like to get my own hands dirty. Far better to summon Levan to do it on my behalf."

Dread flickered like a flame behind her ribs, but she did not let it show on her face. She averted her gaze, looking instead at the miniature gold hourglass on his desk. The pearly grains of ascenite were settled at the bottom.

At her lack of reaction, Lyrian stared out of the window at the city he all but owned. The spires and peaks, the domes and lanterns, dust kicked up from chariot races, all its jewel-toned glory.

"I lost control on the docks," he said quietly—so quietly she almost missed it. "Killing those customs officers was something like a reflex. A desire for a clean cut of the threads. But the rest . . . I saw red. Or *white*—blinding, blinding white. And for the first time in a long time, I lost control."

Again, Saff said nothing, silence her faithful modus operandi.

Lyrian kept talking, every sentence more unexpected than the last. "It frightens me, how far I have strayed from the man I used to be. I was never meant for this life. But I fell in love with Lorissa, and she had all these big ideas, big dreams—she chose me and my unfaltering memory for a reason."

Fear wrapped its branches around Saffron's ribs. These were the sort of insightful words you shared with someone you were about to kill.

"We complemented each other so beautifully," he went on. "But before I was swept along on her undertow, I was a humble amplicator."

Amplicators were pivotal to Vallish society—they magically enlarged crops so that nobody would ever go hungry. The Crown had strict rules over what could or could not be amplicated, because if luxury resources like gold and silver and silk and cotton could be endlessly created, inflation would skyrocket, and it would become very difficult for anyone to sell their wares if nothing was scarce. Supply would far outstrip demand.

Saff's uncle Merin often went on flamebrandy-fueled rants about how the Crown should abandon the outdated notion of "making a living"—a concept born before the amplication spells were perfected—and embrace the idea that in a world where nothing had value, in the traditional sense, everyone would be free. People would still work and make and buy and sell, because humans did not like to be bored. Mal and Merin would still make cloaks, because they loved the art of it.

But King Quintan was old-fashioned, and the *economy* gave him something to control. And, as Merin would drunkenly yell, House Arollan lived in the lap of luxury, and would it be luxury if everyone had it?

"Lorissa was so beautiful, so smart, so powerful." Lyrian's tone was misty with nostalgia. "It didn't start out so violently, you know. This drive for ascenite. But she grew obsessed."

"Why did she want to gather so much?" Saff asked, determined to keep him talking, because if he was talking he wasn't summoning her uncles for slaughter.

Lyrian, however, did not seem to hear her. "I don't *want* to be violent or cruel, but I never seem to have a choice. Take this awful knot of a situation. I can't just let you back out into the world, because you know too much. And I can't keep you as a Bloodmoon, because you're a rat. Once a Filthcloak, always a Filthcloak. And so what am I supposed to do? There's no real option, is there, but to incinerate you?"

Saff withdrew her wand as discreetly as possible. The prophecy had not yet come to pass, so she must not die now. She just had to conjure a way out.

Lyrian took a step toward Saffron, and Rasso's growls intensified.

"I don't want to," he repeated, almost pleading with the animal. "But I would do anything to protect my family. The Bloodmoons are my family, and my family's safety means more to me than anything. I failed them once, the night Lorissa died, and I vowed never to fail them again."

This seemed so at odds with the impression Saffron had from earlier that evening, the sense that Lyrian was impossible to bring down because he had no threads of affection to tug. That was certainly true of the version of him who'd seen red, or white, as he so claimed.

And yet he seemed too to be speaking the truth now. He was highly erratic, a walking contradiction, a game without rules or order. He was volatile, capricious, a pendulum always in swing. And he was all the more dangerous for it.

The kingpin gave a brittle, sad smile as he looked from the fallow-wolf to Saff. "So I'm sorry. I am. But you must die. If it's any consolation, I'll let your uncles live. For once, there's no need for collateral." He raised his wand. "*Sen ammorten.*"

Rasso leapt in the way of the curse.

"*Sen praegelos,*" Saff cried.

The killing curse froze midair.

Saffron edged out of the way, so that if time suddenly flowed again, she'd be out of the firing line.

Rasso hit the floor, falling short of sinking his teeth into Lyrian's chest, and looked back curiously at Saffron.

Heart thumping wildly, Saffron knew her only real option was to run. To flee the mission, a failure but alive. To abandon the thing she had worked her whole life for, to beg and plead her way back into the Silvercloaks so that she might make some oblique difference behind the scenes.

Because what else could she do? The kingpin had resolved to kill her. And Lyrian Celadon was not one to change his mind.

The fallowwolf crossed to her in a flash, nuzzling her hand insistently, as though trying to communicate something critical.

"What is it?" she whispered, confused.

Rasso stared at her, and then at Lyrian's desk, and then at his former master.

She followed the wolf's gaze, and several disparate images coalesced with a sudden, startling clarity.

The golden hourglass, grains of pearlescent ascenite lying at the bottom.

The Timeweaver's wand in the kingpin's hand, power untapped.

The fallowwolf himself, the way the animal had curiously bonded to her.

Everything in her went perfectly still, as though she too were beholden by *praegelos.* Rasso tilted his head questioningly, or *expectantly,* as though he knew what she was thinking and had been waiting for her to finally figure it out.

She pressed her eyes shut, trying to conjure the image of the tunnel carvings that depicted timeweaving. She didn't have an eidetic memory, like Levan, but her brain had retained the word, stashing it in the mental file marked *important.*

Tempavicissan.

It was preceded by something, she remembered. The hourglass turned upside down, to signal the reversal of time.

Slowly, she turned back from the doorknob and looked at Lyrian, at the frail, wizened shape of him, like a shepherd's crook, even more withered when time pinned him in place. The wand was taut with a kind of urgent energy. Perhaps because it had just cast the darkest curse possible, or perhaps because it was . . . waiting.

She crossed to Lyrian and removed the wand from his grip, guided by some nameless force, her heart hammering in her ribs. Then she took the hourglass from the table and turned it upside down.

Rasso purred hungrily, approvingly, as though to say, *Yes, that's it, that's it.*

She tapped the top of the hourglass with Lorissa Rezaran's wand. It felt warm in her palm, not from Lyrian's own heat, but from something brilliant and pure.

"*Tempavicissan,*" she whispered, like a prayer, a litany—

—and the world turned itself around.

An immense smudging, a bleary haze, the feeling of being yanked upward from a great depth. Images blurred around her, Lyrian and Rasso moving backward so unnaturally it made her want to vomit.

Still pressing the wand tip to the golden frame of the hourglass, Saffron felt her lungs squeeze tighter and tighter, compressed through the narrow crevices of time itself, until eventually she could bear it no longer and she tore the wand away.

And then it was several moments ago.

35

...

A Fate Rewritten

LYRIAN'S BACK WAS TO SAFFRON, ONCE AGAIN FACING THE fire. His bony shoulders protruded through the scarlet cloak, and the lambent candlelight caused the shadowy folds of the robes to shift and eddy.

"Or are you just going to confess and let us be done with it?" he was in the middle of saying. "I can have Levan *portari* your uncles here in an instant. It'll all be over very quickly."

Lorissa's wand was still in Saff's palm, and she tossed it at Lyrian's feet like a hot coal. It clattered against his ankle, and he stopped speaking to frown down at it, as though he couldn't remember dropping anything.

Silently, Saffron set the only other evidence back onto his desk. Grains of ascenite flowed through the miniature hourglass, when before they had pooled at the bottom, but Lyrian did not seem to notice the slight disturbance in reality.

"I *wasn't* behind this," she stammered, trying to remember her lines. "Fair trial is not a farce."

Slowly, impossibly, he said: "Does this look like a fucking courtroom to you?"

Saffron could barely hear him over the roar of blood in her ears.

He turned back to her, and she thought she was going to faint from the enormity of what she'd just done. She was weak and dizzy and afraid that he would *know,* and that she would not have the strength to do it again. Her well had never been so empty—a kind of desert aridness that felt like it would never refill.

Rasso rested his head in Saffron's hand and licked her palm, tongue rough and warm.

As he had done already, in another version of time, Lyrian tucked a hand inside his cloak and pulled out a vial of truth elixir. Saff drank, noticing that there was no longer sweet fur on her tongue from the first tincture.

Strange, strange, this is so fucking strange.

Once again, he asked, "Did you leak the shipment information to the Silvercloaks?"

"No."

Saff's heart thundered. She needed this to go differently this time.

A different fork in the path appeared. One she'd been too panicked to see earlier.

"But I got the spell-tracing charm for you." Her voice sounded like it was underwater. "From my informant. It'll lead you to Vogolan's killer. And it won't be me."

There was an almost imperceptible *lurching* sensation, a cart rattling along a preestablished track before abruptly changing direction.

"What's the charm?" he asked, curiosity piqued.

"*Novissan vestigas.*" She omitted the fact it only worked half of the time. He didn't need to know she'd brought him damaged goods. "You'll need to find Vogolan's body, and cast the trace on the starburst where the killing spell met his skin."

Good luck with that.

She'd scattered the rubble of Vogolan's corpse all over Atherin.

But Lyrian's eyes glowed, unperturbed. "I believe I have a workaround for that. *Et convoqan Vogolanphial.*"

One of his desk drawers sprung open, and a small vial the approximate width of a wand leapt into his waiting palm. It was filled with dark red liquid.

He held it up to the light, an almost wistful expression on his face.

"My closest companions submit a blood sample, so that I might find them should they ever go missing. The Whitewings have a habit of holding my most valuable confidants ransom. There's no reason to suspect this spell-tracing charm won't work the same way as a location charm."

Saff's stomach jolted with a missed-step sensation, a hook of pure adrenaline. "My informant said one must hold their wand to the curse's starburst for the trace to have the desired effect. Otherwise it won't know which spell to follow. Vogolan has likely been struck with a thousand curses in his life."

"But *ammorten* was the most recent, and surely the trace is intelligent enough to know that."

He rolled up his sleeves and dipped the tip of the wand into the vial of blood.

Saffron's breath hung suspended in her throat.

Would it implicate her—or her wand?

Or would the spellwork fail, since the charm was already erratic, and the vial of blood was no real substitute for a body?

"Sen novissan vestigas."

There was an infinitesimal pause, charged with expectation and prayer and a rotting kind of despair.

Then a wisp of blue-ish silver vapor spilled from the vial, thin as a strand of cloakiers' thread. It swirled in the air for a moment, like a dog tracking a scent, and Saffron's life hung with it, but then suddenly, impossibly, it snaked across the room and through the thick wood of the door.

"That strand will lead you to the killer," Saff said, letting the lodged breath loose slowly, inconspicuously, trying not to wonder who she'd just condemned to a wrongful, tortured death. It was suddenly very difficult to remain standing, her legs weak and watery.

Lyrian stared after the vaporous string, lost in thought. "Take a seat, Filthcloak."

She obliged, slumping into a leather seat. Rasso leapt onto her lap and curled up in a ball. He was heavy, but the weight was steadying. It settled the sense of unmooring, the sense that everything she knew about magic and about herself had been turned upside down. The fallowwolf was something solid to hold onto when the rest of the world reeled around her.

Lyrian remained standing in front of the fire, his cloak drifting dangerously toward the licking flames. Saff watched hopefully. It would save her quite a lot of hassle if he caught fire of his own accord.

"So the trace has not indicted you. But you cannot deny that everything has been going wrong since you showed up and asked to be branded." Lyrian's tone had lowered to a coiled whisper, and she had to strain to hear him. Another small wrest of control. "You can't expect me to believe that's a coincidence."

"No, not coincidence," Saff agreed. "But the cause and effect isn't what you think. Maybe the Silvercloak contact who gave me the tracing charm grew suspicious about why I needed it. She could've cast a listening spell on my cloak, heard Levan telling me about the lox." She swallowed hard. "I may have made a mistake, but I'm no traitor."

I'm a Timeweaver.

She could not grasp the enormity of it.

"True as that may be, sloppiness can be equally fatal. The Bloodmoons are my family, and my family's safety means more to me than anything in this world."

Saff's stomach gave another strange lurch as the forks in the path intersected, then veered off in different directions again. "And I would never do anything to willingly endanger them. I hope I can make this up to you in time."

She looked at the cruel-eyed man before her, and all at once, she realized exactly how to play him. "I do believe you, you know." She dropped the bravado from her voice, letting it soften and blur around the edges. "That you don't want to be like this. I've heard you say something along those lines a few times since I arrived. I know you would prefer not to hunt or kill."

Her detective's eye caught the slight dropping of tension in the kingpin's shoulders, the way the deep notches of his frown grew shallower. As though she was confirming some truth he had once known about himself but had long forgotten.

Saff allowed herself the smallest exhale.

She was remaking a fate.

It was wrong and exhilarating and strange, for she had unmade not just her own fate but all the other events in all the world that had taken place in those few erased moments.

A monstrous thing.

With a sickly pang, she suddenly *understood* the Augurests' reasoning, even if she did not agree with their methods. There was something unnatural about what she had just done.

Still, she pressed forward. "On the streetwatch, I met plenty of crooks who just loved to cause pain and suffering. But that's not you, is it? It never has been. You do all of this for a reason."

There was a long, ear-ringing silence, his gaze following the vaporous strand as though he could see it all the way to the end. Then a black wall came down behind his eyes, something hard and cruel, something that resembled . . . *epiphany.*

Saints knew what that epiphany was, or how it might implicate her. But it must have been compelling, because somehow, *somehow,* he muttered, "You're dismissed, Filthcloak."

Barely believing her good fortune, Saffron climbed tremulously to her feet and left the room, Rasso at her heel. The corridor was deserted but for the tracing strand, and the shimmering blue-gray vapor sent a sharp yank of dread through Saffron.

And then the dread took a certain form, a certain shape.

Levan.

It has a particular penchant for elm.

His wand was black elm, the same as Nissa's.

Call it Silvercloak instinct, call it deep intuition, call it a strange kind of logic, but she knew beyond all doubt or reason that the strand led to him.

And Lyrian had already accused Levan of the murder once.

The epiphany that had fallen down beneath the kingpin's eyes . . . the blackness of it, the way it had ushered all thoughts of Saffron from his head.

Saints.

She had to warn Levan.

Saff didn't know where the thought came from—Levan was every bit the crook his father was—but it likely had its roots in guilt. She had killed Vogolan, and Levan had not, and yet he would be falling on the sword for her. Deep down, she knew she should let this happen, because it would solve so many of her problems, would neatly sidestep the fact that Levan *had* to know she was a rat, and yet, and yet, and yet . . .

In a horrified daze, she followed the tracing strand, and sure enough, after several winding corridors, it disappeared wispily into Levan's bedroom door.

She knocked loudly, insistently, Rasso still purring at her side.

After the shuffling of footsteps, the door opened inward, and Levan appeared beyond the frame. Without waiting for a single word, Saff pushed past him into the room. Levan held his wand in one hand, peering curiously down at the blue-silver thread buried in its tip, then looked back up at Saff.

Understanding knotted his brows into a frown. He'd been there when Nissa had given her the tracing charm, when she'd warned Saff that it only worked half the time. Driven by childish instinct, he threw his wand to the ground with a clatter, as though holding it was the only thing implicating him.

"But I didn't . . ." he said, as though that mattered at all.

"I know."

The frown deepened. "But the only way you could know is if . . ."

He searched her face, eyes darting and flickering, so much more alive than on that first night. A brow raised in unspoken question.

Saff nodded once. "Yes."

It was a risk, of course, to tell him the truth. It would invite unflattering questions, would tarnish his opinion of her, would cast doubt over the brand's efficacy. And yet she was exhausted from a night of chaos and killing, lies and deceits, and some part of her *wanted* Levan to know what she was capable of. That she would defend herself, if she so had to.

A curious question came to her, then.

Did the prophecy still exist, in this version of the world she had created? Was she still fated to kill Levan? Or had she unmade that fate too?

She sensed, somehow, that they were approaching some pivotal moment, all the tangled twine of the present knotting itself into a terrible future. But had the form of that future shifted?

"What happened?" His tone was low, urgent. "Did Vogolan hurt you?"

"Snapped my arm." Or tried to. "Killed my friend's grandfather in a gruesome and unnecessary way."

Levan clenched his jaw, and Saffron recalled their conversation after the conclave.

To me, Vogolan seems evil just for evil's sake.

Yes.

He killed someone very important to me.

She doubted Levan would hold Vogolan's murder against her.

His brow knitted together. "What about my father? Did he hur—"

"He didn't hurt me, no."

Because I unmade the world instead.

"But what—"

"There's no time," Saff insisted. Slow, calculated footsteps echoed in the corridor outside. Dread smoldered in her lungs. "He's coming. Saints, I can't leave. I'm sorry, Levan. I'm sorry this happened."

Levan finally registered the peril of the situation. He spurred to life, gesturing toward the wardrobe next to his plant-smothered writing desk. "The armoire."

She clambered into the too-small space, enveloped by Levan's clothes. They smelled of him, of lemon and mint and clove tea and leather belts and warm skin. Folding herself into a cross-legged position, Saff patted her lap and Rasso leapt into it. The tight space was cramped and breathless.

Then came the knock at the door.

With a final fraught look, Levan pressed the armoire shut, leaving a tiny sliver of the scene visible where the wooden panels didn't quite meet.

Levan opened his bedroom door, and Lyrian stood on the other side.

The kingpin's son stood almost a foot taller than his father, and yet there was something in Lyrian's quiet, coiled fury that made fear leap in Saff's chest.

Levan's wand had rolled under his bed, out of reach.

He was unarmed.

"So it was you," the kingpin said quietly, almost regretfully, to his son. "You killed Vogolan."

Levan balled his wandless hand into a fist at his hip. "He hurt too many people. Gratuitously, just for the thrill of it. Alucia. Saffron. And you know perfectly well what he did to me—or at least I think you do. Enough was enough."

Alucia?

The life partner Harrow had alluded to?

And what was he *doing*? Was he taking the blame willingly? Protecting her?

Why?

"How did the brand not kill you for the very act?" Lyrian muttered, staring at his son's chest.

"Precisely," Levan said with an air of triumph so convincing Saff almost believed him herself. "The fact I'm alive means Vogolan was a liability, and I acted in the Bloodmoons' best interests. If you don't believe in me, believe in your own magic."

A stunned expression bled across Lyrian's face, as though several more epiphanies were occurring at once. It was the way Saffron likely looked when the timeweaving pearls had finally strung themselves together, and it made her deeply, deeply afraid.

"All along," the kingpin whispered, the words stitched with raw emotion. "It was you all along."

"Excuse me?" Levan said, confused—but also, Saffron thought, alarmed.

"How could I have been so blind?"

"I don't know what you're—"

Lyrian shook his head ferociously. "You can overpower it."

The brand?

Levan shared her bemusement. "I averted major disaster tonight. I stashed the lox. I tried to protect you from the Silvercloaks."

"I've been a fool, Levan," Lyrian moaned. "You're my son. My flesh and blood. How can I kill you? You're . . ."

"You don't know what you're saying," Levan said curtly, and Saff had no idea how he kept so cool, so detached, in the face of a death threat from his own father. "Go and get some rest. We can talk about this—"

"*Sen debilitan,*" Lyrian said suddenly, stabbing his wand at Levan.

And without a wand, Levan couldn't block it. He froze, so suddenly and absolutely that it felt like a black hole. One of Sebran's favored spells on the streetwatch, paralyzing not just the body but the mind as well. Levan was still *aware,* in some kind of animal sense, but his thoughts were thoroughly immobilized, and now this devastating mage, so inexplicably powerful, so ruthlessly ordered, so perpetually in control, was at once power*less.*

Rasso growled, and Saffron clamped her hand around his mouth.

"No. Not now. Please," she whispered, and he heeded the urgency in her tone.

Lyrian reached out his spare hand and cupped his son's jaw. The kingpin's stature was suddenly so small and *sad.* A father studying his child, wondering how he had so badly lost his way. Thinking of all his failures as a parent.

"I'm sorry, son," Lyrian said, his voice hoarse. "But you leave me no other choice. *Sen ascevolo, carcanduan.*"

Carcanduan. Cell two.

Levan's body levitated a few inches off the floor, then drifted out of the room.

The kingpin followed.

And Saffron was left pressing her face into Rasso's warm fur, feeling the beat of the animal's heart against her cheek, reeling over the terrible new fate she had carved for the kingpin's son.

36

...

Shard of Deminite

CROUCHING IN THE ARMOIRE FOR WHAT COULD HAVE BEEN hours, Saffron could not process the night's events.

She was a Timeweaver. She was more powerful than she'd ever realized, a force of nature so potent that many feared it enough to invoke genocide.

She was *powerful,* in the same way Levan was powerful.

She was so powerful it was frightening.

The thought was a bolt of pure elation. Without Lorissa's wand and hourglass, it would be almost impossible to weave again, but she'd go to every wandmaker in the city if it meant finding one with a weaverwick at its core. She'd trawl shady antiques shops and dusty estate sales until she got her hands on a miniature golden hourglass filled with ascenite.

It was a purpose, a reroute, a new path forward, and she would take it gladly.

The victorious surge in her chest was underpinned by a writhing dread, but she could not think about Levan now. No matter what was happening to him at the hands of his father, she had to move. She could not save the world, nor the kingpin's son, while hiding in a closet.

As she pushed the doors of the armoire open, light flooded in, casting a glow over the robes she'd been folded between. Something shimmery amongst the raiment caught her eye. Amidst the scarlet and navy hung two long golden cloaks, each embroidered with pale silk. Elaborate runes flowed vertically down the lapels, and a pearlwillow—the symbol for knowledge, in the *Lost Dragonborn* world—was stitched onto the breast pockets. Baudry Abard's favored garb. The needlework was slightly clumsy, an endearing wonkiness to the tree branches, an uneven spacing to the runes. The fabric pierced in places, where wrong stitches had been unpicked.

Her heart stilled.

Matching costumes. For the Erling Tandall signing.

She hadn't wanted to wear Bloodmoon red, so Levan had made *costumes.*

Now he was in a cell, at his father's mercy—because of her.

And the truth was that she had come to care about the kingpin's son.

Not just in a primal, I-caught-him-fucking-the-King's-Prophet-and-now-keep-picturing-him-in-a-state-of-undress sort of way, but as a *person,* which was infinitely more troubling. Because the truly unfathomable thing was that Levan was . . . sweet. At least parts of him were. He had re-enchanted her necklace and shown Neatras's daughter mercy and spent hours making Saffron a homemade costume. He learned extinct languages and pored over the same books that had brought her back to life, all those years ago.

Yet hadn't she seen him cause unforgivable pain? Hadn't she dodged his killing curses herself? Hadn't he whispered cruelly in her ear about all the ways he would emotionally destroy her if she betrayed him?

She couldn't reconcile all of it, despite knowing better than anyone that people contained multitudes, that nobody was either all good or all bad, that even those most confident in their convictions were riddled with inconsistencies and paradoxes, that even those with the strongest hold on their magic still did not have full mastery of their minds.

Saff herself was afraid of public speaking, which didn't marry at all with her nihilistic worldview. Her parents had been murdered in front of her. Why would she fear standing on a dais and simply talking? And yet her body reacted independently of her mind, stomach cramps and swooping vision, and no amount of logic could ease that fear.

People were complicated. Levan was complicated. He'd never had the chance to become anything other than what he was. She thought of him being branded as a child, and of their shared wounds, and of his lips on hers and how alive she had felt at his touch.

Which is perhaps why, without thinking of the threats and risks, without assessing every possible outcome, without thinking much at all, she decided to act, driven by pure instinct, by pure . . . *something.*

As she made her way to the cells, Rasso trotting at her heels, fortune somehow favored her. A subtle change of the tides, as though luck were suddenly responding to the newly awakened power in her veins. She did not pass a single soul in the hallways, nor was there anyone guarding the cells themselves. Perhaps the kingpin did not want anyone to know that his son was held captive.

The eight cells were notched along a short, narrow corridor, four on each side. Three had deadbolts drawn across their doors. Cell one contained Nalezen Zares, and presumably cell two housed Levan. She wasn't sure who was in cell six, but she didn't particularly care.

She pressed her ear against the door of cell two, and she did not hear voices—which meant if Levan was in there, he was in there alone. Rasso nudged the door with his wet nose, leaving an imprint on the faded wood. She smiled reassuringly at him and tapped the deadbolt with her wand.

"Good gallowsweed."

She'd watched Levan lock up Nalezen Zares this way, and she hoped the password hadn't changed in the days since. She held her breath for a split second, but the deadbolt sighed loose. When the door pushed open, it took her a moment to process what she saw on the other side.

The light was dim, just a single flickering lantern bolted to the far wall. Levan sat on an armless chair next to a thick wooden table, upon which he rested his hand.

Saffron took a few more steps into the room, narrowing her eyes as they adjusted to the light.

No, his hand was not *resting* on the table.

It was impaled with a thick shard of . . . glass? Metal?

As his eyes found hers, they looked as dull and dead as the night she'd met him in the alley.

"What's that?" she asked gesturing to the shard, throat thick with dread.

"Deminite," he replied, hard, emotionless. "Cursed."

His hand was palm-down on the table, and the shard jutted right through the center of it. It was a big enough chunk of deminite that it must've severed ligaments and crunched through bone. Saff suppressed a shudder.

"Cursed?" she asked, aghast. "Isn't the whole point of deminite that it nullifies magic?"

"Hell knows." Levan shrugged one shoulder, leaving the impaled arm still. "But I heard him cast the magic. *Ver sevocan, nis sanadiman.*"

The same spell pattern as the brand. A kind of dark conditional magic that inspired a primal fear in her.

"What does that mean?"

He fixed his empty stare on a point just beyond her ear. "If I pull it out, all the blood in my body will come with it."

"Saints."

"He didn't have the stomach for killing me, in the end. But I'm not sure this is anything less than a death sentence. The magic . . . he didn't caveat it. No conditions or exceptions. Now nobody can pull it out without killing me. Not even him."

So that was why Lyrian hadn't felt the need to station a guard outside the cell.

There was no freeing Levan.

"I'm sorry," she whispered, horror gathering inside her like storm clouds. This was her fault. If she hadn't yanked time unnaturally backward, if she hadn't chosen a different fork in the path, if she hadn't given Lyrian a defective tracing charm . . .

"Don't be. Vogolan deserved to die." Levan stayed rigid, wooden, so far from the softened man she'd kissed in the warded tunnel as they talked about meeting their childhood hero.

"But *you* don't."

"Don't I?"

A fair question. One she might have answered quite differently mere weeks ago.

"Of course not." She breathed shallowly through the clenched fists of her lungs.

He shifted his weight on the too small chair, but there was no indication he was in any pain. And it must have hurt like all hells.

"Was the rest of it your doing?" he asked plainly. "Did you tell the Silvercloaks about the shipment? Because it's not clear how you're alive right now."

Saffron didn't know what to do with her body, so she closed the cell door behind her and leaned against it, sliding down to the floor. Rasso, instead of curling up beside her, padded over to Levan and rested his furry head in his master's lap. A brief emotion shadowed Levan's face before vanishing again, like a frozen lake splintered with an ice pick then immediately freezing solid once more.

"It wasn't me," Saff replied, the lie feeling easier than it should. A muscle well trained. "Not intentionally. I think my contact cast a listening spell on my cloak."

Levan stroked the bony dome of Rasso's head. "You refused to wear your cloak when meeting your contact."

"My tunic, then. My trousers, my boots, my necklace, every lock of my hair."

"And you wouldn't have noticed that happening?"

She couldn't parse his tone. Accusatory? Disbelieving? Or trying very hard to trust her?

"I've been slightly on edge the last few weeks. It's rather hard to concentrate when you're in constant mortal peril."

The folds of Levan's scarlet cloak rose and fell with his overly steady breath. "I see. And is your contact the woman I tried to kill, then brought back from the brink?"

"Is she *your* contact?" Saff shot back.

He frowned. "What?"

"Back in the tunnel, you said you reached out to your *rat* in the Silvercloaks."

The question sat between them, solid as a body, souring the air.

"I don't think it's wise to share my source," Levan said levelly. "Given your history."

"You're my *mentor*, aren't you?"

A snort of derision. "We both know that's mare-shit."

"So what am I, then?" Saffron asked fiercely, not sure why her heart was pounding out of her chest.

He shook his head, looking up at the ceiling. "Damned if I know."

By the tormented expression on his face, she suspected he was as conflicted as she was.

She remembered Harrow's words: *Levan will never take another life partner. Not after what happened to—*

Alucia, she knew now. But she sensed this was not the time to broach the subject.

"Are they feeding you?" Saff asked instead, trying to temper the strange tension. "Do you need some water? A piss bucket?"

"Don't do that," he snapped, so ferociously that Rasso's ears pinned back in fright.

"What?"

"*Care.*" Levan uttered the word like a curse.

Rasso looked between them, then sauntered back over to Saffron, as though Levan had betrayed him.

"Sorry, how heinous of me," Saff retorted. "Of the two of us, I'm definitely the cruel one. I may start wearing horns and communicating in deviltongue."

"Oh, get off your high horse, Silver. You've only been a Bloodmoon for a few weeks and you've already killed and tortured. You're not better than me. You're exactly the fucking same. Most people think they'd never do these things, but in the right conditions, under the right pressure, *everyone* would."

"I had to." Heat rose in her chest, her throat. "To save my uncles. Why do *you* do it, Levan?" Her voice was low, loaded, aimed squarely beneath his defenses. "Why do you take lives over and over again? Why do you torture with such cold brutality that something must be broken inside you? Because nobody has a wand to your temple. Nobody is threatening your loved ones."

A long, shredding beat. "Aren't they?"

"Tell me, then," Saff urged. "Tell me what this is all about. Tell me why you are the way you are."

"I don't owe you that." His unimpaled hand clenched into a fist. "I don't owe you a damn thing."

"Fine," she muttered, climbing to her feet and turning to the door handle. "Rot here, for all I care."

She turned the handle, and he groaned self-loathingly behind her.

"Urgh. Silver, wait."

She didn't turn to face him. "What?"

"Harrow is coming to my chambers tonight," he said flatly. "Can you let him know I'm otherwise engaged?"

Saffron nodded once, opening the door.

"*Saffron,*" he said, hoarse, and hearing him say her real name for the first time unspooled something deep inside her. "I'm sorry. I hate people seeing me helpless."

She'd felt the same way after being branded. They were so hideously similar.

"You're not helpless," she replied, sullen but softening. "I offered you help. That is in direct opposition to the word *helpless*—"

"You know what I mean. Stop being a pedant."

She sighed, resting her forehead against the door. The wood was cold and smooth.

"Could you . . . bring me some salve?" he muttered. "I have another wound that's starting to fester."

This made her finally turn back to face him. "Another wound?"

He swallowed. "It wasn't my father, if that's what you're thinking." From the closed look on his face, she didn't suppose he'd say any more.

"Which salve?"

"There's a pot in my desk. Third drawer down. Password is, erm . . . *Baudry's bitch.*"

Laughter flared in her ribs, but she kept it caged. "Aren't you forgetting something?"

He frowned, genuinely confused. "No?"

"There's a word most people use when asking for help. Just to give you a hint, it's considered good manners in all cultures except Nyrøthi, in which outright hostility is generally preferred. But I'm not from Nyrøth, and neither are you."

Levan cursed under his breath.

"Sorry, I didn't quite hear you," Saff goaded.

"Please."

"Great," she said, plastering a false smile over her face. "Anything else?"

"No. *Thank you.*"

Saffron gave him a sarcastic mock salute and left the cell, Rasso trotting at her heel.

The smile died as soon as she slid the deadbolt back into place.

That deminite shard was going to kill him. It was just a matter of when.

37

. . .

Levan's Journal

THE KING'S PROPHET WAS WAITING OUTSIDE LEVAN'S CHAMBERS, one soft-heeled foot pressed flat on the wall he was leaning against. His dark red hair was like molten copper beneath the lamplight, and his pale, freckled skin danced with shadows. He peered irritably at a goldenjade pocketwatch.

"Levan's otherwise engaged," Saffron said, without preamble. "He sends his apologies."

Harrow looked up, frowning. "Is everything alright? He never misses our . . . communions."

The image of that impaled hand sent a shiver down her spine. "Something came up."

"Hopefully not his *vock,*" Harrow said mildly. "Do you have him tied up in a dungeon somewhere? He always did like the, ah, *firmer* restraints."

Saffron snorted at the accidental accuracy. "Yes. Exactly."

"Well, I suppose I'll be off, then." Harrow dropped his heel to the ground, standing up to his full height, which was at least half a foot shorter than Saffron. "I don't usually frequent the pleasurehouses—unbecoming, for a King's Prophet—but my well is especially *dry* today."

He turned to leave, and an idea came to her.

"Harrow, wait."

Swiveling on his boot, he quirked a brow.

"Are you an Augurest?" she asked.

Just because he didn't shave his head and tattoo his eyelids didn't mean he wasn't harboring radical beliefs. Historically, most Foreseers swore fealty to the Five Augurs. And if this was the case, he would want to see a Timeweaver like her eradicated.

"Absolutely not." His laughter was high and bright, like the peal of a church bell. "Just like I'm not loyal to any crown, I'm not loyal to any religion either. My only true faith is pleasure."

"And have you always had the gift of prophecy?"

"Ever since I was a boy." His voice was arch, well educated, the subtle Bellandrian accent adding a marbled lilt. "They came so thick and fast I struggled to discern between tenses, for a while. Never quite knew what had already happened, what was currently happening, or what was *going* to happen. My parents thought I was talking in riddles half the time. Why do you ask?"

She was surprised by his openness, but supposed he had no fundamental reason to distrust her.

"I've never had a knack for it myself, but I touched an artifact several months ago, and it showed me a glimpse of . . . something." She talked quickly, breathlessly. It was the first she'd spoken of the prophecy in over a year. "Do you think that could've been a real vision? Or at least an echo of one? Or does the fact I have no foreseeing power mean it's impossible, and I might have just banged my head a little?"

An amused smirk notched a dimple in Harrow's cheek. "*Had* you banged your head a little?"

"I don't know," Saffron admitted. "It's all a bit of a blur."

She didn't know why she felt the need to ask—Aspar had confirmed the prophecy was real in the hours that followed. And yet the captain had devoted her entire life to the Augurs, and so her faith in the power of prophecy was inherently stauncher than most. For some reason, Harrow's libertine perspective held more weight.

Saff didn't know, either, why she so desperately *wanted* him to tell her it had likely been an illusion, a mirage. A trick of the light. She didn't know *why* she so badly did not want to kill the kingpin's son.

Harrow leaned back against the wall. As he shifted, Saff caught the scents of honeywine and sandalwood. "Well, my Five Augurs history is a little wanting, but many scholars believe that wands from that era could store prophecies cast long ago."

Saff absently patted Rasso's head. He was whining; she'd forgotten to feed him amongst all the chaos. She'd need to send a servant for some fresh ewe hearts. "But there would only be five of said wands, wouldn't there? And the first four are locked away in the Museum of Verdivenne."

"Oh, no." He smoothed a loose strand of red hair from his face. "Foreseers were so common back then that most people could conjure a vision or two. They were usually mundane—foretelling weather patterns was the best most could hope for—but there was the occasional big ticket vision."

"But that was a thousand years ago. The prophecy I saw related to something that might happen in the next few weeks or months. Could they have foreseen an event that was over a thousand years away from coming to pass?"

"Er, possibly?"

"And why show itself to *me*?" Saff went on, a year of questions tumbling out of her like small rocks loosening before a landslide. "Someone with no foreseeing ability whatsoever? Plenty of mages must have handled the wand between then and now."

"Well, does the prophecy relate to *you*?"

"It does."

He shrugged, as though this settled matters.

Saffron decided to push her luck, to follow her detective's instincts. "What kind of prophecies do you share with Levan?"

"Aha, now you've overstepped, my darling." He pushed off the wall and blew her an elaborate Bellandrian air-kiss: three smooches, pressed against the tips of his fingers. "Tell Levan I miss his *vock*."

"I probably won't," Saffron replied drily.

Once Harrow's clipped footsteps had disappeared around the corner with a swoosh of navy cloak, Saffron opened the door to Levan's chambers. Rasso padded in beside her, nuzzling at her hip, a smudge of silver-white in the low light of the glimmering candles.

It was late, and exhaustion pressed into Saffron from all angles. A heavy, breathless force that felt like the stifling heat of Lyrian's fire. It had been a fraught few hours inside a fraught few weeks inside a fraught life, and there was still no end in sight. She was back to square one thanks to the botched raids, and she doubted the Bloodmoons would be so lax with their ledgers going forward.

How in the hells would she ever bring them to justice? It would be even harder for the Silvercloaks to secure a warrant after the chaos of the failed dock raid.

But she couldn't think about that right now. She just had to keep moving forward.

The first thing she did upon entering Levan's room was slide a hand under his bed and pull out the discarded wand. Tucking it into her cloak pocket, she wasn't quite sure why she felt the need to retrieve it—only that the idea of it falling into Lyrian's hands felt dangerous, somehow.

Then she crossed to the writing desk and tapped her own wand tip against the third drawer down. "*Baudry's bitch.*" She allowed herself a soft chuckle at the password. Only Levan.

The drawer shook itself loose, and she opened it to find a neat apothecary of various salves and medicinal herbs, all alphabetized and dated as to when they were brewed.

Why did he need to password-protect this?

Almost at once, the question answered itself.

There, in a small wooden trinket box, was a label that said *loxlure.*

Was it used as pain relief in some of his salves? If so, it made sense that he had to keep it under lock and key. Castian was openly an addict, along with Saints knew how many others. Hells, Levan himself had to be tempted. It was the ultimate test of his own self-control to keep it right there in his room. He must have a will of iron to resist day after day.

She grabbed the salve he'd requested—a pale turquoise jar, topped with wax-sealed paper. She wondered why he would ever use a salve on himself instead of healing the wound magically, as he was perfectly able to do. Were some curse wounds immune to *mederan*? She tried to remember from her mother's practice but came up empty.

Saff hated the feeling that more and more of her mother was being lost to the murky past. It was like trying to cup water in your hands; no matter how tightly you pressed your fingers together, it would slowly, inevitably, slip away.

She was just about to leave when another thought came to her.

The notebook in the bottom drawer—the one she'd been unable to pry open the last time she snooped in this room. She'd wondered at the time if it might have been a ledger.

She pulled it out of the drawer, running a finger over its plain spine.

Once more, she tapped her wand and said, "*Baudry's bitch.*"

It fell open on a random page in the first quarter of the notebook.

A journal. The page was dated around six months ago, and Levan's narrow cursive handwriting looped and swirled all over the parchment. Saff's heart leapt into her mouth.

SORDING, 14 MAGNÁRIEL, YEAR 1174

Almost three years since Alucia died. A thousand days, and I have felt every single one.

They say time heals all wounds, but even with my mother's wand and a fallowwolf by my side, I cannot convince the slippery seconds and minutes and hours to obey. To wind back the clock to before Alucia was killed.

What use is Rezaran blood if it cannot move time like a tide? I am a slave to its relentless forward march, leaving everyone I have ever loved dead in its wake. Though in truth, Alucia was never mine to love. That much is horribly clear.

How much loss can one person take before the lure of lox becomes too strong to resist?

Saffron slammed the journal shut, chest pounding.

Alucia had been dead for three *years*?

There was no way even the most gifted necromancer could bring her back. Surely a mage as smart as Levan had to know that.

There were so many questions, and she held all the answers in her hands. But she also remembered what Aviruna said about moral codes within the confines of Bloodmoon life.

The kingpin is not always here. What you do in his absence matters.

She should put the journal back in the drawer and never look at it again. The idea of Levan having access to her deepest thoughts made her prickly, nauseous. She couldn't do the same to him.

And yet . . .

What if he named his Silvercloak rat?

She was here as a detective, first and foremost, and she wouldn't be able to best the Bloodmoons while the rat was still active. Every raid would meet the same fate if Levan was always one step ahead. No tactical team would ever be able to close in when the Bloodmoons knew exactly what was coming.

She had to read it.

It was yet another line crossed, another betrayal of the good person she'd always believed herself to be.

You're not better than me. You're exactly the fucking same.

No. Levan was wrong. She was doing this not to save her own skin, but to bring down the bloodiest, most brutal criminal organization in Atherin's history.

The end justified the means. It had to.

Flipping the pages until she found the most recent dates, she blurred her eyes as she skim-read, focusing only on proper nouns, on capitalized names, hoping to spot a familiar shape. But as she passed through the last few weeks of entries, none of her suspects materialized—not Grand Arbiter Dematus, not Detective Fevilan, and not Nissa Naszi.

She was about to close the journal when something caught her eye.

It wasn't just the name Silver—though that had been mentioned plenty of times—it was the date of the entry. Plenting morning, just after she'd told him where he could find Nalezen Zares.

> *We have a location for Zares at last, but I keep my hopes tempered. It would not be the first time the necromancer has slipped between my fingers.*

I cannot let desperation cloud my mind. Not when Silver has already misted the glass.

I must play this carefully, perfectly. The rat promises to be a valuable source of information, and his father is in the King's Cabinet—yet another thread to pull, when the time comes.

Saffron clasped a hand to her mouth.

His father is in the King's Cabinet.

It was Tiernan.

Tiernan was the rat.

38

. . .

Vær Kynnås

TIERNAN—SWEET, UNASSUMING, SLIGHTLY USELESS TIERNAN—was working for the Bloodmoons.

Once the initial shock had worn off, Saffron supposed that it made sense. He was weak-willed, which made him easy to turn, and his father was a significant figure in the King's Cabinet, which made the whole family ripe for extortion.

How long had this been going on? It could be a legacy rot, stemming from his father and passed down to Tiernan like an awful family heirloom. But from the way Levan had phrased it in his journal, it seemed like Kesven Flane hadn't been used to his full potential yet.

The most likely explanation was that while Saffron was inside the Jaded Saint talking to Nissa that first Laving night, Levan had approached Tiernan outside. Threatened him into cooperating. It would explain why Tiernan had *apologized* to Saffron the following week, having learned just how easy it is to fall from grace, just how fragile the house of cards holding up his life truly was.

His corruption was a stunning blow to the undercover operation, and also to Saffron as a person, but she was simply too tired to think her way around it now. Once she'd delivered the salve to Levan, Saffron finally fell into her bed, exhaustion pulling her under.

When she woke the next morning, the first thing she smelled was the chaos of the raid—smoke and saltwater, blood and sweat and *pain.* Wrapping herself in a silk robe, she padded along to the bath chambers and ran a steaming pool filled with rosehip oil. There, she let the warm water coax the fraught knots from her body, resting her head back against the edge of the pool. On the ledge next to her, Rasso snored on his back, every leg cocked in the air. She couldn't quite remember why she'd ever found him frightening—the shredded Whitewing throat was like something from a distant dream.

In any case, she wouldn't leave the bath chamber until she had formulated a plan for how to deal with Tiernan. Her mission could not succeed while he was still informing for the Bloodmoons.

She should go straight to Aspar, of course, although she hadn't spoken to her commanding officer since the raid. The captain would be at Esmoldan's Baths that evening, but it seemed far too great a risk when she'd only just convinced Lyrian of her innocence. Besides, telling Aspar would mean Tiernan lost *everything.* His career, his freedom—he'd certainly be thrown in Duncarzus—but also perhaps his life.

Would the Bloodmoons kill him to protect their secrets?

She couldn't turn Tiernan in, nor could she emerge triumphant with him still in place. Which meant the only real option was a third hideous thing: somehow incapacitate him until her undercover work was over.

A series of horrible ideas came to her. She could use *effigias* or *debilitan* and stash him somewhere discreet, like a shipping container, but it would be just Tiernan's luck to end up on a trader boat to Royane or Daejin, where nobody would ever find him again. She could bring him to one of the empty Bloodmoon cells, but then he'd be in the belly of the beast, vulnerable to assassination at any given moment.

Perhaps she could confront him herself, convince him to run and hide of his own accord. She could confess her own involvement in the Bloodmoons—if Auria, who'd spotted her on the raided boat, hadn't already told him—and try to understand just how tightly the scarlet tendrils wrapped around Kesven Flane's son.

Finally, the plan solidified. She would go back to the Jaded Saint on Laving night, and if any of the Bloodmoons questioned her, she could say she was meeting her own informant. Tiernan had been there the last two Lavings in a row, and chances were he'd be there again, duty-bound to meet Levan outside.

That was two days away, so Sording would be spent trying to buy a weaverwick wand of her own—in her plain black cloak, of course. Nobody in their right mind would sell a wand that powerful to a Bloodmoon.

THE FIRST WANDMAKER SAFFRON visited had an illustrious boutique on a small plaza, fronted by a forest-green awning with ØSTYRD'S WANDS emblazoned in gold cursive letters.

She was particularly hopeful for Østyrd because he was Nyrøthi, hailing from the northern tundra nation at the very top of the known world. When the dragons fled the Dreadreign, tired of doing House Rezaran's bidding, they sought refuge in Nyrøth. Dragons were said to be the original Timeweavers, and weaverwicks—which came from a curious strand inside their claws—had to be willingly gifted to a mage in order for the power to transfer. They'd become so wary of the Sarthi continent nations that the Nyrøthi were likely the only peoples they trusted with the wicks.

If anyone would have a weaverwick for sale, it would be Østyrd.

When Saff spotted the Crown decree in the wandmaker's window, however, her hopes sank like stones.

> *Following King Quintan Arollan's 14th Amendment to the Public Safety Act of 1074PV, the sale of weaverwicks is prohibited by Vallish wandmakers. Those found in breach are punishable by a maximum sentence of life imprisonment.*

Saffron sighed and stepped inside anyway.

The shop was bright and airy, swirling with dust motes, scented with sawdust and wood polish. The walls were covered floor-to-ceiling with small, locked glass cases, inside which were an astonishing array of wands with neatly written labels. In the center of the room was a large freestanding cabinet with a plaque that read DISPLAY ONLY. Inside were some of the most handsome wands Saff had ever seen, with solid gold handles and jewel-studded tips, the hues of wood so unusual and rare that they must be worth a small fortune.

"Morning," Saff said cheerily, approaching the counter at the back of the shop. "I'm looking for a new wand. Mine is becoming increasingly unreliable." She laid her knobbly abomination on the counter. "If I scorch one more set of my grandmother's curtains, I might be assassinated."

Østyrd sat on a high-backed velvet stool, his feet kicked up on the counter as he shaved a new wand into shape using a strange silver contraption. The toes of his shoes were sharply pointed, in the Nyrøthi fashion, and he had shoulder-length hair the color of ash. Like most native Nyrøthi, his eyes were narrow and slanted—an ancient evolution that provided protection from the harsh white glare of snow and ice. The irises were so pale they reminded Saff of Rasso, whom she'd reluctantly left behind so as not to draw undue attention to herself.

"Enchanted to help, my lady." Østyrd's words had the staccato accent of the tundral north. Running a forefinger down the clumsy length of her own beech wand, he hissed like a cat. "May I ask which wandmaker sold you this . . . *this*?"

"Alexan Renzel, from Lunes."

All at once, the scene came back to her.

Renzel's Wandery was a small, pokey shop tucked in the village of her childhood. Wonky stone walls, dusty rugs, and a single golden-candle that Renzel claimed had burned for centuries. On her sixth birthday, just a month before she started mage school, her parents had taken Saffron to Renzel's for her official Pairing—the momentous day upon which a wand is bonded to a mage.

First, Renzel—a bony, wrinkled fellow with milk-white skin and a gray beard down to his knees—had lowered his hooded hazel eyes and closed a narrow ascenite cuff around Saffron's trembling wrist.

"Sharp scratch," he had said, his vowels full of grit, and tapped the cuff with his own wand—a handsome ebony thing, as long as his forearm.

A small needle had emerged from the inside of the cuff and pierced Saffron's skin, pressing all the way into one of her blue-green wrist veins. She'd fought back a gasp as her blood slowly filled the cuff, turning it from a pearly white to a bright poppy red. It had felt like rather more than a *sharp scratch,* but Saffron hadn't wanted to give the grim-faced wandmaker the satisfaction of seeing her squirm.

"The magical abilities are weak, at this age," Renzel had said to her parents. He had a habit of speaking over Saffron's head, which rankled her. "We need the ascenite to meet with the blood and amplify whatever lies within. Only then can we pair a wand accordingly."

Renzel had plucked a short, squat walnut from his cabinet first. He ran a gnarled finger down its length. "As good a place as any to start. Best suited to confident, steady Enchanters."

Saffron had smiled warmly at her dad, who was himself an Enchanter. Perhaps she'd be like him, charming her way through the world.

But Joran had a strange, semi-strangled expression on his face, glancing sideways at Mellora, who was positively ashen. In hindsight, they'd likely known this was going to be a fraught experience, thanks to Saffron's magical immunity. But she hadn't known that then—practicing illusionwork with her father was still months away. All she'd known was that the forced smiles on her parents' faces made her belly squirm.

As soon as the walnut wand had touched Saffron's palm, there was an uncomfortable lurching sensation in her hand and wrist as the wand recoiled from her—and vice versa. Disappointment had tumbled into her stomach as Renzel grabbed the wand away, but it was still early. She'd find another.

"Perhaps willow, for the humble Healer." Renzel had gazed earnestly through his hooded lids at Mellora, who was visibly pissed off at the word *humble.*

He'd set the sleek, silvery willow wand into Saffron's palm, but the same thing happened. Lurch, recoil. A lick of pain where the needle still penetrated her skin. A strange, expectant energy emanating from her parents.

They'd gone through almost two dozen wands of all shapes, sizes, and woods, and each had the same effect. In the end, Joran had quietly said, meeker than Saffron had ever heard him, "I think we'll take the first. The walnut."

But Renzel had shaken his head fiercely, his wiry beard having somehow grown fuzzier and more unkempt as proceedings had worn on. "My good sir, I'm afraid I cannot sell you a wand so clearly *repulsed* by the mage it would be beholden to. No offense, dear," he'd added, addressing Saffron for the first time.

Eventually, Joran had persuaded Renzel to sell a partly damaged old beech he'd stored in the back, having planned to mend it for over a year. Saffron had left the shop with a beat-up wand case, a sting in her wrist, and the feeling of being approximately one inch tall.

Twenty-one years later, Saffron finally realized the true reason none of the wands had felt right: she needed a weaverwick.

"Alexan Renzel," said Østyrd now, several hundred miles away from that poky hole of a shop in Lunes. "A cantankerous fellow, if memory serves."

"He didn't want to sell me a wand at all," Saffron admitted. "I think he thought I was a Ludder, but I made it through mage school just fine."

"Well, let's see if we can find you a more suitable instrument," said Østyrd, laying down her old wand with a thinly veiled *ugh*. "Do you have an official specialization?"

"No, only Mage Practer." There was no sense in lying. "But . . . I was wondering whether you might have any weaverwick wands hidden away?"

Østyrd's face darkened immediately. He folded his arms over his chest and narrowed his pale eyes. "Did you not see the official decree in the window?"

"I did, but—"

"Well then, you ought to understand that I could lose my freedom. Indulging your whims and curiosities hardly seems worth my life."

"I know," Saff said hurriedly, apologetically. "And I understand your hesitation. Do you know any wandmakers who might be more . . . rebellious?"

She tried for a conspiratorial wink, but his expression remained impenetrable.

"Even if I did," he said coolly, "you'd still be hard-pressed to find what you're looking for anywhere on the continent. Most weaverwick wands were destroyed in the Great Purge of 1024. Vallin, Eqora, Bellandry, and the Eastern Republics all complied with the International Council's decree."

"What about Mersina?" Saff asked hopefully. A small, anarchic island off the coast of Aredan.

"A law unto itself, as I'm sure you're aware. Rascals and thieves and mercenaries, the lot of them. But not especially known for their dragon relations, and without dragons . . . no wicks, no weaving."

Saff sighed inwardly. Some distant part of her knew this—had studied the period of history surrounding the Great Purge at university, even. Back then, it hadn't felt so personal, so critical to her survival, and so her memory had simply let it slip away. But the realization came back to her now in full force: Lorissa Rezaran's wand was likely one of the only weaverwicks left on the continent. And the kingpin had rather a firm grip on it.

"But the dragons retreated to Nyrøth, did they not?" she pushed, hoping for *something* that might help her. "Surely a northern purveyor so esteemed as yourself would have access—"

"My lady, I have been rather explicit in my stance on this." Østyrd's tone was like the cool clink of metal on glass. "There are no weaverwick wands for sale here."

Frustration threatening to boil over, Saff turned on her heel. "Alright. Sorry for the trouble."

As she was leaving, however, Østyrd piped up in a curious sort of voice, "Although . . . my lady?"

She turned to face him questioningly.

"You might try Rezaran's Runes, over on Tamoran Place." He was once again shaving the other wand, gaze fixed on the project with a forced intensity. "They're a strange lot—not strictly wandmakers, more like trinket collectors—but they're fanatical about Timeweavers. They might have something."

Hope fluttered in her chest like batwings. "Thank you. I appreciate it."

"*Vær kynnås,*" he replied.

Her Nyrøthi wasn't great, but Saff knew the expression roughly translated as "fare fine," or more accurately: "good luck, you strange creature, because you're going to need it."

Tamoran Place was only a few streets over, but as she rounded the corner, the acrid smell of smoke was unmissable. Metallic, floral—magical fire, no less. She knew what she would find before she did.

There, in the center of the narrow, cobbled street, a building had burned to the ground. The townhouses on either side were immaculate and unscathed—the shop had been the clear and only target. Now the street looked as though it were missing a tooth.

Dread blackening her vision, Saffron crossed to where the shop once stood. On the ruined flagstones of the shop floor, a clear symbol was drawn in dark charcoal.

The Augurest eye, its iris a spiral.

Saints. This city was growing more divided by the day. From the fresh smell of the smoke, Saff suspected this arson was a recent act. She only hoped the mages inside had escaped with their lives.

For the rest of the day, Saffron tried all the other wandmakers she could think of, but nobody could help. Feet aching from the miles upon miles she'd walked, she dejectedly made her way to her final destination: Artan's Antiques. At the very least, she should secure an hourglass of her own.

Artan's Antiques was a shop of unparalleled dust and chaos. All manner of old objects levitated at various heights, and it was incredibly difficult to navigate without almost being decapitated by a flying semi-globe. (Globes of Ascenfall were always half spheres, since the ever-storms of the Carantic Ocean and the serpent-riddled Serantic Ocean lay between the pangea, the continent, and the other side of the world.)

As she perused, Saffron's eye was drawn by several curious artifacts: a pair of rings engraved with some Ancient Sarthi she couldn't translate, a neat silver set of what looked like enchanted butt plugs, and a blackwood ornament of a mourncrow with a peculiarly lifelike gleam to its eye. Tucked in the backmost corner, a pair of eerie human-shaped statues stood sentry. They were oddly blank, bearing only the faintest outline of recognizable features, and seemed to exist somewhere between solid and *not.* If Saffron had to name their color or material, she almost certainly couldn't. They made her skin creep and prickle, so she tried not to meet their eyeless gaze.

Artan herself was a lithe, narrow-faced mage with long, flowing hair the color of straw. She was wrestling with a leather-bound grimoire, which gave her shock-bolts whenever she tried to touch it.

"Afternoon," she said merrily, trapping the tome beneath her heeled boot. "How may I help you?"

"I'm looking for a small golden hourglass with pearls of ascenite inside." Saffron was so exhausted that she didn't bother to be oblique. "One that could fit in the palm of my hand."

Artan nodded enthusiastically. "I know the type of artifact you seek. We have one or two in the attic—but they're extremely old, so they cost a pretty penny."

"How much?"

When Artan told her the amount, Saff had to stifle a gasp. It was far more than she had in her vault—and she had a *lot* in her vault.

"Saints," she said miserably. The whole day had been a bust. "I can't afford that."

As Artan ducked out of the way of a scrying mirror, the grimoire wriggled free of her foot, and she muttered a heretical curse that made Saff like her all the more. "We also offer part-barter, if you have anything of impressive age or value."

"No. Nothing like that."

"Oh!" Artan exclaimed, peering at Saffron's chest. For a horrible moment, Saff thought her brand might have been on show. "What's that pendant around your neck?"

"This?" Saff clasped her hand to the wooden oval. It was sky blue, reflecting an acquaintance. "It's from my parents' old enchanted front door."

"Such unusual spellwork," Artan replied, amber eyes twinkling. She was a pretty mage, with a purplish birthmark on her cheek in almost the exact shape of a griffin. "May I see?"

"It's not for sale," Saff said instantly, but she held it out for Artan to examine anyway.

"I've never seen anything like this. The magic . . . it's Bellandrian in origin, I believe. From the Charlet region. An ancient order?" She shook her head, voice reverent, almost elegiac. "But no, surely not." She blinked up at Saff. "This is fascinating. I'd accept it in lieu of the ascens for the golden hourglass."

Oh, Saints.

Saffron's head waged war with her heart. There was no way she'd ever be able to afford the hourglass with money alone, and she wouldn't be able to timeweave without one. And timeweaving, for Saff, was fast becoming a matter of life or death. Of surviving in the Bloodmoons.

But the necklace was the last thing she had of her parents—hells, it *was* her parents, what was left of their bodies and souls. To relinquish it now . . . she had already betrayed so much of her past, her childhood, her family. Yet this power had remained untapped in her for so long, and she couldn't bear the thought of letting it lie dormant any longer. It was the only potential way to keep her loved ones safe.

And for her loved ones—for Mal and Merin, Nissa and Auria and even Tiernan—she would give anything.

"Alright," she mumbled, her guts immediately writhing with regret as she unlooped the necklace over her head. She felt naked without it, as she had when they'd taken it from her in Duncarzus. Its absence felt physical, painful, like air against an open wound.

As she handed it over, she thought not just of her parents, but of Levan, and the concentration on his face as he brought it back to life. He'd done that for no obvious reason other than to make her the smallest bit happier. The memory felt like a bruise.

"A pleasure to barter with you," Artan chirped, oblivious to Saff's inner turmoil. "I'll go and retrieve the hourglass from the attic."

While Saffron waited, she rifled through the rest of the shop's eclectic collection, searching for anything else that might help her survive the coming weeks. Her gaze landed on a curious palm-size object: black quartz, with over a hundred flat, symmetrical sides, each one engraved with an Eqoran rune. It was deathly silent and absolutely still, yet it thrummed with a kind of dark, virile energy.

"Oh, yes, a strange little artifact," Artan said, returning from the attic with a maroon velvet pouch in her hand. "A *saqalamis.* Painmaker. When held in the palm, it generates a stunning amount of pain without leaving a scar—very rare, only a handful in the known world. Eqoran Timeweavers used them in the darkest hours of the civil war."

Saffron thought of the deep wound on her arm, carved with a crude shard of glass in the home of Nalazen Zares, and asked, "How much?"

Artan named her price, and Saffron paid it. There was a strong chance it wouldn't work—magic never did, on her body—but she was willing to experiment.

"It must be activated in Eqoran. *Az'alamis.* Proceed with caution, friend."

Saffron left the shop with both the *saqalamis* and the miniature hourglass tucked in her cloak pocket, the velvet pouches warm against her palm.

Forgive me, Mum and Dad, she thought.

Forgive me everything.

PART

FIVE

—

TIMEWEAVER

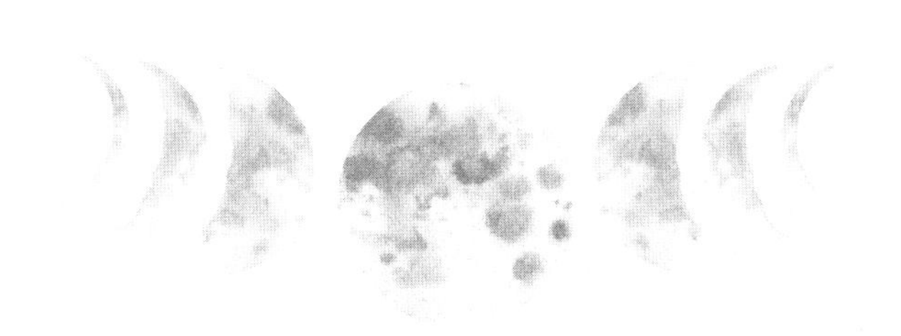

39

...

A Pain Buried

SAFFRON SPENT THE FOLLOWING DAY TINKERING WITH HER newly acquired golden hourglass, but no matter how many different ways she tapped its top and intoned the spell words, time remained resolutely steadfast. Without a companion weaverwick wand, it was essentially a mantelpiece ornament. Even Rasso, who had initially delighted at the appearance of the hourglass, lost interest after several hours of fruitless work.

The whole time, she thought about Levan pinned to that table.

Why did she care, why did she care, why did she *care*?

Why, when she tried to sleep at night, did she think of him reading *Lost Dragonborn* by candlelight as a child? Why did she think of him screaming beneath the furious heat of the scorched poker? Why did she think of him furrowing his brow as he enchanted the wooden pendant around her neck?

An hour before she was due to leave the mansion for the Jaded Saint—where she would confront Tiernan about his own scarlet rot—Saffron went to Levan's chambers to pick up another pot of salve and his beloved copy of *Lost Dragonborn*. She had the vague instinct to take it to Torquil's Tomes to be signed by the author, but forced the childish idea deep down inside.

Don't do that.

What?

Care.

Instead, she brewed a cup of his favorite clove tea—noting with vague surprise that the loose-leaf packet read FOR THE CURING OF ANGUISH—and went to his cell with the salve pot and weathered book tucked beneath her arm, the steaming cup in her hand.

Levan sat in the same stiff position he'd been in when she'd first brought him the salve—there weren't many other options with a hand pinned to the table. The bags under his eyes had darkened to a bruised purple. His hair was stuck up at all angles, as though he'd run his free fingers through it repeatedly, and even his scarlet cloak looked disheveled. Thick stubble covered the lower half of his face.

"Thought you could use some entertainment," she said, resting the tea and the book on the table. "Might stop you from losing your mind."

"Already lost." He grimaced. "But I appreciate the sentiment."

She gestured to the book. "We never did make it to the festival." She thought of the handmade costumes hanging in the armoire, unused, and something panged in her heart.

"Was that today?" he asked, voice bleary. "I've lost track."

Saff leaned against the nearest wall, one heel kicked up. She studied Levan, the slump of his shoulders, the sheen of sweat at his temples. There was a twist of sadness in her chest at the thought that his own father, the man who was supposed to protect him from the world, had inflicted such horror on him.

"Have you slept at all?"

He shook his head. "Can't."

Because every time he did, his hand would jerk against the shard.

"Any ideas on how to free yourself?"

She knew—or she *should* know—that he would manage it, because the prophecy foretold as much.

He would live, only to be killed by her.

But there was a chance she'd knocked them onto a different path entirely after her timeweaving. Was their original fate still cast in curious white smoke? Or had it been unwritten the moment she remade the world to save herself?

How did fate and time intersect?

"None," Levan replied. "I have a whole grimoire of spells in my head, and I've turned over every page, but not one of the usual spell-stripping enchantments would work on deminite. Still don't understand how my father got the curse to take in the first place."

"Maybe he's bluffing."

Levan shook his head. "Already tried pulling the shard the tiniest amount, and all the blood in my body rushed toward it."

She took one look at his hand, and soon wished she hadn't. A gray pallor spread from the wound outward, the color of mountain ash, his veins unnaturally stark. The deminite now had a pinkish hue from the blood it had already consumed, reminding Saffron of the ascenite cuff at her ill-fated wand pairing. She could still feel that piercing burn in her wrist—but it was nothing compared to the massive hunk jutting through Levan's hand.

"Has your father returned since the night he . . ."

"No. Aviruna's been bringing me food. And, as you so tactfully put it, a piss bucket. But she can't keep doing that forever."

A fair observation. His father seemingly had no end state in mind. He hadn't wanted to kill his son, but he'd sentenced him to certain demise regardless. So why keep Levan fed and watered? Was he stewing in his office, frantically trying to find a way to undo his hideous curse? Or was his son out of sight, out of mind?

"You don't look well," Saff said gently, gesturing to the sweat on his forehead. "The wound you mentioned . . . is it still infected?"

"Charming, thank you. But no, the salve's working."

"What's the wound fro—"

"Drop it," he said shortly. "Has my father approached you since . . . ?"

"No."

He relaxed the tiniest amount, and it only made him look more exhausted. "Alright. Good."

There was a knot of emotion in Saffron's chest she couldn't pick loose: threads of guilt and shame, yes, but also fear and desire, all interwoven with the memory of how his lips felt on hers. The taste of clove tea, the furrow of his brow as he pored over her necklace. The hard planes of his body, the rich unspooling deep below her navel. Two golden robes, sewn by hand, left hanging in his armoire.

Somehow, she would fix this. She would steal Lyrian's weaverwick wand, find a way to harness her new powers, and save Levan. Despite everything he was—everything he would always be. Because he wasn't *just* a torturer and a killer. Hells, she was those things too. He was also a dragon nerd, a whimsical Enchanter, a knower of ancient languages, a bereaved son and potentially a widower, a consumer of anguish tea, and a gifted writer, if his journal was anything to go by.

I cannot let desperation cloud my mind. Not when Silver has already misted the glass.

"Where's your necklace?" he asked, gesturing to her bare clavicle, and her hand went automatically to the space where the wooden pendant should be.

"Lost." She swallowed away the lump of emotion. "I think the chain snapped when I was in the city."

"I'm sorry. I know what it meant to you." Something bright and protective flashed over his face, if only for a moment. It reminded her of the look on Nissa's face when she'd found out Saffron would be tortured and branded, and it touched her that he knew just how acute this loss was. "If I somehow make it out of this situation alive, I'll enchant another. It won't be the same, I know. Won't be your childhood door, or the bodies of your parents. But it'll be something. A place for your hand to go when you're feeling too much."

"You've seen me do that?" Her cheeks burned at the thought of him watching her when she wasn't looking.

He nodded wearily. "When you stopped to help that lox-stricken mage on Lancen Place, your hand clutched the necklace like a touchstone. Like you were trying to summon your mother's strength." His gaze met hers again, and something shimmered behind his blue eyes. "I see you, Silver. For all that you are."

Everything in Saffron's body froze for a moment, parsing his words for a more dangerous meaning.

Was he trying to insinuate that he knew she was still a Silvercloak?

A Timeweaver?

Or was she just paranoid?

"And what am I?" she asked carefully, leaning back against the wall in an attempt to look nonchalant.

"Stubborn. Smart. Sarcastic." A curious smile. "Complicated. Brave, in a way most would consider reckless. Afraid, though you'd never admit it. *Good,* though you've started to doubt it."

Saints. She'd always considered herself hard to read.

Yet Levan remained a book mostly closed to her. Nissa was the same, keeping her emotions under lock and key, and the key buried beneath several tons of densely packed earth. Was that Saffron's *thing*? Did she just enjoy the challenge of breaking them open, cracking the spines, dog-earing their pages?

"You know what's unsettling?" she asked, determined to turn the focus back onto him.

"What's that?"

"That you must be in horrible pain, yet there's nothing on your face to suggest as much."

A muscle feathered in his jaw. "Never show what hurts. It'll only be used against you."

"Still, your ability to keep your face still as marble is a little frightening."

His lips quirked. "Would you like me to cry?"

"Maybe a solitary tear. For dramatic purposes." Saff's gaze went to his scarred mouth. "What happened to your lip?"

His free hand touched the silvery indent. "I fell out of a tree when I was a kid. Magic was in short supply where I grew up, so it didn't heal smoothly."

Saffron couldn't fight the laughter. "So ordinary. I was expecting some kind of tragic backstory."

But at the joke, his face darkened, shut down. "I'm not *tragic.* Don't think of me like that."

"My parents were murdered when I was six," Saffron retorted. "I think I have the monopoly on tragic backstories. And you might not feel like you can show the world your pain, Levan, but you can show *me.* I won't use it against you."

His blue eyes had cooled, somewhat. "There's no way of knowing that."

And he was right, wasn't he?

If she did what she came here to do, it would ruin him.

Yet she still found herself wanting to take that pain away.

And she most certainly did not want to leave. Being around him made every inch of her feel awake, alight. It felt like playing high-stakes polderdash, like the first sip of a blackcherry sour, something dark and rich and alluring, something you knew you *shouldn't* want, but that made it all the more intoxicating.

"Are you sure you're alright?" she whispered, fighting the treacherous urge to go to him. He looked so tired.

But he just grimaced, those walls thrown up higher than ever. "Obviously fucking not, Silver."

"Sorry," she muttered, feeling stung, red-cheeked. "I forgot about your anti-caring policy." She pushed her heel off the wall. "Have a lovely night, Levan."

This time, when she went to leave, he did not try to stop her.

40

. . .

Tiernan's Confession

SAFFRON WAITED IN THE JADED SAINT FOR SEVERAL HOURS, but none of her old cohort appeared.

Nursing a small goblet of honeywine, she sat at a table by the entrance, surrounded by vines and candles and statues of mournful Saints, willing her friends to walk in, heads thrown back in laughter, but they never did.

Her brain rifled through the very worst possibilities with a sort of terrible inevitability. Nissa hadn't made it out of the raid, after all. Auria's hideous airborne weapon had turned on her. Tiernan had died on the dock, drowned by the wall of water Castian conjured.

In this world, the worst always came to pass.

Still she drank, and she waited, and she ruminated on Levan's words.

I see you, Silver. For all that you are.

From the way the conversation had evolved thereafter, it hadn't seemed nefarious. Neither an insinuation that she was a rat, nor a Timeweaver. But still the comment had left her unsettled, uncertain of the terrain she was attempting to navigate.

Brave, in a way most would consider reckless. Afraid, though you'd never admit it. Good, *though you've started to doubt it.*

It was an intimate thing, to be seen so completely.

A little after darknight, once she had thoroughly decimated her own emotions, she finally admitted defeat and left the tavern.

"Saffron?" came a timid voice from the alley behind her, and she swung on her heel.

Tiernan.

His frenetic gaze darted behind her, looking for a second figure. "Are you alone?"

Of course. He was here for Levan. *Ordered* to be, most likely.

"I am," she said, feeling uneasy. "Is everyone alright after the raid? Nissa? Auria?"

His face twisted. "They're alive, but Ronnow . . . Ronnow drowned." A thick swallow. "By the time Paliran and the other Healers got to him, it was too late to save him. He had a family. Two kids."

"Oh, Saints," Saff moaned. Ronnow had always been kind to her, had shared his old notes when she was struggling with the procedural exams.

And now he was dead, thanks to Tiernan's betrayal.

She should be furious that his corruption had compromised everything she had worked for, but in truth, she harbored no judgment toward him. He had always been governed by fear, but he wasn't a bad person. And she knew better than anyone how impossible it was to escape the Bloodmoons' snare once you were in its grasp. The scarlet rot, once it had set in, had no known antidote.

"Are you alright?" she asked, remembering the grace he had shown her with his apology.

"No, but also yes." Tiernan ran his hands through his mousy curls, clenching his wand tight. "After everything that happened . . . I asked Auria to marry me."

"Tiernan!" A brief spark of joy in her chest, like flint to dry leaves. She had forgotten what it felt like, the kind of happiness that flared from within. "Tell me everything?"

"The morning after the raid, I just realized . . . we face death every single day. Every single mission, every single arrest, it could go so violently, irrevocably wrong. Look at Ronnow, look at his bereaved family.

So why put off happiness? We could leave that warm common room one day and never come back."

"I'm hoping Auria said yes?"

Saff's tone was light, but everything in her sank. This joy was not as uncomplicated as it had first appeared. Because now that Tiernan had been turned by the Bloodmoons, marrying Auria would make her compromised by association.

Every person in this city is mapped out in my head. Every strand of love and kinship between them shimmers before me, begging to be plucked. The most efficient means of compelling, other than compelling itself, is to tug those threads until they hurt.

The dark tendrils were spreading ever further into the Silvercloaks, into Saffron's found family.

And Tiernan had to know that. He had to know that his proposal was a manacle.

He laughed sincerely. The lanterns in the alley lit him from behind, casting a halo of golden light over his frizzy curls. "To my immense surprise, she said yes."

Saffron smiled, as warmly as she could muster. "I'm so happy for you two. Is your father pleased?"

Something bitter snapped across Tiernan's face, as though he'd been struck. "I haven't told him yet. He's a horrible snob, and her family makes gelato. Or . . . they did. Her grandfather was found murdered by the Bloodmoons." A pained grimace. "By the people holding puppet strings over our lives."

Our lives.

It was essentially an admission that he was indeed the rat, but Saffron couldn't bring herself to ask for details yet. "Is Auria alright? After Papa Marriosan . . . ?"

Tiernan's lips pressed into a flat line. "You know her. She's thrown herself even deeper into her work. Eighteen-hour days, barely eating or sleeping. She got the fourth classification, but hardly cared, just became obsessed with chasing a fifth. I'm worried sick, but what can I do? I love that woman, Saffron." A shard of emotion bobbed in his throat. "So much of my life I spent trying to make my father proud of me. I used to polish his cabinet of ministerial awards by hand, promise him I'd follow in his footsteps. I made my fingers bleed practicing the violin because I knew he liked orchestral music. I studied twenty hours a day in university and still didn't graduate top. Auria did. But it's funny, with her . . . I find myself not caring about my father. I just want to make her happy. Make *her* proud."

Emotion pealed through Saffron's chest. "And I have no doubt you'll do that."

"But I'm not, am I?" Tiernan looked behind her anxiously once more, as though Levan might be concealed by invisibility elixir, hidden in the shadows. "I'm not making her proud at all."

So he knew that *she* knew.

"You were there that night," Tiernan said in a low voice. "On the docks. Auria saw you in a scarlet cloak."

A sharp pang of shame, even though hers was not a true betrayal. *She* was undercover. *She* was still acting in the Silvercloaks' best interest. But she didn't want Tiernan to know that, because it might make him shut down, stop confiding in her. He had to believe they were in the same situation, or he wouldn't talk.

"What happened, Saff?" He took a step toward her, intensity rising in his stare. "How did they get you?"

She shook her head fiercely. "I can't talk about it."

A long, weighted beat. "I understand."

There was a haunted look carved all over his face. Even when he'd been talking about marrying Auria, there was a quiet desperation to it, a dark undertow of fear.

Which of his loved ones were being held at wandpoint? Auria herself? Was he living in such excruciating fear that he had almost entirely shut down?

Only one way to find out.

First, she needed absolute confirmation. "Tiernan . . . the night of the raid. Someone tipped off the Bloodmoons that a tactical team was moving in. And that person was you, wasn't it?"

At once his eyes snapped open, unnaturally wide. He trembled violently, like a fly trapped in a spider's web. His hand clenched tighter around his wand, and slowly, shakily, he lifted it to his throat.

Saffron realized what he was doing a moment too late.

"Sen ammorten—"

"*No!*" Saffron screamed, the sounds echoing around the alley, and there was a spark of bright light, and she withdrew her own wand to cast *praegelos* but it was too late, she was too late, and Tiernan fell lifelessly to the ground.

Rasso howled at the moon.

It all happened so fast, so impossibly fast, just like the night her parents were slain.

How quick it was to end a life, to turn all that rich and complex essence into a pile of flesh and bones.

How much tragedy could unfold between one heartbeat and the next.

She threw herself over his body, shaking him by the shoulders as though convincing him to wake up, wake up, but he was gone, everything that made him Tiernan was *gone,* there would be no marrying Auria, no spawning brilliant, wide-eyed children, no rising through the ranks to prove his father wrong.

As she clutched at his face, his chest, his hands, she thought of the night they first met on the streetwatch. The two of them had been placed with two more experienced watchers, spending the evening shadowing them on their patrol of the city. Tiernan had cowered behind Saffron the whole time, terrified of his own shadow, seemingly mortified by the moans of the pleasurehouses, petrified of the merest suggestion of a scarlet cloak.

But ten minutes before the shift was over, he had seen something the more senior watchers missed—two silhouetted figures on a rooftop, dark cloaks flapping and billowing, one pushing the other to their death. Tiernan slowed the trajectory of the falling body enough that the ground's impact did not kill them.

Saffron had known then that he had *something* to offer the Silvercloaks—what he lacked in pride or courage, he made up for in astute observation and clever, nonviolent solutions.

As the shaken victim was giving a statement half an hour later, Tiernan's mother had emerged from nowhere, having been cloaked in invisibility elixir and tailing him all night. Her face pale and tearstained, she'd thrown her arms around him and told him how proud of him she was—because she didn't think he'd survive that first shift.

Tiernan later told Saffron and Auria that her quiet lack of faith had been worse than his father's outright vitriol. Because if your own mother couldn't see the strength in you, who would?

I do, Auria and Saffron had said at once, and it had not been a lie. By then, Saffron had learned there were all different kinds of strength.

And now he was dead because of her.

Over and over she tried to bring him back—*ans visseran, ans visseran, ans visseran*—but just like it had with Nissa, nothing happened, nothing ever fucking did. She withdrew the miniature hourglass from her cloak pocket, half believing that sheer desperation might conjure a miracle with her wickless wand, but no matter how many times she tapped it, turned it, *begged it,* time marched resolutely, unflinchingly forward.

"*Please,*" she begged Rasso, grabbing him by the soft, ridged shoulders, staring deep into his doleful white eyes. "Please save him."

Rasso tilted his head to one side but did nothing, *could* do nothing, and Saff whimpered, letting her face fall into her hands, sinking her bottom back onto her heels, all the conviction leaving her in one terrible swoop, and she thought that this was it, she could take no more, this was something she would never come back from, would never *let* herself come back from, because everything everything everything was *her fucking fault.*

A mother and father left behind a desolate daughter.

A kingpin's son would bleed a slow, slow death.

A beloved Silvercloak left behind a grieving fiancée, the image of a confetti-strewn wedding now nothing but an open grave.

Not to mention Neatras, Kasan, Ronnow, and however many others had served as collateral damage in this doomed quest for revenge.

Tiernan's body grew cold beside her, death's fingers curled around his soul. He looked so small, so fraught, so afraid. The only thing that could save him now was a necromancer, but—

The idea came to her sharp as a fishhook, and she sat bolt upright so suddenly that Rasso started.

She knew *exactly* where she could find a necromancer.

41

...

The Crypt

SAFF BURST INTO ZARES'S CELL TO FIND THE NECROMANCER lying flat on her back, legs kicked up against the wall, crossing and uncrossing her ankles while whistling a tune. Around both wrists were dark purple scars, symptoms of constant severing and reattaching. Her lank hair was splayed around her, greasy and matted at the ends. Saffron almost retched at the oily stench in the room.

"If you bring back one innocent person for me, I'll free you." Saff's words all rolled into one.

Zares raised a dark, hooked brow, folded spindly arms over her sunken chest, and said nothing.

"I'm sorry about what happened back in your house. I don't even know why we were there, why you're so important. But helping me now is the only way you'll ever be free of this. Because he won't stop, you know. Levan. He won't stop until you finally break."

Another beat, in which Zares weighed her options—and quickly realized this was her only one.

She rolled her body sideways, dropping her feet from the wall, and pushed herself up on her elbow. "Now?"

"Now," confirmed Saff, relief flooding her veins.

This was going to work. Tiernan would marry Auria. He would prove his father—and his mother—wrong.

She tried not to think about the lore surrounding the Risen, the ancient belief that the undead never truly came back. That some fundamental spark in them would be dimmed, extinguished. They would be *almost* themselves, but not quite, and such uncanny variance could drive their loved ones mad.

She tried not to think of Segal's milk-white stare, the emptiness of his movements, as though he could retrace old steps but not choose new ones.

It was better for Tiernan to rise, albeit a little altered, than for him to stay gone.

Wasn't it?

Zares clambered shakily to her feet, and Saff took her by the snarled, bone-cold hand.

Getting Tiernan's corpse to the warded tunnels unnoticed would have been impossible if it weren't for Levan's Bellandrian wand—which she'd pocketed the last time she was in his room. Somehow, she'd been able to conjure a *portari* spell almost immediately, powered by a raw, animalistic desperation that hummed through her very bones. One moment she, Rasso, and Tiernan were hunched in the darkened alley outside the Jaded Saint, and the next they squeezed through the fabric of the world to the concealed entrance of the tunnel. Miraculously, nobody had been coming or going from the mansion. The only sounds were the scuttle of inkmice and a vague dripping noise somewhere deep in the bowels of the building. She'd left Rasso guarding Tiernan's body, so that nobody stumbled upon it and tossed him in the incinerator.

"*Et portari, Tiernan Flane,*" Saff whispered now, gathering all her power into a piercing kernel.

Levan's wand obliged.

With an earsplitting pop, Saffron and Zares dropped into the dark tunnel as though from a great height, limbs crumpling beneath them as they collapsed next to Tiernan's body. Rasso licked at Saff's salty brow and nuzzled his face into her stomach, as though he'd missed her enormously. Corpses were famously not great company.

It was all Saffron could do not to faint. Her well was dangerously depleted, between the *portari* and the fruitless attempts to resuscitate Tiernan, but she wasn't in the mood to pleasure herself in front of a necromancer at the moment.

"This is who I need you to revive. He's only been dead for quarter of an hour."

The necromancer looked from Tiernan back to Saff. "Fine." Then, "You really don't know why they brought me here?"

Saffron shook her head, breathing shallowly.

Zares gave a scathing snort. "He wants to bring his mother back."

"Sorry?"

"Lorissa Celadon." Zares wiped her mouth on the back of her rancid sleeve. "Her son wants to bring her back from the dead."

Saffron frowned. "But she died over twenty years ago. That's not poss—"

"Exactly what I tried to tell him." Zares shrugged. There was a sort of hateful canine snarl to her mouth. "No matter how much ascenite you use to power your crypt, over time the body—"

"Crypt?"

"That's why they're so hell-bent on hoarding ascenite. It's the only thing keeping the old queenpin viable, but they need more with every passing day. They can't sustain her for much longer."

The whole world sharpened to a single point of realization, a truth that should have been so obvious finally revealing itself.

The grand purpose. The why of it all.

The reason Lyrian and Levan Celadon did what they did.

Their plan was pure, desperate delusion. And yet Saffron understood it, deep down. Sometimes she thought there was nothing she wouldn't do to bring her parents back to her.

Mellora and Joran would be fully decomposed by now.

But for the old queenpin . . .

Could it be possible, in a crypt of raw ascenite?

First things first, she had to revive Tiernan. Then she could worry about Lorissa Rezaran, about the Bloodmoons' twisted mission, and about how to finally end it.

She would have to give her wand to Zares—the necromancer's had been confiscated long ago. Yet despite the knowledge that Zares had been branded, that she could not betray Saffron without losing a hand, something about handing over her own knobbly beech filled Saff with unease. It would be worth the risk, to bring back Tiernan, and yet—

—there was a slamming sensation against her head, an elbow hook to the temple, a starburst of agony across her vision, and she collapsed to the ground, everything bleached white.

Zares howled a lupine howl, her hand severed clean from her wrist, but instead of succumbing to the pain, instead of crumpling to the ground in agony and despair, the necromancer clambered inelegantly to her feet and ran for her life.

Vision still vignetted, Saff lifted her wand and aimlessly incanted after the disappearing figure, "*Sen effigias*."

But Zares's footsteps were already vanishing up the tunnel, and the spell fell dramatically short. The wards would let the necromancer pass too thanks to the brand on her chest.

Hope deserted Saffron with the sudden completeness of an eclipse. She could barely cling onto consciousness, let alone pursue her mark. Bleary-eyed, she stared up at the carved markings on the tunnel wall, the depictions of elegant timeweaving almost mocking her for what she could not do without a wick.

Her shoddily conceived plan had been a shambles. Rushed, poorly executed, an embarrassment to her Silvercloak training. She should've restrained Zares until the last possible minute. She should've been more alert for an attack, should've anticipated that the necromancer may have considered her hand a fair price for freedom. Saff had let desperation and impatience addle her judgment, let them undo years of hard-fought savvy.

It was clear now that Zares had been distracting her with stories of Lorissa Rezaran, but did that mean they were not true?

No. It had chimed the tuning fork in Saffron's chest, plucked the instrument she had begun to recognize as her detective's instinct.

Lorissa Rezaran, preserved in a crypt for twenty-one years.

A *crypt*.

Saff sat bolt upright, heart pounding with realization, still dizzy, still nauseated. The tunnel tipped around her, and she tried not to look at the necromancer's snarled hand lying next to her best friend's corpse. A museum of her failures.

Focus. Something Levan had said on the night of the raid, as he was using *portari* to help them escape, came back to her: *Cryptmouth Tunnel.*

Cryptmouth.

Again came that chime, that tuning fork, her instincts clarion clear.

Dazed, she tentatively touched her fingers to the nearest tunnel wall.

The crypt was behind the markings. It had to be. What better way to honor a mother long gone than with art about what her blood had been able to do?

Climbing shakily to her feet, Saffron's mind reeled. If she could just get into the crypt—a crypt so piled with ascenite that it had kept a corpse viable for over two decades—maybe she could leave Tiernan there until she found another necromancer. *Or* until she could find a weaverwick wand and rewind the clock to before she confronted him.

She slid a palm along the rough wall, hoping to find a seam of sorts.

Nothing.

Using her own wand and then Levan's, she tapped at various spots on the markings—the words, the hourglass, the figures—and tried every password she could think of. *Fair featherroot. Baudry's bitch.* Even, through absolute desperation, *Dragontail.*

Nothing.

She recited the timeweaving spell over and over.

Still nothing.

Just as she was about to give up—about to accept that the tuning fork in her chest might be off-pitch—a final idea came to her.

Maybe Lyrian kept an hourglass on his desk for a reason. Maybe it was a key, of sorts.

She pulled her own hourglass from her cloak pocket and tapped it with her wand.

"*Tempavicissan,*" she whispered, and the world did not turn itself around, but a section of the wall in front of her melted into the ground.

Everything in her leapt. Grabbing Tiernan by the ankle, she hauled him over the threshold, then tapped her hourglass again. The wall closed behind her, and she exhaled slowly, looking around.

They were in some kind of entry chamber, every square inch made of ascenite, the surrounding air cold and metallic. The walls, the ceiling, the floor, all of it *glowing* in a way plain ascenite did not, like the shining pearl-silver of a waxed moon. Enchanted with a kind of embalming power to keep Lorissa viable?

Scattered around the atrium were piles and piles and piles of coins, of smelted bars, of ascenite rings and necklaces and diadems, all gambled away by the helplessly addicted citizens of Atherin. More ascenite than Saffron had ever seen in her life.

The space was entirely devoid of noise. No longer could Saff hear scuttling feet or distant dripping, just a silence so absolute that it made all the hairs on her body stand on end. The unrelenting cold held her spine pin-straight.

From the entry chamber, an open doorway led into another space beyond. Leaving Tiernan just inside the threshold, Saff passed into a room six times the size of the atrium.

The central chamber's ceiling was domed, a little like an Augurest temple, but hewn from raw ascenite rather than tempered purple glass. The floor tiles were carved into seven-pointed stars, starting with a single star in the center and spiraling outward in concentric circles. Silver sconces were bolted to the walls, flickering with a blue-ish light, and several other arches branched off the space: more vaults, filled floor-to-ceiling with ascenite treasures. Something cold rose in Saffron's chest, a sense of awe and horror at what the Bloodmoons had built.

Right at the apex of the chamber was a raised platform—a block of solid ascenite worth more than the entire village of Lunes—upon which Lorissa Celadon, or Lorissa *Rezaran,* lay in death.

If Saff hadn't known any better, she'd have said the corpse was an ice sculpture—almost entirely devoid of color, shining blue-white like a Nyrøthi glacier. The scarlet cloak was a shock of blood in the otherwise pale, pearlescent chamber.

Lorissa's chestnut hair was plaited in a thick braid, resting on her chest beside folded hands. Her lashes were black crescents against her muted skin, and her lips were a deathly lilac. She looked so much younger than Saffron would've expected—Lyrian was in his sixties, after all—frozen in a moment of early motherhood, her own life just beginning. The body still smelled, but not of death. Of *magic.* Something clean and bright and metallic, with an underpinning of roses and earth.

There was something so mesmerizing about Lorissa, even in death. A kind of luring charisma, an innate demand for respect.

A chill scraped down Saffron's spine, like a shovel over frosted earth. She had seen many a dead body before, but there was something profoundly disturbing about the corpse before her, about the glowing crypt in which she lay. It was so unnaturally silent, so *still,* like the *praegelos* charm itself, like the whole of reality hung suspended, awaiting the queenpin's next breath.

She could not bear to look away.

There was a legendary cliff on the southwestern tip of Daejin, sky-high stone cutting into the Serantic Ocean. The waves famously crashed over the Shard of Khulin with such astonishing height and force that it defied all nature—almost a thousand feet of towering water, if the lore held any truth. A vast yawning mouth of ocean biting down on the jutting bluff, minute after minute, century after century.

It was often said that to witness the waves of Khulin was to lose one's mind, because the human head could not make sense of such magnitude. The fertile grassland atop the cliffs remained unfarmed for a thousand years, because no shepherd would work in such proximity to the waves. Daejin was frequently left out of trade routes, because no sailor worth their salt would willingly enter those waters.

Lorissa's crypt made Saffron feel as though she was looking over the Shard of Khulin.

Awestruck, terrified, vaguely insane.

It was so damn *quiet.*

With immense effort, she hauled herself back to the atrium, remembering why she was here in the first place.

Tiernan's body looked so frail, so angular, as it slumped against a large open chest filled with ascenpearl necklaces. In the sickly blue glow of the crypt, he too bore that glacial pallor, though without any of Lorissa's innate gravitas. The sense that he was an ice sculpture, not a person, was only intensified by the silver cloak spilling around him—

the only bolts of color were the sapphire brooch at his throat and the burgundy starburst at his chin.

Saff dragged her friend's body into the vault farthest from the entrance. Hopefully the kingpin would only come to visit his wife, not check on the surrounding loot.

"I'll come back for you," she murmured, kissing her fingertip and touching it to Tiernan's forehead, then the tip of his nose, then the jutting point of his chin, a mourning tradition from northern Vallin. One she'd been too traumatized to do for her parents.

A single tear spilled down her cheek. The salty warmth of it was even starker in the clean ice-brightness of the crypt.

She had endured so much, lost so much.

How did it still hurt like this?

She knew it had been a mistake to allow her fellow cadets to breach her emotional barriers. She *knew* it would only ever end like this. And yet she had done it anyway.

"*Tempavicissan,*" she said, as clearly as she could, tipping her hourglass and scraping her wand against the top.

The tunnel wall sank, and the threshold appeared.

The breath leaked out of her like water through a hole in a pail. She had cast too much, her well wholly depleted. Her legs were weak, foal-like, but she smoothed down her cloak and fixed a look of strength onto her tear-streaked face.

She was going to see Levan. And she was going to confront him about everything she had just uncovered.

42

...

A Well Refilled

When saffron entered the cell at around four in the morning, Levan's head lifted off his chest. He'd perhaps been dozing, but the red rims around his eyes suggested he hadn't had any real sleep over the last three days.

"Silver," he said, a hoarse murmur, and it raked down her back like nails.

His hair was damp, his face clean shaven. A bucket of soapy water sat on the floor beside him, a cloth resting over the edge. The clean tang of citrus soap oil hung on the otherwise stagnant air.

"I know why you're doing it," she replied softly, pressing the door closed behind her.

"Why I'm . . . ?"

"Hoarding ascenite like the mountain dwellers in *Lost Dragonborn.* Obsessively tracking down necromancers."

As ever, he held his features perfectly still.

"I found the crypt. Your mother."

Levan's face remained impassive, but his eyes weren't as cold and empty as they usually were. They churned with anticipation. "So then, from the date . . . you know the truth about yours."

She hadn't noticed a particular date. "What do you mean?"

A fraught pause, in which Levan clearly realized he'd said too much. "No. Nothing."

Saffron's limbs had been heavy with tiredness, but a sudden chill shook the exhaustion off her like leaves from a winter tree.

"The truth about my . . . mother?"

Her heart pounded, as though her body knew something her mind did not.

Levan shook his head, freshly washed hair gleaming in the low lantern light. "Forget it."

"Would *you* forget it?" She took one step toward him, then another, planting her palms on his broad, firm shoulders and forcing him to look at her. The warmth of his body spread up through her hands like she was holding them to a hearth. "Tell me, Levan."

Averting his gaze, he carefully studied his pinned hand. "Twenty-one years ago, my mother died during a heist in Almere. Just over the Bellandrian border. Segal had a scroll of all the registered necromancers in Vallin. A few villages away, in Lunes—"

"Was my mother," Saff finished, with a thunderclap of understanding.

"They came to your door in desperation."

"How do you know?"

"Segal told me, when he saw we were getting closer. Your parents died because my mother did." Levan looked up at her through dark eyelashes. "Ever since I found out . . . it's felt like our fates have always been braided together."

At the very moment she was hunched over her parents' bodies, weeping and pleading with the world to undo it, a young Levan was doing the very same just a few miles away.

She had always felt it: a shared grief, a shared pain, a shared fate.

If she hadn't turned that doorknob, her parents would still be alive.

And so would Levan's mother.

It was a revelation so enormous that Saffron couldn't hold it in her head. She didn't know whether to turn and run from this room, this house, this life, far, far away until she could *breathe* enough to process it, until her ribs knotted themselves back together again—or to give herself away to the pain, to run straight into Levan's arms, the way the prophecy foretold, the way destiny had written it from the beginning.

"You genuinely believe you can bring your mother back?" she asked gently. "After all this time?"

"That belief is the only thing that keeps me upright."

The image of Lorissa Rezaran lying motionless in that crypt burned blue-white in Saff's mind, and she thought that maybe his conviction was not so misguided.

Levan shifted uncomfortably in his wooden chair. "Can I ask a favor?"

She nodded, ears ringing, dimly aware that her palms were still upon him.

He gestured to the ground. "Castian brought me soapy water to wash, but I can't undress with my hand pinned. I've managed my hair and face, and my bottom half, but . . . can you cut this sleeve off?"

Saff removed her hands from his shoulders, pinching the cuff of his cloak between her thumb and forefinger. Pulling out her wand, she drew upon her near-empty well, hoping there would be a final dreg, a shallow scrap, to produce this simple magic.

"Sen incisuren."

A small, unconvincing tear appeared at the cuff.

Saffron discarded the wand and carefully ripped the fabric with the grain, all the way up to his shoulder, then across the chest, so that the cloak—and his black tunic—fell away from his arm.

At the sight of what lay beneath, Saffron gasped sharply.

Carved in a neat tally line were dozens—if not hundreds—of equally spaced scars. Some were fresher than others, the skin around the top five raw and inflamed.

"Levan, what the hell are those?"

But some part of her already knew.

"My kills," he replied gruffly, not meeting her eye.

The freshest cuts, red and gnarly, had to be the mistaken-identity Brewer, the three Whitewing assailants, and Tenea.

"That's why you needed the salve," she said flatly. She didn't know *why* she felt so angry at him, only that she did. A kind of protective, emotionally charged anger. "Why do this to yourself?"

He shrugged, but it was far from nonchalant.

"I always thought you didn't feel anything about the bad things you do. You told me your emotions are essentially scar tissue."

He made a *pfft* noise, puffing the air through his lips. "I feel everything at full and terrible force. I just keep it inside, where it belongs."

Levan shrugged the cloak and tunic off the rest of his upper half, dropping them to the ground. Gingerly, to protect his impaled hand, he dipped the washcloth back into the citrus-oiled water, squeezed out the excess liquid, then washed himself.

Saff found it almost impossible not to watch.

His body was a map of the person he was. It was lean and toned from his running and combat training, knots of muscle in his arms and shoulders and chest. His stomach was more concave than she suspected it usually was, with two hollow grooves either side of his belly button, the sharp *V* of his hips disappearing into his waistband.

And there, right over his heart, was the unmistakable pink-silver of a burn scar. Old, but undeniable.

"So you do have a brand."

He stopped for the briefest moment, tense, but said nothing.

"When did it happen?"

"I was ten."

"Your father?" Saff was almost afraid of the answer, because there was a very good chance she'd want to murder Lyrian if so.

"Vogolan held the poker, but my father gave the order."

His tone betrayed no bitterness or anger, but he must have been writhing with it.

"How could he do that to his own son?" The thought of Joran giving her so much as a paper cut was unfathomable.

Levan's jaw clenched, but he did not reply.

There was also a betrothal tattoo where his rib cage kissed in the middle of his chest. A traditional sprig of holly, with two leaves and two berries.

Alucia.

She couldn't bring herself to ask what happened. There had been too many painful revelations for one night, and her exhaustion had returned with a vengeance.

Levan washed his torso, his pinned arm, pale skin glistening with the citrus oil. But when it came to his back, he struggled awkwardly with the angle of it, flicking the cloth between his shoulder blades without achieving very much, and when he tried to wash his unpinned arm, he couldn't fold his wrist the right way.

"Do you want me to do it?" Saff asked, before she could think about what she was suggesting.

Levan froze for a beat, swallowed so hard his throat bobbed, then handed her the cloth.

His back was rippled with muscle, every groove and ridge shadowed by the flickering lantern light behind them. She ran the cloth over the sharp lines of his shoulder blades, and he shivered as the cold fabric brushed his warm skin.

Still standing behind him, she delicately held his hand as she cleaned the inside of his pulsating wrist, the crook of his elbow, the bulge of his bicep. For some reason, it felt more intimate than the impassioned kiss they'd exchanged, and he seemed to have temporarily stopped breathing.

She didn't want the moment to end, so she squeezed the cloth and rubbed it against the back of his head, soaking away the excess oil and moisture. His hair felt impossibly soft. Every other part of him was hard, honed, a stoic construct against the world, but his hair felt like skimming the bolts of satin her uncles used for the royal cloaks. As her nails scraped over his scalp, he let out a long, slow sigh. She felt the reverberation all the way up her arm.

In that moment, every other emotion fell away, leaving only *want.*

It wasn't just the generalized arousal she always felt after too much casting—the simple animal of her body trying to replenish its magical well.

It was deeper, richer.

Darker. Altogether more terrifying.

Tentatively, heart racing, she planted a kiss on his tufted double crown, the hair scented with grapefruit and blood orange and lemon zest. She cupped a palm in the crook between his throat and his collarbone, then traced kisses down his neck, the skin warm and tender, his pulse skittering against her lips.

Levan's breathing turned ragged as he laid his free hand over hers. "I'm not a good person, Silver."

She pulled her mouth away, but only slightly, so that her breath still caressed his throat. "You told me to abandon childish notions of good and evil or I wouldn't survive here."

Dropping the cloth to the ground, all the exhaustion had suddenly left her, but so too had that jittery, uncomfortable adrenaline. She coursed with a pleasant flutter, a raw anticipation, the air around them charged, crackling with something singular and intimate.

He tilted his head back against her hand, the lantern illuminating every ridge of his throat, and he sighed his surrender.

Still standing behind him, she traced her forefinger up his sharp jaw then brought her lips to his. They were upside down, the angles all wrong, and surely his throat was pulling tightly, but he breathed against her, ragged, and as they kissed softly, uncertainly, that familiar unspooling began in her chest, her stomach, between her legs.

She crossed around to the front of him, trying not to look at the brand on his chest or the scars on his arm or the sprig of holly between his ribs, and kissed him again, deeper now that the angle was right, his tongue darting against hers like an invitation.

All thoughts of crypts and corpses vanished from her head.

If that made her a bad person, so be it.

She was driven once more by that deep nihilism, a sense of reckless abandon, the feeling that they both might die at any moment, all the fear and danger and pain coalescing into something wholly intoxicating. As she kissed him beneath his ear, along the hard ridge of his shoulder, over the puckered skin of the brand, the frantic pattering of his heart sounded like *victory*, that she could coax some kind of reaction from this stoic, closed-off mage.

Running a palm over his chest, his bare stomach, the *V* of his hips, she tucked a thumb into his loose waistband, behind the stiff leather of his belt, and an involuntary moan tore itself from his lips.

"We can't," he muttered, swallowing hard. "The power dynamic—it's wrong." Saff thought he meant because he was held prisoner, but then he added, "You're here against your will."

Their faces were inches apart. Her eyes searched his, finding nothing but desire behind them. "And yet you're the one pinned in place, and I'm the one who could hurt you if I so wanted to."

His pupils flared dangerously. "Hurt me, then."

Saints.

There was a hitching feeling in her chest as she worked the buckle of his belt free. He shimmied in the chair so she could tug down his trousers and his underwear, leaving him naked beneath her.

When she took him in her hand—palms still soft and slick with citrus oil—he inhaled sharply. She started slowly, questioningly, feeling him throb against her palm; when he gave her a strained nod, she went faster, digging the nails of her free hand into the back of his neck, their lips almost but not quite touching.

For a moment he hung his head back, letting his eyes flutter closed. When they reopened, something fierce and bright had awoken in them.

His unpinned hand lifted the fabric of her tunic, caressing her rounded hips, the soft dip of her waist, going higher until he found the low teardrop of her breast. His deft fingers found the silver bar piercing her nipple, tweaking the metal sharply enough to send a lance of pain-pleasure through her.

Magic collected at the bottom of an empty well, rich and golden and pulsing.

Heat pooled between her legs—or rather a kind of clashing of warmth and coolness. Letting go of him, she kissed his cheekbone, his jaw, the ridges of his throat, as his hand traveled toward her own waistband and then underneath. She couldn't suppress the moan as his fingertips found the throbbing point of her, stroking in soft circles, the heel of his hand pressed into her lower stomach.

The residual citrus oil built into a tingle, then a pleasant kind of burn, so at odds with the gentle stroke of his fingertips. Her pale curls fell around his face as she stood over him, and the air between their mouths was hot, wanting.

Magic surged inside her, something sentient, alive.

Levan's eyes stared up at her as though she were the most beautiful woman in Ascenfall, as though she was a savior sent from the Saints, as though she held his heart in her very palm, and the vulnerability of the gaze undid something in her.

His hand pushed lower, deeper, until his fingers were inside her, slowly rotating, finding the pulsing spot and pressing against it over and over. The tingle of the citrus oil, the way he cupped her and caressed her, the blazing intensity on his face . . . it all built into something rich and pure and all-consuming. She gave herself over to it, a surrender, a card game, a long drink of blackcherry, all the things she should not crave but *did.*

The curling pleasure swelled and pulsed until it was a towering, peaking thing, magic filling her well until it spilled over, and then there was the shuddering cascade, a tidal wave, a soft whimper into Levan's neck. The tingling spread to her fingers and toes, and she shivered as the wave ebbed against the shore.

Drawing away from him, she kicked off her boots and lowered her trousers, pausing before dropping her underwear.

"Do you want to?" she asked softly. "Or do you have too much *power?*"

"The power is all yours, Silver. Do with it what you please."

It was a stirring thought.

She could unmake the world . . .

. . . and she could unmake the kingpin's son.

So often in the last few weeks she had felt utterly powerless, tugged along on the Bloodmoons' vicious undercurrent, collared by the cruel kingpin, forced to do heinous things to save her own life. And so it was little wonder she felt *ignited* now, now that she wielded control, now that it had been willingly given to her.

In her experience, the best sex was born from the gaining or relinquishing of power.

Glad she'd remembered to take the contraceptive tincture amidst all the chaos, she tugged off her tunic and then watched as his eyes roved over her naked body with something like worship.

Gripping the back of the chair with one hand, she straddled his lap and slowly lowered herself onto him. He let out a sharp exhale, and she worked up and down, feeling the citrus oil tingling, a throbbing inside her like a second heartbeat, the fullness so complete that it ached.

His eyes burned with . . . *something*. That shared fate, that mirrored pain. The protectiveness, the unexpected tenderness. He moved slowly, so as not to tear his hand against the shard, his breathing frayed, uneven.

Hurt me, then.

Heeding his command, she moved faster, up and down, her thighs burning from the effort, and with her free hand she grabbed her wand and aimed it at the base of him.

"*Et aflan*," she whispered, and a raw spark of magic shot out to meet tender skin.

Levan jolted, and finally a moan tore from his throat. She arched her back, and he took her piercing in his teeth, sharply enough to send a similar spark of pain-pleasure coursing through her. At her own gasp, she felt his thighs shudder, and he rolled his head back, eyes fluttered closed, unmoored.

His whole body jerked involuntarily, and his eyes flew open, wincing at his hand.

"Sorry," whispered Saffron, pressing her sweat-slicked forehead again his.

"Don't be." He laced his free hand through her hair, planting a kiss so tenderly on her cheek that she thought she might come apart at the seams. "If that was my last time . . . well."

"Don't say that," Saff said, firmly but still softly. "It's not going to be your last time."

He swallowed hard, still breathless. "I'm dying, Silver."

Levan's eyes went to his impaled hand, and Saff's followed. She soon wished she hadn't.

The small circle of ash gray around the wound had spread over his whole palm, devoured his fingertips, and was now lapping at the shore of his wrist.

The shard was a bright poppy red from all the blood it had consumed.

43

. . .

Sen Perruntas

LEVAN WAS DYING, AND NOBODY, NOT EVEN SAFFRON, COULD stop it.

She tugged her tunic back over her head, both sweating and cold to the bone, though her well of magic was full and shimmering once more. "Has your father been back since that first night?"

"Once," Levan replied, still breathing unevenly. "He tried to undo it, to tear the magic out of the shard. Didn't work. He even brought Miret along, but not a single book in that enormous library had any better ideas."

Saffron blew air through her lips. "So there's no way to free yourself?"

"Only one." His mouth twisted into a grimace. "But it's terrifying."

"What is it?" Saff asked, but judging by the clench in her guts, some part of her already knew.

He raked his free fingers through his fluffy, freshly washed hair. "I think I have to lose the hand."

"Levan . . ."

"There's no other way, is there? I've thought about two things on a constant loop since I've been here. How to survive this. And, well, you."

The sweet ache of the second part barely registered over the horror of the first. "You can't lose your hand."

"The longer I wait, the more of the arm it'll leech away, and the worse it'll be."

"Do you think you'll be able to reattach it afterward?" Saffron gnawed at the inside of her cheek. "You're rather good at that."

He shook his head. "It's beyond salvation. The second the shard is removed, the hand will wither and die."

"Saints." Such an inadequate response, and yet what else could she say?

He leaned his head against the back of the chair, letting his eyes flutter closed. "During my literature degree, we—"

"Literature degree?" Saff blinked in surprise.

He looked bashful for a moment. "I got my Knight's Scroll at the University of Atherin. Nobody here knows. But we studied the *Lost Dragonborn* books in immense detail. I wrote my dissertation on all the small ironies of Aymar's redemption journey. And this feels like that, doesn't it?" A bitter laugh. "The first night we met, you watched me cut off a man's hand over and over again in the pursuit of my own interests. And now, in order to survive long enough for those interests to come to pass, I'll have to endure the same."

Saffron found the thought too horrendous to comprehend. "How will you do it? I rescued your wand from your room, but with the deminite shard physically inside your body . . ."

"You'll have to do it for me."

Everything in her bucked against the notion. "I can't."

He opened his eyes. They were bleary with exhaustion, all the sensual charge gone. "It's that or watch me die."

"We can ask Miret, or Segal, or Castian. Your father, even."

Yet Segal was Risen, and Castian was a lox addict, and Miret . . . well. Miret's head seemed to largely reside in the clouds.

Something vulnerable passed over Levan's face. "I don't trust any of them like I trust you."

Irony, indeed.

"Not even Miret?"

"I trust his character, but not his abilities. He rarely uses magic. Only cares for books."

"He could use a blade."

"Not as clean. Magic seals the wound immediately."

"It could be cauterized."

A vehement head shake. "Then I'm left with a seared stump. I know a Healer who specializes in enchanted prosthetics—Tålun. He used to be a bartender at the student union, when he was doing his Knight's Scroll in Modern Medicine. He worked on the prosthetics for those children who lost their tongues a few years ago. I'll find him afterward. He owes me a favor."

Saffron sighed with disapproval. "You can't just go around threatening people into helping you and call it a *favor.*"

"Oh ye of little faith." A curious smile, though he showed no teeth, no dimples. "I saved his life, actually. The union kitchen caught fire and I went in to rescue him. Burned myself up pretty badly, but I healed us both once we were out."

Saffron stared at him. "You're a very complicated person."

But he wasn't—not really. His moral code made a brutal kind of sense to Saffron. He would only hurt or kill if he believed it would help him bring his mother back. Or in self-defense, like those Whitewings on the first night she'd met him.

"You have to do it, Silver." His face was pale, but if he felt any fear, he gave none away. "And it has to be now. The gray is spreading too fast."

A vise closed tight around Saffron's stomach. "Would lox help? For the pain."

"No," he muttered quickly, resolutely, before softening his tone. "It took too much for me to stop. Harrow locked me in an empty room for a week. Even now, the claws are still in me, ready to pull me back under the surface." He swallowed. "Let's just get this over with."

Saffron's mind went to the prophecy, trying to recall whether he'd been one-handed or not. If he'd been in possession of both, that would surely indicate that they'd been knocked onto another timeline, that her unmaking of the world had rendered the prophecy meaningless, that maybe in one world she would have killed him, but not this one, not after she'd taken his hand. But everything was bleary, confused, and she couldn't conjure the exact image of the vision.

Reluctantly, she withdrew her wand from her waistband. "Are you sure?"

"I've done this to countless victims," he said through clenched teeth. "I'd be a fucking coward if I said no."

"Not a coward. Human."

She hesitated, wand suspended in midair. Mere moments ago, she'd relished in how much control she had, how the situation was entirely in her hands, and yet now that power felt tainted. A curse, a burden. All at once, she wanted to give back the reins.

"There's not all that much that can go wrong," Levan said gently, trying to reassure her. "The worst thing you can do is hold back, or you'll only sever it halfway. Better to go too hard and send the hand smashing into the opposite wall. I'd rather this didn't take multiple attempts."

Her mouth was as dry as dust. "Do I need to make a tourniquet first?"

"No. The magic seals it immediately. I won't bleed out."

"Levan . . ."

She'd been prepared to experience infinite brutalities in the Bloodmoons, but this was not one of them.

"Do it now," Levan said, in a way that suggested he had steeled himself, but it wouldn't hold for much longer.

She cupped his face in her hands, and something raw and fearful fleeted behind his eyes. She didn't know what she wanted to do: to kiss his lips or his forehead, to stroke his cheek, to comfort him or to bolster him, to say sorry or something entirely more ruinous.

Instead, she gave him a single stoic nod and raised her wand. Her heart in her mouth, she rested the tip just below the protruding bone of his wrist, and she knew that if she didn't do it now, she never would.

She'd been able to carve out an eye with a letteropener while the victim begged for mercy. Surely she could do this. The horrors she'd experienced had inadvertently prepared her.

"Sen perruntas."

The magic shot from her wand as a silver-white blade, and the knife-edge was through the wrist in a flash so fast it was almost invisible to the naked eye.

In fact, she might not have been sure it happened at all, were it not for Levan's suppressed roar, teeth clenched, the sound ripping from his throat but bitten down before it could escape fully formed.

He yanked his freed wrist away from the table, clutching his forearm to his chest, panting raggedly, eyes pressed shut.

Sure enough, the wound was clean, sealed over with something remarkably skin-like.

Pinned to the table, the severed hand was still as stone. Chest scudding, Saffron took a deep breath and pulled the shard from it—because maybe, if she acted quickly enough, she could reattach the hand.

But as soon as the shard was loosed, the hand did something no hand could ever recover from. It withered and crumpled like a crushed tin can, all remaining blood seeping into the deminite, taking with it clumps of flesh and muscle, frayed skin and wet strings of ligament. Soon the shard was a dark crimson, the hand a mangled collection of bones.

Saffron dropped her wand and rushed to Levan, who wasn't making a sound but trembled violently, his remaining hand clamped around the other wrist. There was only the faintest tint of ash gray near the stump.

"Are you alright?" she asked stupidly, but what else was there to say?

"Just go, Silver."

"I'm not leaving you."

"Please." The word was serrated. "I don't want you to see me like this."

"No, Levan. I need to help you to—"

"*Go.* Now."

Horror churning in her stomach, she fled the cell, wondering whether he would ever look at her the same way again. Would he always associate her with this? With one of the most painful moments of his life?

She left the deadbolt hanging open, so that he could leave, and just as she reached the end of the corridor, she heard Levan's earth-shattering roar.

It cost her everything she had not to go to him.

Back in her chambers, Saffron knew that there was so much she needed to *do.* She had to find a weaverwick wand, for her own protection. She needed to harangue Segal for his scroll of necromancers, so that Tiernan might rise again. She needed to make contact with Aspar, to come up with alternative plans after the botched raid, to let her know about the now-deceased rat in her ranks.

But all she *could* think about, all she could see in her mind's eye, was Levan.

Levan hurt. Levan alone.

Levan studying literature, poring over old texts and discussing them with Miret. Levan practicing ancient languages until the sound was just right on his tongue. Levan wielding the most complicated and beautiful magic she'd ever witnessed. Levan running for miles and miles, sparring and brawling, until his body was slick with sweat, exhaustion sinking into his bones. Levan enchanting her necklace. Levan bringing Nissa back, because he could tell how much it meant to her. Levan grieving his lost love, Levan growing addicted to the very substance he'd brought into the city, Levan suffering his way out of it in a sealed room. Levan mourning his mother. Levan hunched over Lorissa's body, pleading with his own magic to bring her back, and his magic refusing to rise.

Leaving him in that cell caused a physical ache, a knot of pain between her ribs.

And she knew then, in her heart of hearts, that she *had* to have nullified the prophecy when she unmade time. She had to have thrown them onto a different path, because right now, nothing in the world could make her want to kill him.

Yet . . . House Rezaran had unmade time over and over again during the Dreadreign, and still the first four Augurs' prophecies had come to pass.

There was a feeling in her chest—a gathering snarl of certainty and dread—that these events concerned themselves with the fate of the world, somehow. It all felt so fucking *significant.* She was no Foreseer, and yet, somehow, she knew that she and Levan were at the center of something enormous and devastating, something that would end in mutual ruin. Something that would not just unmake them both—it would unmake everything.

Of course, it was very possible she was just in love.

44

. . .

Golden Hand

After a few hours of patchy, shallow sleep, Saffron spent most of the next day trying to contact Aspar, but every time she said "*Dragontail,*" Aspar would reply *falling,* meaning it wasn't safe to talk.

Saff was inwardly relieved not to be able to talk freely to her commanding officer—she did not want to relive the botched raid, and she certainly didn't know how to broach the subject of Tiernan. Part of her hoped that she'd be able to find a necromancer and revive him before Aspar ever knew he'd died. Although, in truth, the Order of the Silvercloaks was no place for a Risen. Not only would he be a traitor, but he'd also be the maligned undead. Even if Saffron managed to bring him back, he'd still lose everything.

Everything but Auria. And that had to be worth something.

In any case, her hours of research had proven fruitless. Segal was nowhere to be found—she had no idea where his sleeping quarters were, and thus no idea where his necromancer scroll might be lurking—so she headed to the library to browse every piece of literature Miret could find on necromancy. All the tomes were well-worn, dog-eared on countless pages, others annotated with the swirling cursive she recognized from Levan's diary.

Levan.

Thoughts of him shredded all else.

Had he left the cell? Or had the pain sunk him deep into shock, his organs shutting down, taking his final breaths alone and scared?

That evening, she finally caved to the urge to go to him. In a fit of decisive energy, she leapt from her bed, books scattering to the ground, but as she crossed the room, there was a knock at the door. She opened it barefoot to see Levan standing on the other side, an impenetrable expression on his face. His cheekbones jutted, his eyes bleary with exhaustion. He wore a fresh scarlet cloak, a black tunic and trousers, with leather boots laced up his calves.

At the end of his right arm was a golden hand.

He held it up to the light, and it was unlike anything she'd ever seen—except maybe the enchanted tongues gifted to those poor children in her first year on the streetwatch. This replacement was the exact shape and size of his own hand, and as he clenched and unclenched his fist, it moved in exactly the same way—perhaps even more fluidly, more convincingly, were it not for the brilliant gilded hue, the radiance as it caught the light.

"That's incredible," Saffron breathed, relief flooding into every chamber and atrium of her heart. He was alright.

Levan looked at the hand with a strange expression on his face—somewhere between horror and reverence. "If Tålun doesn't receive the Vallish Distinction Prize for this work—just because he's Nyrøthi—I'll burn the Palace to the ground myself. I've never seen magic like it. It . . . I can feel everything." He ran a golden fingertip down the wooden frame of her door, then lowered his golden hand, cerulean eyes searching hers. "Zares is gone."

Trying not to skip a beat—and trying not to betray anything on her face that might hint toward what happened with Tiernan—she replied, "I didn't think you were going to survive. And the thought of your father getting hold of her . . . you made it sound like he couldn't know."

Levan pinched the bridge of his nose with his regular hand. "Hells. It cost us so much to bring her in."

"Are you angry?"

"Not with you."

"Your father? For what he did to you."

Levan's eyes darkened. "No. I understand it."

"You aren't going to punish him?"

"When my mother returns, she'll want him in one piece."

They stared at each other for several long moments, a thousand unsaid words hanging in the warm, citrus-sharp air. Somewhere behind Saffron, Rasso snored obnoxiously.

"Will you lie with me?" she whispered, nodding her head toward the book-scattered bed.

For a moment, Levan stopped breathing.

And then he followed her into the room.

He surveyed the considerable chaos with something like amusement on his face. There were books everywhere, not carefully arranged like his own but rather strewn facedown on top of her trunk. Crumpled piles of clothes lay in various heaps on the floor. Empty mugs of hot chocolate sat on her ring-marked desk, and the faucet in her sink was trickling for no particular reason.

"You're sort of messy," Levan remarked, raising a single brow.

Saffron shrugged. "Always seems to be something more pressing going on."

He took in the rumpled mess of her bed, topped with leather-bound volumes and single sheets of paper with scrawled notes. "It's quite unclear where I'm supposed to lie, exactly."

"Fine," Saff grumbled.

With a muttered levitation spell and a flick of her wand, Saffron stacked the books on her bedside table, then lay on her side, head resting on the pillow.

Levan perched uncertainly on the opposite edge and slowly, painstakingly, unlaced his boots. He shrugged off his scarlet cloak, then folded it precisely and laid it on top of the trunk at the end of the four-poster bed. When he finally lay down next to her, the mattress sank beneath his weight, but he kept almost a foot of space between their bodies, as though he had no idea how to look at her.

Saff took Levan's hands in hers. The golden hand was as cold as marble.

War waged behind his eyes as he looked down at their interlaced fingers. "Will you ever look at me the same again?"

Saff almost laughed. She'd thought the exact same thing when she'd left that cell, but in reverse. "How do you think I look at you?"

"I don't know." He pulled his golden hand away and rubbed the back of his head. Saffron remembered how soft the hair was there and longed to stroke it again, but supposed he had put distance between their bodies for a reason. "It's my first time being looked at like this."

"What about Alucia?"

He flinched as though she'd struck him. "How do you know about Alucia?"

Saints. She knew about Alucia because of his journal.

Think fast, Killoran.

"Harrow mentioned a life partner," she replied quickly. "And then you used that name with your father, the night I was hiding in your wardrobe. I put two and two together. Then the holly on your ribs . . ."

With a bitter twist of his lips, he laughed unconvincingly. "Alucia betrayed me, in the end. It was never real to her. I was just a piece on a board game."

Self-loathing churned in her gut. "I'm sorry."

"I swore I'd never let myself feel like that again. That's why I kept the tattoo instead of dissolving it." A tense beat. "It was supposed to remind me of the dangers of falling in love."

Saff felt as though someone had reached a hand into her chest and wrung her heart like a washcloth. "What happened? With Alucia."

"She was infiltrating from the Whitewings. It was years ago, before they were as prevalent as they are now. They started out as ascenite bandits, then did well in achullah for a while. Cut it with darkseed to make it more addictive. But once we brought lox into the city, we stole most of their business. They sent Alucia to get close to me, then ultimately sabotage us." A fleeting shot of grief passed over his face. "Vogolan killed her the second he found out who she was."

"Why didn't you retaliate? Against Vogolan, I mean."

He tapped two fingers over his brand. "Vogolan's act was clearly in the Bloodmoons' best interest. Mine would not have been." A narrowing of his eyes. "Which begs the question . . . how did *your* brand not kill you? When you took his life?"

She'd almost forgotten about her confession back in his bedroom. A slip of the tongue, a careless show of her hand.

"Maybe it's because he hurt me first, and it was self-defense," she said. "But I've been going over and over it in my mind, and I think . . . I think maybe he had grown sloppy, stopped acting in the Bloodmoons' best interests. He killed Papa Marriosan for no reason other than bloodlust, in broad daylight and with witnesses, and it's that kind of shortsightedness that makes us vulnerable to the Silvercloaks." The casual use of *us* still made her squirm. "So perhaps the brand believed that in neutralizing his threat, I was not acting against the Bloodmoons, but in our favor."

Levan gave a scornful laugh. "In truth, I'm jealous you're the one who got to do it. I've fantasized about killing him for a long time. Although I'm glad you didn't just *let* him hurt you. You've got fire, I'll give you that."

Saffron rolled onto her back, so she wouldn't have to face him. "I'm sorry Alucia wasn't who she said she was."

Levan tentatively rested his golden hand on her lower ribs. Her diaphragm rose and fell against his crypt-cold palm.

"You're not hiding anything from me, are you?" he said, pressing his forehead against her upper arm.

Even though she was secretly on the *good* side, the *right* side, Saffron felt like the most evil person in the world.

She had to destroy the Bloodmoons, but she didn't have to toy with his heart. With *him.*

"I'm hiding a lot of things," Saff replied, trying to sound playful, but it came out a little strangled. "My favorite gelato flavor is chocolate—"

"Heathen," he said, mock-affronted. "Pistachio is far superior."

She wrinkled her nose. "I no longer respect you as a person, but alright. My favorite song is 'This Way the Griffin Flies—' "

"Saccharine nonsense."

"And my favorite time of year is summer."

He *tsk*ed. "How can someone so beautiful have such bad taste? Autumn is objectively correct."

Her heart hitched at the word *beautiful.* Something she'd been called many times before—something she knew to be objectively true about herself—but there was still something wrenching about hearing it from Levan. Closed off, dead-behind-the-eyes Levan, who had slowly but surely come back to life over the time she had known him.

She shot him a wry smile. "At least we can agree on *Lost Dragonborn.*"

"I suppose that forgives you the other sins."

"My favorite childhood memory . . . there are a lot." Saffron didn't know why she was saying all of this. Maybe because sharing true things made her feel less horrible about the myriad lies. "My dad once enchanted a scarecrow with an entire personality. Jickety Snoot, his name was, and he was an absolute crank. I still don't understand how he did it. My dad's magic . . . it was like nothing else I've ever known." Except *yours.* "Jickety Snoot once made my honeywine-drunk mother laugh so much she peed herself."

Levan stroked her rib with his thumb, and it made it hard to breathe. "My father used to be playful like that too. He would invent elaborate board games for us to play together. Spend hours making tiny figurines for me to paint. Write up the rules in formal scrolls, carve wooden chests to keep the board and pieces in. He even sold a few of them—Flight of the Raven did pretty well up north."

There was a lurching sensation in Saff's stomach. "Holy hells. We played that."

Another of the infinite ways their lives had been braided from the start.

And yet this time, it did not fill her with rightness, but a kind of sickly dread. How could her parents have not known how interwoven they already were with the Bloodmoons? Mellora had been watched for years for her necromancy, and Lyrian's board games had found their way into the Killorans' enchanted family home. The tendrils had snaked around their ankles without them ever realizing, until the knock that turned their front door black.

Then again, maybe her parents *did* know. Maybe there was more to that fateful night than she would ever understand.

But Levan smiled at the revelation that they had played the same game as children, that his father had a legacy beyond brutality. "Small world. And my mother—she was formidable, but she was also . . . I know you probably think everyone here is fundamentally evil, but she was *good,* Silver. She helped people more often than she hurt them. When I was five, she and I helped evacuate an entire flooded village. She wound back time a few minutes and saved a family from drowning, even though it ruined her for weeks afterward. That's all she ever wanted to use her weaving for. To help people. But it wasn't strong enough, no matter how much ascenite she gathered. I think you'd have liked her." A wistful smile. "She would've made a good queen, and she knew that. She knew she'd been robbed of the throne."

A warning bell tolled in the back of Saff's mind. "She had her sights set on the throne?"

His jaw steeled. "Every coup needs an army. The Bloodmoons were hers."

The conversation she'd overheard between Harrow and Levan came back to her.

"I see a bloody uprising. The head of King Quintan on the Palace steps. Just as the pulps depicted."

"A Bloodmoon boot at his throat?"

"I don't know, darling."

"When is it happening? This bloody uprising? Can you discern a season?"

"Darkest winter, at a guess."

"How accurate a guess?"

The hope in Levan's voice . . . it all made sense. He thought Harrow was confirming Lorissa's return. No wonder he wanted to know *when.* No wonder he needled for all the detail he could get.

"And she'll still want that?" Saff asked. "If you bring her back?"

"She'll want to resume her coup, yes. Though losing Zares is a blow." He shifted his weight, and a mattress spring squeaked. "But I'm not angry with you, Silver. What you did in the cell meant a lot."

"I was hardly doing that to make you feel better," she laughed, assuming he meant the sex and not the amputation. "I had entirely selfish motivations."

She tilted her head, and found he was looking at her with a sleepy, reverent gaze. It reminded her of how he looked when they were talking about *Lost Dragonborn*—animated, but also at peace.

"You weren't just tossing a dying man a literal bone?" he asked, a smile tugging at the corner of his mouth, the slightest dimple forming. The scar through his lower lip seemed less stark than usual, but there was a shaving nick on his cleft chin that he hadn't bothered to heal. It was surreal to be so close to him. So close she could see every pore on his slightly crooked nose, every hair in his thick brows, the tiny flecks of teal in his eyes.

"I don't pity you. Not now, not ever." Saffron traced a fingertip over the back of his golden hand despite herself. She lifted the cuff of his cloak, stroking the ridged scars he'd carved with his own wand. The place where the golden hand met his own arm was seamless, somehow. "Just like I hope you don't pity me after seeing me branded."

His eyes fluttered closed, as though the lure of horizontal sleep was too strong to resist. "There are a lot of ways I feel about you, Silver. Pity isn't one of them."

Then his hand went slack on her stomach, his lips parted slightly, and his shoulders rose and fell steadily in slumber.

As she lay beside him, the magnitude of her betrayal sat on her chest like a tombstone. She had let him feel safe enough to sleep beside her. She had tilled the tender earth between them, and watched as they had both sown seeds. And she had done this knowing what she would soon do to him.

Sleep did not find her quickly. Instead, she lay with his hand upon her, breathing gently against his palm, gazing at the sharp lines of his face, and slowly, impossibly, *terribly,* her magical well began to fill. Pleasure not from any physical touch, but from his mere presence, from the mere *thought* of him.

Saints, she was in trouble.

They both were.

45

...

Dishonorable Intentions

Saffron awoke with her head in the nook between Levan's arm and chest, one hand stroking her hair and the other wrapped around her body. It was warm and sweet and terrible, and she wanted to sink into it forever.

She looked up and saw him staring at the ceiling. When he saw she was no longer asleep, he pressed a tender kiss to her forehead, but there was pain etched onto his face. The sight of it was a shock. Normally he kept it close to his chest, buried far down inside.

What did it mean that he was letting her catch a glimpse?

"Are you alright?" she asked, her voice pitching with concern.

"Fine. Better for some sleep."

"You're lying."

He grimaced. "Fine. It hurts like all hells. Happy?"

"Ecstatic. Although the thought of your absurd power being amplified by the pain is vaguely terrifying."

Something stilled in his body, for a brief, interminable moment, but was swiftly gone again.

He cupped her jaw with his golden hand and kissed her on the lips, so tender it was barely a kiss at all. They pecked softly, sweetly, until gradually it deepened. Saffron ran her traitorous hand up his broad chest, up his neck, through his soft, silky hair. His teeth grazed her bottom lip, and that forbidden want pooled in her lower belly, tugging her toward him.

She propped herself up onto her elbow and kissed him harder, her wild silver-blond curls spilling over his chest and shoulders. He pressed a palm to the small of her back, and with a fluid swooping motion, turned her onto her back and flipped himself so that suddenly, he was the one hovering over her.

His body heavy and warm against hers, Levan pushed her curls away from her face and pressed a kiss just below her ear, where her jaw met her throat. He brushed his lips farther down the side of her neck, then pushed her tunic to one side and planted kisses along the ridge of her collarbone.

The more she tried to tell herself how wrong it was, the more she wanted it.

He was a glittering gamehouse, a blackcherry sour, a dark prophecy.

And in this moment, he was *hers*.

His golden hand roved over her body, over the soft rolls of her stomach, the sloping curves of her thighs, the tender insides of her wrists, and the hard groove of her spine. She longed for him to find the throb between her legs, but he took his sweet time, alternating between fingertip traces and feathery kisses, the occasional dart of his tongue sending desire lancing through her.

She reached her own hands up to him, but he pushed her firmly away. Before she could feel stung, he murmured, "Last time, you had all the power. It's my turn."

Oh, hells.

"Deal," she breathed, an agreement, a surrender.

He reached out and grabbed his wand from the holder on the bedside table, then took both of her wrists in one hand, pinning them up against the headboard. With a quirk of his brow, he muttered, "*Et vinculorium.*"

A length of narrow rope shot from around the curtain of the four-poster bed and tied Saff's wrists in a tight sailor's knot. The two ends secured themselves to the spindly wood of the bed frame, so tautly her hands couldn't move an inch.

A silken shudder tore down her whole body. Nissa had known her way around ropes and chains, but there was something about this situation, this vicious snarl of a romance that could only end in ruin, that made everything feel heightened.

His eyes twinkled in response. "*Sen evanevesstan.*"

Saff's clothes swept from her body to the floor, defying all seam-based logic, leaving her laid bare.

"*Sen?*" she asked lightly, though her pulse was hammering in her chest.

A smirk. "My intentions are far from honorable."

He pressed her legs apart with the hard ridges of his hips and inched back on the bed, laying airy kisses down the center of her stomach, goosebumps stippling her whole body.

When his mouth reached her *there,* her eyes rolled back in her head, and she couldn't stifle the moan. Starting with delicate kisses, he worked his tongue in tiny, soft circles, his hands gripping her hips so hard it hurt. Her wrists yanked at their bounds of their own accord, and the bite of rope into her skin only intensified the feeling between her thighs.

Everything felt molten, alight, a swirling of pleasure that swelled and surged. All the blood in her body rose to the surface of her skin. Just as the mounting sensation was about to swallow her whole, his golden hand moved from her hip and two fingers plunged inside her, filling her with a delicious cold *ache.*

She bit out a raw gasp.

"*Oh, Saints,*" she moaned, submitting to the overwhelming feeling.

"Shh," Levan warned. "Can't let anyone hear us."

"*Saaaaaints,*" Saffron groaned louder, not truly caring who heard her blaspheme.

Levan grabbed his wand with his free hand. "*Sen orisilentian.*"

Her mouth clamped shut, and she could not open it again.

Not when he tugged at her nipple piercing, nor when he slid a third finger inside her.

As his tongue circled her faster and faster, and his fingers slid in and out until the pressure was too much to bear, it was too *everything,* she peaked and then plummeted off the cliff edge of pleasure, her whole body shuddering around him, her magical well filling and then overflowing. Being trapped inside the pleasure, unable to move or speak, only made it more . . . *more.* It kept crashing down in waves, up and down her arms and legs, and she wanted to cry out but she couldn't; she could only tremble silently, deliciously.

Withdrawing from her, Levan knelt back up onto his knees and tore his tunic over his head. Saffron tried not to look at the scarred mess of his arm—tried not to hate him for what he'd done to himself.

He rested his hand on his belt buckle. "Do you want to . . . ?"

In response, she wrapped her long legs around him and tugged him toward her. He fumbled with his belt—the sound of yanking leather and metal buckles sending another wave through her—and then pulled down his trousers. Angling his hips, he plunged deep into her, so hard and sudden that her hands jerked against her bonds, her lips begged to part, and there was the seethe of rope burn and the intense fullness and the lingering tingle of her orgasm and she felt like she was falling off the edge of the world.

He thrusted his hips slowly at first, then sped up so fast his pupils dilated, his forehead glistened, and he dug a hand into Saffron's hair. With his other hand, he picked up his wand, pointed it at her hips, and whispered raggedly, "*Sen ascevolo.*"

Her hips lifted as though suddenly weightless, and the shift unleashed a whole new sensation inside her, as though constantly pressing down on a taut knot of pure, raw pleasure.

Through the glittering haze, she saw a perilous expression appear on Levan's face.

He pressed hard against her chest and whispered in her ear, "Fair's fair, Silver." He pulled back slightly and pointed his wand tip between her legs. "*Et aflan.*"

The raw magic was like a thunderbolt, a fork of scorched lightning, and she could barely see from the explosion of stars behind her eyes. She whimpered against her clamped lips, and moments later, his hips shuddered, digging into her inner thighs, and he sighed into her neck. Their chests were pressed together, frantic hearts beating through their skin, and she felt his every breath echo inside her.

Eventually he pulled away, and she missed the feel of him immediately.

"*Ans oriloquan.*" Her lips came unstuck. "*Ans arrenodan.*" The ropes replaced themselves around the bed curtains, but he didn't seem in a hurry to return her clothes.

"That was . . ." she gasped.

"That was," he confirmed.

They lay breathless in each other's arms for a while. Saff's wrists were red and tender, and her legs still shook from the intensity of the pleasure, but his arms were so strong and firm around her that she felt safe, steadied.

She felt safe in the arms of a Bloodmoon.

She had to *focus,* damn it. She was here for a reason. And that reason was not pure, animal pleasure.

Just refilling the well for what's to come, she told herself.

A neat little lie.

"So what now?" Saffron asked at last. "You're free, and you don't want revenge against your father. So we just . . . carry on like nothing's happened?"

"We'll find another necromancer. But first we need to retrieve the lox I stashed the night we were raided. The gamehouse is running low."

"You said you'd stashed it near Novarin?"

"It's actually nearer Lunes, just on the Bellandrian border. I grew up in hiding, in a tiny hamlet of wooden shacks in the Havenwood. My mother's ancestors were slain centuries ago, but still her parents would not risk civilization. The shacks are abandoned now, but I still go up there, sometimes. It's like she's still there."

Her heart stuttered on the fresh details. He had grown up only a few miles from Lunes, from *her.* They had always orbited around each other, and again this idea gave her an unsettling retrospective foreboding, as though there had been monsters lurking in the shadows all her life.

"How will we get there?"

"We'll have to use our *portari* gate. I've been playing too fast and loose with the *portari* in my wand. Leaves too much of a trace, and the Silvercloaks seem to be getting much better at the art of tracing."

Saff's throat was dry. She was going to have to relay all of this to Aspar. She was going to have to fulfill her mission. And with every detail Levan entrusted to her, the closer she was to that inevitable moment. "When?"

"Tomorrow." He rolled the half-golden wrist stiffly, grimacing. Now that the heat of the moment had subsided, his face had once again paled, and the skin around his eyes was lined with discomfort. "I'm going to find some pain relief that isn't lox. I need my head to be clear."

Now that he'd trusted her with his hurt, Saffron wished he hadn't. It would only make it more terrible to betray him.

"Who will go?"

"Just you, me, and Rasso. Maybe Segal, though he's Risen now . . . Castian? A small crew anyway. Easy enough to *portari* us all away if anything goes wrong." He sighed and sat upright, pulled on his trousers, then checked his watch. Saffron arranged the blanket around her, cold in his absence. "I'm going to go and run and spar and bathe, then reach out to my Silvercloak rat. Leak them some false information so that they're far, far away from the Havenwood tomorrow night."

Saff's stomach flipped over, as though her body had only just remembered that Tiernan was *dead.* Because of her. And sometime very soon, Levan was going to discover his informant was missing.

"I'll see you later, alright?" Levan whispered, pulling on his tunic and bending back down to kiss her on the forehead.

It was only once he'd left the room that the realization struck Saffron hard and true.

She sat bolt upright, heart hammering fiercely in her branded chest.

Levan had used *magic* on her.

And it had *worked.*

The ropes and the clothes were external; her immunity wouldn't have protected her against that.

But he had *silenced* her, and she hadn't been able to say a word.

Which meant he'd found a way around her unique advantage.

Which therefore meant . . . he knew the advantage existed in the first place.

Or, she told herself, his magic was just so powerful that nobody, not even she, could resist it. Had the severed hand caused such intense pain that his power had exploded beyond all recognition? Is that why he had stilled so strangely when she'd mentioned the possibility?

She didn't know which was more terrifying: that he knew she was hiding her magic immunity, or that he was powerful beyond measure.

Pulling her clothes hastily over her head, her mind filtered through her options.

She was approaching the end as a Bloodmoon; that much she instinctively knew. She'd come further than any Silvercloak had ever come before. She not only understood the ins and outs of their operation, but also *why* they did the things they did. She knew what would happen if Levan brought Lorissa Rezaran back.

War. Bloodshed. Terror.

And she knew exactly how to stop it.

All she had to do was tell Aspar everything about their trip to Lunes. With Tiernan gone, the Bloodmoons would not be prepared for a second raid, and surely, *surely* the Silvercloaks would emerge triumphant.

The predatory gamehouses would be shut down, the hideous violence would cease, and the city would once again be rid of the cancerous lox.

Her parents would be avenged. Her fate would be fulfilled.

And yet doing so would see Levan in Duncarzus for the rest of his life—at best. House Arollan had abolished the death penalty several decades ago, but there had been mounting pressure in the pulps and the newspapers to bring it back.

Could she see this man executed on the Palace steps?

It was barely a question.

She knew, deep down in her marrow, exactly what she had to do.

46

...

The Havenwood

SAFFRON WAS TO MEET LEVAN OUTSIDE THE *PORTARI* GATE AT dusk the next night.

The gate was hidden deep in the belly of the mansion, only accessible by ascending to a dimly lit corridor on the third floor, tapping a marble statue of a dragon on each claw, and uttering the word *tempavicissan*. The Bloodmoons truly worshipped the lost art of timeweaving, and it was almost embarrassing that the Silvercloaks had never picked up on it. Then again, no Silvercloak had ever done what she had. They'd never been this close, never slipped under the skin of the beast.

Saffron wondered what would happen if the Bloodmoons found out she was a hallowed Timeweaver—whether it would make her more valuable or more of a target, whether they would love her or hate her for possessing the power they had so doggedly sought for themselves.

Descending the spiral staircase—exposed once the marble dragon took flight down the corridor—Saffron heard voices. Rasso ground to a halt beside her.

Levan was not alone.

"—going?" asked the kingpin, glacially cold. "You think I'll let you fly out of here, after all you've done?"

"The Havenwood," Levan replied woodenly. "To retrieve the lox I stashed. And nothing I have ever done has been against the interests of the Bloodmoons. Your brand makes sure of that."

"You think I trust you with bringing the lox back?" Lyrian snarled.

"I was capable of stashing the lox. I think I'm capable of unstashing it."

Lyrian laughed cruelly. "Not before you pilfer some for yourself, hmm, *dulgo*?"

A dark crimson flared behind Saffron's eyes at the heinous word—the most derogatory word for "addict" in the Vallish language. A member of the King's Cabinet had once been dishonorably discharged for uttering it.

Before she could stop herself, Saffron hurried forward. The staircase opened out into a dark, sparse chamber lit by goldencandles. "Don't you *dare* call him—"

"Silver," Levan uttered in warning, as Lyrian spun on his heel to face her.

The kingpin looked from his son's worried expression to Saffron's furiously curled fist, and a knowing smile spread slowly across his pinched face. "Interesting choice, son."

Saff's stomach clenched.

Never show what hurts. It'll only be used against you.

Defending Levan was another misstep.

The loosening of her tongue, the fogging of her conscious thoughts, was becoming a problem. All her life she had prided herself on her ability to bide time, to assess every threat before choosing a path, and yet here she was barreling into hostile situations, uttering the first misguided threat that came into her head.

Yet she loathed the kingpin for who he had forged his son into. She loathed him when she thought of the order he had given: for Vogolan to brand Levan's heart. It took all her earthly willpower not to slay him where he stood.

"You shouldn't come to the Havenwood." Levan glared at his father. "There's likely a warrant out for your arrest."

"So we blast the Silvercloaks out of the sky if they so much as come near us." Lyrian adjusted the long gold chain hanging round his neck.

An obelisk-shaped pendant of jade dangled at his navel—Saffron hadn't seen it before. Jade was famous for repelling something, but she couldn't remember what. "I'll bring reinforcements. Segal and Castian, of course. Shalion, Tas, Lindelan. Benvornan can cast a cloud formation around us, and Castian can gust it along on the wind. You see, this is how you plan an operation. You don't just charge in wands blazing with no thought to defense. You *think.* It was a mistake for me to ever trust you with things of such import, but it's a mistake I will not make twice."

Saints, Levan, if you don't seek retribution, I will.

Levan fixed a stony expression onto his face. "Fine. But if this goes wrong, the blood is on your hands."

Soon the chamber echoed with overlapping voices. Aviruna Castian looked like she'd been interrupted midway through a lox session. Her eyes were glassy, her limbs languid, her voice slow as molasses. Saffron vaguely recognized four other mages from the conclave after Vogolan's death. Benvornan had the same lank, hook-nosed appearance, and Saff wondered whether they might have been cousins. Segal's milky gaze was still clouded and wrong, a hypnotic quality to his movements, more languid and gliding than was natural.

The *portari* gate stood in the center of the room, as though propping up the ceiling. The empty core of it pulsed with whorls of magic, and on all four sides were ascenite arches carved into the shapes of bucking axelmares—tall, skeletal steeds standing on hind legs, their broad spectral wings unfurled. Axelmares were to *portari* what fallowwolves were to timeweaving and velvines were to pleasure, though the winged steeds were sparsely populated in a country that had banned their favored magic. Most of them had migrated to Bellandry and the Eastern Republics after the teleportation spell was outlawed in Vallin.

As the others filtered in, Levan took her by the hand for the briefest of moments, his brow lowered.

"Nobody's ever defended me like that before," he muttered, voice thick. "At least not since my mother died. It's not worth your life, but I appreciate it nonetheless."

Saff nodded but found she couldn't say anything in return. She cared about this man enough that she'd stick her neck above the parapet to defend him, and yet a dark, churning part of her still urged her to heed caution.

Levan could use magic on her. She was not as safe as she believed. And while she doubted he'd ever willingly hurt her, she still had to stay vigilant. Alert, without letting emotions cloud her judgment. To reassure herself, she clasped her hands around the cool, smooth hourglass and the thrumming painmaker tucked in her cloak pocket—free of their velvet pouches and ready to deploy at a moment's notice.

Once everyone had arrived, they filtered into the *portari* gate in pairs. Lyrian insisted on accompanying his untrustworthy son, and so Saffron stepped through with Castian. She'd only used *portari* gates a few times in her adult life—Atherin was an easily walkable city—but the sensation was the same as the spell itself. A squeezing, a breathlessness, a starring of the vision at the other end.

They arrived in a forest glade.

A full moon illuminated the clearing, round and pearlescent as an ascen coin, the sky around it salted with stars. The spindly trees were unmistakably wyrmwoods—a silver-leafed genus believed to be the preferred kindling of dragons—and the forest floor was hatched with roots, twigs, and dark blue saintmoss. It reminded Saffron so intensely of childhood that her chest ached. That *smell*—somehow earthy and crystalline, like the clearest of lakes and the richest of soils. Combined with the echoing coo of havendoves, it was like a fishhook through her heart. She hadn't been back to these parts for so long.

Chatter rippled through the Bloodmoons as they arrived, but Lyrian held up a forefinger to urge silence. They stood stock-still for several moments until Saffron realized he was listening for the sound of nearby pursuants. Saffron knew it to be pointless, since any Silvercloak could muffle footsteps at the drop of a hat, but she understood the instinct.

Lyrian gestured for everyone to follow in a northerly direction. The knotty wyrmwoods soon became so densely packed that they had to walk single file, the forest floor dark as the bottom of a well. One by one, the Bloodmoons illuminated their wands with an echoed chant of *et lustran.* Tiny balls of white light bobbed and flickered through the trees like fireflies. The ground was uneven beneath Saffron's feet, alternating between snarled roots and blankets of saintmoss, but Rasso leapt and pattered over it with little effort, glancing at her as though to say, *Come on, slowfeet, what are you waiting for?*

The Bloodmoons walked in silence for a few hundred yards until the woods opened into another glade, sheltered from the sky by a thick canopy of interwoven branches and silver leaves.

A dozen shabby wooden shacks were arranged in a circle so perfect it was almost eerie—like a clock face with evenly spaced hour numbers. The structures were uniform in size and shape, but languished in various states of decay and dilapidation, with several rotted roofs and one cabin bearing vicious black scorch marks up the front door.

In the middle of the shack village, like the perfect bull's-eye of an archer's target, was a stone well with a thick parapet wall and a wooden wellhead slick with saintmoss. Surrounding the well were four stone fire pits for outdoor cooking, spaced perfectly in the north, east, south, and west positions.

Saff had the curious feeling of looking at a purposefully designed tactical village. Everything was so precise and symmetrical that it seemed like something a Silvercloak strategist would come up with for a final assessment.

For a moment, they all stood silently as they studied the site, respectful, reverent, as though the shacks were a dozen open graves. Saffron's gaze went from the unsettling clock-face pattern to Levan's face, trying to parse any emotion she found there, but there was none. His guards were up. Saff's should be too.

Lyrian blew air through his lips, looking slightly winded. "I haven't been here in so long."

"It's deserted?" Castian asked.

"The windows are enchanted to make every shack appear empty from the outside," Levan explained. "So even if people still lived here, it would look deserted. But yes, it's empty."

Castian rubbed her anguished face. "How long has it been since the last inhabitants left?"

"Fifteen years, perhaps. But it's always looked this dilapidated. A defensive measure against the Crown. If any royal scouts stumbled upon it, they wouldn't think to report it as an unlawful settlement of Rezarans."

So Levan's lineage was common knowledge amongst the Bloodmoons. Testament to the brand's power, that this information had never leaked to the Silvercloaks.

Segal ran a palm over the moisture-slicked wood of the nearest shack. It came away black with grime. "And if the scouts looked inside a shack?"

"The locks are fairly robust," Levan replied, "but if a scout forced their way through . . . there are tunnels snaking between each shack. We would either hide belowground or seek shelter with a neighbor until the scout moved on."

Castian looked to Levan in alarm. "You lived here too?"

"Until I was four years old."

Lyrian grimaced. "A simpler time. We had family. Community." His regretful gaze dropped to the golden hand at the end of Levan's arm.

"The lox is in our old shack," Levan replied, steering the conversation back to logistics. "If you would like to accompany me."

Saffron had no idea how Levan refrained from slaying his father where he stood, after everything Lyrian had done to him. And yet she knew better than anyone that these things were complicated. Love was complicated, and pain was complicated, and believing you *deserved* to hurt was complicated.

A peculiar, almost wistful expression fleeted over Lyrian's face. "As you wish."

Levan nodded toward Saffron. "Silver, with us. The rest of you keep watch."

The Rezaran shack of many years ago was positioned to the northwest of the settlement. It was the least battered of the structures, but the wood still warped and crumbled in the corners. Inside, the space smelled of mildew and saintmoss, both of which had taken over the shabby furniture. No latrine, no running water, only two small rooms and a storage closet. A small stone hearth was buried in the far wall, still coated with soot and ash.

One room contained two beds—one large, one child-size, which made Saff's heart pang—and a rotting wooden chest, while the other functioned as a tiny kitchen dotted with copper pots and pans, chipped clay plates and bowls, teapots with broken spouts and rattling lids. For them to have not been fixed with simple mending spells, pleasure must have run perpetually low here.

She thought of the scar on Levan's lip. *I fell out of a tree when I was a kid. Magic was in short supply where I grew up, so it didn't heal smoothly.*

Even before the death of his mother, his life hadn't been easy. Saff understood at once why the Bloodmoon mansion was so gaudy, so lavish—because for so long, they'd had nothing.

Lyrian stood in the doorway, grief etched into every line of his face. "It hasn't changed."

Levan cleared his throat. "No."

"Do you come here often?"

"Seldom."

Rasso padded around the space, sniffing every square inch for traces of his old mistress. He leapt onto each of the beds—still made up with moldy bedspreads—and shoved his face into each pillow, inhaling the scent deeply and making a sad, low whimper.

Lyrian picked up a clay mug from the lopsided wooden shelf in the ramshackle kitchen. There were four in total, each with the letter *L* neatly carved into its side. One had stars around the letter, another had flowers, another leaves, another an open book. Lyrian's hand had reached for the mug with the stars, tracing the shapes with a careful forefinger.

"I think I can still feel her here." Lyrian's words were serrated with sadness. "Your mother."

Levan stood perfectly still.

Lyrian's hand went to the mug with leaves, and a wistful smile broke across his face. "Remember when your brother—"

"Let's not talk about him, please."

Levan avoided Saffron's questioning stare.

He had a *brother*?

Lyrian looked up, reverent, lost in thought. "I am sorry, son. For your hand."

Levan nodded once in return, his emotions carefully in check. There was no longer pain drawn around his eyes and mouth, as there had been in Saffron's bed. Had he managed to find some relief? The whiteroot remedy Paliran offered Nissa, perhaps? Or was he simply a master at locking the pain away? She remembered how bland he'd kept his expression while impaled on the deminite shard and wondered.

Still stony-faced, Levan crossed to the storage closet and tugged at the faded brass handle. Inside was mostly empty but for the two large wooden crates with COTTON and SILK stenciled on the sides.

"Still here." Levan allowed himself the smallest sigh of relief, then levitated them both into the bedroom area. With a jerk of his wand, he ushered the crates out of the shack and back into the clearing.

They emerged to find the other six Bloodmoons gathered behind the neighboring abode, murmuring in low, urgent voices.

"What is it?" Levan demanded, straightening his crimson cloak and pulling himself tall.

"This just appeared," muttered Castian, twitching like a dying insect from the lox withdrawals.

Saffron's stomach curled into a fist as she followed their gaze.

A pearlescent barrier, as thin as a spider's web but stronger than freshly forged steel.

Saffron knew what it was immediately. She'd spent many days and weeks of her life practicing how to conjure them.

"A perimeter dome," she choked out.

Nobody could pass in or out until the conjurer dropped it. Not even with *portari*.

She hadn't known whether Aspar would trust her intel again, since the last raid had been so utterly disastrous. And after the captain had heard the news of Tiernan's death, she'd seemed almost ready to murder Saffron herself.

But she had trusted her informant, despite it all.

The Silvercloaks had followed the Bloodmoons to the Havenwood.

And now there was no way out.

47

...

Jebat's Resistance

LYRIAN SPAT A CURSE WORD SO VILE SAFF PHYSICALLY RE-coiled.

The perimeter dome stretched over all twelve shacks, tucking itself behind each of the outer facing walls like a blanket. The domes could only be cast from inside them, which meant the Silvercloak responsible was in one of the shacks. Yet the enchanted windows held up, and from Saff's vantage point, every single abode seemed just as abandoned as when they'd arrived.

Fear swelled in her chest like a balloon.

It all ended here; she knew that in her very bones.

"*You,*" Lyrian snarled at her, a few seconds before lunging for her throat, wielding his wand like a blade. "*Sen ammort—*"

Levan moved in a flash, tackling his father to the ground as Saff threw up a mattermantic spellshield.

Pinning his knees into the hollows of his father's shoulders, Levan held his wand tip to Lyrian's chin. "She didn't do this. She's branded, for hell's sake. This is likely happening because of your idiocy on the docks." Behind her shield, Saffron fought the urge to frown. Did he really still believe in her innocence? Or was he just trying to prevent his father from murdering her? "And if you make another attempt on her life, I'll—"

"Less of the tavern brawling," snapped Castian, hauling Levan off his father in a surprising show of strength—perhaps she was wind-wielding under her breath. "We might need Killoran. *Sen exarman.*" Saffron's wand shot from her hand into Castian's. "Neutralize her, don't kill her. She's leverage. If she's theirs, they won't let her die."

I wouldn't be so sure of that, thought Saffron, livid at herself for losing her wand, frantically recalibrating, reworking her plan. But the truth was, she didn't have one. For the first time in many years, she did not have a plan. She felt trapped in some kind of liminal space, a terrible in-between, neither a Silvercloak nor a Bloodmoon, a helpless passenger in the upcoming wreckage.

Survive, she told herself. *Just survive. That's the only plan you need.*

"Disarmament is not enough. She needs to hurt for this." Climbing to his feet, the kingpin lifted his wand to his mouth. "*Et vocos, Zirlit.*"

Zirlit—the tall Nomarean mage with the monocle and macaw cane.

His response crackled through the kingpin's wand immediately. "*Fair featherroot.*"

Lyrian waited a single agonizing beat. "Kill the uncle."

It took a moment for the meaning to land.

"*No!*" screamed Saffron.

"Yessir," replied Zirlit.

And then the wand went silent.

All the breath was knocked from Saffron's lungs, and she fell to her knees. Pain, hot and bright, flogged her chest, her heart. The magic in her well shimmered with it, ameliorating into something raw and potent, responding to the agony as surely as if she'd been whipped.

Which uncle, which uncle, which uncle—

Her brain scrambled, trying to come up with an explanation for how her uncle might survive, how he might overpower Zirlit, how he might flee with his life intact, but she knew, had *always* known, that in every situation where the worst could happen, it did.

"*Stop,*" Castian snarled at the kingpin once more. "The time for revenge will come. For now, we need to get out. How?"

Levan, breathing unevenly, looked from Saffron to his father, then around at the shacks, reality setting in. "Impossible to know how many cloaks are here."

Uncle Mal, Uncle Merin, who was it, and how, and maybe he could have—

The grief was almost too much to bear. It was a fist banging against her sternum, a blade driven into her gut, a crescent moon carved into flesh. It hurt so fucking *much,* and her magic responded accordingly. Yet without a wand, there was nowhere for this bright, searing power to *go.* It just burned her from the inside out.

Enough.

With immense force of will, Saff shoved the mental image of her dead uncle into a sealed box. Pain would not serve her now. It would muddy her instincts, warp her emotions. She needed to keep her wits about her to survive this—to execute the raid the way it should've been executed on the docks. There would be time to mourn when all the Bloodmoons were in manacles, and she was back in the Silvercloak common room, where she belonged.

Think.

Assess.

Reroute.

The Silvercloaks would have brought at least one tac team of six. Likely two, given how much the last confrontation had escalated. They'd also be able to hear every word the Bloodmoons were saying, so accurate and powerful were their amplifying charms.

Would they move in if they thought Saff's life was in immediate danger?

No. Lyrian had been a single syllable away from killing her where she stood, and Aspar had not given the order to move. Much more important to take the Bloodmoons alive than to save Saffron. The captain was like Saff, good at honoring the big picture. But truthfully, it still stung.

The Bloodmoons swung into an oval formation, their backs to Levan, Lyrian, and Saffron, wands outstretched.

"Castian, set fire to the shacks," ordered Lyrian, no longer spitting with rage but instead coiled with that dangerous, serpentine hatred. "Smoke them out."

Castian nodded. "*Don incend*—"

"*No,*" bellowed Levan, not caring who heard. Castian stopped mid-enchantment. "We. Are. Not. Burning. The. Havenwood." Levan bit out every word through clenched teeth, his gaze swinging around the settlement like a pendulum. "Why are they not moving in on us? Something isn't right."

Saffron had been wondering the same. There were countless ways the Silvercloaks could've approached this capture—they'd drilled so many different set pieces during tactical villages just like this one. So why was everything silent, taut with a pulsing tension?

A few moments later, the answer emerged.

Through the chimneys of every shack but the one they'd just left, a violet mist wafted up on magical air.

Saffron recognized the smell before her brain fully caught up. Pepper and ash and rotten rose petals—the airborne weapon they'd deployed at the docks. Whorls of it drifted around the shacks, through the trees, not breaching the perimeter dome but brushing right up against it, like a velvine against its master's shins.

This time, though, Levan was prepared.

"*Ans espirabullan,*" he said, pointing his wand to his face. A small bubble, made from the same shimmering ephemera as a spellshield, formed around his nose and mouth. Just as the first hacking coughs rippled around the Bloodmoons, he tapped each of their faces in turn—starting with Saffron, she noted with a pang—so that each of them could breathe normally through the crude purple haze.

Beside her, Segal stared at the dome with that strange glassy expression on his face. Sweat poured from him in rivulets, his cloak clinging wetly to his chest, his wand hanging slack at his side. When Levan drew a breathing bubble over his mouth, he didn't appear to notice. In fact, he had the distinct appearance of a mage who'd rather be anywhere else. Like a soldier who would not actively resist orders, but who would also not take their own initiative, would not enter into battle of their own free will. Saffron assumed he was here because of the brand, and the brand alone. Even the Risen were not free of it.

Another small notch in the Silvercloak advantage column—reluctant fighters were rarely effective ones.

This *had* to go differently.

"Alright, the cloaks have shown their hands," Levan muttered, raking his hand through his hair. The words had a strangely warped echo to them. "They're spread thin in each of the shacks. We split up in pairs and take them down one by one until we find the perimeter caster. Silver and I will take the tunnels—it's the most dangerous, since they might be sealed off and we could be trapped, but we'll have the element of surprise."

Saffron's chest thudded like a military drum. The Silvercloaks would almost definitely have sealed off the tunnels . . . if they knew about them. If not, they'd be scrambling at Levan's words.

Silent and grim-faced, the pairings split off into the moonlit village, crouching beneath windows and pressing ears to wooden walls. Saffron felt like a leather belt was strapped too tightly around her chest. Prickling fear stabbed at her hands and feet, and she felt as though she might die at any moment. Like any breath might be her last.

Levan's ungolden hand found hers, and he tugged her toward his childhood shack. At the touch of his skin, bolts of lightning shot up her arms, straight into her heart.

Surely he knew. Surely he knew this was her doing.

A poisonous purple cirrus clung to the shack like the tendrils of some ethereal beast. The front door opened onto the central clearing, so they were horribly exposed as they entered. Even though the Order all knew, by now, that she was dirty, she lifted her hood anyway.

She felt naked and vulnerable without her wand, but the onslaught of *effigias* spells she was expecting never came. Perhaps the Silvercloaks were too busy watching their own doors to mind the windows. They knew the Bloodmoons were splitting up to take them down, and they knew the Bloodmoons would fire nothing less than killing spells. Two lone figures and a fallowwolf creeping into an unmanned shack were a distant threat—but a threat, nonetheless.

Once inside, Levan let go of her hand and pointed his black elm wand at the floor of the storage space.

"Et aperturan."

A trapdoor swung up into the room, revealing a hole wide enough for a single body to slip through. A narrow rope ladder disappeared into the darkness below.

As soon as Levan cast a new spell, the protective bubbles around their mouths evaporated, but the purple mist hadn't infiltrated the shack yet. They could breathe freely—as could the other Bloodmoons, providing they'd also made it inside a shack, but anyone still in the open air beneath the perimeter dome would be vulnerable. Saffron hoped a few stragglers might be picked off by the Silvercloaks this way, tipping the odds more squarely into the Order's favor.

"After you," Levan muttered, gesturing to the opening.

And what else could she do but obey?

Rasso leapt blithely into the chasm in the floor, unmistakably familiar with this strange locale. Saffron imagined Levan—and his *brother*?—chasing the beast around the surrounding woods as laughing children, mere miles from where Saffron herself had floated around Lunes on a flying carpet. With even the smallest detour, their paths could so easily have crossed.

Saff sank to the ground with a click of her knees, swinging her legs over the edge and finding the top rung of the ladder with her left boot. She lowered herself down until her feet found the soft, damp earth at the bottom, then turned to see nothing but blackness stretching out before her.

Levan dropped to the ground behind her, muttering an illumination spell. His wand lit like a candle, flickering white light over his face.

Saints, he was beautiful. Even now, his eyes shadowed and weary, his skin rough with stubble, the scar bisecting his lip somehow starker than ever.

Now they were alone, he took a step toward her, cupping her jaw with his palm. Urgency played out in his eyes, an undeniable plea, a question loaded with dread.

"Was it you, Silver?" he murmured, voice coarse and hollow.

"No," she whispered, stomach flipping over, but she knew he'd see right through it—if he wanted to.

"You're the only one who knew the plan in advance."

She swallowed, forcing herself to keep meeting his blazing stare. "They must've been watching the *portari* gates."

"And that would've given them enough time to pull together a squad of at least eleven?"

"They were likely waiting to move on your father the second he left the wards. They'll have an arrest warrant now, thanks to the killings on the docks. The twelve—because they move in sixes—would have been on standby."

Deep down, Saffron suspected there were twenty-four. Four whole tac teams. There's no way they'd split up one-by-one and go into each shack alone.

The Bloodmoons were vastly outnumbered.

Hope smoldered in Saffron's chest—surely, *surely* this time the Bloodmoons would not weasel free—and yet it was tempered with something sad, something bitter, something that only intensified when Levan rested his forehead against hers.

"I want to trust you," he said. "It's just . . . Alucia . . ."

Saffron's heart split open like a log beneath a woodaxe. "I know. Thank you for not letting your father kill me."

He tilted her chin upward with his golden hand, and touched his lips to hers so tenderly it almost broke her. He pulled back a hair's breadth, as though about to say something, then decided against it.

"Let's go," he muttered, rearranging his cloak in a way Saffron now recognized as a nervous tic.

She followed him down the tunnel. The passageways were dug out like the spokes of a wheel, meeting in the center before spanning back out to each individual shack. Saffron wondered why they didn't connect each shack in a wider circle, but since every part of this settlement was built with defense in mind, she assumed there was a grander reason.

A pattern emerged in which they'd go down each spoke to the center, then back up the next one until they reached the trapdoor at the end. They'd hover silently beneath each trapdoor for a few moments and then repeat the process.

"What are you looking for?" Saffron asked, after the fourth trapdoor remained sealed shut.

Levan rubbed at his temple. "Miret taught me about the energy fields created while casting spells. How to *feel* them and follow them like a kind of sixth sense. It's taken practice, but I can home in on that energy. It's not a sound or a heat or a smell or a sight, but . . . I can't describe it. There are skirmishes going on above us, and it's all overlapping. But I'm looking for a constant thrum from whoever's casting the perimeter dome. If we can incapacitate them, we can *portari* out."

Up the sixth wheel spoke, Levan found the sensation he sought.

"Here," he mouthed, pointing upward at the trapdoor.

Dread lurched up Saffron's gullet.

With little hesitation, Levan climbed up the rope ladder. It was identical to the one beneath his family's old shack, and Saffron finally realized the purpose of the wheel layout. It was intentionally disorienting, a purposeful scrambling of the internal compass, difficult to know which shack you lurked beneath. If you could simply move around an outer circle, it would be far easier for intruders to track their whereabouts.

Manually lifting the trapdoor only an inch or two, Levan pushed his head up high enough to see through the crack, then positioned his wand in the gap.

"*Sen debilitan,*" Levan shot out.

There was a muffled grunt, and then the sound of nothing.

Had Saffron been wrong? Was there only one Silvercloak in each shack?

Levan climbed the rest of the way into the room and gestured for Saffron and Rasso to follow.

Stock-still in the center of the room, blocking off the fireplace, was Detective Fevilan, a gas mask fitted around her nose and mouth, sandy hair falling into her pale eyes as she strained against the paralyzing spell Levan had cast upon her. Saffron wondered why he wasn't casting to kill. To protect her, perhaps, from the hell of seeing her friends slaughtered.

Behind Fevilan, crouching in the hearth of an ashen fireplace, was Detective Tenébo Jebat, also in a gas mask, pointing up through the chimney and trembling with visible effort from holding the perimeter dome. Saffron could almost detect what Levan meant by the energy field. It was somewhere between a hum and a vibration, a pitch and a heat and a magnetic draw.

Levan moved around Fevilan to get a better shot at Jebat, who was trapped in the small space and unable to defend himself while maintaining the effortful dome.

"Sen debilitan."

It struck true.

Every inch of Jebat trembled against the bounds of the cruel curse, and there was a shudder overhead as the perimeter dome crumbled to nothing.

"Let's just get out," Saffron muttered. There was still a chance that the Silvercloaks would round up the Bloodmoons, even without the perimeter dome, and a large, traitorous part of her didn't want Levan to go down with them. "The two of us. Now."

Maybe he could escape. She'd help him flee, hide, arrange exile.

But Levan seemed not to have heard her. Instead, he crouched by the fireplace, studying Jebat's immobilized face. The detective—in his fifties, and nearing retirement—had deep brown Sinyi skin with a craggy, pocked texture. The gas mask was slightly too tight, puckering the flesh around it. Levan ripped it off, revealing Jebat's gold-and-ruby septum piercing and horror-frozen mouth.

"Who told you about this mission?" Levan pointed his wand at Jebat's lips. "*Ans oriloquan.*"

The spell he'd used to loosen Saffron's tongue after sex.

She didn't know what she wanted more: for Jebat to betray her, or for him to stay silent. Because Saints knew what Levan did to people who stayed silent.

"I don't know," Jebat spat out in an odd, stiff tone. The rest of his body stayed immobilized. "Orders are orders."

Levan's jaw clenched. "Who. Told. You?"

"Orders. Are. Orders."

With an impatient sigh, Levan pulled up Jebat's silver sleeve and pressed his wand tip to the veined stretch of wrist. "You'll lose a hand."

Jebat's eyes blazed. "I don't *know.*"

Levan's grip on Jebat's forearm tightened, and he dug the wand tip even more harshly into the wrist, but the cruel words Saffron was waiting for—the cruel words she uttered herself two days ago—never came.

Instead, Levan looked down at his own golden hand, as though remembering the sheer agony of it, and his eyes pressed closed. His chest rose and fell, steeling himself, and Jebat watched with unbridled terror and hatred in his stare. Waiting for the pain.

But then Levan opened his eyes, and that dead expression was back behind them.

There was a wordless exchange between them, coiled with some unnamed force.

Then Jebat said, calmly, willingly, as though he had never resisted at all:

"Aspar has an undercover Silvercloak in the Bloodmoons. I don't know who, but they're close to you."

What—?

No.

The thing that sucked all the air from the room was not that Jebat had all but confirmed Levan's suspicion of her. It was not that he had essentially signed her death warrant.

It was that he had suddenly dropped all resistance entirely.

The world rearranged itself around a singular shattering realization.

Levan was a Compeller.

48

...

Two Prophecies

Saffron turned back to the trapdoor and ran for her life.

Behind her were a few heavy footsteps, then a vicious lupine snarl and the squelch of teeth into flesh. Levan roared as Rasso hung from his forearm, face contorted with pain and fury, thrashing wildly to shake the fallowwolf off.

He knew now, beyond all doubt, that she was the undercover Silvercloak.

He knew now, beyond all doubt, that she had betrayed him the way Alucia had.

And there was no way he'd let her walk out of this alive.

Rasso unhinged his jaw and landed neatly on all four paws.

Both Saffron and the fallowwolf dropped to the bottom of the ladder just as Levan's deathly face appeared in the square of light above. Rasso let out another hair-raising growl, and Saffron fled down the tunnel spoke.

Levan followed.

His magic worked on her. He could compel her to stop if he so wanted to, and yet he chose not to.

She reached the center of the wheel layout, Rasso panting at her heels. Indecision rooted her to the spot like the *sen debilitan* charm. She'd have to choose a tunnel spoke to hare down, but doing so would trap her on that path, since they were all dead ends. She would have no choice but to emerge into the shack she'd chosen, because Levan would be right behind.

If only she had a weaverwick wand. She could try each spoke in turn, then commit to the least tragic of them. The one with the best chance of escape.

Footsteps thundered toward her.

Saffron closed her eyes, reaching her instincts out in front of her like tendrils.

They pointed down one particular spoke, and so she ran, Rasso right behind, to the rope ladder at the end. She climbed up, trying not to think about what might be waiting for her in the shack above. The worst-case scenario was Lyrian, who had killed her uncle, who wanted *her* dead, because surely Levan would not leap to her defense now.

But there was only a one-in-eleven chance of finding the kingpin on the other side. She had to trust the odds, like some twisted gamehouse attraction. She could almost hear the tinkle of coins, could almost smell the rich fruity scent of the blackcherry sours.

Only she was gambling not with ascens but with her life.

Wandless, she shoved upward. The trapdoor swung open into the storage closet. There was a cacophonous racket in the main dwelling, but the closet door was mercifully shut. Rasso sprang into it behind her just as Levan appeared at the bottom of the ladder.

"*Silver*," he mouthed, but the second syllable was severed by the closing trapdoor.

Saffron sat down on top of it, breathing hard as Rasso curled into her lap.

It would not stop Levan; he could catapult them into the rafters if he so chose.

But it would buy her a few moments.

From her lower vantage point, she could see through a narrow gap between the slats of the door into the kitchen. Thudding boots and blasts of magical light, overlapping yells and curses, the rush of enchanted wind knocking bodies off their feet. It was too chaotic to make any sense of, and besides, her mind orbited around one thought and one thought alone.

Levan is a Compeller, Levan is a Compeller, Levan is a Compeller, Levan—

Had he compelled her before?

Would she know if he had?

Back at the Academy, Aspar's secret Compeller had tried to order her during the final assessment. It hadn't worked, thanks to her magical immunity, but she already knew Levan alone could breach those defenses. Could force her mouth shut during the throes of sex.

She thought back to the conversation she'd overheard while hiding in Levan's closet, when the tracing charm led his father to his door.

All along. It was you all along.

How could I have been so blind?

Had Levan been compelling his father this whole time? Had Lyrian finally realized it, and stabbed his son through the hand with deminite so that it could never happen again?

Everything slid into awful place.

Lyrian's jade necklace—a supposed ward against compelling, Saffron now remembered.

The kingpin repeatedly, *doggedly* insisted that he didn't want to do such hideous things, that he'd never had the same bloodlust as his wife.

It was all *Levan.*

"Silver," came a breathless voice through the pane of wood that separated them. He rapped gently on the trapdoor with his knuckles. "I'm not going to blast through. I'm not going to hurt you. I just want to talk."

She said nothing. Almost always the safest option.

"We've both been keeping secrets from each other," Levan said, voice strained, almost inaudible over the frenzy of spells in the main shack.

Saffron still could not speak.

"Do you really think I'd hurt you, Silver? Let me in. I could force you to do it right now. I could compel you to open the trapdoor, or slam it open so hard you crumpled like a tin can, or just kill you straight through the wood. But I'm not going to. Please."

It was true. If he wanted to hurt her, she'd already be dead.

And there was so much she wanted—needed—to understand.

Bile rose in her throat, stinging her tonsils and tongue, as she rolled off the trapdoor.

Levan climbed slowly into the closet beside her, holding his palms in the air—one pale skin, one golden as the sun—as though to show he meant no harm. Rasso's teeth had torn into his forearm, shredding the fabric and drawing thick red stripes of blood, but he hadn't bothered to heal it.

He didn't go straight to her, but instead sank to his knees. He pressed his face against the door into the main shack, then sucked in a sharp gulp of breath. Whatever he'd seen through the crack, he did not relay it to Saff. Instead, he turned to face her, sitting back against the door, resting his elbows on his knees. The deadness had gone from his eyes, making way for a deep and terrible hurt.

"So it was you," he whispered hoarsely. "You're undercover."

Saffron neither confirmed nor denied it, but her silence was damning enough.

He rubbed his weary face. "And so history repeats."

Why did Levan keep falling for the women sent to ruin him? Was it because they were the only ones to show him any humanity—for the sake of getting close to him, for the sake of uncovering his secrets?

Saff swallowed hard. "If you *portari* out of here now, you'll escape the—"

"That's not what it is to be a Bloodmoon," he replied quietly. "Family is everything. Loyalty is everything. My father is in there right now, battling it out with two of yours. Your captain's been hit. She's alive, but barely."

Saints, Saff thought, with a savage clench of her stomach.

Levan twisted his lips as though in pain. "And yet here I am, crouched in a closet talking to you." A disbelieving grimace. "I'm a senseless fool."

"All the times you've tortured people for information when you could've just compelled them—why?"

A muscle feathered in his jaw. "I couldn't risk anyone knowing what I am. It would've been immediately reported to my father, and my father would've realized who's been puppeteering him this whole time. Though he figured that out anyway, in the end."

Saff's chest rose and fell unevenly. "So why control your father at all?"

He gave a dark shrug. "Control or be controlled."

"A bleak worldview."

He gazed at her in turmoil, and she couldn't parse the emotions, because there were so *many*. Shame, self-loathing, a kind of deep internal horror he'd never be able to outrun. A love so complicated neither of them could understand the exact shape of it.

"Do you want to know why I'm so powerful?" he said, voice clotted. "Why I can heal and wield and transmute and compel with such terrible force?"

Saffron nodded, dread curling in her stomach like a slow python.

He leaned his head back against the wall, letting his eyes fall closed, as though they were not in the middle of a brutal battle. "Not long after my mother died, my powers started to develop in earnest. It was clear I had a proficiency for healing, and so my father thought perhaps I could learn the subclass of necromancy and bring back my mother. He kept her preserved, just in case, using every scrap of ascenite they'd gathered over the preceding few years. But no matter how much I studied and practiced, I could never master it." Inhale, exhale, both tremulous. "So one day, Vogolan came to my room and restrained me. Then he hit me with *sen doloran*. The torture curse. Hours and hours and hours he did it, trying to make my magic powerful enough to raise the dead. Pain is power, after all." A flat grimace. "I was seven."

Saffron's stomach twisted. "But it didn't work."

A head shake. "He came back the next day, and the next day, and the next, believing that perhaps he could make my magic *permanently* potent. It went on for years, and while he succeeded in twisting my magic into something monstrous, something unstoppable, I never did learn to raise the dead."

"That's horrific."

He shrugged woodenly. "It's hardly a new concept. Pain is the whole foundation of the Nyrøthi military, after all. They sleep on beds of nails, apparently, and high-ranking officers flagellate themselves every day at dawn. The Daejini have bits of themselves removed, so that the phantom pain might always hurt." He held up his golden hand scornfully. "Even the Eqoran soldiers burn themselves with jeweled lighters when they need a boost."

"Yes," Saffron conceded softly, "but they aren't children, Levan."

His jaw clenched, and she remembered too late how much he loathed pity.

"You could've stopped him," she added, both a question and a statement. "If you were that powerful, you could have prevented Vogolan from ever laying his hands on you."

Another stiff shrug. "A large part of me *wanted* it to work. I would've suffered all the pain in the world to bring my mother back."

"But why did Vogolan care so much about whether or not your mother was resurrected?"

Levan avoided her furious gaze. "I think I've always suspected, on some level, that my father gave the order. Like the brand, he just didn't have the stomach to do it himself."

"Suspected? You could just compel him into telling you the truth."

A nameless emotion passed over his face. "I don't truly want to know. Would you be able to go on, knowing your father had wished that upon you? If I found out for sure that it was him . . . I don't know what I'd do."

There was the deafening sound of wood shattering in the main shack. Saffron dug her nails into the rotting wooden floor. "I'm sorry that happened to you."

"You know what drove me truly insane? It happened at different times every day. If it was always at, say, noon . . . I could've compartmentalized, organized my thoughts around it. But it depended on Vogolan's whims, and so I spent every minute of every hour wondering when it was going to happen. It's why I'm so fucking neurotic now. It's why everything is ordered, regimented."

"Control or be controlled," Saffron mirrored, with sudden understanding. Speaking of which . . . "Have you ever compelled me?"

"*No.*" He shook his head. "I don't *like* doing it, Silver. Especially not to you." He swallowed hard, throat bobbing. From the haunted, hollow look on his face, she knew he was telling the truth.

"How long have you been able to compel? Since the torture started?"

A stiff nod, then a brief pause, as he decided how much truth to share. "The only thing worse than the pain was being powerless. And so I read every piece of literature there is on compelling. I taught myself, with Miret's help. I swore to myself I would never be powerless again."

"You compelled Tiernan," she whispered in horror. "You compelled him into leaking you information, and you compelled him into taking his own life the moment he was discovered."

Levan nodded gravely. "Covering my tracks. I didn't know then that he was important to you."

"Would you have made a different decision if you *had* known?"

Levan did not—or could not—answer.

Other situations cascaded through her mind, cast in a fresh light. "The night we met in that alley . . . why didn't you just kill me? Your power far overwhelms my own. You shot a fair number of killing curses at me, but none of them hit. Yet I don't think you often make mistakes."

At this, he bowed his head. "Because I knew you were coming. And I knew you were important."

Everything in Saffron stilled. "What?"

Levan sighed. "A few months before we met in that alley, Harrow foresaw the scene in Zares's house. He told me that an unfamiliar mage with wild silver-blond curls would lead me to the necromancer—and that the same mage would save my life when it all went wrong. That's all we knew. Not that you were a Silvercloak, not how it would all come to pass. But when I saw you in that alley . . . I knew you were the one. So I had to give the impression of wanting you dead without *actually* killing you. You had to believe you were on the front foot. And that illusion you cast—the alter self. I knew I was striking the wrong one with *ammorten.*"

The room blurred around Saffron. It explained his moments of kindness, even in the beginning—bringing her salve, asking if she was alright every time her brand stung. It explained why he'd warmed to her faster than he should have, and continued to trust her long after it was prudent to do so. It explained so much, and yet it left her reeling.

"Has Harrow foreseen anything else involving us?" she murmured, hoarse.

Levan shook his head. "No. I have no idea how this night ends. I have no idea what lays beyond it."

But I think I do.

"And Zares? Why did she nearly overpower you, back in her house? Why didn't you just compel her?"

"I didn't want you to know what I could do. Some cards are best kept close to the chest. And besides, I'm used to casting to kill. Taking marks alive has always been more difficult, since power rushes from me at full force."

Saffron let this sink in, then whispered, "Is it *all* you? Every terrible thing your father does . . . how much of it is him, and how much of it is you?"

The unspoken question: *Did you just compel him to kill my uncle?*

"Oh, it's mostly him. He wants my mother back as much as I do. I just take over whenever he doesn't have the stomach. But he's been getting better at resisting, even though he doesn't know he's being compelled. That meltdown on the docks, when he kept firing killing spells all over the place—his mind was so embroiled in this unknown battle that I felt it splinter."

Saints.

"Levan . . . is my uncle dead?" She hated how small and scared she sounded. She had spent so much effort making sure he never saw her vulnerable, not even after she'd been branded. But she needed to know. "Or is there a chance your father was bluffing?"

Sympathy crested over his face, and she knew before he replied.

"My father doesn't bluff. I'm sorry, Silver."

A sob cracked free of its own accord.

Levan looked like he so badly wanted to comfort her, to bring her into his arms and kiss her forehead and stroke her back while she wept, but then a kind of reluctant darkness fell behind his eyes, as though he'd forced himself to remember the real reason they sat in this shack, a war raging on the other side of the door.

"You're a rat, Silver." Every word was a crack of thunder. "And now I have no idea what to do. I could kill you or incapacitate you or order you to do what I want. But for some hellsforsaken reason, I can't. So we're at an impasse." Desperation clouded his face. "But you can *choose* to unmake your decision. To change loyalties. All you have to do is freeze time with *praegelos* and get my father out of that room."

Saffron's insides were ablaze. "And what makes you think I'll do that? What makes you think I won't just freeze time and tie you up for my captain to haul you away?"

A long, potent beat. He crawled toward her on his hands and knees, cupping her sweat-slicked face in his cool golden hand. His blazing blue eyes searched hers so deeply it was like he was mining for ascenite at the bottom.

Everything in her hurt.

And then their lips met, and a shiver rolled through her, and he said a single word so softly she almost missed it.

"Hope."

49

...

Sen Praegelos

SAFFRON FELT AS THOUGH SHE WERE STANDING IN A CEMETERY, drenched in the scarlet light of a true bloodmoon. All around her were graves of those already fallen: those she had lost, and those she had fought to save, and those she had killed with her own hand, each headstone a solid, immovable weight upon her chest.

Neatras and Kasan. An uncle, though she knew not which. Tiernan. Her mother and father.

In the front row of the cemetery was a neat line of open graves, awaiting their bodies.

And it was up to Saffron who would claim each one.

An awful power, and yet more awful still not to wield it.

This was the final play. The last square before the Flight of the Raven was complete.

"I don't have a wand," Saffron muttered.

Without hesitation, Levan handed her his.

Saints. He was putting all his trust and faith in her. He was putting his life, his fate, in her hands. And it felt how it had when she'd severed his hand—a curse, a burden.

Saffron pressed her eye against the crack in the pantry door.

Beyond it, the carnage roiled on, even more bodies on the ground. Tas was dead, as was Detective Alirrol. Lyrian, once again casting killing curses with reckless abandon, was flanked by Castian and Segal. Castian wielded wind so powerful that the roof had blown off the shack, while Segal fired vague disarmament curses at the Silvercloaks crouched behind the bed. But there was something wrong with Segal's wand—the spells trickled out in pathetic tufts of mist, falling dramatically short of their marks.

Aspar and Auria, both still in gas masks, tried to strike their opponents with *effigias* spells. One velvine was perched on Auria's shoulders, black-furred and arch-backed, but Aspar's velvine lay dead on the ground, spine snapped, eyes faded from indigo to gray.

Castian gusted the bed frame into the open sky above, sending it smashing into the nearest wyrmwood.

The Silvercloaks were completely exposed.

Not a moment too soon, Saffron gripped Levan's wand and uttered, "*Sen praegelos.*"

The world stood still, and the spell felt strong.

She didn't have much ascenite out here in the Havenwood, but she had Rasso to bolster her, and a magical well full of pain and pleasure. From the intimacy she'd shared with Levan, and from the world-ending hurt of hearing her uncle's murder ordered. From the historic loss of her parents, and from the righteous sense of purpose that had fueled her since. All of it so potent she felt it in her body and her heart, all of it churning together in one fearsome pot.

Behind her, Levan crouched perfectly frozen. The emotion in his eyes was so richly textured she couldn't wholly parse it.

He wouldn't see what she was doing while time was held still. Only the outcome.

She stepped into the room.

The shack was decimated. Copper pots and pans were scattered all over the floor, bent and misshapen. Castian had blown holes in the walls, and a white owl hung suspended over the roof, as though it couldn't resist getting a better look. The colored starbursts of various spells streaked the air, their paths frozen with time. It was almost festive, like strings of twinkling winter solstice lights.

On one side of the room, Aspar and Auria crouched beside Detective Alirrol's lifeless body. Auria's pale face was pinned wide with terror. Next to her, Aspar had been struck square in the chest by a spell Saffron only vaguely recognized—not the pale shimmer of *sen ammorten,* but rather a vicious shining scarlet, like a pool of blood.

Dread coiled through Saffron's stomach. It would kill the captain, albeit slowly. The caster clearly planned to extract information before her demise. Information about Saffron, no doubt.

Castian had been caught by an *effigias* spell—turning to stone from the heart outward.

Up close, Segal's face was the picture of wrongness. His Risen irises were a single shade darker than the whites of his eyes, but now that he was frozen long enough to study in earnest, Saff saw that they were not blank at all, but rather churning from behind, from *within*. She could not say whether the monster who had murdered her parents was still in there, or whether he had become something else entirely—could not say, with any amount of certainty, which would be worse.

Saffron closed her eyes, picturing the cemetery once more.

The open graves, the scarlet moon in the sky.

Only two possible paths forked in front of her.

She could restrain her colleagues, then extract the kingpin, as Levan wanted her to do—but had not *compelled* her to do. Because he wanted this to come from her. He wanted, beyond all reason, for her to choose him.

Or she could restrain the Bloodmoons, and hand the Silvercloaks victory.

It was barely a choice. She had not come this far to turn back now. No matter how she felt about Levan—lust, love, hate, anger, fascination, fear, and myriad other emotions she couldn't name—she could not place that over the fate of Ascenfall.

The fate of her *life.*

She had to finish what she'd started.

All those graves could not lie full for nothing.

She unlooped the manacles from Aspar's belt and hooked them around the kingpin's wrists, thinking all the while of that final assessment back at the Academy. Casting that very first *praegelos* had shone too harsh a spotlight on her, setting this whole doomed carriage in motion. There was an almost pleasing full-circle feeling to it. The great bend of destiny, always arcing back on itself.

Once all the Bloodmoons were restrained—Castian was already semi-stone, so didn't require manacles—Saff grabbed her own wand from Castian's waistband, then pocketed Lyrian's weaverwick. She took Segal's and Castian's wands for good measure, cold sweat pouring from her temples at the effort of holding time hostage.

Then came the hardest part.

She went back to the closet to restrain Levan, knowing that when time resumed, and he realized she had not chosen him, the already broken heart in his chest would shatter. Dizzy from holding the moment still, she manacled his wrists together just moments before time shuddered and freed itself from her grasp.

There were a series of confused yells in the main shack, then Auria's shouts of *effigias* as she incapacitated the Bloodmoons more convincingly, but all Saff could do was stare at the man she had just betrayed.

He looked down at his bound wrists, and when he looked back up at her, all the light was gone from his eyes. All that rich, textured emotion was gone, and he was as dead inside as the night she'd met him in that alley.

And then she felt it.

The uncontrollable impulse to undo the bonds and hand back his wand.

He was *compelling* her.

Crossing the line he had never wanted to cross.

Or at least, she thought he was. The desire to untie him sprung from deep inside herself, her heart and her bones and her soul, like the basest of all instincts. No wonder it took Lyrian so long to realize the truth.

She was powerless to resist.

But how? He had no wand. And yet her body was moving of its own accord, guided by his will. Hands shaking violently, she loosened the manacles and gave him back the wand.

He looked straight through her, as if she were nothing, and climbed to his feet, turning to enter the main shack—and undo everything she had just done to tip the raid in the Silvercloaks' favor.

"*Sen effigias,*" she said desperately, the spell burying itself in his back, and he turned wholly to stone.

It only lasted a moment.

Almost as quickly as he'd become a statue, he became flesh once more.

He peered over his shoulder, cold amusement on his face. "After my father used *debilitan* on me to such devastating effect, I had Miret help me practice breaking free of such curses, over and over until I could barely stand. Then I practiced until I could do it without my wand. Nice try, though."

The horror in Saff was a dark, pulsing thing. Levan's magic was something monstrous and unnatural, borne from more torture than most other mages had any hope of surviving.

And she had no idea how to overcome it.

"*Ans exarman,*" Saff hissed desperately, a basic disarming spell, and his wand leapt from his hand. She scrambled to pick it up from the ground . . .

. . . only to be immediately overcome with the urge to give it back.

She gave it back.

When he'd given her his wand and said *hope,* it hadn't been a risk at all. He'd always been powerful enough to undo whatever she did on the other side of that door.

Gambling isn't reckless if you're good at it, she thought.

"Levan," she whispered, closing the gap between the two of them. "I'm sorry. I'm so sorry. Please, forgive me."

She pressed her body to his chest, felt the slow, steady beat of his heart against the frantic patter of her own. She gazed up at him, trying desperately to distract him with the only weapon she had left: the way they felt about each other.

Levan shoved his wand tip beneath her chin, pushing her face painfully upward. "I always win, Silver." His fingers wove through the blond curls at the back of her head, but it was not affectionate. She fought a yelp as he dug into her hair. "Your magic cannot best mine."

He was right.

There was no other way.

She pressed her breathless lips to his. A surge of emotion crested through her, an existential longing, a desperate desire, and she felt it mirrored in the way his body softened ever so slightly. A subtle yield, but it meant little. She would never be able to overpower him, and they both knew it.

The kiss deepened, intensified.

Saff dug one hand into the hollow of his hip; he let out a low, rough moan.

Her other hand pressed her wand against his stomach.

"*Sen ammorten,*" she said, grief permeating every inch of her body.

The killing spell leapt, a fork of lightning, a death kiss, and Levan staggered back, as though falling into an empty grave.

He was dead before he hit the ground.

50

...

Aspar's Farewell

THE IMPOSSIBLE PROPHECY HAD BEEN FULFILLED.

Levan's eyes peeled open, staring, unseeing, at the ceiling of the shack. A lock of dark brown hair fell into his face, and his scarred lips were slightly parted in shock. His blade of a body, normally so sharp with tension, seemed horrifyingly empty.

She could not have done what she'd just done.

She could *not.*

And yet it had been the only way.

If she'd let him walk back into the shack, it would've been over. The Silvercloaks would have lost, and the Bloodmoons would certainly have executed her.

The enormity of it didn't hit her yet. Instead, there was only disbelief, the same breed of shock she'd felt when her parents died, the sense that nothing this horrific could possibly be real. The feeling of standing on the edge of the Shard of Khulin, unable to comprehend the scale of the waves crashing down upon her.

Pure adrenaline shoved Saff into the room beyond.

The three Bloodmoons were stone statues in the kitchen. In the bedroom, Auria crouched over Aspar's bleeding body, weeping profusely and pouring a series of tinctures down her captain's throat in a desperate bid to revive her.

Aspar gurgled, then hacked up so much blood that Saffron knew there was no saving her.

Saffron crossed the room and sank to her knees before her captain.

"We got them," she murmured, so dizzy she almost tipped, grabbing Aspar desperately by the shoulders. "We got them, Captain. You're going to be commissioner. Stay with us."

But Aspar's gaze was weak, glassy, as the blood burbled down her chin.

Auria yanked Saffron back so hard her fingertips left bruises. "Get away from her," she all but spat. "It's your fault she's dying."

Saff shook her head vehemently. "I've been undercover this whole time. I'm the one who snuck Aspar intel about the first shipment, who told her we were retrieving the lox tonight. Tell her, Captain."

"Dragontail . . ." Aspar tried to say, but it was hard to understand her over the thick gloops of blood spouting from her mouth like a faucet. Moonlight limned every ridge of her shaven head. "Dragontail . . . your father. And he . . . he . . . he would be proud. There's a . . . letter."

Captain Elodora Aspar died in Auria's arms.

A sigh, a shift, a final twitch. And then nothing.

Auria let out a single rollicking sob, turning to Saffron, wand raised, world-ending anger blazing over her face. "Give me one good reason I shouldn't kill you right now."

"Auria, I—"

"My grandfather died a gruesome death because of you. The captain is dead because of you." Auria's skin was pale as bone, framed by frizzy copper hair, and she looked so unbearably young. "The only thing I want more than to see you dead is to see you suffer for the rest of your life. To see you rot in Duncarzus, living every day with the shame of what you have done."

"I've been undercover," Saffron snapped. "Which should be familiar to you, as a concept."

"How can you *live* with yourself?" Auria went on, as though Saff had not spoken. "I thought you were *good.* I saw the very best in you, and now look—"

"It's not that fucking *simple,* Auria! In this world, everything comes with a price. Magic comes with a price, love comes with a price, goodness comes with a price. Sometimes you have to do dark things in the name of the light."

"Is that the bullshit logic you use to exonerate yourself?" A scathing head shake. "In the great arc of humanity, goodness will always win. Nothing you can say will convince me otherwise."

"This *was* a part of the great arc. You have to believe me," Saffron whispered, palms up in surrender. "*I* froze time and tied up Bloodmoons. Would I do that if I weren't undercover? If I weren't still working for you?"

"You were switching sides at the last minute because you knew defeat was nigh."

"Switching sides?" Saff shook her head in frustration. "Because it's so easy to just *switch sides* back into the institution that publicly shamed and imprisoned you? You heard Aspar. She said my father would be proud. Would she say that if I hadn't been risking my life to bring in the Bloodmoons?"

"Aspar was dying and delirious."

Saffron pressed her palms into her eyes, trying to right her pitching vision. "Fine. Nissa knows too, ask her."

Auria's expression grew even colder. "Nissa has been in a coma since the first raid. She went into shock a few minutes after you *portari*-ed out. She might recover, and she might not."

No. Nissa couldn't be . . . Tiernan had said . . .

New horror dawning, Saffron realized he'd only said Nissa was *alive.* Not that she was *awake.*

Something freshly furious reared behind Auria's hazel eyes, as though she could read Saffron's thoughts. "Where's Tiernan? The last time I saw him, he said he was going to meet you. To make amends. I didn't understand why."

A single tear rolled down Saffron's cheek. "He took his own life."

Anger and grief and hatred erupted over Auria's face.

"He's dead?" She was shaking uncontrollably. "You *killed* him."

"*No.* He'd been compelled into informing by the kingpin's son. Who I just killed in that closet, by the way, to save your life. Go and see for yourself."

At this, Auria blanched. "Tiernan was the rat?"

"Tiernan was the rat. He cost us the first raid."

"Don't say *us*, like you're still part of it." Auria trembled from head to toe, looking from Aspar's dead body to the last person who'd seen her betrothed alive. Her palm went to her rib cage, where the betrothal tattoo was likely still fresh. "He can't be gone."

"He might not be. I took him to the Bloodmoons' ascenite crypt. It'll preserve his body until we can get a necromancer to him." A plan galloped into Saff's mind fully formed, a way to convince Auria to let her walk free. "I alone can get beyond the wards into the crypt, since I've been branded. Once all the Bloodmoons are safely imprisoned, I'll get him out. We just need to find a necromancer, alright?"

War waged behind Auria's eyes for several moments. All around them, silence pressed in, as solid as a physical object after the fierce skirmish. Saffron wondered dimly what was going on in the other shacks, who had lived and who had died.

Auria shook her head frantically. "It's wrong. Necromancy is wrong. I don't want him back like *that.* And even if I did, Tiernan wouldn't want me to put him above what's right." She raised her wand in a trembling hand. "*Sen effigias.*"

The statue spell struck Saffron, but nothing happened.

Auria frowned at her wand as though it had betrayed her.

"I'm immune to magic," Saffron murmured.

It was once again true, now that Levan was dead.

Dead. The word, hard and unyielding as stone, sent a peal of loss through her. A physical whip-crack, straight to her well. She had little magic left after holding time still, but what dregs remained glittered from the fresh wave of hurt.

"It's how I was able to receive the loyalty brand without actually being bound by it," she added. "Being branded is hell, by the way."

Her attempt to break through Auria's walls failed, and her old friend took a step closer to her, hatred convulsing all over her face as she drew her blisblade.

Rasso growled and leapt through the air toward Auria.

"No!" Saff yelled. "Leave her."

But Rasso did not listen. Moments before his jaws closed around Auria's throat, Saff gasped out a desperate, tremulous, "*Sen praegelos.*"

The world froze for the second time that night. If it weren't for the pain of losing her uncle, for the pain of killing Levan, for the pain of Aspar dying in Auria's arms, she likely would not have the magical strength left to hold it.

Startled, Rasso landed on all fours, glancing curiously back at Saffron.

"Don't hurt her," Saff whispered to the fallowwolf, trying her very damnedest not to pass out.

If she passed out, the *praegelos* would lapse, and it would be over.

With every ounce of mental strength she had left, she weighed her options.

There was no getting out of this situation without temporarily incapacitating Auria, and if she did that, she'd have an even harder time proving to the Silvercloaks that she'd been on their side all along. She'd be arrested and tossed in Duncarzus until the end of time. Aspar and Levan would stay dead, and Saff's life would be effectively over.

There was a chance, of course, that Nissa would recover well enough to testify in Saffron's favor. But there was an equal chance she wouldn't.

Detective Jebat had known that Aspar had *someone* undercover, just not who. But Saffron had no idea whether Levan had left Jebat alive.

Still dazed, Saffron could've sworn she felt the weight of her parents' gaze from beyond an imperceptible veil. Their love and judgment, their silent pleas. But what were they pleading *for*? Would they want her to do this—to sacrifice her life and freedom in the name of banishing this great evil? Or would they want her to save herself?

She could always flee. Levan's wand could *portari* her anywhere on the continent, but as Levan had said, the Silvercloaks were becoming far more proficient at tracing these things. Even if she exiled herself to another country, everywhere but Mersina and Nomaden had extradition agreements with Vallin, and the chances of her successfully transporting that far in her weakened state were slim.

If she fled, sooner or later she would be caught. Auria would stop at nothing to bring her in—as far as she was concerned, both Tiernan's and Aspar's blood was on Saff's hands.

The *praegelos* charm shimmered and faltered around her as she considered her final option.

Timeweaving.

She had Lyrian's wand, the hourglass, and Rasso. She might be able to unwind this disastrous night, but how far back could she get without all the ascenite she'd been bolstered by in the mansion?

For this not to be so ruinous, she needed Aspar to survive, but Aspar had already been struck by the time Saff and Levan had made it to the shack. In any case, placing herself in the middle of the brutal skirmish to try and block a spell fired at the captain would just as likely result in her own death.

Could she go back even further?

To before the night even began, before the kingpin ordered her uncle's death?

Likely not. She vividly remembered the lung squeezing sensation from the last time she'd weaved, the fierce fighting for breath, the way it had become harder and harder to keep her wand on the hourglass. In Lyrian's office, she'd been surrounded by ascenite from all angles. Here she could rely only on her own well of magic—which was running dangerously low.

Desperation mounted as she realized there was no way out of this . . . unless she made the *other* decision.

Unless she didn't betray Levan.

Unless she went back to before she killed him.

Aspar would die regardless, but Saff could incapacitate Auria instead of Lyrian, let the Bloodmoons flee, stay undercover until she knew whether Nissa would be able to vouch for her. Until she knew whether Jebat lived.

Doing so would win back Levan's trust, and further down the line, there would surely be another chance to bring the Bloodmoons in. This time she would make sure the whole institution of the Silvercloaks knew what she was doing, so that no matter who died in the crossfire, her efforts would be recognized, and she'd be reinstated.

Of all the options, it was the only one that didn't leave her decimated.

She reached deep inside herself and felt a meager smear of magic at the bottom of her well. She had to make it last—make it as potent as possible, so that it might do what she needed it to do.

And so she opened the internal box where she stored all her grief, and held it upside down, so that every last devastating piece came tumbling out.

The terror on Tiernan's face as he had raised his own wand beneath his chin. The wet squelch of an eyeball beneath a letteropener. The mental image of her uncle's fresh corpse, and of his widower weeping alone by a fire.

A killing curse leaping from her knobbly beech wand and into the body of the man she loved.

That fateful night in Lunes, kneeling over her dead parents, knowing that life as she knew it was over.

The grief was a mountain sitting on her chest. She could barely breathe through the weight of all she had lost. It hurt so much, all of it, but pain could always be used. That was the very foundation of their world.

Pain meant you were alive. Pain meant you still had a fighting chance.

Her grandfather's words, slurred at her parents' wake, came back to her.

Let me tell you something about loss, sweetling. You can either yield to grief, or you can use *it. Those are the only two choices, in the end.*

Maybe pain was the only thing that could save her.

Yet now the emotional dam had fallen, throwing it back up felt like trying to best gravity.

Dad, the broken child at the heart of her wept. *You can't be gone.*

Mama? Please. Please, I need you.

She was six years old and cleaved in two.

Looking down at her body, she was surprised to see long limbs, broad hips, the swell of breasts. Because at her very core, in every place that mattered, she was still hiding in that pantry, staring through the keyhole at the corpses of her beloved parents. Some fundamental part of her would be anchored there forever.

She drew from that part of her now, a bucket lowered and then raised.

The solitary smear of magic left in her well glowed bright as ascenite.

Face salt-slick with tears, she pulled the hourglass from her cloak pocket and met Rasso's piercing gaze. Turning the hourglass over and tapping the weaverwick wand to its new top, she threw every ounce of power she had left behind the word: "*Tempavicissan.*"

Then the world smudged around her. An almighty wrench, a backward yank, a star imploding, a fate unbraided, so profoundly wrong that it *hurt,* like all the tissue was being torn from her bones.

Time blurred and uncoiled. Her body scuttled backward of its own accord, across the room and back into the closet.

Levan was dead, and then he was alive.

She might have vomited, but it disappeared through the cracks of time unwritten.

Keeping the wand tip to the hourglass took everything from her, and when she could breathe no more, and her mind was on the brink of collapse, she let go.

51

...

The Saqalamis

THE WORLD BECAME A PALIMPSEST.

With a violent lurch, Saffron found that she was in the middle of talking.

"—makes you think I'll do that?" Sweat dripped down her temples, every inch of her body shaking. Lyrian's wand was clasped in her right hand alongside her own—two wands, when before she'd had none. She tucked them into her cloak pocket as subtly as she could, folding forward onto her knees as though buckling under the emotional weight of the situation.

There was a long, potent beat, in which Levan studied her like an ancient tome. Then he crawled toward her on his hands and knees, cupping her sweat-slicked face in his cool golden hand. His blazing blue eyes searched hers so deeply it was like he was mining for ascenite at the bottom.

And then their lips met, and a shiver rolled through her, and he said a single word so softly she almost missed it.

"Hope."

Here they were again.

She allowed herself to linger in the moment for longer than she had the first time.

Something naïve and hopeless soared in her chest. Levan was *alive.* On this fork in the road, she didn't kill him. His skin was still warm, and his gaze was not yet scrubbed free of emotion. Tears streamed down her face unbidden, and she couldn't bring herself to wipe them away.

The deep, stony exhaustion in her body told her that she had to get it right this time. She would not be able to unmake time again. This was her final chance to salvage the ruins of this night.

"I don't have a wand," Saffron whispered, remembering her lines.

Levan handed her his.

She clambered unsteadily to her feet and pressed the closet door open.

Tas was still dead, as was Alirrol.

In the great reshuffling of time and wands, Lyrian's had vanished, and he bellowed his confusion, crouching behind Castian.

Segal fired his ineffectual curses at the Silvercloaks crouched behind the bed.

Aspar and Auria tried to strike their opponents with *effigias* spells. The bloody starburst on Aspar's chest spread violently over her silver cloak, her gas mask filling with scarlet as she bled from her mouth.

Castian gusted the bed frame into the open sky above, sending it smashing into the nearest wyrmwood.

"*Sen praegelos,*" Saffron whispered, stars dancing around her eyes.

Time stood unconvincingly still.

It faltered and wavered, jerking back and forward, resisting her command.

Stomach dropping, she realized she couldn't hold it.

She tossed the kingpin's wand back at his feet, in a desperate attempt to avoid his—and Levan's—suspicion.

Time shook itself free, a hellhound escaping a leash.

The owl flew freely overhead.

Chaos resumed.

Castian turned fully to stone, mouth agape.

Lyrian spotted his wand, grabbing it in a heartbeat.

Aspar fired her final spell, a furious roar of grief. "*Sen ammorten.*"

"*Sen ammorten,*" yelled Lyrian at the same moment.

It struck Aspar in the head.

Aspar's killing curse struck Lyrian's heart.

They were both dead in an instant.

Silence rang out all around.

Saffron collapsed.

Levan burst into the room, roaring his own grief, hurling himself at his father.

Auria was the last Silvercloak standing.

Segal stared blankly at the felled kingpin.

Whipping around, Levan stabbed his wand at Auria, eyes alight with grief. "*Sen ammorten.*"

Auria fell dead, pale and empty.

Every inch of Saffron wailed *no,* but no sound left her mouth.

Think! she screamed internally. *Reroute!*

Levan now had his father's weaverwick wand in his hand, Rasso by his side, incanting the timeweaving spell over and over, even though it had never worked for him, even though it likely never would.

Auria was *dead,* and Saffron had no more magic.

Unless . . .

She dug into her pocket and pulled out the painmaker. Artan had said that Eqoran Timeweavers had used them during the civil war, to inflict massive, life-saving pain.

Magic had only ever worked on Saffron once before, at Levan's hand. But she had felt the call, the thrum of this device back in Artan's, and some curious instinct told her this time it would be different.

It was the only play she had left.

"*Az'alamis,*" she begged hoarsely, not truly thinking about what she was doing, about how much pain she could stand, about how this infernal device was just as likely to fell her as it was to fuel her, just willing it to *work.*

And it worked.

It worked so suddenly and violently that the world was drenched scarlet.

This pain was not the circular sear of a brand, nor the bright sharpness of a cut, nor the lancing burn of a whip.

This was a rusty nail hammered into every nerve ending in her body. She could not scream, could only fall endlessly down the open shaft of agony, existing only as an afterthought to the pain, unable to move or speak or breathe, only to *hurt.*

She could not drop the *saqalamis,* could not unfurl her fist, and so the pain kept going.

She was the pain, and the pain was her, a long implosion, an utter annihilation.

Then someone ripped the black quartz from her hand.

The world lightened from deep red to faded watercolor. Levan crouched at her side, breathing hard, existential horror on his once empty face, the *saqalamis* in his own hand, disarmed.

And the sliver of magic in her well was liquid gold.

She grabbed the weaverwick wand from his loosened grip and whispered, "*Tempavicissan.*"

Another almighty wrench, more smudged silhouettes, more pain, always pain, why did everything hurt so much?

She let go. The whirling stopped. Levan was no longer beside her, and the *saqalamis* was back in her pocket.

Aspar's killing curse struck Lyrian's heart.

Silence rang out all around, but the blood roared in Saffron's ears.

She collapsed to the ground. When had she stood back up?

Time slid, losing form.

Levan burst into the room, roaring his own grief, hurling himself at his father, and Saffron tossed the weaverwick wand back to his feet.

Auria was the last Silvercloak standing.

Face contorted, Levan stabbed his wand at Auria, eyes alight. "*Sen amm—*"

"*Sen praegelos,*" Saffron cried, raising her own wand, sweat pouring from her temples, every muscle in her body convulsing and twitching, and thought she might come undone from the pain, from the exertion, but there was nothing she would not do to save Auria.

To save *someone.*

Time paused unconvincingly.

Saffron clambered to her feet, stumbling and almost falling again, crossing to where Auria stood frozen.

Time lapsed and then froze again, enough that Levan finished incanting the curse, enough that he must have seen Saffron's glitching progress. The dark magic leapt from his wand, halting in a fork of lightning halfway to Auria as time jerked to a stop once more.

Standing behind Auria, Saff hooked her wrists under her friend's arms and dragged her back in the direction of the door.

Almost there.

Ten feet.

Saffron was going to faint.

Five feet.

Saffron could not faint.

Outside, the air was eerily still, not a twitch of forest sound to be heard, and Saffron understood then why Captain Aspar had so savagely opposed *praegelos,* because it felt wrong, even to Saffron, even to a Timeweaver, to bring all of life, all of reality, to a stop.

The pain-brightened magic in her well was fading to nothing.

Time shimmered and faltered.

Please flee, she urged her friend, her found family. *Please don't be a hero. Please accept the defeat, go away, and regroup.*

I'm sorry, I'm sorry, I'm sorry.

She stumbled back inside, and time resumed with an inelegant lurch.

Levan's killing spell buried itself in the frayed wood of the shack.

Saffron fell to her knees, and Levan looked straight at her, and he *knew* that she had used *praegelos* to save her friend, yet his expression was so mired with grief that she couldn't cipher how much he hated her for it.

"I'm sorry," she whispered, unsure who she was apologizing to.

"Find the fleeing cloak," Levan snarled at Segal, before turning his attention back to his fallen father.

But Segal too was on the floor, staring at his hands as though they belonged to a stranger. Almost inaudibly, he whispered, in abject horror, "I can't feel it. I can't feel *any* of it. Pleasure, pain. I feel nothing—I thought, but . . . this . . . I haven't felt anything since, just old magic, and now . . . *NO.*"

A shudder clutched his whole body as he realized the enormity of it.

Without pleasure, without pain, his well would never refill.

The true cost of being Risen.

For most mages, it was a fate worse than death.

Some innate part of Saffron recoiled at the idea, but she could not find any sympathy for the man who had slain her parents. And besides, his wallowing gave Auria ample time to escape into the Havenwood, to rally the surviving Silvercloaks and regroup back at the Order.

Saffron had saved someone.

She had saved someone, but there was something badly wrong with her body. She felt like a claw, a husk, a snarled mass of mangled bones. The *saqalamis* had done something permanent, something terrible, though she couldn't put her finger on *what.*

There was still pain, and for that she was grateful. Without it, she'd have feared the same fate as a Risen.

"Please," Levan moaned, grabbing fistfuls of Lyrian's cloak. "Please. Come back. Come back."

A tear slicked down Saffron's cheek, and then another.

Twenty-one years ago, Levan had knelt over his mother's body, begging her to come back to him. Now, because of her, because of the woman he had trusted against all his better judgment, his father had fallen to the same fate.

Both times she had unwoven and rebraided the strands of time, Levan had suffered in her stead.

"*Ans visseran, ans visseran, ans visseran,*" he pleaded, but the necromancy spell still would not heed his command.

"We can take him to the crypt," Saffron murmured, louder than before but still not *loud,* and she didn't know if Levan heard her. "We can bring him back when we bring your mother back."

But Saff didn't believe it. Not really.

Surely there wasn't a magical well deep enough to bring Lorissa back to life after twenty-one years. Not even as perfectly preserved as she was. And it could be several more years before they found a necromancer skilled enough to even attempt it.

Besides, now they knew that to rise from the dead was to never feel pleasure or pain again. It was to be, for all intents and purposes, powerless. *Empty.* There was a slim and distant chance that a necromancer could revive them, yes, but they would not be as they were, as they had been.

Levan seemed to realize this too, his horrified gaze slicing between his father and Segal, slowly coming to understand that, in so many ways, his parents' deaths were more permanent than he had ever been willing to accept.

He did not cry, but his breathing was ragged, his shoulders shaking, and Saffron knew that pain so well, what it was to be an orphan, what it was to have your life carved into a *before* and an *after*, and in that moment, she would have done anything to take the grief away. To mend it, and to mend her own. To mend the world.

But perhaps . . .

No. Surely it could not be done.

And yet . . .

Words like *before* and *after* no longer held the same weight. They were a tide, a force of nature so powerful they were seemingly absolute, and yet a gifted enough Wielder could alter the flow of the sea. And so it went with time.

She'd just unraveled several minutes without *any* ascenite around her.

The desire had been so intense, so raw, and the belief so unwavering, that time had obeyed her regardless.

What if . . .

What if time could be unmade not by minutes or hours or days, but by years?

House Rezaran had done it, during the Dreadreign. Unwritten and rewritten the same decades over and over until they unfolded exactly as they wished. They'd done it so ruthlessly and so often that the very fabric of the world had eroded, running time back and forth through the loom of reality until it was so gossamer thin that patches began to fray and disappear.

Unmaking time so significantly was terrible, but it was possible.

And it therefore followed that it was possible for Saffron.

Could she unwind the world until she was once again six years old?

Could she save her parents?

Could she save Levan's?

Could she go back and *not* turn that Saintsforsaken doorknob?

If she didn't, Mellora wouldn't be distracted, and she'd bring back Joran, proving herself to be a necromancer. She would revive the queenpin. The Bloodmoons wouldn't kill the Killorans for silence—having a necromancer in their cards was far too valuable. The Killorans would be branded, but they would all escape with their lives.

Saffron would not be so decimated with sadness that she spent six years in silence. Levan would never have to grow up inside that same grief, would never be tortured to within an inch of his life on his father's order, would never be crippled by obsessive, cyclical thoughts.

And all the people who had died because of her would live. Neatras, Kasan, Papa Marriosan. Ronnow, Alirrol, Tas. Lyrian, Vogolan, for better or worse.

Captain Aspar.

Tiernan.

Her uncle.

This revenge mission had been an elaborate gamble, a desperate bet in the gamehouse of destiny, and the sunk cost was too high to turn back now. She had sacrificed too much to walk away.

But if she could keep going long enough to undo it all . . .

It would require an unholy amount of ascenite. More than existed in the crypt, in the whole of the mansion—hells, in the whole of the city. But the Bloodmoons had the means to accumulate more and more. For the next few months or years, her motivations would perfectly align with Levan's.

They both wanted ascenite, and they both wanted to bring back their parents.

The prospect filled her with a deep, bright glow.

She could make this right, but she had to go all in.

Her enormous sunk cost could still pay off, in the grand gamble of fate.

She might have to keep torturing and killing, keep covering her tracks, fully invest herself in the Bloodmoons and in her goal. But it would all be worth it in the end, when she was back with her parents in that round, ramshackle house in Lunes, all the pain she'd caused vanishing between the cracks of rewritten time. Was it still killing, if you knew you would undo it later, and the victims would be none the wiser?

Then came the axis tilt, the perspective shift, the great pitching of the world beneath her feet.

A thunderclap of terrible understanding.

Oh, she thought, horrified and fascinated in equal measure.

This is how villains are born.

EPILOGUE

• • •

Levan

ELMING, 26 SABÁRIEL, YEAR 1174

It's been three days since my father died, three days since I became kingpin, and three days since I learned what Silver truly is.

A Timeweaver.

One minute in that closet she was relatively calm, steady, with no wand in her hand. A split second later, she was weak, breathless, sobbing, with my father's—or really, my mother's—wand in her palm alongside her own.

Did she think it would escape me, what she had done? I remember enough of my mother's lost art to spot those tiny inconsistencies, to recognize when the fabric of reality shifts from one moment to the next.

The truth is all too clear. The first time she made her decision, she chose to betray me. In another timeline, I died at her hand.

Saffron Killoran unmade my world.

And now I will unmake her.

Acknowledgments

SILVERCLOAK IS MY ELEVENTH PUBLISHED NOVEL, AND YET writing acknowledgments never gets any easier. Not just because I'm petrified of missing anyone, but also because it's oddly emotional. Hell, I'm an emotional person anyway, but just thinking about how many people touched this book is a fundamentally awe-inspiring thing. The old adage of these things taking a village is a cliché because it's true.

First and foremost, thank you to my incredible agent, Chloe Seager. Where do I begin? This whole book is dedicated to you, but I need to thank you again here, in a much more earnest manner than you're really comfortable with. Simply put, I owe you everything. You're the first person in this industry to ever believe in the very wildest of my dreams, to not urge me to think smaller or safer. But also, thank you for just being a really great pal and general delightful presence in my life. Please never leave me to become an Olympic surfer.

And to the rest of Madeline Milburn Literary Agency—you have all changed my life with your hard work and faith in my books. Maddy Belton, whose keen editorial eye shaped this story for the better—you are a fantasy genius, and I bow down to you. Hannah Ladds and Casey Dexter, thank you for everything you do on the screen adaptation side. Valentina Paulmichl and Georgina Simmonds, thank you for the frankly phenomenal work on the translation deals for the whole trilogy, and sorry for screaming at you down the phone on multiple occasions. Kelly Chin, for being always On It. Hannah Kettles, for keeping me on the straight and narrow with my paperwork (sorry for being so wholly inept). Rakhi Kohli, for your *Silvercloak* excitement right from the very first draft. And to Giles and Madeleine, for being really rather cool overlords.

Del Rey, on both sides of the Atlantic. I've admired and coveted you immensely for so many years, and I still can't believe my books are on your list. Thank you endlessly to my editors, Emily Archbold and Sam Bradbury, who are two of the most talented and lovely people in publishing, and who always catch my little Easter Eggs. And also to the full teams who brought this book to life, including (deep breath): Barbara Bachman, Marcel Iten Busto, Angie Campusano, Keith Clayton, Maya Fenter, Regina Flath, Paul Gilbert, Ashleigh Heaton, Tori Henson, Sarah Horgan, Becky Hydon, Rachel Kennedy, Erin Korenko, Alex Larned, Julie Leung, Issie Levin, Ada Maduka, Madi Margolis, David Moench, Amy Musgrave, Tricia Narwani, Mhari Nimmo, Jordan Pace, Kay Popple, Elizabeth Rendfleisch, Susan Seeman, Scott Shannon, Sabrina Shen, Robert Siek, Jason Smith, and Rose Wadilove.

Elliot Lang, thank you for the frankly astounding US cover art. It's sharp and dynamic and cool and modern yet also timeless—better than I ever could have dreamed. You have a fan for life. And thank you also to Dan Simpkins, who worked utter magic on the UK cover—I leapt from the sofa and cheered when I saw your mock-up. Francesca Baerald, for the incredible world map—which is going to be hung on my office wall forever.

Thank you to Kate Potter, the first person to ever read *Silvercloak,* for the countless hours spent talking through every single tiny detail of this story. It wouldn't exist in its current form without you—your suggestions and insights made it infinitely better. (You're also an all-round wonderful human who keeps me happy and functioning on a day-to-day basis.) To Imi McDonnell, who reached the final page of the novel and messaged me a string of profound obscenities while I was onstage doing an event, trying not to laugh at all the curses appearing on my watch. And to Steven Eggleston, who read it (twice) during the week the book spent on submission, and whose immediate passion and obsession for the story made me think I might actually be onto something.

I'm fortunate enough to count a pretty boastful number of absurdly talented authors as my friends, and to list them all here would probably nudge this book's page count into the quadruple figures. So just a few special mentions—to V. E. Schwab and Sarah Maria Griffin, my cabin retreat pals and coincidentally two of my favorite writers. And to H. F. Askwith, my oldest writing friend (we met as babies on our journalism BA in 2010 and followed each other to the creative writing MA in 2015!) and someone who continually energizes me. The rest of you know who you are—thank you.

To my best friends in the world: Toria, Lucy, Nic, Lauren, and Hilary. To my dog, Obi, who cannot read but deserves to be thanked regardless. To my brother, Jack, who shares my love for all things fantasy, and my sister-in-law, Lauren Wilson, a phenomenal author in her own right (look her up, she wrote *The Goldens*). To Mum and Dad, my dearly missed Gran, and everyone else in my big mad family. And to Louis and Blair, who I love with all my heart. I would unmake the world for either of you.

And finally, to you, the readers. None of this exists without you. Thank you for following me on this journey.

ABOUT THE AUTHOR

L. K. Steven is an award-winning author from the northernmost town in England. She has written several young adult novels as Laura Steven, including *Every Exquisite Thing, The Society for Soulless Girls,* and *Our Infinite Fates.* When she's not writing twisty science fiction, fantasy, and horror, you can probably find her trail running, reading chunky novels, baking cookies, venturing on *Pokémon GO* safaris, playing chess with old men, or ignoring her husband and son to perfect her *Stardew Valley* farm. *Silvercloak* is her adult debut.

laura-steven.com

Instagram: @laurasteven

TikTok: @authorlaurasteven

Ascenfall
Nyrøth
Mount Pyre
Tundra of Bones
River Karken
Molda Isles
Bhondriel's Bluff
Kylgard
The Tomb Trees
Hrimir
Mount Fyrariel
The Coldwaters
Serantic Ocean
Kanai
River Marrik
Valgard
Stone Sea
Taimen
Shisai
Daejin
Brasden
Fair Firth
Malsea
Bay of Silence
Novarin
Shard of Khulin
Dragon's Droppings
Royal Riverlands
Holy Hills
Vallin
Gate of the Gods
Port Quran
Atherin
Forest of Parlin
Wielder's Cove
Summerhills
Saint's Vale
Cape Fala
Sarosan
Murias' Bay
Aredan
Lake Aquiriel
Sekani Archipelago
Crone's Finger
Sleepless Sea
Kada River
River of a Thousand Palms
Kintaso
Idera
Holy Plains
Mersina
Sinyo
Zirane
Divine Peaks
Royane
Ni Layi
Mabasi
Joribal
River Borou
River Dean
Verdant Plains
Emerald River
Arawo
Kudano
Yemabu
Ni Baso